Unravelled

The Revealed Series – Book 2

Alice Raine

Acknowledgements

As always, my first thank you must go to you readers. I can never express in words how grateful I am for the support you give, and I truly hope you enjoy this second instalment of the new series.

I've never really had 'writer's block' as such, but I must admit that there were a few tough times while writing this book. Getting the flow right has taken me considerable amounts of time, and during that process I must have written and re-written practically the entire book multiple times. I can't thank Helen L., Katie N., or Helen N. enough for their support through this process – girls, your advice, feedback, and help has been invaluable.

An especially big thank you must go to Helen L. – the constant emails and phone calls I made to you while re-jigging the manuscript must have driven you insane, but you stuck it out and your help was immeasurable.

Eve K., a huge thanks for sharing your knowledge on prop making and prosthetics, it has been hugely helpful. Joanna R., thank you for the technical advice on film studios, and for keeping me sane over numerous coffees!

A special shout out goes to Cara Millar, who helped pick the name of the film studios I have used in this book – Dynamic Studios. Thanks for entering the competition, Cara.

Once again I need to extend a huge thank you to everyone at Accent Press for the hard work and dedication that goes into supporting my writing. Alex, I have the greatest respect for what you do as my editor, and can't thank you enough for keeping me on the straight and narrow and correcting my mountains of grammatical errors.

For all my friends and family who have ended up missing out on time with me because 'I have a deadline and I need to stay in and write,' thank you for your unerring support: it means the world to me.

Alice xx

Chapter One

Allie

'No! You can't change your mind!' I held the phone away from my ear and winced as the excited voice of my best friend screeched down the line. 'It's perfect timing! You *have* to come out here!'

Of course the 'here' was Los Angeles, where Cait was currently staying, and the 'perfect timing' was my going out to visit her while both she and Sean – my fabulous and *famous* boyfriend – were in the same town.

The same fabulous and famous boyfriend I'd now been apart from for eight, long torturous weeks since he'd had to fly back to America at the end of February. Depressingly, Sean had easily returned to the actor's life of glitz and glamour, leaving me in soggy old England while I worked my final term at school. And, boy, had the two months dragged. It had felt like eight years, not eight weeks.

Wrinkling up my nose I frowned, my stomach quivering with nerves at the thought of jumping on a plane and flying out to LA tomorrow. Gripping the phone tighter I shook my head, even though I knew Cait wouldn't be able to see the gesture.

'I'm not sure it's such a great idea any more. I mean, he's Sean Phillips, for God's sake. He'll be at home in glamorous Hollywood and then there'll be me, Little Miss Nobody, stuck to his side looking like a right plonker.' After eight weeks of separation I was starting to have some doubts and question the suitability of our relationship. Some *serious,* sleep-depriving, nail-munching doubts.

I heard Cait blow a dismissive raspberry and couldn't help but smile slightly as I imagined her pretty face scrunched up peevishly. 'From all you've told me so far, I don't think he'd let you feel out of place at all. I bet he's the perfect gent.'

A perfect gent? He probably was. He certainly looked the part anyway. He might not be a suit wearer like Bridget Jones' Mr Darcy, but boy, could Sean wear jeans and a tight T-shirt like nobody's business. Not to mention how sinfully good he looked bare-chested and in pyjama bottoms …

That gentlemanly picture might not be quite as accurate to describe his bedroom antics though, because Sean had already proven that he could be quite demanding and rough when the mood took him. Feeling my cheeks flush, I tried to push the arousing images out of my mind and focus on my call with Cait.

'Hmmm. I'm not so sure he wants me to visit any more,' I admitted thoughtfully, stirring my hot chocolate with far more vigour than necessary. My clumsy actions caused some of the added marshmallows to slop onto the coffee table and I grimaced at the mess. Picking one up, I popped it in my mouth, savouring the rush of sugar as it melted over my tongue.

'Why? Has something happened?'

Dumping down the spoon, I shrugged to myself and drew in an anxious breath. 'Not really … I don't know, he's just seemed a little more distant on our last few Skype calls.' I knew I was probably making a mountain out of a molehill, but I was just unable to move past how tense Sean had been when we'd spoken in the last two weeks. He'd been frowning a lot too, which, although not an unusual expression for Sean, was one he hardly ever used with me anymore. Until recently, that is.

It had all made me think something had happened, but when I'd questioned him about it he'd just looked a bit awkward and blamed it on tiredness from long filming hours. Despite Sean's reassurances, something in my gut wasn't convinced, and I'd begun to wonder if something *had* happened in the last two weeks.

Or someone. After all, he was out in LA, surrounded by clamouring fans and glamorous celebrities, so there must be temptation around every corner.

A shudder ran through me at the thought of all the women who would be vying for his attention over there in the sunshine. No doubt Botoxed beauties with bikini bodies and tans to die for. Ugh. Hardly comparable to my girl-next-door looks, pale skin, and smattering of freckles.

Plucking another marshmallow from my drink I tried to push my gloomy thoughts aside. Perhaps Cait was right and I was making too much of his tenseness. It was most likely just tiredness.

'That's probably because he's getting frustrated with the distance and missing you like crazy,' Cait said with certainty. It was true that it felt like years since I'd last seen him in person. 'Even more reason to plant your skinny butt on that plane tomorrow and get over here,' she concluded merrily.

'My *skinny butt*?' I exclaimed, attempting to imitate the bizarre accent she'd just used. 'You've only been over there a few weeks and you're already starting to talk like an American.'

I heard her soft giggle down the line and realised just how much I'd missed having Cait around since she'd started travelling. I was so lucky to have such a genuine, loyal friend. The brief flying visits she made to the UK were always great, but I couldn't wait to spend some real, quality time with her. 'Am I? Really?' She sounded almost proud of the fact she was rapidly deserting her roots and I couldn't help rolling my eyes.

'Has he still been demanding that you text every night? And using that soppy nickname for you? What is it again? Sweetie Pie? Pudding-Pop? Something like that?' Cait asked, and I just knew she was grinning and massively taking the piss.

'Gorgeous girl,' I corrected quietly, smiling as I thought of the words rolling from Sean's tongue in that lovely rasp of his. Just thinking of his ridiculously sexy voice made goose pimples pop up on my arms.

'I prefer Sweet Cheeks,' Cait teased with a chuckle.

'And yes, he's still using it.' My friend was most amused by Sean's term of affection, saying that calling me 'girl' made me sound far younger than I actually was – twenty-six – and Sean far older than his thirty-eight years. Personally, I loved it.

'And yes. We still message every night.' I loved this habit. It was only a quick message to say good night and let him know I was home safe and sound, but it was a constant reminder of our connection and gave Sean the compulsive reassurance he needed. Cait thought it was sweet, if somewhat obsessive – which it was – but I knew the traumatic story behind Sean's possessiveness and understood his concerns. Besides, what girl wouldn't want to know they had a gorgeous Hollywood star waiting for a text from them?

'Well, there you go then – everything's fine. You're just overthinking things. Please say you're still coming?'

Glancing down at the coffee table I saw my plane ticket sitting there almost expectantly. Picking it up, I licked my lips thoughtfully as I flapped it between my fingers.

Sighing, I leant back, amused by the bizarre reality of my life: to the world he was Sean Phillips, movie star and all-round heartthrob, but to me he was the man I'd been secretly dating since January. *My Sean*. At least I hoped he was mine. I think he was, but then why had he been so tense recently? I hated the way I continuously went over the same concerns in my mind. Being apart for the last eight weeks had been so much tougher than I'd anticipated and seemed to be driving me just a little bit crazy. In addition to making my heart grow fonder, the absence also added to my nerves about our long-term compatibility.

The reason for my hesitation was never far from my mind – just the teeny tiny fact that he was a globetrotting actor and I was a mere school teacher (soon to be *ex*-school teacher) was always nagging at me. It was all so surreal; *me*, dating Sean Phillips. I mean, when did things like that ever happen in this universe?

An impatient huff down the line brought my attention back to the present as I guiltily realised that Cait was waiting for my reply. 'Come on, Allie, don't leave me hanging,' she begged. 'You have the ticket booked anyway, and besides, when else am I going to be in the same frigging city as your new fella? It's fate, like I said. Perfect timing.'

Now it was my turn to sigh. Cait had a point – my ticket *was* booked, and had been for nearly a year. Now that my student loans were paid off and I had some savings under my belt, it was time to indulge my two passions: travelling and writing. Those plans had been made before I'd met Sean, so now not only was I one day away from finishing my teaching job, but Cait was in Los Angeles *and* filming had taken Sean there too. In a way, it *did* seem as if the fates were aligning to steer me towards the glitz and glamour of LA

Who knew where it would go? Biting my lower lip with a nervous frown, I chewed on it as my mind went into overdrive *again*. I guess I'd find out for sure tomorrow. Although seeing as I had to endure a long-haul flight of more than fourteen hours to get there first, it was going to be more like two days until I'd see Sean. Even that seemed a million miles away. Could we make our relationship work or was a teacher dating a famous film star just a crazy fantasy? I suppose I'd get to see if my concerns had any grounding once I was there.

'OK, OK, of course I'm still coming.' Smiling as I listened to Cait's giddy laughter I glanced at the empty suitcase across the room. It looked like I had some speedy packing to do.

Chapter Two

Cait

The day of Allie's arrival was finally here, and I was so excited I could hardly sit still. As friends went, Allie was top of the pile – loyal, strong, supportive, and stomach-clutchingly funny – so it really wasn't surprising that I was so keyed up about seeing her soon and exploring this amazing city together.

Actually, thinking about it, even though she would be landing later today I probably wouldn't see her for at least another day or two, because Sean was picking her up from the airport and I suspected they'd want some time to catch up. Images of romantic kisses and heated reunions briefly swept through my mind, but I didn't let myself dwell on exactly what that 'catching up' might involve, because I felt my cheeks immediately begin to burn. Even at twenty-six, I still blushed like a schoolgirl whenever the topic of sex was raised. It was a ridiculous and annoying trait, but seemingly unavoidable.

Rolling my eyes, I stood up from the tall kitchen stool and wandered across to the industrial-sized coffee machine in the hostel kitchen. This place was only a budget backpackers' joint, but they provided very tasty, very *free* coffee every morning, which was a definite point in its favour as far as I was concerned. Pouring myself a refill, I turned and leant back on the counter, still too twitchy with excitement to sit down. The caffeine couldn't have helped, either. Even knowing I would have to share Allie's time with Sean couldn't put a dampener on my day. My bestie was on her way, and after three years of living on entirely different continents we would finally be in the same city again.

As I sipped my coffee, I thought about Allie's whirlwind romance with Sean. After spending eight weeks apart she must be so excited to see him – and perhaps a little nervous if our phone call the other day was any indication. Part of me (a deep down, long-buried part) was actually slightly envious of their relationship. Not because he was famous – that didn't bother me at all. The part I was curious about was the closeness they shared. From Allie's descriptions, they seemed to be utterly head over heels for each other and could hardly wait to get back together after their time apart.

Pursing my lips, I absently played with the elastic bands around my wrist as my thoughts briefly darkened. A closeness like that with a man was something I would never experience, even if the idea did occasionally intrigue me. Having gone through a particularly traumatic relationship when I was younger, I now didn't date. At all. *Ever*. A fact that Allie found particularly frustrating, but was something I saw as a necessity to keep myself safe. No relationship could ever be worth the trauma I had gone through.

Shaking off the shudder that ran up my spine, I drained my coffee cup, washed it, and hung it on a hook before taking a deep, calming breath. Locking my feelings and memories away inside me – something I was now particularly good at – I replaced my smile and turned back to the room feeling far calmer.

I needed to find some distractions to fill my time for the next day or two, because knowing Allie would be here soon was driving me nuts with excitement. It was still early, so maybe I could burn off some of this fidgety energy with a run, and then head out at lunchtime to register with a few more employment agencies.

Even though the hostel was cheap, I was essentially

living off my savings and so couldn't afford to stay for much longer without finding work. Seeing as Allie was going to be here for at least a month, I had decided that I may as well try to get a temporary job and extend my stay too.

As I made my way out of the large kitchen, I heard a familiar piece of music from the lounge area that made me pause. Turning my gaze to the television, I saw the opening credits of one of my favourite shows, *Fire Lab*, and found myself humming along to the theme tune as my grin got wider. I wasn't a massive telly watcher, but this show was based around an arson unit in LA and had it all: drama, action, a touch of romance, and of course, Jack Felton. A man so handsome it should be illegal. Just as thoughts of him entered my mind, there he was, gracing the screen with his dark-haired godliness, warm brown eyes, and chiselled jaw.

Before I could stop it, a small appreciative hum left my throat, drawing the amused attention of the lone occupant of the sofa.

'He's quite a hunk, isn't he?' the girl said, as she grinned at me in agreement then turned back to the TV to join me in my ogling.

My cheeks flushed traitorously, but the girl's attention was firmly rooted on the TV and I felt myself relax. I might not date, but I *did* occasionally window shop – after all, I was a twenty-six year-old woman, not a ninety-year-old nun. Jack was my latest crush, and since he'd been signed as the lead in *Fire Lab* I had become quite a closet fan of both the show and him. According to the gossip magazines I sometimes read, he lived in LA too – not that I'd seen him, of course, but the fact that I was in the same city as him always gave me a little thrill when I stopped to consider it.

It was tempting to linger and indulge in watching the

programme, but I tore myself away and turned for the stairs. Work was needed, and today was the day to find some. Now I just had to pound the tarmac for a nice cleansing run and then dust down my suit to hit the employment agencies.

Chapter Three

Allie

So here I was. Los Angeles International arrivals terminal. Thanks to some strong winds on the way I was over an hour early, and grateful to finally be able to stretch my legs properly. I was also so excited that I felt sick. Although admittedly that might be down to the chickpea and beef sandwich I'd had on the plane about two hours ago, because it had smelt decidedly dodgy and hadn't tasted much better.

As I made my way through the throng of people attempting to exit the airport I felt my phone vibrate in my handbag and smiled, glad that I had remembered to turn it back on after landing. Dragging my suitcase away from the chaos of the luggage carousel, I tucked myself out of the way and then dug around amongst the debris in my handbag – Kindle, chewing gum, hair brush; you name it, I had it – until I finally found my phone.

Seeing a message from Sean, my stomach bunched with excitable nerves, but my face curled into a smile nonetheless as I slid my thumb across the screen to open it.

From: Sean
Checked your arrival and saw you were early so I'm here already. Look for a driver with your name, I'm in the car. Hurry up. I can't wait to see you. S x

A pang of disappointment settled in my chest – I'd been half hoping for a romantic reunion in the arrivals lounge, with Sean sweeping me into his arms and spinning me about frivolously while I giggled and smothered him in sloppy kisses. *Pfft.* I made a dismissive noise with my lips and rolled my eyes – that was the stuff of movies, and although Sean might be a film star, he'd already warned me that the reality of dating a famous person wasn't going to be easy.

Popping my phone back in my pocket I made my way through Customs with a small accepting smile on my face – Sean had an established reputation in Hollywood and often drew crowds, so meeting me in the car made sense. But I was still a little disappointed.

Exiting into the main terminal building I was met by a sea of expectant faces belonging to the families and loved ones waiting to greet their relatives. It was so busy that I actually found it a little overwhelming at first, and the huge glass building seemed to elevate the noise around me to astronomical proportions until I was almost wincing.

Glancing repeatedly around the crowd, my eyes finally caught sight of a smartly suited man holding a placard with my name upon it, just as Sean had said. What Sean hadn't said however, was that it would state my full name – Alexis Louise Shaw. Bastard. I'd told him how much I hated my first name, and I could just imagine him sat in the car having a good chuckle to himself.

Tentatively making my way across, among the jostling crowds, I began to feel the bundle of nerves in my stomach expanding. I was so excited about seeing Sean again, but simultaneously I was nervous. It had been a full two months since we'd seen each other in person, and given that our relationship was so new, the distance had made me jittery. Not to mention the tense Skype calls. Forget edgy, those had made me full on paranoid.

The suited man silently nodded at me as I reached his side and gave him a hesitant smile. 'Good afternoon. You must be Miss Shaw.' Seeing my jerky nod, he gave me a smile. 'My name is David. I'm here to pick you up on behalf of Mr Phillips,' he informed me in a deep American accent.

His very being exuded professionalism: perfect posture, crisp white shirt, flat cap, and a black suit that wouldn't have looked out of place in *Men in Black*. Taking the handle of my case, he inclined his head towards the exit doors. 'The car is just outside.' He set off in the direction of the exit signs before flashing me a gleaming white grin. 'I hope you brought your sunglasses, because we're having a bit of a heatwave at the moment. It's sixty-nine degrees Fahrenheit today, far warmer than usual for this time of year.'

His words were like music to my ears because back in the UK I'd left behind one of the coldest, wettest Aprils ever recorded. Bring on the rays. The sticky warmth of the day engulfed me as we exited the terminal and I smiled happily, tipping my face back to briefly soak up the sun. It might only be the end of April, but David was right about the heatwave – it was far hotter than I'd been expecting.

Lowering my gaze again I found David waiting patiently for me and looking rather amused by my impromptu sunbathing session. Flushing with embarrassment, I began to move again, following him like an obedient puppy until we reached a long queue of cars waiting by the kerb. As I gazed at the different vehicles my eyes widened. I'd literally never seen so many expensive cars in one place. I suppose it was a sign that you were in Los Angeles when the majority of cars sitting in the short stay car park were Porches and Mercedes.

Opening the boot of a sleek black limo at the front of the line, David slid my case inside before holding the back door open and leaning his head in. 'I'll just be a few moments while I pay the car parking fee, Sir.'

I barely noticed David disappearing because my entire body was now aware of the fact that Sean was just a few feet away. Would he be pleased to see me? Would everything be OK between us? And would the attraction be the same? God, I hoped so. The hairs on my arms stood to attention, my stomach was spinning like crazy and my heart had started accelerating so quickly that it felt like a bass drum pounding in my chest. In fact, I felt decidedly lightheaded as I dipped my shoulders to enter the car and only just managed to persuade my trembling fingers to pull the door shut behind me.

This was it – reunion time.

I was barely in the car before I was engulfed in the glorious sight, smell, and strong arms of Sean as he took a hold of my upper arms and literally dragged me across the car and onto his lap, causing me to yelp in shock and then giggle happily.

Over the course of just a few seconds it was like a hormone bomb had exploded inside the car. We didn't even bother to say hello, instead we became a blur of clutching fists, exploring lips, and lusty moans, rapidly reacquainting ourselves after our separation. God, I'd missed him so much. The relief from his keen response washed over me in blissful waves, relaxing my previous insecurities until I felt like a pliant, boneless mass of lust poured like a second skin across his body.

This was hardly elegant. I was sitting sideways across Sean's lap with my skirt askew and rumpled, but I still managed to shamefully grind down on his groin. My fingers greedily slid through the silky strands at the back of Sean's head, eliciting a groan of pleasure from him as I tugged to pull him even nearer, not satisfied with our already close contact. Sean's hot tongue delved between my lips, twining with mine as he hummed his appreciation into my mouth. Taking hold of my hips in a similarly tight hold, he jerked me down so I could clearly feel the heat of his groin against me through our clothing.

Our breaths were mixing and combining in my mouth, his taste so familiar and divine that I really couldn't believe I'd lasted eight weeks without him. Grumbling something unintelligible against my neck, Sean lifted me, hitching up my skirt at the same time as shifting my legs so I was now straddling his lap. Giving a sharp, upward thrust he prodded the growing evidence of his excitement against me. *Right* against me. Oh God. We were joined so firmly that there was no disguising the hot length of his excitement pulsing between us against the thin lace of my knickers.

I didn't care where we were, I wanted him. *Right now.*

It appeared that Sean was on the same wavelength, because one of his hands pressed down between us and dug underneath my skirt until his fingers found the damp lace at my groin. 'Hmmm. Lace. These feel too nice to rip off. Shame,' he muttered as he pulled the fabric aside and slid a finger along my quivering flesh to my clit.

My eyes rolled back in my skull at the unbelievable pleasure as a gargled moan left my throat. That felt so bloody good. I was so desperate for him that I nearly yelled out, 'Rip them off! I don't care!' but instead, I brought myself back to the moment and set about doing my own burrowing until my fingers found, and hastily undid, the zip of his jeans.

From the moment his hot, hard cock surged free into my palm, there really was no doubt about what was going to happen, it was just quite a surprise to me how *quickly* it happened.

One second I was groaning my appreciation of his talented fingers as I reciprocated by gripping his firm shaft, then the next moment Sean had lifted me and, after impatiently flicking my knickers out of the way, had dragged me down to line up my entrance with his waiting cock.

'This is going to be so fucking good,' he muttered hotly. The sounds of my yelps and Sean's groans then filled the car as he nudged the first few inches inside me before becoming wedged. Sean was rather well graced in the manhood department, and I vividly recalled how I'd found fitting him in a bit of a challenge at the start of our relationship, but I'd adjusted over time. I suppose after the few months apart where my body had gone without sex, I just wasn't used to this type of generous intrusion any more.

Never being one to turn down a challenge, I impatiently wiggled on his lap, trying to push myself down and causing Sean to growl against my mouth as he gripped my hips to stop me. 'For fuck's sake, don't hurt yourself,' he murmured, licking two fingers and lowering them between us to add more lubrication. He really didn't need to; I could feel that I was wet enough. I just needed time to stretch a bit.

Lifting his face to kiss me, Sean held me half-impaled on him, my body relaxing as his slow, luxurious kiss worked its magic, making me accept more of him until at last he was fully sheathed inside me.

Our foreheads met, damp with sweat, dilated eyes burning with desire as we grinned at each other and took a second to absorb how great it felt to be reconnected again. Really, *really* flipping great.

The noise of a car door closing followed by a polite cough from behind me had me rapidly tensing and letting out a small shriek as I hastily sat upright. Giving a quick glance over my shoulder I belatedly realised that the privacy screen was down, and that David was now in the car and waiting patiently for instructions.

Holy fuck.

I was panting hard, turned on like a lightbulb, and horrendously aware that I had Sean's cock buried inside me twitching away happily. My cheeks filled with a heated blush so rapidly that I must surely have been depriving other body parts of much needed blood. Oh God. This was utterly mortifying.

Wincing with embarrassment, I rapidly turned back to Sean to hide my flaming face, but instead of seeing my chagrin reflected in his own expression, I instead found a wicked grin gracing his lips. Jesus, did he not care that we were basically having sex in front of the driver at this very minute?

Raising my eyebrows at him in amazement I shook my head and tried to focus on staying calm. Unfortunately, that failed completely, and my attempts at focusing merely made me hugely aware of the soft warmth of his pubic hair as it nestled intimately against mine. *Bugger, bugger, bugger.* Just then, his rigid cock gave a jerk inside of me, as if taunting me for my embarrassment. The audience wasn't giving him performance issues then.

What the hell should I do? If I climbed off his lap it would leave Sean uncovered and make it even more obvious what we were up to, but apart from that I was flat out of ideas. The feeling of Sean's hands gently smoothing over my bottom and onto his thighs grounded me slightly and made me realise that maybe, *just maybe*, David couldn't see exactly how intimately joined we were. Yes I was straddling Sean's lap, which was embarrassing enough, but he still had his trousers on, so if my skirt was down at the back David might just assume that we were having a reunion cuddle.

A very hands-on reunion cuddle. Which technically we were, just with a bit more groin action …

I couldn't believe I'd lost control like this in front of David. How shameful. I'd been about thirty seconds away from some serious backseat bouncing manoeuvres too. Now *that* would have been really embarrassing.

'Traffic's pretty heavy so it'll take a while to get out of the airport grounds, sir. I'll let you two … um … catch up, and once we're on the freeway you can let me know where we're heading.'

'Perfect. Thanks, David,' Sean replied, sounding cool, calm, and in complete control. I gave him an astounded look, which he brushed off with a smile as he casually leant around me to close the privacy divider. He was buried inside me balls deep, how the heck had he managed to sound so … *normal*? If I were to try to speak I had no doubt that it would come out as a wobbly, incoherent squeak.

We both remained rigidly still – apart from Sean's cock, which was still lurching inside me like crazy – as the mechanical whirring of the screen hummed for about fifteen seconds, and then there was silence, signalling we were now alone.

A huge breath left my lungs as I registered my heart clattering against my ribs and lowered my head onto his shoulder in relief. 'We can stop, or are you OK to carry on, my gorgeous girl?'

That had been a close call, but now we were alone, joined at the groin and desperate for release, so there seemed only one thing to do. Get on with it.

Instead of answering him audibly, I raised myself onto my knees, the soft leather of the seat giving a whisper of sound as I pulled him almost completely from my body. I saw a flicker of disappointment cross his features, presumably because he thought I was going to stop things altogether, before I let my body drop back down, our hips clashing as I seated myself fully on his lap and once again had him imbedded inside my body.

His head flew back against the seat in shock as his fingers gripped painfully into my hips. '*Holy shit!* Give me some warning before pulling a move like that,' he cursed, his eyes widening in shock for a second before refocusing on the task at hand. 'You'll be the death of me, woman …' he muttered hotly as one hand dug into my hair, wrapped a portion around his wrist, and then dragged me forward to meet his lips. As our mouths collided feverishly he gave an upwards jerk of his hips that had me crying out in pleasure. '… but what a way to go,' he added with a devilish grin.

I might have been the one on top, but there was no doubt who was leading this reunion. With my hair gripped tightly in his fist, and his other on my bum guiding me up and down, his hips thrusting repeatedly into me, all I really had to do was hold on for the ride. And what a ride it was. Sean was so deep within me that I was building towards my climax practically from the first thrust.

'Touch yourself for me, Allie. Rub your clit,' he suddenly urged me, clearly reluctant to give up his hold on my hip or hair. Following his instruction I lowered my right hand and found my clitoris already swollen and sensitive, a gasp leaving my lips on the first contact. Sean's eyes were glowing, his enjoyment obvious as he bit on his lower lip and delivered a particularly hard thrust that had me seeing stars. I was so close …

With my fingers working against myself my knuckles kept brushing against his length as he jacked it in and out of me and I couldn't help but look down to watch. I'd never felt him like this before – never touched his cock as it entered my body, I mean, and I found it such a turn on that I briefly left my clit and rubbed at the base of him, finding him slippery from my arousal.

'Little tease,' he moaned, a smirk curling his mouth as he gave my hair a gentle tug to bring my head back up to him. Sensing our impending climaxes, Sean upped the ante, moving harder, faster, and deeper, and then just as I was about to slip across the blissful brink of my orgasm, he sealed our mouths together in a deep, searching kiss. His move successfully swallowed my cries of pleasure as I came, his tongue twisting with mine, and then seconds later he ground himself up inside me and came with so much power that I felt him give a series of almighty jerks before the warmth of his release flooded me.

No words were necessary for several minutes as we merely sat there in silence, clutched together, each holding the other up as we regained our breath and quietly enjoyed coming down from our incredible high.

When I finally mustered the strength to lift my head from his shoulder Sean cupped my jaw and flashed me a cheeky wink. 'I think we skipped the "hellos" and moved straight to the reunion fuck,' he mused, a smile pulling at his lips as he raised his hand and ran it gently through my damp hair, presumably attempting to flatten it after his earlier grabbing and tugging.

'Hello, my gorgeous girl.' His belated greeting made me chuckle as I lowered my lips to nuzzle his neck and then returned it with a shy one of my own.

'Hey you.' Lord knows why I suddenly felt shy. We'd just fucked like bunnies in the back of his limo *and* he was still inside me, so there was no place for bashfulness between us now.

With another wink Sean reached beside us to a central console and pulled out a box of tissues. Carefully lifting me, he let out a hiss of pleasure as his softening length slipped from my body, and then with great care he wiped me clean and pulled my knickers into place for me.

Helping me to shift from his lap, he gave a satisfied chuckle – probably at my complete inability to control my flopping, post-orgasmic body – sorted my skirt out for me, and then settled me close beside him on the seat.

He looked so boyish and yet devastatingly handsome, his hair now thoroughly messed up from my exploring fingers as he grinned his trademark smile and adjusted his jeans, popping himself back inside. I just couldn't drag my gaze away from him, not after so long apart. Luckily he seemed just as affected by our reunion, because his eyes remained focused on me the entire time which caused him to fumble with his zip for several seconds.

A huge breath filled my lungs as I sought out his hand and linked our fingers. I had missed him so much, and now we were back together, that fact hit me in the chest like a sledgehammer. It was crazy how connected I felt to him, but I was incredibly relieved that the mere sight of him still affected and aroused me just as much as it had when we'd first met. Part of me had been worried that our separation might have dulled the intensity of our bond, but that certainly wasn't the case; the car was still filled with the fizzing energy of our link. My heart was still pounding, stomach somersaulting, and the lust coursing through me was making me feel young and reckless.

Not to mention horny, hot, and damp in all the right places. We'd only just done it, but I could go again right now.

'My gorgeous girl,' he murmured into the hair by my temple, his warm breath making me shiver with delight as he seemed to inhale my scent before finally pulling back and gazing down at me with heavy-lidded eyes.

'I've missed you so much,' I replied in a whisper, hugely satisfied by our lovemaking but still embarrassed to have been caught out by the driver. I was British – we simply didn't do things like *that* in public and the knowledge that I had probably flashed him a good portion of my knicker-clad arse was still filling me with embarrassment.

'I can't believe David caught us. Do you think he realised what we were up to?'

Sean gave an unconcerned shrug that only a male could give, looking rather proud of the fact that he had had his way with me in the back of the car. 'Probably. But don't worry, he's seen far more explicit stuff in his rear view mirror.'

My entire body tensed as I ripped my hand from Sean's and swivelled on the seat to glare at him. Was he seriously just casually confessing to all the dirty deeds he'd done in the back of this car? Surprisingly, Sean dropped his head back and laughed heartily, not looking at all put out by my sudden anger.

'Not from me!' he chuckled. 'David's only been driving with me a year, but before that he used to work with a boyband – C-Plus, you know, the ones at the top of all the British charts?' My anger now stowed away again I gave a vague nod of acknowledgement and he continued. 'He said they were a nightmare, always pulling girls and having a right good go in the back of the car while he was driving them around

'Apparently the lead singers, the twins with the blue streaks in their hair, were real exhibitionists. They liked to have freaky threesomes and leave the privacy screen down on purpose …'

Raising a hand to stop him, I grimaced and shifted uncomfortably. 'Please tell me they didn't use this *exact* car?' Ugh, the thought of what substances would be on the leather was not a pleasant one.

'Nah, this one is owned by the film company, mostly used by stuffy directors, but I managed to wangle it for the day to impress you,' he said, flashing me a cheeky wink. 'Driving me around must be boring in comparison, but David reckons it's far more preferable.' I wouldn't have cared what car he picked me up in, but the fact that he had specially arranged to get a limo made me feel all warm and fuzzy.

'I can't wait to get you in bed,' Sean suddenly growled, his few words disintegrating my fuzzy feeling and firmly replacing it with one of lust and longing as my core clenched. With the memories of our recent encounter still thick in the air and desire pinging between us, it was a statement that I wholeheartedly agreed with. Smirking to myself, I let the gorgeous, loved-up feeling swell inside me, leaving me with a heady sensation of euphoria and contentment that was almost making me sleepy.

Just then, there was a short buzzing noise over the intercom, which was apparently some sort of signal from David, because Sean lowered the privacy screen again. A quick glance out of the windscreen showed that we were out of the airport grounds and on some sort of large motorway, but as I became aware that David was glancing at us in the rear view mirror I felt my cheeks heat. There was no way I could look him in the eye, not after what he had just witnessed. It was just too embarrassing so I quickly averted my gaze and looked out of the side window.

'Straight to the hotel, sir?' David asked, breaking me from my contented, lusty bubble and making me frown in confusion. Hotel? What hotel? I thought we were staying in Sean's apartment. That had certainly been the plan when we'd spoken last week, anyway.

'Uh ...' Sean's eyes briefly flickered across to me, looking distinctly nervy, and then turned back to the driver. 'Yes please, David.' What had *that* look been about? And why the flipping heck were we going to a hotel?

'No problem, sir. There are some roadworks on the 405, so I'm going to detour slightly across town onto the 110. It won't add much to the journey, though. Should be about a thirty minute drive.'

Sean was suddenly looking really uncomfortable next to me as he murmured his thanks and reached around me to raise the privacy screen again. In just a few seconds we were isolated in our own little world, but the lust and desire that had been swirling in my system earlier had been completely flattened by his mention of a hotel.

Mere seconds ago, I would have whooped my excitement about having another thirty minutes closed away with Sean, and would probably have promptly set about ripping his clothes off, but now, after just a few innocent words from the driver my horniness had been thoroughly doused and I was suddenly sitting on the cold leather seat feeling wary.

'Seatbelt,' Sean murmured, still giving me an odd look as he reached across to try and fasten me in. He hadn't been worried about seatbelts earlier when he'd laid claim to my body, I thought grouchily. A mixture of concern and irritation rose in my system, causing me to slap his hands away and click myself in before turning back to him with a frown.

'We're not going to your new apartment?' I asked in a confused whisper.

'Uh, no … actually, something's come up, but I've booked you into a really nice hotel. Let's go there and I'll explain.' The slightest twitch at the corner of Sean's eye gave away some hidden tension and I felt my stomach drop. Was something wrong? Narrowing my eyes, I stared at him. It certainly looked as if something was wrong. As well as his sudden fidgeting and avoidance of eye contact, his words 'I've booked *you* into a really nice hotel' were screaming around my head like a klaxon – I wouldn't even be staying with him now! This was all incredibly strange and I felt distinctly alert despite my post-flight tiredness.

Nerves made both my mind and mouth go into autopilot. 'What came up? I thought you were looking forward to showing me your new apartment?'

Sean shifted on his seat and cleared his throat several times, his cheeks flushing again, but clearly not from lust this time. 'I was. I mean, *I am*. But I'm not staying in the new place at the moment.' Scratching at the back of his neck I watched as Sean's cheeks reddened further, a seemingly nervous reaction that did nothing to calm my anxiety. 'It's just details to do with the series … the production team have moved me into a house closer to set, that's all.'

Hmm, I could have sworn that one of the reasons he gave me for his choice of apartment was its convenient proximity to the set … but trying to recall the exact details of a conversation from nearly seven weeks ago was decidedly tricky, especially seeing as my mind was currently in overdrive.

He'd certainly greeted me with enough enthusiasm when I'd got in the car – the slight ache between my legs, swollen mouth, and damp panties were evidence of that – so I didn't want to appear desperately needy or defensive, but an obvious question presented itself in my mind which I couldn't help but ask. 'Why can't I stay with you, though?' I persevered, bitterly disappointed that I had come all the way here to spend my time alone in a hotel. Not that I couldn't happily entertain myself, of course, but when the original plan had been to stay with Sean and catch up, this new alternative certainly seemed a poor second option.

'Our relationship is still so new, Sean, we've barely spent any time together. I … I guess I was hoping to rectify that.'

Letting out a frustrated breath, Sean looked at me, his usually vibrant blue eyes cloudy and shadowed by a deep frown as his brows knitted together. 'I know, I wanted that too.' Running a hand through his dark hair it spiked up all over the place as if he'd had a small electric shock, and, because of whatever product he used, it stayed that way, making him look like a handsome scarecrow. Under different circumstances I'd have smiled fondly and leaned over to smooth it down for him, but now I was edgy and unsure what was going on, so I kept my distance and joined my hands in my lap.

Perhaps he saw my frown or the way my posture had stiffened, because Sean leant across and pried my hands apart, taking one into the warmth of his and lifting it to his lips where he kissed the palm several times. 'It's just that it's a property owned by the film company and only employees can stay there. I'm sorry, Allie.'

Oh. Well, I suppose that could logically explain things. Plus I knew he'd been working horrendously long hours this week, which could perhaps be the reason for his twitchiness. Gazing at my pale hand clutched in his tanned one, I let out a long breath, trying to release my paranoia and instead enjoy soaking up the warmth of his lips on my skin. It was infinitely reassuring, and I felt my nerves begin to unravel under his loving attentions.

Giving in to the seductive kisses he was fluttering along my wrist, I smiled, deciding that I was being overly suspicious and needed to chill out and appreciate that we were finally back together. I was tired from my long-haul flight, my brain not fully functioning yet, which was probably the cause of my insecurity and suspicion.

As we wound through traffic, the car once again began to fill with tension, but this time it had nothing to do with my earlier paranoia and everything to do with the red hot waves of lust that were once again flowing between us and seeming to heat me from the inside out.

Our months apart had left me decidedly horny, and now that we'd had sex once I couldn't seem to get it out of my mind. Sean's continued attention to my arm wasn't helping matters in the slightest either – his lips were still on my wrist, licking and nibbling at my thundering pulse point and making my blood feel like liquid fire in my veins. His free hand had settled on my bare knee a few seconds ago and was now working a trail up my leg and under the hem of my skirt to my inner thigh as if he was intent on initiating round two. Oh goodie. His tickling and massaging was leaving my skin increasingly hot, my entire body needy and flustered until I squirmed on the seat and let out a long, low, lusty moan.

Chuckling, Sean met my gaze, his eyes dilated with desire as he blinked slowly, a sexy smirk curling his lips. 'I'd like nothing more than to lift up that sexy little skirt, rip off your knickers, and fuck you again,' he informed me in a deceptively casual tone, as if he were discussing something mundane like the weather and not using deliciously crude language to describe the very thing I desperately wanted him to do to me.

'But for the things I plan to do to you next we need to make it back to the hotel. The quicker the better,' he murmured, before licking his lips again and huffing an impatient breath. 'We shouldn't be too much longer. Help distract me from your tempting little body, Allie,' he suggested with a wry smile, once again attempting to adjust his crotch with a wince. It seemed from the bulge in his jeans that Sean felt just as insatiable as me.

Thinking back to his last words I blinked several times, staring at him uselessly. I was bright red, could barely think straight, and he wanted me to conjure up a distraction? My brain was only just managing to keep my body functioning normally, let alone attempting to focus on thinking. His salacious words were still spinning in my brain, and my body had been well and truly whipped up into a frenzy, but as I let my gaze wander out of the window I saw a poster for AT&T, the American telecommunications company, and an idea hit me.

'Actually, I need to get an American pay-as-you-go SIM, can we quickly stop at a shop?' My voice sounded thick with desire, and breathless to the point where I was seriously doubting the ability of my legs to carry me into a store in their jellified state, but he'd asked for a distraction, and hey presto, I had provided one. I should have sorted this out before leaving home, but in the midst of all the packing, stress, and last-minute jobs it had been forgotten.

Sean laughed, but then dug his fingers into a ticklish spot by my groin – that hollow of skin just where the hip, stomach and groin meet – making me jerk and yelp, before he shot me an intense but amused stare. 'Did you not hear what I just said about needing to get back to the hotel *quickly*?' he grumbled, a faint smile finally gracing his gorgeous lips. 'But OK, we'll stop, as long as you really are quick.'

Nodding once, he lowered the privacy glass and reluctantly informed David of our slight detour before looking back at me, his eyes filled with an exhilarating mix of lust, love, and happiness. Returning his heated stare I licked my lips, deliberately dragging my tongue slowly and teasingly across my lower lip and successfully drawing his attention.

'I want to get you into bed just as much, Sean, believe me. I'll be quick as a flash,' I promised him in a low tone, my words causing a growl of appreciation to rumble from Sean's throat as he took my hand and gave a firm squeeze.

'Don't mention flashing,' he complained with a wince as he yet again tried to make his groin more comfortable. 'Now I'm just picturing you on your hands and knees with that gorgeous arse of yours flashing up at me enticingly. *Fuck*.' I couldn't stop the giggle that bubbled up at just how wound up Sean was, but one thing was for sure – if he was this focused on sex now, then things were set to be *explosive* between us by the time we got back to the hotel. My core quivered at that thought and I had to forcibly drag my eyes, and hands, away from him to stop the urge of throwing myself at him again.

As it turned out, there was a convenience store just off the main road only a few minutes later, and David assured us that even though it wasn't really a touristy part of town, they definitely did temporary SIM cards.

'You stay here, I'll just be a minute,' I told Sean as the car cruised to a stop in the lay-by opposite. Not that it was likely that he would have accompanied me anyway, I supposed. I could just see the headlines now, *'Hollywood heartthrob buys crappy disposable SIM Card from 7-Eleven.'*

I'm not entirely sure what made me do it – perhaps Sean's barely constrained lust was permeating my body, but suddenly I felt uninhibited and wild. Leaning over, I placed a scandalous, open-mouthed kiss on his mouth, briefly sucking his lower lip as I brazenly used my free hand to cup his groin and give it a firm squeeze, all the while hoping that David wasn't watching.

Lurching below my touch, Sean grabbed at my wrist and let out a long, hissed breath, his eyes shooting wide open. 'Christ, careful, Allie, one more touch like that and I'll come in my jeans.' I was thrilled by his response, rather proud to find him still rock-hard underneath the faded denim. Good. I'd make use of that as soon as we got to the hotel. I'd been so horny for the past two months that I couldn't wait to jump on him, and almost told David to skip the shop and take us straight back … but I *did* need the SIM card. My mum would panic if I didn't call her tonight, and it would cost a fortune from my UK number.

Sliding reluctantly from the car I gave one final, lighter caress to his manhood and giggled to myself as I heard a growl of frustration, followed by a series of heated curses. Grinning to myself I hurried through the muggy heat into the store, in a ridiculously good mood and thinking this day really couldn't get any better.

Chapter Four

Cait

Running had definitely been a good idea. I tended to get extremely fidgety when I was excited about something, and Allie's imminent arrival was exciting me to near explosive levels. I was super jittery and could barely keep still. Where was she now? Still in the air? Or had she landed yet? I was almost bursting at the seams with anticipation.

As my legs got into a nice, steady rhythm I started to relax into the run, my body working off the excess energy rather pleasantly as I began to mentally plan a list of sightseeing that Allie and I could do together. As I jogged energetically around the corner of a small community building in the park, I ran headlong into something solid and unrelenting like a hapless bird into a freshly washed window. There had been no warning or possible way to prepare myself, just *wham*.

I was vaguely aware of hard muscles and warm skin beneath my fingers before I went tumbling backwards, the impact from the stranger's broad, strong frame so powerful that it sent me cascading unceremoniously to the ground.

'Oof!' The air rushed from my lungs as my back hit the sun-warmed tarmac, winding me instantly and sending stars spinning in front of my eyes.

Unfortunately, any vague remnants of my composure were lost seconds later when I tried to draw in a breath and couldn't. Instead, awful retching noises began to escape from my heaving chest as I desperately tried to breathe, while simultaneously clawing at the stony ground in an attempt to sit up and gather some speck of my shattered dignity.

I failed on all counts.

My composure appeared to have deserted me and made a run for the hills, because air simply wasn't returning to my lungs and I was still wallowing around like a beached whale.

My iPod was blaring The Prodigy in my ears, but over the fast, rhythmic beat I vaguely heard a man's voice. 'God, I'm so sorry! Are you all right?'

I was sprawled on the floor with breath sawing from my lungs like a blocked drain and he was asking if I was all right? Did I flipping look all right? As I blinked in shock behind my sunglasses a multitude of sarcastic replies flew through my brain, but with my head spinning and my poor lungs winded, I couldn't actually voice any of them, choosing instead to check my stinging palms for scratches, which were thankfully minimal.

Tugging one earbud out so I could hear, I tried to calm my spinning head. 'Winded …' I finally managed to croak between rasping breaths. Blimey, I hadn't been winded like this since I was a kid and fell off of the rope swing in my back garden. I'd forgotten how ridiculously uncomfortable it was. I felt like someone had kicked me square in the chest with a hobnailed boot.

It suddenly occurred to my poor shocked brain that as well as being marginally injured, I was also lying on the ground by the feet of a man. He was towering over me, which might not bother some, but after my … *harrowing* … history with men – one man in particular – my brain began screaming at me how vulnerable my position was.

My cruel mind flickered back to memories of the last day with my ex, when I'd been in a similar position collapsed by his feet. He'd flipped out so badly that I'd had to run from him, but that hadn't deterred him and he'd chased me, and when I'd tripped and fallen to my knees he'd caught me …

A huge, painful shudder wracked my entire body as I came back to the present and my defences leapt to full alert. In my panic to put some distance between myself and the man, I momentarily dropped backwards and scrabbled myself away on my bum as I raised my face to assess him for signs of danger.

My elbows protested at the mistreatment, but it wasn't until he spoke that I vaguely began to come down from my panic. 'Whoa, careful! Just sit still for a second.' He sounded concerned by my tarmac floundering, hadn't leapt upon me, and was maintaining his distance, so I decided he didn't seem to be a threat and marginally relaxed my over-sensitive defences as I tried to focus on getting my breath back.

His blue baseball cap and wraparound sunglasses were swimming in front of my hazy vision like a mirage, which was definitely not a good sign. Letting out a low wheeze I winced and rubbed at my chest with the heel of my hand in an attempt to soothe the constricted muscles around my lungs.

'If you're winded you need to allow your diaphragm to expand properly. Here, let me help you stand.' His low, husky tone seemed vaguely familiar, and for some reason sent shivers dancing down my spine.

As I sat on the floor gasping desperately for breath and picking tiny, gritty stones out of my palms, I felt my panic returning as he suddenly held out a hand to help me up. I did *not* touch men, and I didn't let them touch me either. Regardless of my sprawled position on the floor, this guy was not going to be an exception to my strictly-enforced rule.

God, this was embarrassing. I couldn't believe I'd fallen so awkwardly. Reluctantly looking at his outstretched arm I shook my head. 'I'll be fine, thank you,' I grumbled wheezily as I began to try and clamber to my feet.

Unfortunately, no sooner had the soles of my feet landed back on the ground than I started to sway and stagger until I felt him gently slipping his hand to my lower back to steady me as I stumbled about like a drunken idiot.

As innocent and well-intended as it may have been, his touch almost caused me to choke on the limited oxygen I was managing to pull into my lungs. Electricity seemed to fizzle across my skin, stabbing me like a thousand pinpricks and sending terror shooting straight to my brain.

I wanted to vomit. Not from the fall, or my winded condition, but from the sudden contact of his hand on my back. My body simultaneously managed to feel frozen and horribly over-sensitised. As much as I wanted to move, I couldn't get my leaden legs to function, and then as a true indication of my descending panic, my vision started to go patchy. I needed to get away before I passed out, which judging from my spinning head, wasn't far off.

The five points where his fingers were touching me were now burning sparks singeing my skin, making it crawl unpleasantly as it once again reminded me all too bitterly of the one man I'd known who could cause such a visceral reaction in me. Greg – my fucktard of an ex; the one who had chased me until I'd had to crawl away from him on bloodied hands and knees. Right from the start of our relationship he'd always liked to place his hand possessively on my back in the *exact* spot that this man's fingers were currently settled. Needless to say, being touched on my back was now a pretty major trigger.

A huge shudder of fear racked my body and I jerked my head backwards sharply as my eyes shot to the jogger again, my heartbeat skyrocketing in my veins as my dark, terrifying memories flooded back to the surface. Seeing brown hair and broad shoulders, not Greg's wiry frame and blond mop, I almost fell to the floor again in relief.

He's not Greg.

Trying to tamp down the panic that had wrapped me in its icy vice, my right hand groped for the elastic bands on my left wrist and began to rhythmically ping them – this was my technique for controlling my anxiety – the sharp snap on my skin helping to bring my brain back from the brink of meltdown.

'You look really pale. Maybe you should sit down for a minute,' the stranger suggested, using his palm on my back to turn me towards a nearby bench. I let out a small hissed breath at his continued touch, but followed his advice and stepped to the bench before practically falling onto it as the man took a seat beside me.

Pulling out my second ear bud to remove the disorientating beat of the music, I straightened myself a little more and steadied my thoughts to try and restore my confidence.

Eventually managing to get a grip on my spiralling emotions, I slid along the bench to the furthest end so I was as far away from him as possible. It wasn't much distance, probably only a foot, but it made me feel infinitely more reassured. As if sensing my discomfort, his hand also dropped away from me and rested on the bench beside his thigh.

With his distracting touch gone I finally felt my chest expand properly and I sucked in several refreshing lungfuls of air while giving the elastic bands another quick, reassuring pluck.

Glancing across, I saw his eyebrows dipping behind his shades in a frown as if he was trying to work out my skittish behaviour. He'd be a while; even I couldn't work myself out sometimes. Lowering my head I stared at the ground, wishing he would just go and also wishing I'd never bothered to leave the hostel this morning. This had hardly turned out to be the refreshing start to the day I'd needed.

Taking in another fortifying breath, I felt steadier and decided to finally give this guy a proper look. The first thing I noticed was that his head was dipped, and even with him wearing a hat and shades it was obvious he was giving my wrist – and elastic bands – a peculiar look. Damn it. I hated being looked at like that. Clenching my hands into fists I stopped with the plucking and forced them to lie still in my lap.

From his light cotton running shorts and fitted blue T-shirt it seemed apparent that he had also been out for an early morning jog, before his collision with me had so rudely ended both of our fitness fixes, not to mention having very nearly sent me spiralling into a full meltdown in the middle of the park.

Edgily allowing my gaze to further assess him, I noted that his broad shoulders seemed to be attached to a toned body, with tanned, strong arms. He had incredibly muscular thighs lightly covered with soft brown hair that drew my gaze for several seconds longer than was probably polite. I'd never seen legs quite so … well, I wasn't exactly sure what it was I thought about them, but they were making my stomach tumble slightly and for some reason I couldn't seem to be able to look away.

Swallowing loudly, I finally tore my gaze away from his almost mesmerising muscles and let my eyes drift up towards the safer territory of his face. It turned out this wasn't much safer, because even with the top half of his head hidden under a low hat and sunglasses, I noticed that he had an angular, very manly, very *bearded* chin, and a lovely, slightly lopsided, half-smile, which he was now dazzling me with. It was a shame about the beard, really, because with a body like his and his cute smile, I suspected that the face hidden underneath all that shaggy fur would have been quite attractive too.

'Hi. Feeling better?' he enquired, and I nodded in response as a smile began to curve the corners of my lips and my gaze lingered on the full, appealing mouth I could see behind his beard. Frowning, I suddenly tensed, jerked my shoulders back, and looked away from him towards the gravel trail beyond. What the heck was wrong with me? I didn't ogle men, *ever*. In fact, I hadn't dated once since Greg. He'd put me off for life.

Narrowing my eyes behind my shades, I licked my lips and felt a trickle of unease settle in my belly at the strange reaction I was having to this guy.

He continued to sit quietly, allowing me the time I needed, and after several seconds of contemplation the only reason I could come up with for my odd reaction was self-consciousness, because from all I could see I had just run headfirst into what appeared to be a rather handsome man. I might not date, but I wasn't blind. This guy was clearly well built *and* good-looking, and my pulse quickened as horrendous embarrassment washed over me.

Shakily swallowing, I ran a hand through my sweaty hair and quickly decided that it was time to make a hasty exit before I could embarrass myself any further.

'I'm OK now ...' My voice sounded far from normal, all high and tremulous, probably caused by my diaphragm still trying to recover from my fall, or perhaps nerves from my odd reaction to him. 'Bye ... th ... thanks ...' I managed to say shakily.

Although why I was thanking the man who had just run me down I had no flipping idea. Rolling my eyes at my stupidity, I pushed myself up and turned on wobbly legs but as I began to walk carefully away I heard him click his tongue impatiently behind me.

'Wait, you're bleeding. Hang on, I'll have a look at it.' Reluctantly I turned back and saw he was indicating my right arm. Pushing my sunglasses up onto the top of my head, I glanced down and saw a trickle of blood running from a small gash on my elbow, and belatedly felt it sting. It wasn't anything too serious and could easily wait until I got back to the hostel, but before I could protest and get on my way, the stranger had risen from the bench and approached me.

Whipping off his cap and sunglasses he proceeded to wipe the sheen of sweat from his head and then took hold of my arm as he crouched down to get a better look.

Staring in horror at where his hand was now holding my arm, I felt my entire body tense again as black traces of fear began to seep back into my consciousness at the edge of my vision. For fuck's sake, I'd only just got my previous panic attack under control. I could seriously do without all of this constant touching.

Breathe. I ordered myself calmly. *Breathe.* But I couldn't, and any semblance of calmness shattered as panic began to engulf me. Annoyingly, because he was holding on to my right arm I couldn't even use my stress-relieving elastic bands to ease the situation.

I tried to tug my arm away from him, almost desperate to ping the little strip of elastic, but he held on and looked up at me curiously.

A gasping, panicked wheeze left my lungs, and I watched in astonishment as he slid one finger under the thin lace of elastic on my wrist and gave it the tiniest tweak for me. My skin flared with the snap, which was just enough to bring me back to earth and out of my anxious daze.

How bizarre. My mouth opened in shock at that surprise move, but just like that, I found I could breathe again. It was almost as if he had sensed my need for it. But how could he possibly know?

'You OK?' he asked softly, his tone ridiculously reassuring and causing me to nod at him jerkily. Perhaps it was his soothing tone or his strange ability to read my need, but for some reason I realised that the touch of this man didn't scare me any more, not half as much as I'd expected, anyway. It was almost … soothing, as if he'd managed to connect to my inner demons and push them away for a while.

As he continued to hold my arm I struggled to deal with this new phenomenon. I didn't do bodily contact, so how could I be allowing this *and* beginning to enjoy it?

Annoyance was easier to deal with than the mix of other emotions like curiosity, confusion, and attraction which were now swirling in my chest, so instead of giving in to the strange new sensations I focused myself on his presumptuous behaviour and felt my hackles rise. How dare he just assume I was fine with him grabbing on to me, and how *dare* he ping my elastic band? That was my nervous habit to indulge – not his!

Wincing, I realised I was letting my fears rule me again and being hugely over-sensitive. This guy certainly didn't seem to be a threat. From his actions and words so far, he was clearly only trying to help me, but like an irritating rash, my past experiences were still haunting me.

Calming my fluctuating nerves, I licked my dry lips and looked back to his face, wondering despairingly if there would ever be a day when my past didn't make interactions with men so bloody terrifying. Probably not. Sighing heavily, I blinked at my miserable prediction.

'Are you sure you're OK? You didn't bang your head when you fell did you? You seemed to zone out there for a second,' he asked again, still crouched by my side with concern obvious on his face.

As I saw the curious lift in his eyebrows I fully realised the extent of everything he must have witnessed over the last few minutes: elastic band plucking, tense body spasms, jerky breathing … God, the list of my crazy quirks was almost endless. I must have come across as such a wierdo.

I pasted a small smile on my face, determined to act like a normal human being for once, and nodded. 'I'm fine, thank you. I didn't bump my head, and this is just a small cut. I'll survive,' I answered feebly, completely avoiding his mention of me zoning out.

His eyes narrowed, but thankfully he didn't push it, and I breathed a sigh of relief.

It was rare for me to look men in the eye, but nothing about this encounter had so far been run of the mill, so I allowed myself a closer inspection. Now that I could see his features without the cap and glasses I took in his brown eyes and sweat-spiked hair. Drawing in a long, quiet breath, I blinked rapidly before gasping. Surely not … Suddenly everything seemed to happen in a strange dreamlike fashion. Even through his exercise-induced sweat and bushy beard, I knew who he was, and as the clarity of recognition hit me I found my legs rapidly turning to a consistency similar to jelly and threatening to give way. Again.

With eyes now as wide as saucers I looked at his hunched form to double-check my initial suspicions. As my eyes roved over his features and registered that I was indeed correct, I felt myself wavering on leaden feet as a further wave of dizziness swept over me. Fearing I might be about to fall over again, I had to reach out and support myself on his firm shoulder, which went against all my self-imposed rules about initiating contact with men, but was a necessity if I wished to avoid a second liaison with the tarmac.

There was literally no way I couldn't hold on to him. I felt so dizzy that I really might fall over if I let go. Once again, touching him made my skin prickle, this time not with fear but some other bizarre reaction that I couldn't quite place. I ignored it best I could, trying to push the strange sensation aside with a firm shake of my head as I dealt with the other peculiar reality currently on my mind – there was no doubt about it, the man who had knocked me down and was now kneeling at my side performing impromptu first aid on me was none other than Jack Felton, my current celeb crush and the guy I'd fondly watched on the television earlier this morning.

Holy shit balls.

When I'd first arrived in LA I'd read in a gossip magazine that Jack had been spotted running in this park, and that knowledge *might* have slightly swayed my choice in jogging spot, but only because it had been exciting to imagine using the same running trails as him. I'd never in a million years thought I'd actually see him. Or get run down by him. This park was huge, over four and a half acres of wooded tracks, so to be honest, I was still struggling with the unbelievable odds as I sat there gawking up at him.

'It … it's you …' I mumbled, unable to control myself as my mouth finally caught up with my brain. I tilted my head to the side to properly look at him. *That* was why his voice sounded familiar, because it *was*.

At my belated recognition, an amused expression spread across his face, crinkling the corners of his eyes and making my heart beat just a little faster behind my ribs.

This was at once both utterly exhilarating and completely mortifying, because before me was Jack Felton (admittedly a heavily bearded version) which was so surreal and exciting that I could barely comprehend it. But on the other side of things, that meant that this rather successful film star and general all-round heartthrob had just witnessed me lying on the floor with my legs splayed and grunting like a hippopotamus in heat.

As a blush seared my cheeks, it vaguely occurred to me how amusing Allie would find this when I told her. She knew I had a bit of a soft spot for Jack, but talk about random coincidences! First her getting snowed in with Sean Phillips, and now me getting practically slam dunked by Jack Felton. Two run-ins with Hollywood hunks in less than four months. Who would have placed money on that? Not me, that was for sure. What a small, crazy world.

Looking disbelievingly at him again while simultaneously registering his alarmingly warm brown eyes, I replayed my unladylike fall and subsequent panic attacks and internally cringed. Crap, crap, crap.

Ignoring my humiliated look he gave me a casual shrug. 'Yeah, sorry to disappoint you. They were going to send George Clooney to knock you over, but instead you got me.' Actually, if I was offered a choice between Jack Felton and George Clooney, I'd pick Jack every single time.

The way he brushed off my earlier nerves and was joking to put me at ease was incredibly sweet, but then he smiled up at me as he began to examine my cut and I found myself almost unable to breathe. God, that smile. My stomach performed an enormous flip just from the sight of it.

'I'm surprised you recognised me with this monstrosity,' he commented as he almost lovingly stroked his beard. Unaware of the impact his incredible smile had had on me, he flashed me another one and went back to tending to my arm as he continued to speak. 'It's for an episode of the show. Thankfully I can cut it off soon, bloody thing is so itchy.'

The presence of the beard had totally thrown me. His character in *Fire Lab* was always clean shaven, so I'd never seen him with one before. I wasn't usually a fan of beards, but I had to say, this one looked pretty good. Or perhaps that was just down to my fondness for the man displaying it …

'Well, it's your lucky day. I'm wearing new trainers today so have these with me in case of blisters,' he explained as he pulled two plasters from his shorts pocket with another of those heart-stopping half smiles that he was evidently rather good at.

This was so strange on so many levels. For one thing, he was famous, but instead of being on a television he was standing in front of me large as life. Secondly, he was touching me. Not only was I allowing it, but it wasn't freaking me out, and finally my body was reacting to a man in ways that I hadn't experienced for a long time. A very, *very* long time.

Talk about messing with my head.

Trying to shake off the peculiar feelings swirling in my stomach, I swallowed and dragged up my usual sensible side with significant difficulty. 'Ah, always prepared? You must have been in the Scouts,' I quipped lightly, relieved that I at least sounded calmer than my thundering heart and churning stomach indicated.

'Actually, Scouts was on the same night as drama club and I chose to go to the latter … much to the disappointment of my father,' Jack commented casually before glancing up at me. 'My dad was quite old-fashioned. He believed that Scouts was for boys and drama was for girls, and thought that by choosing drama club I was attempting to discreetly tell him I was gay.'

Jack upped his half smile to a grin, and in response I became slightly light-headed. Wow … when it was turned up to full power, his smile really was something else. Like a

4D, surround sound, all-singing, all-dancing, out-of-body experience. I'd seen it enough times on television, but in the flesh it really was quite breath-taking.

I knew he was still talking to me, but I was finding myself rather distracted by his smile and the way the corners of his eyes crinkled so appealingly.

'I'm not, by the way,' Jack added as he carefully peeled the paper back from the plaster. I didn't understand, and started to panic that maybe he had said something important I had completely missed while I was lost in my ridiculous swoon. Pocketing the papers from the plaster, he glanced up with his captivating eyes again.

'Gay. I'm not gay,' he clarified with another grin. Actually, the reason I chose drama club was because I fancied Miss Bright something rotten … now that woman had *great* legs …' He grinned wickedly at me, and I was horrified to feel my heart react by attempting to kick its way out of my rib cage like a wild kangaroo. 'That plus my interest in acting, of course,' he added with a charming quirk of his eyebrows.

Struggling not to sigh out loud like a pathetic teenager, it suddenly occurred to me that Jack might be mildly flirting with me. The warm glances, smiles, and attention seemed to imply so, or perhaps he was always this friendly and charming with everyone he met (and collided with) while running in the park.

As I gazed down at him, I felt that peculiar feeling niggling at my stomach again; a heavy, warm sensation, making me suddenly acutely aware of a growing dampness between my legs. A flush bloomed on my already heated cheeks as I just about died from embarrassment. Bloody hell, I was actually aroused – and all he was doing was touching my arm.

What the heck was going on? I'd shut myself down so strictly since Greg that I literally couldn't remember the last time I had felt properly sexually attracted to anyone, but long-forgotten emotions were now flooding my system and making it abundantly clear that that was definitely what I felt.

Shaking my head, I blinked wildly. I'd never reacted to a man like this, not even with Greg at the start when he'd been a total charmer and seemingly lovely. As Jack continued to clean my elbow with a tissue, I made a huge effort to shake it off, and instead of focusing on the chemical reaction happening in my body I drew in several long breaths and stared intently at the beautiful park until my composure began to settle again.

Finally feeling in control enough to risk a glance at Jack, I looked down at the top of his head where he was still tending to my arm. I was standing there like an idiot staring at the parting in his hair when Jack glanced up and caught me looking at him. Guiltily, I flushed immediately, but Jack merely flashed me another stupendous grin, winked at me, and then continued with his task.

A wink? Raising my eyebrows in surprise I sucked in a shocked breath ... surely *that* counted as flirtatious? I thought I'd been imagining it earlier, but after that, I was becoming more and more certain that the glances Jack had been giving me over the last five minutes were, in fact, appreciative ones. The odd thing was, I wasn't entirely sure how I felt about it. History had taught me to run as soon as a man showed even the remotest interest in me, and I usually did, and yet here I was allowing this virtual stranger to flirt with me.

There was no way someone like Jack would be interested in me. I knew I was pretty – my friends always told me so, anyway – but I had some serious issues, some of which he had witnessed first-hand, so really the chances of him looking at me that way were slim.

I very nearly laughed out loud at the wandering direction of my thoughts. How ironic that I avoided even considering romantic attachments to men and yet here I was, openly weighing up the possibility that he might find me attractive. Smiling wryly, I decided that even if I was in the market for a boyfriend – which I most definitely wasn't – then I wouldn't even be in Jack's league. In fact, I was probably so many rungs *below* his league that I almost snorted out a dry laugh, putting his glances down to nothing more than him being friendly.

Even with my dismissal of his attention, I couldn't help but notice that the sensuous, curling heat was still settled in my stomach. But before I could consider it further, my thoughts were distracted as Jack finished tending to my elbow and stood up.

With a satisfied nod, he smoothed the plaster down carefully with warm fingers, sending a shudder of pleasure running through my body that I desperately tried to disguise as a stretch. God, I was pathetic.

My unprecedented reaction was leaving me floundering and making a mockery out of my supposed self-security and the rigid defences I'd built up over the years. I had no idea how I could be so ridiculously attracted to a man I had literally only met five minutes ago, but that certainly appeared to be the case.

Jack's fingers seemed to linger on my elbow for a touch longer than was necessary as his eyes observed me intently and a thick silence fell between us, making me feel incredibly exposed. His silent, curious gaze was unnerving, but when it dropped to my lips and remained there I very nearly whimpered.

Actually, it was worse than a whimper, because I suddenly realised to my horror that I was panting so hard that I was wheezing. Quite audibly, actually. Which incredibly embarrassing, but hopefully could be passed off as a side-effect of my fall. Jerking my arm away, I raised my eyes to his and was immediately hit with his penetrating gaze again.

Before my poor confused brain could make too much of it, Jack's expression cleared as he ran a hand rakishly through his ruffled hair, a gesture which proved to be totally pointless because no sooner had he lowered his arm that his brown mop of hair tumbled haphazardly across his forehead again.

'Not bad, eh?' he said, tipping his fur-covered chin towards my elbow and smiling proudly at his first aid skills. I nodded weakly as I tried to recover a grip on my shredded composure and decided that now was an ideal chance to make a swift exit.

'I can't run now that I've cooled down. I'd probably pull a muscle,' Jack joked. 'Shall we walk together for a while?' His voice sounded pleasant and light but I could have sworn that he looked just a tiny bit hopeful.

I think I was officially delusional. I felt my forefinger begin to slide up my wrist and I gave one of the elastic bands a ping. I saw Jack's eyes follow the movement with interest, his gaze narrowing briefly as he looked at my reddening skin.

With my nerve endings completely frazzled from Jack's closeness, I tilted my head trying to commit the image of his handsome face to memory before I left, then shook my head with far more force than necessary.

'Uhhh, actually, I think I'll keep running.' I had found that meeting Jack in the flesh had done nothing to cool my stupid crush on him. Quite the opposite, in fact, so in my nervous state I spoke hurriedly, knowing as the words left my tongue that they sounded abrupt and rude.

My confused emotions suddenly made me feel really defensive and irritable. Why was he flirting with me anyway? Was he so used to women literally throwing themselves at him that he didn't care if they were sweaty and red as long as he stood a chance of getting laid? My lip curled in annoyance as flashes of Greg skimmed through my mind again.

Was Jack just as shallow and narrow-minded as Greg had been? Were all men completely obsessed with nothing but sex? I wasn't experienced enough to know, but unfortunately my only encounters with the opposite sex so far had certainly suggested so.

Jack was famous and astonishingly good-looking – and clearly knew it. He probably had this effect on most women. Perhaps it was a game to him, fun to see how flustered he could make us. Tensing my jaw, I cursed myself, my finger pinging the elastic band almost relentlessly and making me wince. How could I have got so carried away? I never let my guard down around men. Least of all handsome ones. I felt hot annoyance coursing up through my veins at my own naïvety.

Definitely time to leave. Not to mention forget the crush I had on him and avoid all future urges to even think about him. Giving one last look toward Jack, I scowled at my own stupidity before spinning on my heels and walking away from him without another word.

Chapter Five

Allie

The tourist SIM cards were easy enough to locate – there was an entire rack of them just inside the door under the cool breeze from the shop's air conditioner. Selecting the cheapest one that did what I needed (pay-as-you-go with unlimited international calls and texts) I darted across to the till, keen to get back to Sean and see exactly what naughtiness he had planned for us this afternoon.

As I stood in the queue daydreaming, I conjured up images involving me, him, lots of sweaty skin slapping, and a king-sized bed. A filthy grin spread on my lips, but whatever it was he had up his sleeve I knew that I would enjoy it because I would be with him.

As the queue shuffled forward, I was trying to work out which of the American notes and coins I needed when my eye caught the headline of a newspaper stacked to my right. Picking up a copy I read the headline again and my brain stalled, unable to digest the words no matter how many times I went over them. Quickly skimming the rest of the article I suddenly felt sick to my stomach, my blood turning cold in my veins and my head spinning as I tried to work out what I was seeing.

It couldn't be true. Could it?

My brain was too caught up in the sudden confusion to notice that the cashier was now free. Someone behind me gave a cough, and then politely nudged me forward, where I blinked out of my trance and realised it was my turn to pay. Handing over a note to pay for both my items I didn't even bother to wait for my change as I stepped away from the busy counter in a complete daze.

Tucking the paper under my arm with trembling fingers, I stumbled towards the exit, barely knowing what to do next. My head couldn't process what I'd just read, but that didn't stop me replaying the headline over and over in my mind.

What should I do? I could hardly stay hidden away in the shop all afternoon. Eventually Sean would send David in to check where I was and I'd look like a complete idiot. Working on autopilot I made my way towards the exit and back towards the waiting limo, barely noticing how my skin instantly dampened from the humid day.

Surely the headline was just a load of rubbish. People always said you should never believe what was printed in the papers, didn't they? But my mind flicked back to Sean's twitchy behaviour earlier and I felt concern settle heavily in my stomach. Did this explain why I was suddenly being placed in a hotel? I shook my spinning head, feeling utterly confused, because he'd been all over me in the car, and *inside* me, so it didn't make any sense whatsoever.

By the time I had crossed the pavement David was holding open the car door for me and I slid in, automatically looking towards Sean as my heart seemed to cramp in my chest, with a pain so sharp that I almost had to reach up and rub at it.

'Get a SIM card?' he asked, obviously completely unaware of my inner turmoil. Somehow I nodded and pretended that nothing was wrong, even managing to return his smile, albeit weakly, and deciding that I needed to test the water to see if this headline held any truth, or if it was just made up tat only worthy of the bin.

If I were less enthusiastic in my return to the car than he'd been expecting, Sean didn't say anything, but he did pull me across the seat and tug me in for another breath-taking kiss. At first I was about to push away and question him about what I'd read in the paper, but his lips were like a magic balm and I found myself instantly dragged under his spell and helpless to resist.

Knowing that we had some serious issues to discuss I gave myself two minutes reprieve to soak up his delicious attention, just in case it would be the last time I ever got to do so. Caving to his persuasive mouth I parted my lips as his tongue massaged against mine, exploring leisurely as his hands dug through my hair.

'You kept it long,' he growled appreciatively as his fingers threaded through the long tresses he had always adored. He was right, I had deliberately avoided having it cut for six weeks just so it would be as he liked it, but with the headline still floating around my mind I had to wonder if it had been a wasted effort on my part.

If the newspaper article was true, then it made a complete mockery of his warm welcome – or perhaps that should be scorching welcome, because the car sex had been smoking hot and right up there on my list of top ten Sean shags. To be honest, all my best sexual experiences had been with Sean. Previous boyfriends just paled into non-existence in comparison.

As much as I wanted to dismiss what I'd just read and give myself over to his seduction, the photographs that accompanied the article seemed to be imprinted on my brain like a singed, smoking brand and were endlessly taunting me, making it impossible to fall completely under his spell.

I needed to find out the truth, and I needed to find it out now. Puffing out a sigh I untangled myself from his arms with some difficultly and sat up straighter, only to be met by Sean's desire-flushed face and a questioning look. It was all so incredibly perplexing that I wanted to scowl at the confusing mess, but trying to keep my wits about me I faked a smile that hopefully looked convincing.

'Sorry, I just needed to come up for air for a second.' That lie should easily pass unquestioned, because we had both been getting well and truly carried away yet again. Sean smiled, licking his lips and nodding as he raised a hand to brush some stray hairs from my cheek.

Keeping myself alert I dodged his hand and swept my hair back myself, earning a small frown of disapproval from him. 'So the film company are picky enough to stop you having any guests at the house? That seems a bit tight,' I said lightly, scrutinising his reaction carefully and hoping that I would see nothing to make me doubt his honesty with me.

Unfortunately, I saw the complete opposite: his eyes widened at my words, brows dropping in concern, and he definitely shifted uncomfortably in his seat, all causing my heart to sink even lower in my chest.

We might not have been together very long, but I always had a sense for when someone was lying. I put it down to being a good reader of people – although Cait called it my 'bullshit detector' – and right now I was sensing some seriously fresh, steaming bullshit, because I could spot Sean's nervous tics a mile off. He was shifting in the seat repeatedly, pursing his lips nervously, and had a twitch in his eye that was impossible to miss.

Any one of these alone made it screamingly obvious that Sean was anxious about something, but add all three together and it seemed to scream 'guilty'. It definitely didn't make me any more confident about the way this conversation was going to go.

'Um … yeah … they are,' he stuttered, completely avoiding eye contact, at which I nodded, deciding to just confront him head-on.

Pulling in a deep breath I tried my best to strengthen myself for what was coming as I tugged the newspaper out from under my handbag. 'So it has nothing to do with this?' I said blandly, a horrible suffocating feeling spreading in my chest as I opened the paper to show him the front page headline.

'Sean Phillips and co-star Savannah Hilton turn fictional love into reality with their new engagement.'

Sean might be an actor capable of faking expressions to make a living, but as he ran his eyes over the paper there was no disguising that he looked as shocked as I felt. No, actually, shocked is the wrong word. Shock would indicate that he was unaware and had just found out, but it was clear that he knew all about the story. 'Horrified' would be a more accurate description. He was more horrified to be caught out.

Suddenly he was doing a very good impersonation of a puffer fish – eyes bulging, mouth opening and closing several times, and a vein popping up on his left temple as his wide eyes flicked to mine.

'Fuck!' His hand scraped through his hair so violently that he must surely have ripped several chunks out from the roots before he flung his arm back down onto the seat in defeat. 'I didn't want you to find out this way, Allie … I was going to tell you …' His words petered off as he shook his head, shoulders practically deflating before my eyes, but all I could focus on was the fact that he hadn't even attempted to deny it.

So it was true?

Shit. Even though I'd been worried, I hadn't actually thought that Sean would really deceive me like this. I'd half expected him to laugh it off as a bluff of some kind. But no. What the hell did I do now? I was so stunned that I ended up just sitting there in silence as my heart quietly began to break apart inside my chest.

'It's not real,' he blurted suddenly, snapping into the shell of my shocked thoughts. Blinking, I flailed the paper at him, pictures and all, just barely missing his head and then proceeded to have a complete meltdown.

'It looks pretty bloody real to me, Sean!' I snarled. Shocked at how aggressive I had sounded, I ran a shaky hand through my hair as I tried to get a grip on myself. I'm not sure I'd ever snarled before in my entire life, but my throat was so tight from the anger, hurt, and confusion roiling inside me that it had been the only tone I'd been capable of forming.

'No! Allie, no. I swear to God, it's just hype set up by the PR people to encourage the fans and get higher viewing figures.'

My breaths were shallow and wheezy as I felt on the verge of breaking down. If it was just a PR stunt, why hadn't he told me about it? Staring at the face of the man I loved, the man I thought had loved me too, I tried to work out if I actually knew him at all.

Ignoring the anxiety in his voice and face, I squared off my glare with his eyes again. 'It's not real? So you and I can still be together?' I questioned feebly, not knowing what else to say.

Cringing slightly, Sean winced and I felt another piece of my heart wither. 'It's not real, but it needs to appear genuine for the public. You and I will need to keep things quiet until I can straighten it all out.'

Straighten it all out? It seemed pretty straight to me – I'd travelled half way around the world to be told that my boyfriend was actually 'engaged' to someone else.

'Look, let's go to your hotel and I'll explain,' he murmured softly.

My world was practically shattering before my very eyes, but Sean somehow sounded calm and flat and almost dismissive of my shredded emotions, so much so that I could barely take it in, my frayed nerves immediately snapping again.

'Ah yes, the nice hotel you mentioned earlier?' I growled at him, feeling quite disgusted. 'Like I'm some kind of mistress? Hidden away in a hotel so no one sees your bit on the side?' Spinning on my seat I faced him fully, my eyes bulging and my heart racing to the point where it sounded like it was going to burst in my eardrums. I felt sick with shock, but utterly furious. He could have told me this yesterday before I flew half way around the frigging world!

Sean paled at my agitation, visibly panicking and fidgeting on his seat so repeatedly that it was like he had ants in his pants. Watching him squirm I briefly wished that he did have ants biting his arse. Really big fuckers that would itch for weeks. It would serve him right for putting me through this shit. His eyes darted around my face as he chewed on his lower lip so frantically I was surprised I couldn't see any blood.

'Of course not! Just let me explain, Allie, please.'

Glancing down at the article I felt my stomach turn sickeningly as I looked again at the pictures, all of Sean with some waif-like beauty clinging to him. Clearly the 'Savannah' that the article referred to.

There was no way I could ever compete with her; she was as skinny as a chopstick, with beautiful brown eyes like a deer, flawless skin, and sleek, shiny chestnut hair that fell all the way to her non-existent waist. Oh God ... was that why he liked my hair long? Because it reminded him of her? Fuck. The very idea made me want to shave my head as I began to feel sick to my bones. Just looking at the pictures made me feel dowdy, fat, and distinctly snarky.

'You want to explain, Sean? Fine. You say this is all fake, but you look pretty flipping friendly in this picture,' I said, jabbing viciously at a photo in the newspaper. 'You have your hand on her arse, for fuck's sake.'

Sean visibly withered before my eyes. 'I do … but that's not a recent shot. It was taken last year, well before I'd even met you.'

Last year. Before he'd met me. When it was OK to put his hand on her arse? My lips pursed with instant displeasure – not from jealousy, although I was jealous – but because I distinctly remembered him telling me that he hadn't slept with anyone for at least two years before meeting me, and yet here was some lovely pictorial evidence that distinctly suggested otherwise.

'Have you ever dated her? Or do you make a habit of groping women's arses in public?' I demanded, my tone seething with barely contained pain.

Sean flinched and then fiddled with his sleeve, a reaction that spoke volumes. 'Uh … yes … that photo was taken early last year during the last season. Filming lasted a few months and we went out once or twice. That was it, just a couple of dates.'

It seemed he'd lied to me at Christmas when he'd told me he hadn't slept with anyone for two years. And when he'd said the rumours of him dating his co-stars was untrue.

Bloody bugger it. I was usually so good at spotting a liar that I couldn't believe I'd missed all this bullshit. And to top it all off he was engaged to her, but apparently that was made up too?

Shaking my head, I blew out a long, trembling breath, desperate not to cry. It seemed that I'd been so swept up by the intensity of the connection between us that I'd fallen for everything he'd said hook, line, and sinker. God, how could I have been so stupid? I felt so naïve it was unbelievable.

Swallowing hard, I nodded as a bitter taste rose in my throat when my eyes fell to a different picture with a date of just over two weeks ago. 'And have you "dated" her recently? Since you've been back in America?' I asked bluntly, my emphasis on the word dated making it obvious that what I actually meant was fucked.

'No, Allie, of course not. But Savannah can be quite … demonstrative. Her behaviour set a few rumours off again. I always set her straight through, Allie. Always.' Apparently not in public, I thought bitterly as I stared at the pictures.

'This photo was taken at an awards ceremony three weeks ago and you have your arm around her again,' I murmured in stunned disbelief.

'That's just for the cameras. Besides, it's not on her arse that time,' Sean pointed out, which almost made me cackle with demented laughter and slap him around the face for his stupidity – as if that made it better! It didn't matter where the fuck on her body his hand was, it was the fact that his hand was anywhere on Savannah Hilton that was irking me.

Shifting again, Sean looked like the epitome of discomfort; there was a slight sheen of sweat on his forehead and panic was contorting his usually handsome face. 'Because having a beautiful woman draped all over you must be so tough to deal with,' I spat. Blowing some loose hairs out of my face I shook my head again and stared at the article.

Before I could make further comment, I suddenly drew in a horrified breath. 'Oh my God … she's wearing an engagement ring …' A huge, sparkly diamond took pride of place on her ring finger, clearly on display as she showed it off to its full potential.

My wide eyes flew to his and I saw Sean blanch of colour and then frown. 'She is … but I didn't buy it or give it to her, Allie. It's fake.' The glittery ring didn't look particularly fake to me, and neither did their cosy embrace. 'She looks gorgeous … and you look like you're about to kiss her,' I whispered faintly. As sick as my words made me, it was true. Leaning in closer to the picture I squinted as I took in the details of their stances. She had one arm around his waist, but it suddenly occurred to me that the other, the one with the ring, was practically tucked in the front of his flipping trousers. How had I not noticed that before?

'Christ. Sean, she's practically wanking you right there on the red carpet.' Which was perhaps a small over-exaggeration, but seemed necessary. He was supposed to be dating me, didn't he realise that that meant only I could touch him like that? Or did he simply not care?

'Don't be ridiculous,' he barked, but I could tell from his stormy expression that I had hit a nerve. Either that, or he was finally losing his patience with my freak-out.

'I'm not being ridiculous, Sean, her fingers are below your fucking belt!' OK, so perhaps I needed to rein in my voice a little, because I had definitely just yelled loud enough to rattle the window glass.

My shouting apparently snapped Sean's composure too, because suddenly he was leaning forward, his eyes blazing and tendons stretching in his neck. 'Fine, OK, you want to know the truth? Savannah did try to kiss me that night, Allie,' he spat, his face reddening with growing anger. 'Repeatedly, in fact. The whole fucking crowd was chanting for me to do it too, and yeah, she looked fucking hot so it would have been easy to give in.'

As he glared at me I felt another part of my heart crumble away. At this rate there would be nothing left of it by the end of this car journey. His spiteful words felt like they had stabbed me in the chest and I dragged in a ragged breath as pain lanced through me, only just managing to hold myself together. 'But I didn't kiss her. You want to know why? Because I love you. You, Allie,' he growled. 'I could never do that to you, and on top of that, I would never want to do that.'

As reassuring as his words were no doubt meant to be, my mind just kept replaying his earlier phrase. And yeah, she looked fucking hot so it would have been easy to give in. I doubt I'd ever looked 'fucking hot' in my entire life. Not to the standard that Savannah did, anyway. How long would it be until he did give in and kiss her?

I felt hot bile rise in my throat and had to swallow hard to avoid throwing up in the back of his posh car. This was suddenly all waaay too much for my poor jet-lagged brain. His spiteful words had been the last straw. A dry sob broke from my throat as my face finally crumpled and I buried it in my hands, determined not to cry, but not knowing how to avoid it as I felt tears building.

'Christ. Please don't cry,' Sean begged, his voice softer and sounding almost as shattered as I felt. 'I'm sorry. I'm freaking out and some of that came out wrong … Look, I know how this must seem, but let me try and explain.'

Lifting my head, I stared at him and then shook my head sadly. 'Actually, I'd rather not hear it, Sean. Besides, these pictures make it all very clear,' I stated decisively, making an on-the-spot decision to save my heart while I still had a vague chance to salvage at least a small portion of it.

'I knew deep down that trying to date an actor would crash and burn, I just didn't realise it would happen so quickly,' I muttered with a grimace. 'I've made plans to meet Cait. I'll stay with her.'

'What? No, you can't do that!' Sean spluttered as I rummaged through my bag. Grabbing my phone I loaded an email from her letting me know the name of her hostel and leant towards the driver, lowering the privacy screen until I saw David glance at me questioningly. 'Can you take me to LA Digs Hostel please? It's on Hollywood Boulevard,' I asked as I felt panic and hysteria build in my stomach.

'Allie. Please,' Sean said in a near desperate tone, one of his hands reaching out for me.

'Don't touch me!' I shrieked, terrified that if I felt the reassuring warmth of his skin on mine that I would cave and fall into his arms.

'Don't say that. I have to touch you, Allie, you're mine.' Is that why he touched her too? Was she his as well? The thought sickened me to my core. His voice lacked its usual conviction, his concern obvious in the way his hand hesitated in the space between us, desperately seeking my permission. But he wouldn't be getting it, not today. Not ever, if he really was involved with that woman.

'Not any more I'm not.'

'Allie, no! You don't mean that ...' His voice was choked, eyes wide with panic, but I'd had enough. This was all too much. The car pulled to a stop in some traffic and suddenly I couldn't bear to stay in the enclosed space with Sean for another second, so I decided to grab the opportunity the crowded downtown roads presented me with. In other words, I planned to high tail it out of there.

'I do. I might not be some famous superstar, but I'm worth more than being your secret bit on the side. Besides, I'm clearly too regular and boring to date you and your "fucking hot" fiancée. Good luck with the new series.'

And with that I was gone. Grabbing the door handle I pushed it open and slid out into the road, somehow managing to rip the boot open and grab my suitcase before Sean had followed me. Leaving the boot open I dashed onto the sidewalk dragging my case carelessly behind me and lost myself in the crowds almost immediately. I had no idea where I was, but I didn't care. Hearing Sean yelling my name somewhere behind me, I hunkered my shoulders down to hide myself as I zigzagged through the bustling crowd, but I didn't glance back, not even as the first hot tears finally escaped my eyes and began to slide silently down my cheeks.

Chapter Six

Sean

There was a split second where I simply sat there, staring at the open door with my jaw hanging loose in shock. Then I was jolted from my stupor by David in the front seat swivelling to look at me with a stunned expression on his face. The last twenty minutes quite apparently more than made up for my subsequent lack of drama as his employer.

Ignoring him, I burst from my seat as if a rocket had been shoved up my arse, then launched myself through the open door. Cursing as the bright sunshine temporarily blinded me, I squinted and made a haphazard dash in towards the pavement.

'Allie!' Shading my eyes, I winced at the penetrating light and frantically looked in both directions, trying to catch a glimpse of her long, blonde hair. It was just my luck we had stopped in a main shopping area, so the bloody pavements were chock-a-block with sodding people.

Pushing through the crowd for a few seconds I stood in the midst of the jostle and yelled her name again, spinning in all directions. There was no sign of her.

'Fuck.' Cursing under my breath, I strode back towards the car and slammed the boot shut before rounding back to my door. Placing my foot on the floor of the car I stood up and rested a hand on the roof, scanning the crowd from my slightly higher vantage point. Ripping my phone from my pocket I dialled her number and shoved the phone to my ear, waiting impatiently for it to connect. It rang and my heart soared. Please answer, my gorgeous girl. My silent plea was to no avail though, because my call continued to ring until it clicked to answerphone.

Disconnecting, I banged my hand on the roof. 'Shit!' There was still no sign of Allie, she wasn't answering her phone, and I was starting to draw the attention of quite a few people in the crowd. Wasn't this just fucking perfect?

'Sir?' Blinking away from my search I scowled down and saw David, now standing beside the car looking up at me and flashing wary glances at the gathering crowd.

'Perhaps you should get in the car, sir. I can park up and then you can try and find her? It's just that we're causing a bit of a blockage.'

It was only after he spoke that I vaguely noticed the honking of car horns behind us and looked over my shoulder. David was being polite when he said we were causing a 'bit of a blockage', because behind us there was a substantial line of cars and several irritated drivers standing beside their vehicles.

Acceptance fell on me like a heavy weight – Allie was majorly pissed off with me and clearly didn't want to be found. She had successfully melted into the crowd, and realistically no amount of aimless wandering by me was going to find her. 'No, leave her to cool down. Let's go,' I murmured, dropping down and stepping back inside the car before slamming the door as hard as I could. The fierce tug and heavy thunk gave me some satisfaction, but not nearly enough to dissipate the agitated energy bubbling up inside of me.

Fuck. I could barely think straight. My breathing was so loud and ragged it was as if I'd just run a marathon. As the car pulled forward I caught sight of David throwing me several concerned glances in the rear view mirror.

What a total shit storm. I couldn't believe Allie had run off like that. What the hell should I do? My phone was still gripped in my hand, so I dialled her number again, praying that she might answer this time. Again it rang, but just like last time the call went unanswered and I tossed it on the seat beside me with a grunt. Running a hand across my face, I found it drenched and slippery and wiped it on my jean-clad thigh with a curse.

I cast my eyes down towards the abandoned newspaper and scowled before reaching across and grabbing it. Ripping my fingers violently through the pictures of myself and Savannah, I screwed it up and threw it to the floor in disgust, then watched with growing concern as my hand visibly trembled in front of me.

Pounding heart, sweaty skin, edgy nerves, shaking hands ... If I wasn't careful I was going to have a panic attack right in front of David. Fuck. He knew I could be temperamental, but I'd rather avoid him seeing that particular spectacle. Pulling in several breaths through my nose I tried to lower my stress levels. Jesus, I really needed to try and expel some of this energy before it totally overwhelmed me.

Allie was gone. God knows how she would find her way around. Fuck. The thought of her alone, upset, and lost in an unfamiliar city was too much to bear and as the car began to pull forward I felt the wall of control within me crumble. Dropping to my knees on the floor I hammered my fist onto the opposite seat with a frustrated snarl. It felt good, freeing, and then before I even realised it I was repeatedly smashing my hand down onto the unresponsive leather as a loud yell roared from my lungs.

Over and over I hit the seat, until my chest was screaming at me to stop and I was dripping with yet more sweat. Flopping forward, I rested my head down, my body practically curled into the foetal position as I tried to pull some air back into my protesting lungs.

Finally mustering enough energy to sit up on my haunches I blinked several times, feeling surprisingly calm after the tirade. Examining the seat for damage I saw none, a sweat patch from where I had rested my head the only evidence of my unprovoked attack. Giving it a vague wipe I pushed myself back into my chair, fastened my seatbelt, and raised my eyes to look forward.

'I apologise, David,' I murmured, my voice scratchy and sore after yelling. I wondered what the hell he must be thinking after witnessing my mini-breakdown, but seeing me thrashing the hell out of a seat was probably better than seeing me in a full on anxiety attack.

'No apology needed, sir,' he replied politely. 'How can I help?'

Sighing heavily, I kept my eyes pinned to the pavements passing by outside, just on the off chance I might spot her. 'I'm not sure you can, I've well and truly fucked up this time.'

'Perhaps I could take you to the hostel she mentioned, sir?'

My gaze snapped away from the crowds and focused on David's in the mirror. That was it. I could go there and wait for her, talk to her and try to explain. It was the prefect plan … except for one minor detail. I was Sean Phillips, and I tended to draw a crowd whenever I went out around town over here. Sometimes being famous was a complete pain in the arse. I glanced down at my jeans and shirt. I might only be dressed in a smart casual outfit, but I had no hat with me to even vaguely help hide my identity. It would be just my luck to get recognised and prompt some bullshit story in the papers.

Fuck. This situation seemed utterly hopeless. Scowling, I dropped my head forward in defeat and sighed heavily.

'No. You better take me back to the house.'

Back to the house, back to my all-star American life, and back to Savannah.

Chapter Seven

Cait

What a bloody waste of time the day had been. I think the run in with Jack Felton first thing had rendered my brain incapable of even simple conversation, because all of my interviews at the job agencies so far had flopped. Big time.

I briefly tried to recall the encounter with him again. Pah, who was I kidding? I didn't need to try and remember it – it had been on my mind constantly since I'd walked away from him. I'd even accidentally called one of the job agency guys Jack by mistake when his name was Peter, which had gained me a disapproving frown and must have looked completely unprofessional.

Yeah, all in all, persevering with my job hunt after the Jack interlude hadn't been one of my better ideas. Being stubborn though, I hadn't wanted to accept that a man had left me as ruffled as I felt, so I'd tried to brush it aside and carry on as normal. Unfortunately, I had failed dismally. I'd be completely stunned if I even managed to get one job offer thrown my way after my pathetic performance today.

Groaning at the bizarre reaction he had caused in me, I closed my eyes and tried to get a grip on my senses, but it was no good. The way he'd looked, smelt, and felt as he'd gently cleaned the cut on my arm seemed to be imprinted on my brain for posterity.

The whole occurrence was so unbelievable that it felt much like a dream now. Had it really happened? Opening my eyes, I glanced down at my elbow and saw the reddened skin and carefully applied plaster. So that was a yes. Biting my lip, I shook my head. Talk about surreal. Wandering towards some shade I leant back on a wall and pulled my water bottle from my bag for a much needed drink. The way I felt, I could do with vodka in this flask, not water, but I'd have to make do until I got through these final interviews and could get something stronger.

As much as I might not like to admit it, I was still decidedly shaken from it all. My heart rate hadn't quite returned to normal either, and I was fairly sure it had absolutely nothing to do with the nerves from my job interviews and everything to do with a broad-shouldered, brown-haired man who now seemed more like a hallucination than a reality.

Thoughts of Jack vanished for a second as I caught a glimpse of a woman dashing down the pavement opposite. Gosh, for a moment there she looked just like Allie, except her hair had been a touch longer. Frowning, I craned my neck to try and see her again, but she'd been swallowed up by the bustling crowds. Glancing at my watch, I shook my head. It couldn't have been her; I was fairly sure Allie wasn't even due to land for another hour yet. Besides, Sean was picking her up. God, my brain really was frazzled if I was conjuring up images of my best friend out of thin air.

I felt a small twinge of disappointment that it hadn't been her, because while my protective nature was trying to persuade me to keep my run-in with Jack to myself, I was also quite tempted to unload the details of my encounter onto someone, and my best friend would have been the perfect target.

Leaning back on the wall again I stared up above the crowds and buildings to the blue sky and lightly played with the elastic band on my wrist. Actually, all things considered, keeping this to myself was probably for the best. Feeling so nonplussed because of a man was not a feeling I liked, or usually tolerated, but if I told Allie about my literal run-in with Jack Felton it would end up with her getting waaay overexcited, and trying to persuade me that it was time to get back on the dating scene. Which it wasn't. I knew she had my best interests at heart when she tried to encourage me to meet someone, but I couldn't do it. Shuddering, I rubbed at the goose pimples suddenly peppering my arms and took a long calming breath.

I would never open myself up vulnerably like that to another man as long as I lived. Never.

Chapter Eight

Allie

Thank goodness for the little man on the street corner selling maps to the stars' houses, otherwise I think I would have been lost in this bloody city for the rest of my life. He must have noticed the overwhelmed expression on my face as I stood at the street intersection, shielding my eyes from the bright sunshine and reading the multitude of street signs in a vain attempt at orientating myself. Or perhaps he'd spied the dried tracks of the tear I'd let escape after fleeing from Sean. Whatever the reason, the man came up to me with a smile and held out a map. 'You look a little lost, sweetheart.' He had a thick American drawl, a kind smile, and a bright red trilby balanced jauntily on his head.

A little lost? He had that right – my life had turned to shit, and apart from the fact that I knew I was in Los Angeles, I had no flipping clue where I was.

'Thank you so much.' I breathed in relief. Taking the map, I started to dig in my pocket for some change, but he held up a palm and shook his head. 'No charge. You look like you're new in town.' Blinking several times at the unexpectedly kind gesture, I very nearly burst out crying again, but luckily I mustered up my British grit and managed a weak smile instead. 'That's incredibly kind of you.'

'Where are you heading to?' he asked, taking the map from my hand and unfolding it for me.

He seemed like a nice guy, but I was new in town and didn't want to tell a complete stranger my exact destination. I did, however, distinctly remember Cait mentioning that she could see the famous pointy roof of the Chinese Theatre from her hostel window, so it seemed a sensible landmark to head for. 'I need to get to the Chinese Theatre on Hollywood Boulevard,' I said, hoping it might magically be just around the corner.

'OK, that's not so far.' Turning the map, the man squinted at the jumble of roads for a second before pointing. 'You're here at the moment, Melrose Avenue. Follow this road straight up for four blocks,' he said, pointing to the traffic-filled street behind me, 'then you'll be on Hollywood Boulevard. Turn right, and in no time you'll be able to see the theatre. You won't be able to miss it, it'll be the one building with crowds of people outside.'

I nodded my thanks, but I had no idea how long 'four blocks' would take me to walk. It sounded short enough, but I wasn't exactly experienced with American city design. Seeing my uncertainty the man smiled again, revealing a set of bright white teeth with one sparkling gold tooth smack bang in the middle. 'Even with your suitcase it'll take you just over half an hour to walk, or you could grab a cab and be there in ten minutes.'

After thanking the man profusely, I clutched my new map tightly and went for the lazy option of getting a taxi. I couldn't believe I hadn't thought to jump in one earlier, but I supposed the shock had numbed the sensible part of my brain. As I stood there on the edge of the pavement trying to flag down a cab, I ended up staring almost blindly at passing traffic. I felt raw and hollow inside, like today had all been part of a strange, distressing dream.

A cab pulled up, giving me a honk to wake me from my stupor, which briefly relieved my melancholy as I sighed my relief and slid in. It smelt a bit like cabbage, and the plastic seating was far less luxurious than Sean's limo, but it did have one distinct advantage – it didn't contain Sean.

After the long haul flight and the shock of Sean's bombshell, I was a bit dazed – major understatement – and all I wanted was to get to the hostel so I could find Cait, sit down, and then probably cry again as I confessed my woes. Luckily, the cab ride didn't take long at all, and after paying my fare the car pulled away, leaving me standing alone on a wide pavement.

Looking up at the hostel building I squinted, trying not to be too judgemental – but if I'm being honest, the hostel looked like it had seen better days. Waaaay better days. Perhaps last decade it had looked good, but now it just looked … run down. And that was being generous. The paint was shabby, the roof wonky and there were large cracks visible around some of the windows, but I was still so stunned by the morning's events that I didn't really care. All I wanted was to get inside and find Cait.

Since fleeing the limo, my brain had struggled with something to focus on other than Sean's hideous deception, so finding Cait had become my goal. My best friend always knew what to do in crappy situations, so she would hopefully have some words of wisdom for me. That was what I was banking on, anyway, and as a result I needed to see her desperately.

Trudging up the five steps to the entrance, I bounced my poor battered suitcase behind me and found that the foyer beyond the huge red front door was much more welcoming: light and airy with high ceilings, soft, comfy-looking sofas, and several huge plants climbing their way towards the large windows. Any slight signs of the building's age were cunningly disguised with a bright and cheery paint job depicting a rainforest. All in all, I liked what I saw and felt my shoulders marginally relax.

I like to think myself a very open-minded individual, but I couldn't help but stare slack-jawed at the young guy manning the reception. Every single inch of his exposed skin was covered in an ornate swirl of Oriental-looking tattoos, even on his face. His lips, ears, nose, and eyebrows were dripping with a multitude of different piercings. Wow. I bet airport security was a nightmare for him.

He even had a small metal bar through the skin of his wrist. I'd never seen someone with a pierced wrist before and it made me briefly wonder what other hidden body parts might contain metal. I'd place money on the fact that there was some in his pants, and my cheeks heated. His hair was fastened into a multitude of dreadlocks and plaits with various colourful ribbons and strings entwined throughout it, and looked distinctly like it hadn't been washed for a while. A very long while.

Talk about a walking work of art. I was so fascinated by him that I think I stared for a good two minutes before realising the girls in front of me were finished and that he was politely waiting to serve me.

Thankfully, after a bit of shuffling of incoming guests, the tattoo guy managed to get me a bunk in the same dorm as Cait – who he informed me wasn't back yet – and then kindly gave me a hand up the stairs with my suitcase.

We stopped at a door and I had to bite on my lower lip and blink several times to stop more tears from flowing. The name plaque on my dorm read 'Hollywood Heartbreakers' Hangout' and I shook my head in disbelief. How ironic. Pursing my lips to stop myself having a meltdown in front of the tattoo guy, I nodded my thanks and made my way inside, thankfully finding the room quiet and empty.

What a day. First, I'd pretty much dumped my very own Hollywood heartbreaker, and now I was going to be sleeping in a room with the same name. How depressingly apt.

Had I really finished with him? God, I felt exhausted – physically, emotionally, and mentally – and had so much to think about that I could barely comprehend it at the moment. Dragging my case to the only empty lower bunk, I decided to rest my tired body before attempting to sort out how I was going to proceed with Sean. Hopefully Cait would be back soon and I could share my woes with her. She might not be experienced with relationships, but she was always level headed and great at giving sensible advice.

I'd just dumped my suitcase down beside my allocated bed when my phone rang in my handbag. Plonking wearily onto the mattress, I felt the wiry springs protesting with a series of unsatisfied squeaks and winced – my planned rest might not be the most comfortable one I'd ever had.

Pulling out my phone with a sigh I desperately hoped it would be Cait calling, but suspected that it may well be Sean. Again. My phone had rung fourteen times in the cab ride over here, all from Sean, and all that I'd stubbornly ignored.

Looking at the screen I saw his name flashing, and my face folded into a sad, resigned frown. Sighing heavily, I decided to get it over with now while I had some peace and quiet in the room, so I connected the call and raised it to my ear. 'Hi.'

'*Allie.*' My name came through the earpiece in a whispered, desperate wheeze that made me close my eyes tightly as scorching tears built up behind my eyelids. He sounded as emotionally fraught as I felt. 'What the fuck were you doing jumping out of the car in the middle of the goddamn road? You could have killed yourself!'

His soft tone had lasted all of two seconds, and now he just sounded monumentally pissed off. He wasn't happy, that much was clear, but almost as soon as Sean had expelled his frustration, I heard a long, rushed breath down the phone as if he were deflating like a used balloon. Talk about a rollercoaster of emotions. He seemed to be fluctuating wildly between his feelings, which wasn't helping me to settle either.

'I'm sorry, I'm sorry … I didn't mean to shout. Thank God you're safe.' My eyebrows rose as I heard his voice trembling. Or perhaps that was just my dodgy phone signal, I was still using my UK SIM, so the call sounded a bit tinny. 'Are you checked in to the hostel?'

I'd only just connected the call and already I wanted to end it. Even hearing Sean's breathing down the line was painful – too painful. The gnawing, raw pain in my chest felt as if my heart was literally tearing in two, making me physically rub at my sternum uselessly, but I still couldn't bring myself to hang up on him.

Sighing, I nodded and hissed out a curt 'Yes.' As heartbroken as I was, thankfully my anger was still bubbling inside me and just about helping to keep tears at bay.

God, this was awful. I'd never experienced emotional pain like this before. Keeping the phone clutched to my ear, I rolled onto my side and curled my body into a protective ball, staring blindly out at the room as silence stretched between us.

'I hate the thought of you staying there,' he muttered, sounding agitated again. 'Make sure you lock your room, Allie. I need to know you're safe.'

A dry, ironic laugh escaped my throat as I surveyed the basic surroundings of my room: three bunk beds, six wooden lockers, and a threadbare carpet. That was it. Sean would go ape shit if he saw this place, and a small vindictive part of me suddenly felt the urge to hurt him as much as he had me. 'I'm in a dorm room with six other girls, there's no locking the door, Sean.'

There was a pause, several clunking noises as if he had briefly dropped the phone, and then a yell echoed down the line. 'What?' Moving the earpiece away from my head, I winced. He sounded like he'd almost exploded on the other end of the line. I couldn't see him, but I'd place money on the fact that his eyes would be bulging and he'd be doing that tight lip pursing he did when he was agitated.

'You're staying in a fucking dorm? With no lock? This is LA, Allie, you can't stay somewhere without a lock!' His voice grew higher with every word until finally he expelled a huge, rushed breath. I just knew that his eyebrows would be dipped into one of his deep, daunting frowns by now. No doubt I was driving him insane.

'I'll be fine, Sean,' I muttered defiantly. I had enough money to go elsewhere if I wanted, but if things with Sean really had collapsed like they seemed, then I may as well save my cash and go back to my original plan to travel for a while. Seeing the world would certainly help to take my mind off of Sean, for a while at least, after all, it wasn't like I had a job to get back to, and seeing a few more countries might be exactly what I needed.

'I need to see you, Allie, please. I said some really stupid things in the car, and I'm so sorry, but you can't just run away without even talking about it.' He sounded like he was in a foul mood, which just added to my annoyance, because if either of us had the right to be throwing a strop right now, it was me.

'What you said in the car ... about not being mine any more ... please say it's not true. Say you're still mine.' His plea was whispered in a voice so small and weak that it made my chest compress. I was still his – my heart was, at least – but was he mine? I wanted to ask, but my throat had closed with unshed tears. Pushing myself back up to a sitting position, I drew in a long breath, trying to force my battered emotions to the side and think rationally about all that had transpired since I'd landed in LA.

I loved him, that was undeniable, and for that reason I wouldn't just write him off, but I also wouldn't lower myself to sharing him or hiding away like some dirty little secret – my pride simply wouldn't allow it.

What I needed was a clear head, and that was something I certainly didn't have at the moment. With my emotions running wild and a serious case of jet leg setting in, my head felt like it was stuffed with cotton wool. Pulling another huge breath into my lungs, I then released it from between clenched teeth and made my decision.

'Look, I'm jet lagged and emotional. I need to get some sleep and cool off, then we can talk. This has been a hell of a day.' I hadn't answered his question, but it was about the best I could give him right now.

There was a long silence, broken only by the sound of Sean's ragged breathing. 'OK.' He sounded thoroughly dejected in his agreement. 'Look, Allie, I know you're pissed off with me, but just do me one favour, will you? Don't stay in that bloody hostel tonight. There's a room booked at the Beverly Hills Hotel in your name, go there, please?'

It was rude, but I didn't even bother replying. 'I'll be disconnecting this number immediately after this call to swap to my temporary US number. I'll call you in a day or so when I've calmed down. Goodbye.'

As soon as I hung up I sent both my mum and Cait a quick text letting them know what my new number would be, and told Cait that I had arrived and was at the hostel waiting for her. Then I switched my phone off and swapped the SIM card to the American pay-as-you-go one I'd bought earlier, grateful I had opted for one that gave me a new phone number so that Sean couldn't call me back. Clicking the plastic cover back in place, I turned it on in case Cait called, then stowed my phone in my handbag and put my bag under my pillow for safety before flopping down on it.

As I stared up at the slats of the bunk above me, a cold sensation swept across my entire body before a series of shudders shook me. My seemingly perfect life appeared to have unravelled before my eyes and I felt like I was rapidly descending into shock. Maybe I was – it wouldn't be surprising after the hellish day I'd had. I didn't know what to do, or how to proceed, but I was exhausted, so maybe sleep would help evade this feeling of grief that was swamping me like a suffocating blanket.

As much as I wanted to escape into the quiet darkness of sleep, I couldn't even begin to settle my hammering pulse. Sleeping right now felt like an impossible task, especially with several mattress springs poking me in the arse and lower back, but I would persevere and try. I was perched on top of an emotional breakdown, I could just feel it, and I needed to be unconscious to forget my hideous morning, even if only for a little while.

Unfortunately, instead of falling straight to sleep, one of my hands felt out to the cold sheets next to me, and I couldn't help but let out a dry sob at the realisation that I wouldn't be curling up with Sean tonight. Every time my fingers clenched and unclenched in the sheets I felt a sharp, stabbing pain in my heart, the loss of Sean leaving my chest, and life, feeling raw and empty.

The dry snuffles began to turn to cries, and then before I could get control over myself my entire body was jack-knifing with huge, heaving sobs. Tears began to fall from my eyes, burning my cheeks and soaking the sheets as the full anguish of the day finally hit me.

Chapter Nine

Sean

I must have sat there stock-still, staring at the phone in my hand, for at least five minutes. Allie had actually hung up on me. Hung up. Shaking my head, I lifted the mobile to my ear again just to triple check that the line was dead. Compete silence. Fuck. I couldn't believe it.

In our short time together, Allie had come to understand how obsessed I was with keeping her safe. She knew how vitally important it was for me to be able to get in touch with her, so surely she wouldn't go through with her threat to disconnect her number? By this point my hand was clenched around my phone so tightly that my knuckles looked snowy white in the pale light of my bedroom, and I was amazed the plastic casing hadn't given in and crumpled in my fist.

Quickly hitting the re-dial button, I waited impatiently as the number went through, but after several quiet clicks there were three loud beeps and then an automated voice. 'The number you are calling is currently unavailable, please leave a message or contact the service provider for more information.' Swallowing hard, I pressed the disconnect button as I felt the blood draining from my face.

She'd actually done it.

Now there was no way I could get in touch with her, and judging from the mood she was in, she wouldn't be sending me her nightly text to tell me she was OK either. This was my very worst nightmare coming true before my eyes. What the fuck was I going to do?

A wheezing breath left my lungs and I found myself struggling to draw in new air to replace it. Had she really meant it when she said she was no longer mine? Fuck. Roughly thumping my fist into my chest I tried to knock some air into my useless lungs as my chest tightened in the first stages of a panic attack. This had been simmering in my system all day so I wasn't really surprised it was finally getting a proper grip on me – my muscles clenching, lungs shutting down, and heart pounding at a frighteningly furious rate. Fuck.

My vision went blurry as my brain went into full-on anxiety mode so I did the only thing I could do, and let out a groan, allowing my failing legs to sink me down onto the mattress. Trying to steady my swimming head I rested it in my hands, the cold plastic of my mobile pressing into my temple uncomfortably.

Right from the start, when I'd felt how potent our connection was, I had always suspected it would be this bad if I ever messed things up with Allie – or God forbid, lost her. The hellish two weeks after our first snow-bound week together had proved that to me; we'd been apart and not even technically a couple and the stress of that separation had just about done me in.

The accident with Elena all those years ago had completely screwed me up when it came to women. I hadn't even loved Elena, but the thought that she might have died because I hadn't been there to save her had never gone away, always lodged at the back of my brain like an annoying little itch. I'd avoided developing overly emotional relationships with women ever since, only allowing myself a fling every now and then, and always with women I knew I'd be able to walk away from.

But then I'd met Allie.

She had dropped into my life on that snowy day last December like a bolt from the blue, all long legs, blonde hair, innocent eyes, and that gorgeous smile. And her spunk was something else entirely. She hadn't taken my moody shit at all, which had endeared her to me even more. The way I instantly felt about her had hit me like a punch to the gut. Right from the start I'd known that I was connected to her on some weird, cellular level, and that I would be getting myself into deep water if I started a relationship with her.

It was the very reason that I'd tried to resist it at first, attempting to push her away by being stroppy and unapproachable. Not that I'd tried very hard; I think I'd managed to last two days until I was seducing her in my office and fucking her on the desk.

My experience with Elena had screwed me up, that was for sure, but after much counselling and therapy, I'd managed to regain stability over my need to control everything in my life. All except for Allie, that was. There was no controlling her, not really. She might let me lead our bedroom activities, but there was no doubting who had who by the balls.

Luckily Allie had been amazingly understanding when I'd explained what had happened with Elena all those years ago, and had helped me develop some strategies to minimise my concern for her safety. One of those was a daily text, which had been working a treat to put my mind at ease about her well-being before I went to bed. But now it looked like I wouldn't be getting those messages any more. Not tonight, anyway.

Blinking hard, I tried to clear my eyes as I glared at the phone again as if it had just personally stabbed me in the heart. I have no idea how I resisted the urge to fling the bloody thing at the wall. But I held back, just. If Allie chose to call me – and that seemed like a pretty big 'if' – but if she called, I needed my phone to be in working order.

My free hand came up to run through my hair as I tried to work out what the hell had happened in the last forty minutes. A complete fuck-up, that's what had happened. To summarise – I'd screwed up, big time.

Dropping the phone onto the covers, I scrubbed at my face with my hands, trying to ease the ache growing behind my eyeballs. Why did I ever try to shield Allie from all this shit with Savannah? It must look like I was a completely deceitful arsehole.

In hindsight, it was blindingly obvious that I should have just told Allie as soon as it happened. She'd have understood. But now, if I tried to explain, it would just look like I was trying to cover my tracks.

Fuck. I couldn't believe the way I'd snapped in the car and taunted her with the fact that Savannah had tried to kiss me. And yeah, she had looked fucking hot, so it would have been easy to give in. Wincing, I scrubbed at my face again, unable to believe that I'd been so heartless. My recklessly yelled words and the pain they had caused in Allie's beautiful eyes were going to haunt me forever.

What an unbelievable mess. In reality, what it came down to was this: for some stupid fucking reason I'd chosen the show over my girl. My job provided for me, supported me financially, but at the end of the day there were other roles out there I could get, and quite frankly it wasn't exactly like I was short of cash.

Up until now I'd always lived for my job. My career had been it for me, but since meeting Allie it had become crystal clear that she was it for me. She made me complete. I should have told the studios, and Savannah, to piss off the second this engagement farce was brought up.

Wincing, I tried to acknowledge the horrible, sickening fact that my screwed-up deceit had turned the one woman

I'd ever loved against me – my smiling, loving, gorgeous girl. God, the thought that she might hate me was like a dagger to my heart.

My fingers twitched with the need to do something, anything, that might help. What I needed to do was focus on how I could make things right. I tried to imagine how Allie must be feeling, and in return my stomach sank so low that I actually felt sick. No doubt she felt confused, alone, and utterly betrayed. Every fibre in my body wanted to go to her, drag her into my arms and comfort her, but I knew that would only make matters worse between us.

God, I hoped she'd go to the hotel and not stay in that awful hostel. The thought of her sleeping in an unlocked room in LA was almost enough to send me further into a panic. I'd give her a few hours to cool off and then go and see if she'd checked in. Maybe she'd even agree to speak to me.

Drawing in a deep breath, I was relieved to find my lungs working far better than they had been a minute ago. It seemed that forming a plan of action had helped me step away from the brink of my panic attack. Thank fuck for that. My hands lowered to the soft bedding below as I vaguely came back to reality and looked around the room.

Shaking my head at my situation I very nearly laughed. I was sitting on a bed which I slept in at night, but it wasn't my bed. It was a bed in a room which was mine temporarily, in a house I didn't own – or even like – instead of being in my beautiful new apartment, in my superking-sized bed with Allie tucked by my side. Talk about a cold, hard reality check.

This was turning out to be one of the worst days of my entire fucking life.

A second later my phone rang beside me, and I nearly leapt through the ceiling in my rush to grab it in case it was Allie. My heart sank when I saw the name on the screen though – Joe, my personal trainer. Blowing out a breath that rushed between my teeth, it felt quite a lot like my entire life was deflating along with it.

As usual, there were no pleasantries with Joe, he just got straight to the point once I'd lifted the phone to my ear. 'You're late. I'm downstairs, big boy. Come and get it.' With that, he hung up. Tossing the phone on the bed I stood up and allowed myself a derisive smile; that was the second bloody person to hang up on me in less than three minutes. Was I really that repellent?

On autopilot I undid the top few buttons of my shirt and peeled it over my head, tossing it in the vague direction of the washing basket. It certainly didn't seem as if I could do much with regards to Allie at the moment, so a workout would be a good distraction and might help me burn off some of my nervous energy. Smashing the stuffing out of the car seat had helped marginally, so having Joe to take my anger out on might be even more cleansing.

It was almost perfect timing, really. Not that this was a coincidence; he was a regular visitor. During shooting I was contracted to 'work out a minimum of five times a week and maintain a suitably muscular physique'. Which, given that I was acting in a supposedly 'serious' police drama, spoke volumes about the type of audience they were aiming at – bored housewives who might like to drool over the hotties on the TV. One of those hotties being me.

Sighing, I pulled on a workout vest and some shorts, rolled my neck, and tried to clear my mind a little before descending the stairs to find Joe – all six foot eight and sixteen stone of him – impatiently waiting for me in the hall and looking at his watch with a scowl. I didn't let his weight fool me: this guy was solid muscle from head to toe. He was also a miserable git, much like me sometimes, but there was no denying his skills as a personal trainer. There was never any slacking with Joe, that was for sure.

'For being late you can do an extra set of everything today,' he told me with a smirk, but I just heaved a sigh and rolled my eyes. Perhaps a good workout would help me sleep tonight, because one thing was for sure – if I didn't hear from Allie today, I would probably be up all night worrying.

'Don't start, Joe, I'm having a really crappy day,' I muttered, my mood almost as dark as his raven hair. 'I hope you brought some wrist wraps for boxing, because I need to hit something. Hard.'

Chapter Ten

Cait

The sun was hot on my face, but my feet felt lovely and cool in the long grass now I had removed them from within the confines of my smart shoes. Wriggling my toes amongst the bright green blades, I smiled at how funny I must look, sitting here in the park with bare feet and wearing my suit. A complete mismatch, but goodness, did it feel good to rest my weary, blistered soles.

Four hours of traipsing around various employment agencies within the city and I was still jobless. But now in addition, I was sweaty and irritable to go with it. Looking down at myself, I grimaced. Thanks to the humid day I looked like a crumpled, sticky mess. Which was oddly close to how my brain felt whenever I thought back over my run-in with Jack. Overheated and screwed up, that's how the encounter had left me.

Pushing him from my mind I wiped my damp brow on my palm and pushed my hair back behind my ears. I hadn't anticipated that it would be so hard to get a job in a city as large as LA, but so far all I'd had was knockbacks and a couple of numbers for bar work. Besides the fact that I had accepted the contact details out of politeness, I knew there was no way that I would be following them up. Bar work I did not do. In fact, any job that prompted direct, and possibly unwanted attention from the opposite sex was an immediate no-go for me. I knew my rigid rules limited me jobwise, because obviously most jobs involved some interaction with men, but bar work in particular just seemed too risky for me.

Actively encouraging men to flirt with me just to get bigger tips? Ugh. No thank you. A brief glimmer of my ex flittered through my mind again and I pushed it away with a shudder, my thumb instinctively raising so I could bite nervously on the skin around the nail. Tutting at the resurfacing of my old habit, I shook my head in annoyance.

That was twice today I'd allowed my fucktard ex-boyfriend to infiltrate my thoughts. Blowing out a dismissive raspberry, I scrunched up my face in annoyance. I had already wasted enough of my life on him, he didn't deserve to occupy one more second of my time. Although, due to the anxiety issues he'd left me with, he frequently did.

Blinking away the bitter feelings that always came with memories of him, I let out a long, calming breath and closed my eyes for a second to enjoy the sun. I was done for the day, so I could relax now. I still had no job, but right now I was so hot and bothered that I didn't care.

Shrugging off my suit jacket, I carefully folded it before placing it on the grass beside me. My shirt was stuck to my back from the heat and I rolled my shoulders, trying to free the cotton from the rivulet of sweat running down my spine. Ugh. I needed to invest in some breathable shirts. Briefly wafting my blouse I enjoyed a cool breeze on my heated skin before pulling my bag onto my lap to check my phone.

Drawing back the zip I smiled when I saw a small Tupperware tub tucked inside one of the pouches. It must've been from Julie, one of the cooks at the hostel. Seeing as I'd been there over a month now I knew some of the staff quite well, and was quite close with Julie. She was a bit of a mother hen, and always spoilt me rotten when she could, saying I need fattening up.

Prying off the lid I grinned when I saw an orangey-coloured muffin coated in sticky, cream icing. If this was what I suspected – a carrot, walnut, and pumpkin seed muffin with butter cream topping – then it was my favourite from Julie's baking range. Her vast baking range. Julie single-handedly kept the hostel café stocked with homemade cakes and biscuits, all of which I had sampled, and all of which were delicious.

Inside the lid was a small, star-shaped Post-it note with the words 'Good luck with the job hunt! J x' written on it in a curvy, wayward scrawl, the words now half obscured by some melted icing. Smiling to myself I poked my finger into the soft topping, popped it in my mouth, and immediately sighed with pleasure. That woman made the best vanilla butter icing I had ever tasted in my life, and it instantly made me feel better about my crazy Jack-and-job-hunt-filled day.

Who cared if I'd been mown down by a sexy film star and then failed to get a job because my mind had been so fuddled from it? Not me, not when I had this delicious muffin to distract me.

I was nearly finished with my muffin – which was acting as a very late, but delicious, lunch – when I felt my phone vibrate in my bag. Popping the last bite into my mouth, I licked my fingers clean as best I could and then pulled my mobile out.

Seeing a text from Allie, I only just managed to supress my squeal of delight as I forgot about my slightly sticky fingers and frantically opened up the folder to see what it said.

From: Allie
Hey you, change of plans, instead of meeting Sean I'm at your hostel. It's a long story. See you when you get

back. I'm turning this phone off now, if you need me my new number is 213 672 1243. A xx

Frowning, I immediately found my fingers moving to the elastic bands on my wrist, absently plucking them in concern before a sting of pain had me realising what I was doing.

Saving her new number, I stowed my phone back in my bag and stared out across the park thoughtfully. Why was she at my hostel? Not that I was complaining, I couldn't wait to see Allie, but still … why the sudden change of plans? I couldn't think of any good reasons why Allie would be staying at the hostel instead of with Sean, so kicking myself into gear, I pulled on my slightly sweaty socks with a grimace, donned my shoes, and set off to find out for myself.

Chapter Eleven

Allie

A skinny brunette sashayed her hips as she crawled over a naked, aroused, and moaning man. As she tossed her long hair over her shoulder I got a glimpse of not only her face, but the man's too, and my heart just about stopped in my chest. Savannah. *And Sean.*

I wanted to move away, but I couldn't. Instead I stood frozen to the spot, watching like some sick voyeur as long, tanned limbs entangled around sculpted muscles slick with sweat, and manicured fingernails clawed at reddened skin in the heat of passion. Sean allowed the attention on his body for a minute or so, before rolling Savannah over as he pinned her arms above her head and began to worship her stick-like body with his talented fingers and lips.

The hairs of his chest brushed her dark nipples, the peaks hardening further before he greedily sucked them into his mouth and then reared back to plunge his hot, hard length inside of her as they both groaned out their pleasure into the room …

'Hey, sweetie, wake up.'

The voice caused my mind to move away from the sickening dreams as reality slowly began to filter in. 'Allie? Wake up, babe.' I became aware of hands on my shoulders shaking me awake, causing the sick fantasies to evaporate as the battered mattress below me once again began poking me with its aged springs.

It was just a dream. Ugh. But a horribly vivid one. Swallowing hard, I sucked in a breath as I tried to force their remnants from my mind's eye. At least I *hoped* it was just a dream. Ugh. Swallowing down the urge to throw up, I pushed the lingering images of Savannah to the side of my mind as I felt the soft, warm hand on my shoulder give another gentle shake.

'Allie, are you awake? Too much sleep will make your jet lag worse,' the familiar voice informed me as I blinked my bleary eyes. It took me a second or two for my stomach to stop churning and I breathed in several deep, cleansing breaths to try and speed up the process. Drawing in another breath, I opened my eyes wide, rubbed a hand over my face, and slowly sat up, immediately banging my head on the bunk above me and wincing.

'Ugh … actually, we might already be a bit late. Crikey, you look rough,' Cait said from beside me, her head cocked curiously as she examined me with a searching look so amusing that it managed to elicit a small, dry chuckle from me. Gingerly rubbing at my bruised head, I tried to smooth down my bed hair, my fingers becoming tangled in the long strands until I gave up and limply dropped my arms back into my lap with a heavy sigh.

'Hi, Cait.' My voice was croaky and sore from the tears I'd cried earlier, which as well as giving me a dodgy throat had probably made me look pretty dreadful too. I'd fallen into a troubled slumber with tears rolling from my eyes before I'd had a chance to wash off my make up or sort myself out, so I no doubt looked like death warmed up at the moment.

'Well, my initial urge was to leap around gleefully because you're finally here … but having got a look at you, I'm reconsidering. You look like you might snap in half if I so much as hug you,' she said, still analysing me as if I were some curious and newly discovered specimen.

'So ... why do you look so wretched, and why are you here? At the hostel, I mean.'

She didn't beat around the bush, did she? I'd barely woken up, and I was facing an inquisition already. Mind you, I couldn't blame Cait; I would be just as curious if I had found her in the state I was in.

'I thought you were staying with Sean,' she added thoughtfully.

Sean. I hated how pathetic the mere mention of him made me, but no sooner had Cait uttered that name than I let out a low groan and felt my bottom lip begin to tremble. I wasn't usually much of a crier, so this complete loss of control over my tear ducts today was decidedly annoying.

With an impatient grunt I stood up and ran my hands almost violently over my face to try and snap myself out of my wretched state. 'It's a long story,' I said. 'Well ... long-ish,' I corrected. In actuality, it wasn't so long at all, was it? Sean was engaged to his co-star – or some peculiar set up where in the eyes of the world he was, anyway – and I wasn't prepared to be a part of it. That summary made it seem quite a short story. Not to mention bone-jarringly depressing.

Shaking away my dark thoughts, I stepped toward Cait's slim, lithe frame and pulled her into a fierce hug. I did this for two reasons: firstly, I desperately needed the comfort of a hug, but secondly, it was a good way to break eye contact and stop her giving me such a penetrating assessment. The familiar smell of my best friend's perfume was infinitely reassuring though, and I felt a little of my usual spunk returning as her warmth seeped into my chilled body. There were many good reasons why this girl was one of my best friends, and her quiet composure and strength in times of need was one of them.

'I don't suppose there's a good bar around here, is there? I could do with drowning my sorrows and using you as a sounding post.'

Leaning back, I watched Cait as she observed me with narrowed eyes. Her gaze was full of curiosity and unasked questions, and I could tell she was trying to work out what was going on but was just too polite to force it. Being quite a private person, Cait never needlessly pried into other people's business, but I could see that even she was tempted to push me and ask me to spill the beans. The problem was, there was a high chance that I was going to cry, and the only way to lessen that possibility was to get a bit of liquid courage inside me first.

Seeing my resolute features, she finally relented and nodded. 'As a matter of fact, there is. I could use a drink too, I've had a pretty crazy day myself.' Before I could ask why, Cait glanced at her watch and then grinned. 'And if we hurry we'll catch the start of happy hour. We'll need to smarten up, though, it's a pretty exclusive place.' Snorting out a laugh, she rolled her eyes, 'Mind you, this is LA, they're all pretty exclusive places!'

Smart clothes … right, I could do that. Swivelling back to my suitcase, I whipped the zip around and dug about for my wash bag and a suitable change of clothes, quickly selecting a navy, knee-length cocktail dress with a pattern of tiny white flowers and a pair of blue heels. I loved this dress, and it should be more than appropriate for a night of drinking in a posh establishment. 'Let me freshen up, I must look a right state.'

'Hmmm,' was Cait's thoughtful response as she obviously continued to try and work out exactly why I was a soggy, tear-stained mess, but I left her hanging. She'd know the whole sordid story soon enough, so it may as well be when I was looking a bit more refreshed and had a strong drink in my hand.

When I arrived back from a quick wash, I found Cait had changed into a smart pair of black trousers, a teal, long-sleeved top, and some funky high heels as she stood beside one of the wooden lockers, nodding happily.

'It took a bit of effort, but I managed to fit your case in,' she announced proudly, jerking her chin at a locker which was now crammed full of my belongings. 'It's almost embarrassing, Allie, no self-respecting traveller brings a bloody suitcase. You need a backpack.'

I felt like making a comment about the fact that probably not many 'real' backpackers would be carrying a pair of designer high heels like the ones she was wearing, but I kept quiet. Seeing how Cait was usually so reserved and nervous around men she never really got that dressed up or exposed much skin, so it was nice to see her wearing the flashy shoes. Besides, the suitcase was hardly my fault, I hadn't exactly been intending on doing too much moving around.

But instead of mentioning any of this, I just rolled my eyes and chucked my wash bag and discarded clothes on top of the case before sliding a coin in the locker slot and slamming the door shut.

'Whatever. We haven't all been swanning around the world for the best part of three years like you, Cait,' I retorted with a grin, linking my hand around her elbow and turning for the door. It was time to escape the Hollywood Heartbreaker's Hangout, even if just for a few hours.

'This bar does the best cocktails,' Cait said as our high-heeled feet clicked off the main drag of Hollywood Boulevard and onto what seemed to be a residential side street. Walking a few more steps, I realised we were approaching what could only be described as a very eccentric wooden house. It didn't look much like a bar at first either, but as we got closer I saw it was adorned with fairy lights and complete with cherry red leather Chesterfield couches on either side of the front steps.

My eyebrows rose significantly. Blimey. What a quirky place – a beautiful, retro-looking building, complete with bay windows that reminded me of the Victorian-style houses I loved at home. It almost looked like part of a film set, a view further enhanced when I saw the sign displaying its name: No Vacancy.

'Wow … this place is incredible,' I murmured, my mind momentarily distracted from thoughts of my problems as we walked through the front door and entered the beautiful, wood-panelled entryway. There were a few other customers inside, loitering around the bar or seated in one of the various groups of plush sofas, but seeing as it was still early, the bar was empty enough for me to easily gaze around in awe.

'I thought you'd like it. I know you love a bit of history.' Leading me towards the bar, Cait slid a cocktail menu towards me and climbed up onto one of the tall, red leather bar stools. She sat with a rod-straight back, as always, and looked every bit as elegant as her surroundings in her fancy shoes, with her chestnut hair flowing down her back.

'Apparently Charlie Chaplin used to own this place when it was just a home.'

Cait was pointing to a part of the menu that had the history of the bar on it, but I got side-tracked by a sore-looking patch of skin on her thumb. 'Hey, what's this?' I asked, my protective tone immediately coming to the surface.

Pausing in her conversation, I saw Cait glancing down at her thumb and cringing at the trace of blood on the poor skin around the nail. Damn it, I'd thought she'd stopped this habit.

Back when things with her ex had started to get weird, Cait had begun to subconsciously pick her thumbs so much that they'd been red raw, even bleeding on occasion, like today. One day at school we'd been in the staffroom and I'd noticed and tentatively commented on it., sShe hadn't confessed her exact worries, but I'd guessed it had been to do with her then- boyfriend, Greg. He was a manipulating bastard – , worse than manipulative, – and I'd hated him from the start.

Shrugging, Cait's eyes flashed to mine guiltily. 'I don't do it that much any more,' she started defensively, causing me to raise one eyebrow high. Pulling back her sleeve she showed me her wrist, and I saw two small elastic bands. One yellow, one green.

'My therapist suggested these bands. Instead of picking my thumbs, I give them a quick ping when I'm anxious. The sting is usually enough to help focus my mind.'

Oh. Well, I supposed that seemed like a suitable method of control, even if it did still involve inflicting pain on herself. 'What's the significance of the colours?'

Smiling, Cait fingered the two small bands. 'Nothing. They were the only elastic bands I could find at the time.'

'So why the red skin on your thumb?' I asked with concern, because from the small trace of blood it was obvious that she had been picking. 'Why not pluck the elastic?'

Looking self-conscious, Cait shrugged again. 'I dunno, really.' But the flush in Cait's cheeks said otherwise, so I raised an eyebrow to spur her to elaborate. 'I had a weird start to the day … and then some job interviews, so that was all a bit stressful, and something reminded me of Greg which is never good, then to top it all off I got your message about you being at the hostel and I was worried. I guess I still do it sometimes without realising.'

Smiling sympathetically, I felt my heart give a tug for my friend. She was so brave going off travelling after everything she'd been through, but even though she'd been determined that the incident with Greg wouldn't ruin her life, the emotional scars he'd left were clearly still affecting her.

'What do you mean you had a weird start to the day?'

Her blush deepened, but she adamantly shook her head, her hazel hair drifting around her face like a veil. 'It was nothing important. Anyway, tonight is for you. What do you think about this place?' Whatever it was, she clearly didn't want to discuss it so I let the subject drop and looked around the room again before nodding. I was seriously impressed, and quickly became even more so when I got a glance at the cocktails on the very extensive, and very tempting, menu. This was perfect – and exactly what I needed. Once our drinks were ordered, a barman with an impressively bristly handlebar moustache set about preparing them, flinging the cocktail shaker around, spinning it, bouncing it, and showing off in an attempt to entertain us, which worked a treat.

Once we had our colourful beverages in hand, Cait led me away from the main bar into a second, even quieter, room and we slid onto a red leather sofa side by side.

After taking a sip of my drink I sighed appreciatively at the cool, delicious fruitiness. It had quite a kick to it too, I realised, as I felt a pleasant buzz settle in my throat and quickly warm my stomach.

'Come on then, there's only so much my patience can take. Spill the beans, what's happened?'

With a sigh I placed my drink down and gently gripped the stem of the glass in an attempt to keep my fraying emotions in check. Swivelling it several times as a distraction to my tumbling stomach, I pursed my lips and gave Cait a recap of my morning, right from my heated, lust-fuelled reunion with Sean in the back of his car, to his weak reasons for me needing to stay in a hotel, and finally finishing with my discovery of the newspaper article about his engagement to Savannah and his lame reasons for it.

Sitting back with a huffed breath I looked to Cait and saw her gawking at me, her cocktail raised halfway to her mouth and frozen mid-sip. 'Engaged?' she whispered almost theatrically, to which I scrunched up my face and nodded.

'Although according to Sean it's not real.'

'Blimey. I vaguely try and keep up with celebrity gossip, but I haven't seen a thing about that,' she pondered thoughtfully, before her cheeks flushed and she gave me an odd look. 'And you had sex in the back of his car?' she whispered in a tone which, although shocked, also sounded marginally curious. But then she blinked rapidly, her lashes fluttering like butterfly wings before she shook her head, looking embarrassed as her cheeks flooded with colour. 'That just slipped out, it's hardly the most important issue at hand, sorry, Allie … I lost my focus for a second there.'

Snorting out a dry grunt I rolled my eyes and sipped my drink. 'Yeah, it was a first for me, actually,' I admitted sadly, wondering if the car would be the last time I ever got to experience something new with Sean.

'Let's get back on track and see what we can find out.' Placing her glass on the table with a decisive bang, Cait began digging through her handbag before pulling out a mini iPad and flipping open the turquoise cover. My eyebrows rose in surprise, and even under the current circumstances I found myself laughing wryly.

'I thought you were some poor, hard-up traveller?' She flashed me a grin and went back to her task of opening up an internet search. 'I have two luxuries: a nice outfit to go out in,' she said, 'and my iPad.' Narrowing her eyes, she typed something on the screen and sat back while it loaded.

'Besides, I might stay in hostels from time to time, but I do work, Allie. I'm not that hard-up.' She finished with a fond smile as she turned her attention to the iPad.

Her fingers began speeding across the screen, face intent and focused. Placing the iPad on the table Cait then sat back and rolled her shoulders to straighten her posture before turning to me. 'So, you want me to go through it? Or shall we leave it?'

As tempting as it might be to avoid all things Sean and simply drink myself into a blissful cocktail oblivion, I needed to know if there was any substance to the supposed engagement rumours. Drawing in a deep breath I steeled myself for an unpleasant few minutes to come and nodded. 'I need to know. What does it say?' At that moment a waiter poked his head around the door, eyeing our half-depleted glasses. 'Another round, girls?' he enquired with a bright smile.

'Yes please. We have a personal trauma on our hands so keep 'em coming, I'll start a tab,' Cait instructed him in a serious tone as she characteristically avoided all eye contact with him, but then downed the last swig of her drink and waggled the glass in the air.

'You want me to mix in a few shots for you too?' he asked with a surprisingly sympathetic look on his face.

'Hell yes,' I announced with a watery smile. 'No tequila though, please.' Years of drinking had proved time after time that tequila was not the drink for me – it made me veeery ill in the most unpleasant of ways, and always led to hangovers that seemed to seep straight from the bowels of hell. With a nod, he was off, leaving me to turn back to the iPad with a sense of heavy trepidation settling in my stomach. 'OK, give it to me.'

The tip of her tongue poked out in concentration as she scrolled through the search results before bringing up an article from just over three weeks ago. Leaning across, I scanned the article with her. Along with the text there was a picture which made my heart constrict painfully in my chest; Sean, dressed in black jeans, a fitted white T-shirt, and looking tanned and unfairly handsome, was at the centre of a group of eight people walking along a pavement. It was dark and none of them were looking at the camera, so I could only assume that they were on a night out when the picture had been captured.

The painful part of the image was Savannah, though. One of her tanned arms was firmly gripped around Sean's waist while the other was pressed into the centre of his chest, her blood red nails standing out proud against the white of his shirt and making me want to pluck them out one by one with a pair of pliers.

Closing my eyes I took a second to stabilise myself and then opened them again, chewing painfully on my lower lip. Even walking along the bloody street she was all over him – it couldn't have been a comfortable position to walk in, but she was still managing it, as if laying a claim on him. Bitch. So many expletives ran through my mind that I had to forcibly roll my lips together to stop myself having a meltdown.

'He's frowning, and he's not got his arm around her, so maybe she's just trying her luck,' Cait pointed out. 'Let's see what it says …' We both fell silent for a second as we skimmed the article, which was fairly sparse in details and didn't really tell me anything new, apart from one interesting fact – Savannah had been the one to announce the engagement, on her own. Sean hadn't even been present when she'd made a statement at some public event she had attended.

Interesting. That didn't seem like the usual behaviour of a happy, love-struck couple, did it? Perhaps Sean was telling the truth.

A bitter taste rose in my throat. It might all be pomp for the public, which I still needed to be convinced of, but regardless of whether or not it was fake, I'd been in regular contact with Sean since he'd been over here – since Savannah had made her announcement – giving him more than enough opportunities to tell me about it, but he'd chosen to hide it from me. That hurt more than I could even comprehend at the moment.

As if sensing my growing distress, the barman suddenly appeared at our table with a tray containing two more colourful cocktails and two small shot glasses filled with a clear liquid and topped with a blue, floating substance. 'A special shooter of my own creation,' he informed us as he placed our drinks down with a flourish. 'Just the thing to sort out trouble,' he added with a conspiratorial wink before disappearing again.

'So, what do you think?' I asked tentatively, taking a sip of my cocktail. It was just as delicious as the last one and as the cool liquid slid down my throat it seemed to make the events of the day just a tiny bit more bearable. Maybe I should back-track to my earlier thought and get blasted on booze.

Cait skimmed the iPad results once more and then bounced her head a little from side to side as if weighing up the options. 'Some of these articles back up Sean's story saying that the engagement came out of nowhere and seems a little too conveniently timed with the promos for the new series. It seems from those pieces that fake engagements and relationships are actually quite common in Tinseltown.'

Giving me an intent look, she raised her eyebrows. 'If you want my honest opinion, then from the brief meeting I had with him at your house in January, he's clearly crazy about you, so I think he's probably telling the truth.' Sliding her iPad back into her bag, she turned to me with a sympathetic smile. 'You love him, don't you?'

This wasn't something I'd actually confessed to Cait. She knew I was crazy about Sean, but it wasn't exactly the type of thing you could discuss over a phone call, so I'd never really divulged the exact depth of my feelings. Swallowing loudly I slung back my shot, relishing the burn in my throat, and then nodded my head decisively.

'Yep.' My voice was thick with emotion, but I was definitely getting a good buzz from the alcohol. My limbs felt looser, and my melancholy certainly seemed easier to deal with, which could only be a good thing.

'Wow,' she whispered softly, giving my arm a supportive rub. 'Well, granted he's not dealt with this situation in the best of ways, but it seems to me you have little choice in the matter. You should cool off for a day or so, but then you need to meet up and give him a chance to explain it to you.'

Tipping my head back, I stared up at the ornate ceiling rose that surrounded the elaborate light fittings, and drew in a few deep breaths as I tried to settle my swirling emotions. That was basically the same conclusion I'd come to, and I found myself nodding as I lowered my head.

'Has he called you?' I was about to explain that I hadn't given Sean my new number, but we were interrupted by Cait's phone as it chimed on the table. Glancing at the screen she smiled, 'It's my mum. Even after three years of travelling she still likes to check in with me most nights,' Cait joked, but I saw a slight tightness around her eyes and immediately suspected that her mum must still be paranoid about her safety after the trouble with Greg, much like I was.

Our conversation drifted through easier, less stressful topics as we caught up on each other's news, but after a few more expertly mixed drinks from our moustached cocktail master, the conversation came back around to my man troubles with Sean. Levelling her glass at me, Cait nodded sagely, looking more than a little tipsy. 'I know I don't have all the specifics, but this town is full of fake, fickle fools. Stories get invented every hour, none of them with a shred of truth to them. Don't you dare let him off easy, though, Allie, celeb or not, you need to make sure he treats you right.'

I knew that Cait's warning came from her own personal experience, and felt a brief pang of pain for her again, but Cait wasn't hanging around for any pity tonight, ploughing straight on with more advice. 'I think you should give him a few days to stew, just to make him realise that he shouldn't have hidden it from you, and then go and see him.'

Nodding, I took a second to absorb her words. Sean had always treated me perfectly up until now, I thought miserably, feeling a tight lump settle in the top of my throat. He'd perhaps been a little domineering in some of our sexual encounters, but I rather liked that side of him.

'Of course, my advice is partly selfish,' Cait confided with a small smile to brighten our moods. 'Because if you are staying away from him for a day or so then it means I get you all to myself!'

Grinning at Cait's tipsy words, I nodded my agreement before suddenly feeling quite overwhelmed and immensely glad that my best friend was here with me when I needed her the most. To try and distract myself from the tears that were suddenly threatening to spill from my eyes again I finished off my drink. Alcohol might have seemed like a great idea earlier, but mix it with the exhaustion of my flight, not to mention the high emotion of the day, and I was quickly wavering towards a meltdown.

Placing my empty glass down I stared at it fixedly, willing my eyes to dry and the room to stop spinning, when my stomach gave an almighty rumble. Hmm, that had probably been my third cocktail on an empty stomach, and that wasn't counting the shots the barman had prepared for us.

Standing up, I looked intently at my drinking partner. 'I need to go and get something to eat,' I announced. I was surviving on the airplane food I'd eaten that morning, and with all the drinks I was consuming I'd be steaming drunk soon if I wasn't careful. Actually, testing my balance with a few adjustments of my stance, I decided I didn't feel too drunk at all. Maybe the cocktails were more fruity than alcoholic, but still, dinner was definitely needed in the very near future.

Cait assumed her tour guide role, collecting up our few belongings, seeing to the bill, and ushering us to the door. It wasn't even nine o'clock yet, but out on the street, the serious party goers were just starting to crawl out of the woodwork looking like catwalk models, several sending complimentary wolf-whistles our way.

Crikey, I don't think I'd ever attracted so much attention on a night out before. If I really was about to find myself being young, free, and single again, then I suppose at least it looked like I was in the right town for it.

Cait

As we stumbled along the pavement I tried to distract myself from the dark night sky by thinking back over all I had discovered this evening. I could barely believe what Allie was going through with Sean, it was like some far-fetched movie, and it was awful to see my best friend this upset, especially when I didn't know what I could do to help.

However miserable it might seem at the moment, though, I had hope for them. I'd met Sean back in the UK, admittedly briefly, but I'd seen the way he'd looked at her – his eyes lit up when she was in the room and the connection between them had practically buzzed in the air. He was a man in love, it was clear to see, so I had faith in his commitment and believed his side of the story even if Allie was cautiously dubious.

I just hoped with all of my heart that Sean would get his arse in gear and sort this mess out quickly, because I knew that Allie was too stubborn and too proud to hang around for long if she was being messed about.

Thinking back to my own vague man issues of the day, I decided that I had been bloody lucky that Allie hadn't wangled the story of my run-in with Jack out of me. She was normally the first to spot my guilty blushes if I was trying to hide something, so I could only assume that her issues with Sean had distracted her from pursuing it. I was still certain that keeping the Jack incident to myself was the best course of action, for now at least. Allie was trying to deal with all her own problems at the moment, the last thing she needed was me turning into a simpering mess just because a man had made me feel a bit peculiar.

Feeling myself tense as we passed a group of lads out for a night out, I remained stiff and wary all the way back to the hostel, only relaxing once I was back in the reception's familiar surroundings.

Taking a deep breath to compose myself I looked at Allie and felt my heart clench at the sadness I could see in her eyes. Apparently noticing my pity, she forced a bright smile onto her face. 'I'll be OK,' she assured me, her voice firm but quivering just slightly. 'So, I was thinking we should get some comfy clothes on, grab something to eat from the hostel cafe, and then as the resident Los Angeles expert you could help me devise a list of some distractions to keep me occupied tomorrow.'

Nodding my agreement eagerly, I linked my arm through hers as we set off for the dorm room to change.

Formulating fun sightseeing plans I could do. None of that would involve me thinking about a certain tall, dark-haired jogger …

Chapter Twelve

Allie

Cait had been a little tense on the walk back to the hotel, presumably because it was dark and we had passed several groups of guys out for the night who had made attempts at conversation with us. They were all harmless though, and it made me wonder for the thousandth time just how Cait had managed to spend the last three years travelling if she was still struggling with her anxiety to this extent. She was a brave one, that was for sure.

Now we were back at the hostel, Cait seemed more relaxed, and I was glad to say the drinks had also done me the world of good too, the girly chatting helping clear my head to the point where I actually felt I might be able to give Sean a call tomorrow. Or perhaps at least text to give him my new number. As insignificant as it may seem to others, the thought of breaking our routine and not sending him my nightly text was almost too painful to consider.

Heading up the stairs we decided to change into more comfortable clothes and reconvene in the kitchen for a cuppa before bed, some much-needed food, and a chat about what we could do tomorrow.

After changing into tracksuit bottoms and a loose T-shirt I decided I should call the Beverly Hills Hotel to cancel the room that Sean had reserved for me. There was no point in him getting charged for a room I wasn't even going to use. A quick internet search had the hotel's number on my phone, and then seconds later I was listening to a very OTT greeting in a sing-song American accent. 'Good evening, this is the Beverly Hills Hotel and Suites. You're speaking to Carolyn, how may I help you tonight?'

Once I had given my name and explained that I wanted to cancel the booking, I heard a pause down the line followed by a soft, embarrassed cough. 'Um, I'm afraid I can't do that, ma'am. The suite has been paid for in full by a gentleman, two hours ago.' If she had recognised Sean, the receptionist was keeping quiet about it.

'Suite?' I repeated weakly, suddenly feeling a little dizzy at how ridiculously grand his gesture was.

'Yes, ma'am. The gentleman has booked you a garden bungalow for the next three weeks. He came in to see if you were checked in. When he found you hadn't arrived he paid the balance in full and then left.'

Pursing my lips, I leant back on the cool, tiled bathroom wall and closed my eyes as a wave of nausea swept through me. A garden bungalow. If that didn't reek of a desperate attempt at an apology I didn't know what did, and the fact that he'd seemingly done it all anonymously annoyed me too, reminding me that I was essentially his dirty little secret.

Ending the call in a daze, I stayed in the bathroom for a few more minutes just in case I did throw up, killing time by splashing cool water on my face and rinsing out the alcohol taste from my mouth. Even after lingering for nearly ten minutes, I could still feel my stomach swirling with renewed anger at his deception. But far worse than the anger was the hurt, and the horrible, achingly-deep sense of loss that I was starting to feel at the thought of my relationship being over.

Blowing out a breath I puffed my cheeks and tried to shake off my frayed nerves. Drying off my face I decided I couldn't very well hide in the toilets forever, so I made my way back to the kitchen where I found Cait chatting with two other girls and the tattoo guy from reception, who I had learnt was called Marlon.

As I got closer I saw that he was leaning over an intricate sketch of a wizard, adding some details with a fine-tipped pen. 'My next tattoo,' he said when he saw me looking.

'Oh, wow. It's good. Where's it going?' I asked instinctively, because from what I could see of him there wasn't a centimetre of his skin that wasn't already inked.

Looking up at me he popped the cap on his pen and stood up with a smirk, his dreadlocks swinging as he did so. 'I got some spare flesh that ain't marked yet. You wanna see?' he said, reaching for the fly of his baggy jeans.

Beside me I heard Cait spitting out a full mouthful of tea, a good deal of it splattering warmly on my wrist as I held up a hand towards Marlon. 'I'll take your word for it!' I shrieked, glancing across to see Cait recoiling in panic behind me and banging into the fridge.

Thankfully, Marlon just burst out laughing and fell back into his seat with a grin and a wink before carrying on with his sketch. Poor Cait would probably have exploded if he'd popped out his flesh. But I have to say, my mind was now positively boggling about the possible locations for the tattoo.

Distracting me from my thoughts, Cait (who was now incredibly red in the face) plonked some toast on the table and handed me a cup of tea which I accepted gratefully. After blowing the steam from the top I multi-tasked, sipping and grabbing a slice of toast and taking a hasty bite.

'Mmm, that's good. Thanks.' I felt almost instantly better as some nourishment hit my stomach. 'I couldn't cancel the hotel room at the Beverly Hills, it's fully paid for up front.' I told Cait through my mouthful, feeling a stab of guilt that Sean had paid out so much money for a suite that was going to sit empty for three weeks. Although if he hadn't concealed all this stupidity from me in the first place he wouldn't have had to try and hide me away, so really, it was his fault.

My words apparently got Cait's full attention, because she practically dropped her mug as she looked at me with wide eyes. 'You have a room booked, and paid for, at the Beverly Hills Hotel? That's the hotel you meant when you said Sean had booked you a room somewhere?'

Nodding glumly, I raised my tea to my lips again and took another sip. 'A suite, actually,' I offered with a shrug. 'A garden bungalow, I think the woman said.' Cait and Marlon were now both sitting with similar expressions of shock on their faces, mouths hanging open and eyebrows raised high.

'What the hell are we doing in this dive then?' Cait exclaimed loudly, 'No offence, Marlon,' she added, flashing an apologetic wince at him.

'None taken, I just work here. Ain't like I own it or nothing,' he said, going back to his drawing.

I raised my own eyebrows as I bounced my gaze back to Cait. 'Why? Do you want to go?'

Rolling her eyes, Cait grinned and nodded vigorously. 'It's the flipping Beverly Hills Hotel, and the suite is booked and paid for ... so yeah, I kinda want to go there.' she said with added exaggeration in her voice as if it was the most obvious thing in the world, which thinking about it, it probably was. Why stay in a five story budget hostel when we could be living it up in a five-star hotel?

'Wow. Wow. Wooowww.' Cait was standing in the middle of our garden bungalow with her head thrown back and arms held out wide as she spun on the spot, causing her long, brown hair to flow around her like a floaty, chestnut, silk scarf. 'This is amazing! I don't think I've ever stayed anywhere so posh before!'

'I know; me neither. But we may as well make the most of this luxury while we can!' And luxury it was – the room was huge, done out in cool creams and tans and furnished so beautifully that it screamed class and expense. The two bedrooms were exquisitely decorated: sumptuously covered king-sized beds, foil-wrapped chocolates on the pillows, beautiful furnishings, and tempting roll-top baths in the stone tiled en suites.

The master bedroom was basically in a wing of its own, down a corridor, round a corner, and completely separated from the rest of the rooms, so we left that until last in our exploration. Arriving at the doorway in front of me, Cait suddenly stumbled to a halt. Wondering why she had stopped so abruptly I looked around her and followed her gaze towards the bed. There was a single red rose on the quilt, sitting upon an envelope, and as I gazed at it I felt my heart accelerate in my chest.

'Why don't you look around and I'll go and order some room service for a late snack? I'm starving, and that toast can't have been enough for you either,' Cait blurted, giving me the opportunity for some time alone. Nodding, I smiled weakly at her as she left. Her soft footsteps disappeared down the corridor until I was embraced in a heavy silence. My chest felt tight. Was this some perk left by the hotel staff, or had Sean been in here? As stupid as it was, I inhaled to see if I could get any lingering trace of his smoky, spicy scent, but disappointingly all I smelt was the clean aroma of the bed linens and the soft smell of some beautiful flowers on the chest of drawers to my right.

Forcing my shaky legs forward I hesitantly advanced to the bed. Without even moving the rose I could see that the envelope had my name written across it in Sean's elegant, sloping script, and this tiny thing brought the events of the day crashing down on me. I missed him so much. My throat tightened with emotion a second before my legs went soft below me, causing my body to sink down onto the edge of the mattress. I felt completely and utterly drained. Picking up the envelope with trembling fingers I held it in my hands for a few seconds before drawing in a deep breath and then sliding the flap up to remove a single sheet of paper.

Allie,

I went to the hostel but you weren't there. I checked here but you haven't checked in either, and I can't phone you because I no longer have your number. I'm going out of my mind.

This situation is completely messed up. I understand how it must seem to you, but you must believe me when I say there is nothing between Savannah and me.

I see now that I shouldn't have tried to keep it from you. I thought I was protecting you, but instead I've pushed you away. I can only say how very sorry I am for that.

You know how much I hate not being able to contact you – I won't sleep not knowing if you are safe or not. I recognise why you want to distance yourself from me, but please, please, if you are reading this just let me know you are safe.

I love you. Please don't give up on me, my gorgeous girl. I will sort it, please just be patient.

Yours, Sean x

A fluttering, wispy breath slipped from my lips, followed by several hot tears that slid down my cheeks and dripped onto the letter. Not wanting to smudge his writing I collapsed backwards onto the bed and clutched the note to my chest while squeezing my eyes closed. God, I was trembling. Literally shaking from head to toe.

I'm not sure I'd ever felt this emotionally raw in my life. It felt as if someone had ripped me open and left my nerves exposed to the elements until they became flayed and oversensitive, and then just for fun, had set me on fire.

The worst thing was that I didn't have a clue how to proceed. I *did* believe him when he said it was all a PR scam, but could I live with the knowledge that he couldn't date me officially? Couldn't even be seen in public with me, but would frequently be pictured with his hands all over Savannah? Shuddering, I closed my eyes. That was not the kind of relationship I wanted, or deserved.

I rubbed at my arms, trying to calm the burning, tingling sensations that were running across my skin, until my stomach suddenly gave a loud grumble. Sitting up, I composed myself with several long breaths and then flattened the paper and carefully placed the note on the bed.

Running my eyes over his words again I shook my head at his obsession with my safety. It slightly irked me that he didn't seem to trust me to take care of myself, but deep down I couldn't stay mad at Sean for that. I knew it was just his insecurity from the fatal accident that had happened with his ex when he hadn't been present.

Picking up the rose, I twirled it between my finger and thumb and lifted it to my nose, inhaling its subtle scent. Rolling my lips into a tight line I absorbed the contents of his note and felt my heart soften in my chest. He'd made some big errors in judgement recently, but the note seemed genuine. Besides, if he'd actually turned up here and at the hostel then it showed that he was prepared to take some serious risks with his career in his attempt to find me.

The chiming of a bell rang from the other room, probably signalling the arrival of our midnight snack, so I numbly stood up and placed the rose on top of the note.

I didn't have much of an appetite, but from the repeated rumbling of my stomach, my body was clearly still in need of sustenance so I had to force something down.

Standing there looking at the delicate petals of the rose I acted on a whim and snapped a quick photograph of the opened letter and flower, and then attached it to a text, adding his number from memory and pressing send. I hadn't added any words, but after his heartfelt plea I was compelled to at least let him know that I was at the hotel, and was OK.

A brief frown fluttered on my brow as I immediately realised my error. Bugger – by sending the message I'd just inadvertently given him my new number. I knew I should be irritated and pissed off with him, and to a certain degree I was, but the knowledge that he now had my phone number made me feel a little more … connected. Reassured, perhaps.

Even at this late hour my phone immediately began to ring in my hand, flashing up Sean's familiar number. He was still awake? Because he was worried about me? Or because he was out partying somewhere with Savannah?

A shiver of jealousy shook my body as I thought about him being out somewhere with women swooning all around him, but then my brain focused on the fact that he was on the other end of the line. Just one press of a button and I would hear his gravelly, sexy-as-sin voice. But I felt on the verge of a breakdown, and far too raw to speak to him so I left it to ring in my hand as my stomach knotted guiltily.

It seemed to ring forever, as I just stood there limply, holding my phone and staring at it with glassy eyes as hot tears flowed down my cheeks. The room sounded eerily silent when my mobile finally stopped, but the quiet was broken a second later as a text message pinged and my heart gave a little kick. Biting on my lower lip I tensed my body and opened his message.

From: Sean
Allie, thank you for letting me know you are safe. Can
we speak? Please? x

I considered just ignoring his message, but no matter
how much I knew I should, I didn't have it in me. Besides,
if I didn't reply he'd probably phone me again and again,
which would aggravate my already frayed nerves, so I
replied, keeping it brief and to the point.

To: Sean
I need to clear my head, Sean. I'm going to catch up
with Cait for a day or so, but I promise I'll text you
when I'm ready to talk. x

Given the circumstances I knew it was stupid to add a
kiss on the end, but no matter how shitty the situation, I still
loved him, and I couldn't help myself from expressing it. It
seemed that was often the case around Sean, I thought, as I
left my phone on the bedside table and walked out to join
Cait for a late dinner.

Chapter Thirteen

Sean

After giving me an intense work out of core exercises, running, and press-ups, Joe dug around in his kit bag and pulled out two sets of gloves. Raising one eyebrow I took in his arrogantly expectant expression and glanced between the options he was presenting me with – one set of full cover boxing gloves, and one set of small, light, fingerless martial arts gloves. He seemed to be offering me an easy option of boxing against the punch bag, or the harder option of hand-to-hand sparring.

Bring. It. On.

After the day I'd had so far, I was more than up for some grappling and tussling to help relieve my stress, and so I reached forward and grabbed the smaller gloves with a cocky grin.

Wiggling his eyebrows at me, he began to don his own battered gloves, which had certainly seen some action over the years. Joe was a good fighter – more than a good fighter; before he'd gone into personal training he'd actually spent two years on the professional mixed martial arts circuit, racking up some impressive wins and gaining himself a good deal of respect within the world of cage fighting.

He could knock me out in the blink of an eye if he wanted to, but I had a small protection policy working in my favour ... Joe wasn't allowed to hit me in the head. Seeing as these weekly workouts were part of my contract with the film studio, he wasn't allowed to include anything in the training which could damage my looks, a stupidly protective clause, but one that worked in my favour when it came to fighting with the big guy. Luckily, it didn't go both ways, so I could attempt to do any damage to him I liked – if I could even get within touching distance.

I usually felt pretty bloody pleased with myself if I even managed to land a few light punches on him during a session, but the stress with Allie must really have pumped me full of adrenaline, because today I managed to take Joe down to the mats not once, but twice. On the second occasion I even earned a grunt of praise, followed by a swift leg sweep so I ended up flat on my arse while he picked himself up with a smirk. Smug git. He always liked to be the last man standing.

Joe was long gone now. I was showered, had picked at some dinner, and was now sitting on my bed in some pyjama bottoms. Smiling sadly, I picked absently at a loose thread on the knee. These were Allie's favourites, she'd said something about how they hung 'just right' from my hips. I wasn't entirely sure what that meant, but from the wicked twinkle in her eyes I could only assume it was a good thing.

Sighing heavily, I sat back against the headboard. My body was feeling the stresses of a hard workout, fatigue making me weary as tiredness burned my muscles, but mentally I just wasn't willing to give in and sleep. My mind was still full of thoughts of Allie and the way she'd run away from me earlier, and no amount of treadmill pounding or wrestling with Joe was going to distract me from thinking about her for long.

I was seriously tempted to head out to try and find her again, but my two attempts earlier this evening had been unsuccessful. First I'd ventured to the hostel. To avoid recognition I'd dressed in my scruffiest clothes: a rumpled T-shirt out of the wash bin and a pair of cut-off jean shorts, outfit completed by a beanie hat and shades. I hadn't been spotted by any fans, but unfortunately the guy behind the counter had adamantly refused to give out any guest information. He'd looked half stoned, so I'd even tried to bribe him with a fifty dollar note, but the moralistic bastard had staunchly refused my attempt. I'd probably have had more luck if I'd had some weed to offer him instead. From there I'd returned home and changed, then donned the same dark glasses – this time twinned with a cap – before heading to the hotel. I looked, and felt, like a complete idiot wearing dark glasses at night, but if I could avoid being recognised then I would. Unfortunately Allie, my stupid, stubborn, gorgeous girl hadn't checked in there either, so I had no clue where she was.

Seeing as I was paying for the suite, the hotel staff had at least allowed me access to the rooms and I'd left a note for her, hoping with all my heart that she would rethink sleeping at the hostel.

It was nearly midnight now, so surely Allie would be home by now? Wherever her 'home' for the night was. I was absently spinning my phone in my hand when it vibrated. Bolting upright, my heart leapt and blood surged through my veins when I saw a notification of a message from an unfamiliar number. Could it be her? I wasn't a religious man, but I definitely sent a quick prayer up to whoever might be listening, begging for it to be from Allie.

I barely even gave myself time to hope before my finger was swiping across the screen and eagerly opening the message. The message itself was blank, but there was a picture attachment which I quickly clicked. The picture opened and I couldn't help the huge breath of relief that left my lungs as I realised that it was from Allie. Finally! It showed the opened note that I'd left for her and the rose. It seemed to be her way of telling me she was safe, and the relief that pounded in my heart was almost overwhelming.

I could only assume that she wasn't ready to talk to me yet, but I quickly saved the number as 'Allie USA', and pressed call anyway. I was too keyed up to remain seated, so I leapt from the bed, phone pressed to my ear, and began pacing up and down as the ringing tone rolled on and on. Damn it. I'd half expected her not to answer, but I would have given anything to speak to her, even if only briefly. I knew why she was pissed at me, and I totally got it, but I wanted, needed, to hear her voice so bloody badly.

Pulling up the message again I typed out a quick reply asking if we could talk. I knew what her reply would be, if I even got a reply, but I had to try. Staring at the phone as I waited impatiently for a response, my brain was practically pulsating from the mental effort I was putting into willing her to text me back.

Finally my wish was granted, and the phone vibrated in my palm again. I was like a giddy teenager as I immediately opened the message, desperate to soak up her words, no matter what they might be.

From: Allie USA

I need to clear my head, Sean. I'm going to catch up with Cait for a day or so, but I promise I'll text you when I'm ready to talk. x

As frustrating as it was to see that she wanted space, it was probably quite a good thing. My filming schedule tomorrow was from dawn to dusk, and seeing as mobiles were banned from set, making any kind of contact would have been practically impossible. She'd said she would text me when she was ready to talk, but I couldn't help myself from sending one last message before bed.

To: Allie USA
Okay, my gorgeous girl. Think things through, but think of me too, because you will be constantly on my mind. Sleep well. I love you. Sean x

A day apart, maybe two. I could do that. I'd give her the space she needed to come to terms with my crazy-arsed world, and then we'd talk. I knew I could be persuasive when I wanted, so if she was still reluctant then I'd simply have to engage my full-on charm and hope that I could bring her around.

The phone was still sat in my palm with her words illuminating the screen. I must have read the message twenty times, my gaze hanging on each word and committing them to memory, but the part that really had me captivated was the 'x' at the end. As my eyes lingered on the small letter I felt my lips curl into a tiny, hopeful smile. She'd added a kiss. I couldn't seem to take my eyes off of it. Did that mean she genuinely did just need some time to cool off and still loved me? God, I hoped so.

Chapter Fourteen

Allie

The duvet slid from my body, exposing my heated skin to the coolness of the room, the movement of the soft material gliding off my legs waking me in confusion before two strong hands grabbed my ankles and tugged me down the mattress.

Before I'd barely even regained consciousness a hot, hungry mouth descended between my legs, sucking and licking and causing me to yelp and push myself to my elbows. Between my legs was a dark brown head that I recognised very well. Sean. Not taking his lips away from my flesh, he tipped his head slightly so our eyes met, the gleam of mischievous intent in his blue gaze instantly igniting my desire for him. One of his hands snaked up over my stomach, splaying across the skin and pressing me back down into a lying position. 'Relax. Let me take care of you, my gorgeous girl …' he murmured, every word sending delicious vibrations across my oversensitive skin.

His tongue was now lapping at my clit with firm, sure movements, as two of his fingers began to explore my opening. Finding me wet, he pressed them in high and deep before beginning to gently thrust. Oh that felt heavenly. It was so tempting to just let him continue, but given all that had happened yesterday, we really needed to talk, not fuck. 'Sean …'

'Shh …' he muttered, before effectively silencing me by adding a third finger to the mix.

'Oh, God …' He was filling me so distractingly that I forgot about talking and clawed at the duvet on each side of me instead.

His fingers kept on plunging, curling inside of me to tickle at my g-spot as his other hand danced across my chest between my nipples, giving both of them gentle rubs and tweaks to harden them. Once I was panting, begging, and writhing around to his satisfaction, he gripped one erect peak and gave it a fierce twist that had me coming apart and climaxing around his fingers as my back arched off the bed and a ragged yelp left my lips. He really was so good at this, mastering how I liked a touch of pain mixed in to heighten my pleasure, and always managing to deliver it in just the right dose.

Gazing down with heavy eyelids I saw him standing at the end of the bed, staring up at me hungrily, one hand palming his cock and working up and down at a rapid pace. 'I want your mouth on me, Allie, sit up,' he murmured, and my eyes rolled shut briefly at that hint of the commanding tone I so loved.

Pushing myself bolt upright I parted my lips and blinked several times before frowning in confusion. My body was heated with arousal, heart pounding, and my clitoris was still pulsing frantically with the after-effects of my climax, but Sean was nowhere to be seen.

Both the bed and room were empty. What on earth? Glancing down I gasped in shock when I saw the duvet pushed back from my body and my own right hand between my legs while my left hand lay on my reddened nipple.

Oh. My. God.

Realisation of what I had done dawned on me … I'd dreamt that Sean was here, and had apparently rather effectively serviced myself in my sleep. My cheeks flamed as I shifted myself back up the bed and towards the pillows.

Sean being here had felt so real, but as I propped myself against the headboard and looked down at my glistening fingers it was increasingly obvious that my mind had merely conjured him up as part of my fantasy. Bloody hell. That had been one hell of a self-service orgasm too.

On very, very, rare occasions in the past I had woken up feeling like I'd had a small orgasm in my sleep, but as far as I was aware this was the first time that my body had actually joined in with the dream to such an extent.

Grabbing a tissue from the bedside table I wiped my fingers and flopped back, still shocked at how real that dream had felt. Mind you, my head had been full of thoughts of Sean before I'd fallen asleep, so I suppose it shouldn't really surprise me that I had ended up dreaming about him. I was just a bit shocked at how erotic it had been.

At least it was better than imagining him having sex with Savannah, I supposed. Ugh, after dreaming the same sickening thing several times now I had started to panic that the skin-crawling dream of them sweaty, entwined, and humping rampantly was going to become a recurring nightmare. Dreaming about me having sex with him was far, far more preferable, and long may it continue.

Sighing miserably I ran a hand through my hair – it was Sunday morning, and after my text to Sean on Thursday night I had avoided calling or texting him since. That was three complete nights, and two long days without him. How I managed it I'm not sure, but I had. In that time, sleep had been evasive, leaving me feeling decidedly like an insomniac, although clearly from that steamy dream I was obviously sleeping at some point during the night.

I knew that some non-contact time would allow Sean to stew over his errors, hopefully making him repent his stupid decisions, but unfortunately, as well as letting him stew, it was torturing me too, because I was missing him like crazy and was desperate to meet up with him to see if we could sort out the issues between us.

Cait had to take most of the credit for my discipline over the last forty-eight hours though, because I would have crumbled and called him if she hadn't provided near-continuous distractions. I'd been given a tour of the hotel neighbourhood, which was pristine, glitzy, and amazing. A tour of the hostel neighbourhood – which was fairly grimy, not that glitzy, and distinctly less lovely – and then she had kept me entertained with drinks out, walking in local parks, and playing games by the private pool at the bungalow.

All in all, I had barely been left alone for more than a few seconds so hadn't had a chance to mope apart from when I was alone at night.

This morning I'd somehow managed to last until just before eight before I even considered rolling out of bed in search of coffee. The superking-sized bed, luxurious mattress, and Egyptian cotton sheets might have had something to do with my ability to snooze this morning, but the more likely reason was my exhaustion finally getting the better of me.

Rolling out of the bed I blushed as I felt the smooth dampness between my legs and recalled my dream again. I wasn't a prude by any means – in my months apart from Sean I had sorted myself on numerous occasions when I'd felt horny – but still, I couldn't believe I had done it in my sleep! Shaking myself out of my groggy, slightly embarrassed state with a full body stretch, I picked up my phone to check for any new emails.

To my surprise, there was a new text message alert on the screen. With slight trepidation I checked the sender and saw Sean's name, but the date read as 10.49 p.m. last night. Frowning, I wondered how I'd missed it; I'd checked my phone before bed and hadn't seen it. Pulling in a deep breath I opened the message and skimmed my eyes across it.

From: Sean

I'm trying to be patient, Allie, but I can't take this any longer. I need to speak to you. I'm on the film set tomorrow until four, but I promise to call after that, please answer. Goodnight, my gorgeous girl. Sleep well. xx

Sleep well? Huh! Hardly. Although, I had woken up rather pleasantly, I thought with another blush. Allowing myself a small smile I decided that I liked the fact that he'd upped his usual one kiss to two. For some reason that made me ridiculously happy and I held the phone tightly against my chest, trying to absorb some of his reassuring warmth from the cold plastic.

The space and time, although torturous, had at least made me feel ready to speak to him. I loved him, and believed him, so all I needed now was his reassurance that this engagement situation wasn't going to last for too much longer. When he called later today I would answer his call and be calm, level-headed, and sensible. Perhaps all this stupidity with Sean, Savannah, and me would be behind us quicker than I'd expected. At least I hoped that would be the case.

Delving in my suitcase, I pulled on a loose T-shirt and some pink running shorts before leaving my bedroom and navigating my way towards the bar area in our bungalow on a quest for caffeine. The bar was complete with marble top and two leather stools, but as well as a vast selection of alcoholic beverages it housed a smart coffee machine, which was my focus this morning.

I would have thought that eight in the morning was quite an early hour for a seasoned traveller like Cait, but she was already sitting by the bar reading her book, as she had been both previous mornings too. I suspected she had been getting up early on purpose to make sure I had company if I was feeling low, which was really rather sweet, and a very Cait-like gesture.

Seeing her sipping at a steaming mug I licked my lips in anticipation – hopefully that meant there was a fresh pot of coffee waiting for me somewhere.

'Morning, sweetie,' Cait crooned when she saw me. 'Coffee?'

'Yes please. Morning.' Slipping onto the second stool along the bar I watched greedily as Cait filled a large mug for me, topped it with milk, and then handed it across. 'God, that smells amazing.' Lifting the mug of delicious-scented nectar to my lips I sipped and groaned in near ecstasy. 'And it tastes even better.' I sat in silence for a few moments, letting the bitter taste dance over my tongue before commenting, 'You're up early again.' Placing my mug down I glanced up at Cait to find her studying me closely. A flush crept onto Cait's cheeks and she shrugged, feigning casualness.

'I was worried about you. I thought after your … jet lag … that you might be up early, so I decided to get up and keep you company.' I translated that to 'I thought after your shitty week you might not be able to sleep so have been getting up early to make sure you weren't moping around pathetically'. Even with her dreadful lie I appreciated the effort and smiled gratefully.

'Thanks, hun. I'll be OK.'

'No problemo. So, you got any plans for today? It looks like the weather is going to be glorious again.'

'Um, no. I'm expecting a call this afternoon, but apart from that, nothing. I was hoping to keep myself busy again, do you have any ideas?'

Plonking her mug down so some coffee slopped over her hand and the counter, I saw Cait's eyebrows rise. 'Back up there, lady. You're expecting a call?' Her tone made it obvious that Cait wanted the gossip, and so with a sigh I explained I'd had a message from Sean last night, and was now expecting to speak to him this afternoon.

'It sounds like a step in the right direction,' Cait agreed with a pleased nod as she licked some coffee from her thumb. 'So, back to my plans for distraction. How does a bit more sightseeing sound? Starting with the best pancakes you'll ever taste, squeezing in a few more landmarks, and finishing with some lounging on the beach?'

Smiling, I nodded gratefully. 'That sounds pretty perfect to me.'

When Cait had said that I'd eat the best pancakes I'd ever tasted, I'd assumed she was going to cook them, but that wasn't the case, and now, at just gone nine o'clock we were sitting in a booth in Blu Jam Café on Melrose Avenue, a place apparently renowned for its amazing pancakes. I was impressed with the décor; exposed brick walls and a high vaulted ceiling made for quite a stunning breakfast setting.

'It's just as well we're relatively early, this place gets rammed later on when all the cool kids wake up with hangovers and sugar cravings,' Cait told me as she sipped on her second coffee of the day.

Every now and then my mind would drift back to thoughts of my planned phone call with Sean, but when my pancakes arrived ten minutes later I quickly became engrossed in a blur of syrupy, blueberry, battered goodness and thought of nothing except how bloody good they tasted.

Placing down her knife and fork with a satisfied and rather inelegant grunt, Cait leant back and rubbed her stomach. 'I swear they get better every time I come here.' Grinning, I nodded, pleased to see Cait really tucking into her food for a change. She was too slim in my opinion, but then again, she always had been slender, so perhaps it was just her build.

Using my last bite of pancake to collect the remaining syrup on my plate I then popped it in my mouth, savouring every chew until it was gone. 'They were amazing. You were right, best pancakes I've ever eaten,' I confirmed as I licked the traces of sugar from my lips. 'Let's have five minutes to digest and then hit the sights.'

Just over twenty minutes later, Cait and I were staring avidly at the ground outside the Chinese Theatre. If the crowds out here were anything to go by, then this place must be one of LA's most popular tourist spots. The forecourt was infamous for its amazing array of hand- and foot prints belonging to the rich and famous, but I'd seriously underestimated how exciting I'd find it. At this rate I'd have a bad back from the constant hunching as I read the names.

'Look, here's Harrison Ford!' I yelped, dragging Cait across so she could look at the square containing his prints. I'd had a bit if a crush on Harrison Ford ever since I saw him in Indiana Jones. A bare-chested, whip-wielding historian with a wild side? What's not to love? Crouching lower I couldn't resist placing my hand in his print, where it was dwarfed by the imprint of his fingers. 'Wow. Big hands and feet, you know what that means …' I said teasingly, looking at Cait and seeing her flush.

'Yeah. Big shoes,' she replied dryly, refusing to rise to my bait. 'Look, you can see from the sole print that he was wearing Converse like yours,' she commented, probably to divert my rude comment. Cait always avoided conversations about anything remotely sexual; it was another one of her defence mechanisms. I would sometimes persevere in an attempt to get her to loosen up, but this time, her diversion worked a treat as I checked out his shoe marks and saw she was right.

'Ha! I wear the same shoes as Harrison Ford! How cool is that?' The fact that half the population of the world also wore Converse slipped conveniently from my mind as I placed my right foot into his indent and snapped a picture on my phone.

After taking several more photographs and even managing to jump onto a quick ten minute tour of the interior of the theatre, the two of us were back on the busy pavement outside. Glancing down the street, Cait suddenly drew in a quick breath and pointed urgently along the road.

'Quick! That's the bus we need!' She took off at such a rate that I didn't even have time to stop and ask where we were going, having to practically sprint to catch up with her.

Once we were on and seated with tickets clutched in our hands I exhaled in relief and leant back in my seat. 'This is one of the Hop-On, Hop-Off tour buses, we don't need many of the stops but it's probably cheaper than keep paying for taxis.'

The bus was actually a really great introduction to the city, and I enjoyed a bit of people watching while we made our way past brightly colourful billboards, American diners, and wide, tree-lined boulevards. After about twenty minutes we passed by a very affluent neighbourhood of huge sprawling houses, which Cait informed me was called Cheviot Hills, and then began winding our way down towards the coast.

'And this is Venice Beach,' Cait announced as the bus pulled to a stop by a beach which stretched its beautiful, golden sands in either direction far as the eye could see. Jumping from the bus we stood for a second soaking up the view as a warm breeze tickled my skin. I smiled at how relaxed I suddenly felt. This place really was a perfect distraction from my troubles.

Peeling off my T-shirt I stripped down to the cooler vest below, but predictably Cait stayed as she was, in her tunic dress and three-quarter length leggings. I didn't pass comment on the fact that it was roasting hot, because I knew the reason Cait didn't expose great amounts of skin – her bastard of an ex. To be honest, the fact that she was wearing short-sleeves and knee-length leggings that not only uncovered her forearms but also the bottom of her legs was a pretty big step forward for her, because usually she was covered from top to toe.

'So, do you want to walk, or sunbathe?' Cait asked, but something over her shoulder caught my attention and after staring for a second I grinned like an idiot and spun Cait around to look with me. Behind some yellow and blue fences there was a vast array of tanned, toned, half-naked men lifting weights in an enclosure before us.

Wow-oh-wow. I had been so taken with the sea view that I had barely noticed this lot. It was certainly a heck of a lot of budgie-smuggling action in one small area. Not to mention some serious testosterone levels. I liked muscles on a man, but perhaps not quite this big. Jeez, some of these guys had boobs bigger than mine.

'Oh, yeah. Uh … this beach is famous for its outdoor weights area,' Cait stuttered.

Unfortunately, seeing the muscled men nudged my mind back to my own decently toned man. As I allowed myself to think about Sean for the first time in several hours I pulled my phone from my pocket and checked for any calls. Nothing. Admittedly, it was still only early afternoon, but as it was getting closer to the time of his proposed call I could feel my stomach tightening with nerves.

Leaving the weightlifting boys to their thing, we made our way to a quieter spot on the beach and decided to indulge in some sunbathing. It was certainly a nice change from the cold UK weather, but as we whiled away several hours lounging in the sand, I became twitchier and twitchier as my phone remained staunchly silent beside me.

As the afternoon dwindled to early evening and I still hadn't had a call from Sean, I could feel my mood dropping lower and lower. Bloody man. I would not cave in and call him. I'd honestly thought he would stick to his promise to call me today, but it looked like he simply couldn't be bothered with me after all. He was probably too busy socialising with his celebrity friends to even think about little ol' me.

In our last hour at the beach I must have checked my phone a million times, probably to the point where Cait was getting tempted to snatch the thing and chuck it in the sea. But there were no calls. No texts either, and by the time five thirty rolled around and we were on the bus heading home, I was in a severely bad mood. Like apocalyptic levels of stroppy-ness. As far as I was concerned, Sean Phillips could take his snivelling apologies and shove them where the sun didn't shine.

Cait checked her watch and glanced up. 'It's been a fabulous day, but I need to pop back to the hostel now – I've got a meeting to finalise the social event I said I'd run with them tomorrow. Shall we eat there? It'll be cheaper than the hotel menu.'

Cait was watching me carefully, and there was concern obvious in her voice – she'd clearly seen me repeatedly checking my phone, not that it would have been easy to miss.

'Actually, I think I might have an hour or two alone, if that's OK with you? I might head back to the hotel and do some writing. It always helps take my mind off things.' I stayed vague about what the 'things' were, even though it would have been pretty obvious that I was referring to one thing in particular. One *man*.

Cait didn't look convinced at all, but I knew I would make miserable company, so I nodded my head again. 'Honestly, go to your meeting and get some dinner then we can meet up for hot chocolate when you get back to the hotel.'

Looking reluctant, she relented with a sigh. 'OK, but only if you're sure?'

'I'm positive, I'll be fine.' And I would be fine, once I'd cursed Sean's name a few times, anyway. 'If you need a hand with the event tomorrow, I'll help out,' I offered. 'What is it exactly?'

'Just a meet and greet for the newbies to help them settle in to travelling, but help would be great, thank you. I kinda got roped into volunteering by Julie, the cook.'

It sounded quite interesting, and besides, anything would be better than sitting in a posh hotel waiting for a call that clearly wasn't going to come.

With plans made, I jumped off the bus at the closest stop to the hotel and left Cait to go to her meeting. My best friend had done an amazing job at keeping me occupied, but the events with Sean had finally caught up with me and I needed some alone time. I'd said I was going to do some writing, which I might, but really, after being snubbed by Sean, I just needed to sit down and work out what on earth I was going to do next.

Chapter Fifteen

Cait

As soon as I'd finished my meeting with Marlon and Julie, I grabbed my phone to check on Allie. I'd seen her mood gradually drop this afternoon and I was worried about her, but she often liked to write when she was thinking, so there was really nothing else I could do until she decided she wanted to talk. I checked my phone, sagging in relief when I saw a message from her telling me she was safely tucked up at the hotel.

Phew. OK. Now I wasn't worrying about Allie I could crack on with the shopping list that Julie had asked me to get for tomorrow's event. As well as being the in-house cook, Julie was assistant manager and pretty much ran the hostel, but she was so likeable that I really didn't mind giving her some help every now and then. Picking up my bag, sunglasses, and cap I smiled warmly at the three other volunteers that had been roped in – Jen, Sally, and Isla; girls that I knew fairly well now from around the hostel – and we set off for the local 7-Eleven.

Fifteen minutes later, we were loaded down with enough ingredients to make about a million cupcakes – at least that's what it seemed like – and after sharing out the bags were heading back towards the hostel.

Turning my face upwards I smiled as the rays from the evening sun warmed my cheeks. This was one of the things I loved about America, the long, warm evenings. It was just gone seven now, and although it was still warm it wasn't sunburn temperature any more, so I paused to pull off my cap and run my fingers through my hair in an attempt at arranging it in some sort of style.

An excited murmur suddenly ran through the girls as they drew to a sudden stop on the pavement, their heads bobbing up and down as they bounced on the spot like a trio of meerkats. Throwing them an amused glance I shrugged in confusion, wondering what on earth had got them so keyed up.

Jen spun around with eyes wide like saucers, her cheeks flushed. 'I totally forgot! It's the American Television Awards ceremony at the theatre tonight! Famous people everywhere! Who fancies some celeb spotting, girlies?' Her words were met with an uproar of yeses from the others, and I then proceeded to watch in silent astonishment as our small group of usually normal girls changed into a giggling mass of red cheeks and excitable arm flapping. God, they were like a pack of rabid animals.

As amusing as their transformation was, I grimaced. Hanging around street corners hoping for a glimpse of a famous face wasn't really my scene. I read the occasional gossip magazine at the hairdresser's, but I certainly didn't go harassing celebrities in the street like a stalker.

Except for when I had bumped into Jack Felton a few days ago, of course, but that had been totally accidental, not stalker-like, and let's face it, was probably more his fault than mine. Burned into my brain for posterity, but totally accidental, I thought with a blush, a strange, squiggly feeling settling in my stomach.

Hmm. I was doing exactly what I'd promised myself I wouldn't – thinking about Jack Felton. That was dangerous territory, so as a distraction I tapped Jen's arm and made my excuses, telling her I would find a bench in the sun and wait for them. She couldn't understand my nonchalance where it came to celebrities, looking completely perplexed by my decision to miss out on the 'fun', before rapidly forgetting about me as she turned back to the crowds.

Unfortunately, there were no benches on this street, so I settled myself in a doorway to the side of the red carpet area at a safe distance from the energetic crowd, but close enough that I could keep an eye on the girls. I might not be keen enough on celebrity spotting to risk getting squashed in the middle of a writhing mass of people, but observing from a distance might make interesting viewing.

Over the course of the next twenty or so minutes, I watched a procession of limousines come and go as they dropped off their cargos of celebrity actors, actresses, directors, and writers, all dressed to the nines and practically reeking of wealth. While I recognised some of the faces and was quite enjoying myself, I was glad I'd chosen this spot and wasn't in amongst the throng of spectators, because they buoyantly surged back and forth with each new arrival, and I knew that I would hate all of that bodily contact. It was making my skin crawl just imagining it.

Absently spinning my baseball cap on the end of one finger, I was thinking I might head back to the hostel to drop my shopping with Julie and then see if Allie had finished writing and wanted to hang out, when my thoughts were rudely interrupted by my pulse suddenly leaping in my chest.

The cause for my near heart failure was the dark brown head of hair bobbing out from the latest limo. That hair cut was awfully familiar. In fact, the more I stared at it, the more I became sure that I'd spent at least ten minutes staring down at the top of it very, very recently. As the stooped figure finally unfolded from the car and stood to its full height and waved to the crowd my suspicions were confirmed … it was Jack Felton.

As stupid as it was, I momentarily flattened myself against the wall in case he saw me, but then scoffed a dry laugh and rolled my eyes at my stupidity – with all the clamouring fans surrounding him the chances of him even looking this way were slim to start with, and then even if he did he was hardly likely to recognise me. Our encounter on Thursday morning had been so brief he probably didn't even remember me.

Resuming my original position against the doorway, I found myself watching Jack with interest, and then promptly groaning as memories of our encounter – the ones I had been stringently trying to forget – flooded my mind. I pinged my elastic bands in an attempt to supress my body's traitorous reaction, but unfortunately my eyes were still glued to him, so it didn't seem to be working.

In the four years since I'd left my ex, I hadn't so much as romantically thought about a man, let alone let one touch me. Jack's touch as he'd cleaned the cut on my arm had been so gentle, tender, and as much as I might not like to admit it, it had made me feel … well, I'm not entirely sure what word would describe it, but I'd definitely felt something out of the ordinary.

The blush on my cheeks in no way dwindled as I continued to look at Jack, and it occurred to me that his beard was gone, leaving his angular jaw cleanly shaven and looking far more appealing than the facial fur had been.

He was fully decked out in a sleek, black tuxedo, white shirt, and black bow tie, and predictably looked absolutely gorgeous. Swallowing hard, I realised that my elastic bang pinging had now reached excessive levels and winced as I looked at the reddened skin. Looking back at Jack, I forced my hands into fists to stop the pinging temptation and then let out a long, low breath that sounded quite a lot like a lusty moan.

Lusty was probably about right, really, because the suit made his broad shoulders look even more impressive than the tight running T-shirt had, and I wasn't even going to let my brain focus on how great it made his bum look. For a guy who was nearly forty, he looked pretty flipping amazing, and easily passed for thirty.

Tipping my head back, I stared at the pale pink dusk sky, drew in a breath, and then let it out slowly through my teeth, hating the way I seemed to be losing control of myself again.

Sod it, why hadn't I left sooner? I could be tucking into a large pepperoni pizza and curled up on the sofa with Allie right now. The last thing I needed was a ridiculous and totally unrequited crush on a bloody Hollywood star. I knew I shouldn't look, but I found my eyes drawn back to Jack again as he stood on the red carpet, one hand tucked casually in the pocket of his suit trousers as he waved to the crowd.

At that moment, an absolutely deafening roar went up and I turned in time to see Brad Pitt emerge from the next sleek black limousine at the kerbside. Blimey. Brad Pitt? Even I was quite impressed by his arrival. The crowd were going crazy for him, but I found my gaze sneaking back towards where Jack had been standing, and saw that he was now almost completely alone with a slightly ironic smile twisting his lips. It seemed that he had been deserted by the press and fans in their desperate attempt to get a glimpse of Brad. Poor thing.

Suddenly, like a ridiculously cheesy scene from a slushy movie, Jack's head turned in my direction. The moment could only have been improved if it had occurred in slow motion, with some dramatic music in the background perhaps, and some hi-def colouring to improve the look of my clothes.

The next second he was looking straight at me, his head tilting slightly as he observed me, before a flicker of what might have been recognition sparked in his eyes and he broke into the most immense grin I had ever seen. Crikey, that man could smile. I actually felt my breath catch in my throat as I weakly attempted to smile back and nod a hello to him.

What happened next couldn't have shocked me more than being slapped in the face by a huge cream pie, because without so much as another glance at the preoccupied crowd, Jack was suddenly vaulting the rope barrier and making his way hastily towards me with a rod straight back and easy strides.

Swallowing loudly, I pushed off from the wall, my mouth hanging open in shock as I wondered if I was hallucinating, but no, after several forceful blinks it seemed that Jack Felton was indeed making a bee line for me, and … what on earth was he doing? I watched as he began loosening his bow tie with one finger, and then quicker than was surely possible he had removed it and begun work on undoing his jacket and shirt as well.

Holy heck ... Was he going to completely strip? Had he lost his mind? Both of these questions were answered seconds later as Jack stopped his strip tease after revealing a sky blue T-shirt hiding under his dress shirt, and then he was at my side.

'Can I borrow that hat? Thanks.' Jack didn't give me time to respond. Instead, he simply grabbed the baseball cap from my hand, jammed it on his head, shoved his jacket and shirt into my shopping bag, and proceeded to steer my stunned body away from the theatre.

'So, how's your elbow?' he asked casually, as if he hadn't just leapt over a barrier and run away from an awards ceremony.

Dazed by his actions, I found his words caused me to blink back to reality and blush as my stomach dropped to my boots. Well, that settled that then; he definitely did remember me, but I was too flabbergasted by the events of the last few seconds to even speak.

'You thought I didn't recognise you, didn't you?' he quipped lightly, but I was apparently still struck dumb. 'I might be getting on a bit, but my short-term memory isn't that bad. Besides, I wouldn't forget a face as pretty as yours in a hurry.'

I immediately narrowed my eyes and felt myself tense. So, a smooth talker, was he? I was particularly sensitive to anything remotely complimentary, even if there was a chance that the sentiment was genuine and non-sleazy, so his words had effectively raised my defences within seconds.

Since Jack's leap from the red carpet, everything had happened so quickly that I had barely registered we were moving, my feet on autopilot as he slowed down and started to walk casually, as if we were a normal couple out for an evening stroll. We could probably get away with it too if it weren't for his ridiculously shiny dress shoes and my stiff posture, which was so tense he practically had to drag me.

Small tremors of awareness began to dance across my back, and to my horror I realised that at some point Jack had placed a hand on my lower spine. How had I not noticed that immediately? Normally even a light contact from a man passing me on the street would have me stiff as a board. But no, this one had definitely escaped my attention, because his hand remained planted almost territorially as we walked and I felt my entire frame stiffen. At least it felt territorial to me, but that was because when Greg had placed his hand there he *had* been marking his property, not that I'd realised that at first.

My reaction wasn't quite as violent as it had been last time Jack touched my back, but how he managed to place his hand in *exactly* the same spot that Greg had favoured I had no idea. It was creepy, and certainly made my mind recall elements of my past that I'd rather forget. Swallowing hard, I remembered how Greg had started shoving my lower back to knock my balance, then tugging me toward him so I'd had no choice but to grab him for support. He'd always claimed it was accidental, but now I knew better. Controlling fucker.

Sidestepping jerkily, I moved away from Jack, and thankfully his hand eventually dropped away from me, allowing me to sigh in relief and give one instinctive pluck at the elastic band on my wrist to clear my mind. I noticed him giving me a quizzical glance and felt my face flush as I turned away, tucking my head down. Frowning, I avoided his gaze, keen not to give any indication of the torrent of emotions flying through my mind and body at the moment.

As we walked I saw Jack's eyes moving back to mine, and now that I had marginally reeled in my minor panic, I met his gaze. I couldn't quite summon a smile, I was still too tense for that, but I was at least looking at him, which was a step in the right direction, and one that I didn't usually make. He was staring at me intently, his brown eyes glimmering as if he were curious about something – probably my neurotic elastic band tugging – but then he shook his head and the trace of a smile curled his lip.

'I didn't even say hello, did I? How rude of me. Hello again. Meeting you twice in a week, what a small world, eh?' He sounded relaxed and genuine and I nodded jerkily, thinking along much the same lines. Thankfully, he didn't mention the fact that I'd practically run away from him last time we'd met, an omission I was immensely grateful for. His voice might be light and casual, but his warm brown eyes seemed to be burning into me and holding me captive as he continued to assess me.

If that wasn't bad enough, he then totally blew me out of the water by smiling. Oh, that smile. It was so lovely that it knocked the wind out of me. I really needed to not look at him when he smiled like that, but it just seemed too difficult to drag my eyes away.

I started to squirm, feeling well and truly under scrutiny, a sensation I found quite confounding because I really shouldn't like it – it certainly wasn't something I was used to, but with Jack I didn't mind as much as I thought I would.

The way this man made me question the very rules by which I lived my life was distinctly unnerving. Why couldn't I look away from him? His gaze was almost bloody magnetic. As we continued along the pavement I actually started to wish that he would make the first move and stop looking at me with those captivating eyes of his, because that might help me settle down a bit. It didn't look like I'd get my wish though, because he was even managing to stare straight at me as we walked. Clearly Jack favoured eye contact way more than I did.

Trying to calm my rampaging nerves, I straightened my back – a habit that helped to improve my confidence – and plastered a small smile on my face. 'Hello, Jack. It's, uh … good to see you again,' I lied feebly. It wasn't good to see him again. In fact, it was terrible; my heart was pounding so hard that my chest hurt, the back of my neck was starting to sweat, and to top it all off, my body was reacting to him in that same strange way as it had last time, heating and imploring me to move closer to him.

Nope, after trying desperately hard to forget our run-in at the park I could safely say that all in all, it was *not* good to see him again – it was disastrous.

As we walked I realised he didn't even know my name and was just wondering if I should introduce myself when he spoke again. 'Did I get away with it?' he murmured, but at that moment I think I might have been slipping into a mild state of shock and had to work particularly hard to process his question. Glancing over my shoulder, I saw that the theatre was some way away now, but I could still see the huge crowds busy snapping Brad Pitt in various poses. It certainly didn't seem as if anyone was looking for Jack.

'Uh, yeah, I think so …what exactly *is it* that you're doing?' I asked in an almost accusing tone, still annoyed at myself for the confusing way I felt around him. After I'd left him in the park I'd blamed my peculiar reactions on the shock of my fall, and assumed that if I'd met him under normal circumstances I'd have been fine. But I was far from fine, and the way my stomach was clenching and my heart was racing was definitely *not* normal.

'I bloody hate those events but I promised my manager I would come along to be seen. Well, I came along, didn't I? I was seen, wasn't I? I never said I would stay for the whole thing,' he said in a rather proud tone, a satisfied smile sitting on his lips.

Just then, my eyes caught a glimpse of a huge mountain of a man, dressed in a smart black suit, and pushing through the crowd with a thunderous expression on his face as he charged toward us.

'Uh … actually … there's a guy that seems to be looking for you,' I whispered, wanting to cower away from the obviously angry man who was now almost upon us.

Stopping, Jack turned and watched as the suited man reached our side. He was tall, even taller than Jack, broad shouldered, and very red in the face. If he hadn't been so furious then he might actually have been quite good looking in an older man kind of way, with grey-blond hair, an angular jaw, and crystal clear blue eyes. But he *was* livid, his eyes were narrowed on Jack and his brow pulled into such a deep frown that they almost met in the middle.

'For fuck's sake, Jack. I was on the other side of the red carpet, you can't just divert from the plan like that.'

Rather confused by the entire situation – first Jack's appearance by my side, and now this random man – I stood in shock, my eyes flicking between the two of them as my nerves built up and I began to wonder how I could discretely make my get away.

'My apologies, Flynn, you're right. But I'm not going back in there, so have a few hours off. I'll call you when I need you,' Jack said calmly, his composure opposing Flynn, who looked like he might combust at any second.

Flynn's eyes darted to me and narrowed even further, before he let out an irritated breath, spun on his heel, and walked away without another word. What a charmer.

'That was my delightful bodyguard,' Jack explained sardonically, giving the gigantic man an amused glance as he stormed off.

Bodyguard? Blimey. 'You have a bodyguard?' I asked, surprised, the very idea of it seeming peculiar to me. But then, thinking about it, he *was* pretty famous, so perhaps it was run of the mill for someone like him.

'Yeah, not for day-to-day things, but I have a few slightly crazy fans, so at big events like this Flynn comes with me. Sorry for his abruptness, he doesn't have the best manners, but we were in the military together years ago so I know I can trust him.'

Wow. Bodyguards, crazy fans, and now I discover that Jack used to be in the military? This was information overload.

Moving closer again, Jack somehow looped my arm through his so we were joined at the elbow. A spike of terror pulsed trough me at his sudden touch and this time I couldn't be casual about my reaction; my entire body jerked away as my eyes flashed to his in panic.

'Please don't keep touching me!' I squeaked, rubbing at my elbow joint as if the skin was burnt before lowering my hand and beginning a frantic picking at the elastic bands by the poor abused skin of my wrist.

My eyes were darting around restlessly, and I saw confusion on his face, followed quickly with concern as he held up a palm in a placating gesture. 'I'm sorry, I didn't mean to s ... shock you.' Given my wildly over-the-top reaction I'm sure the phrase he'd wanted to say was 'I didn't mean to *scare* you', but he was no doubt attempting to be discreet.

Immediately, I flushed with embarrassment, but when I said I hadn't let a man touch me in four years, I meant it, and now Jack had done so numerous times in the space of a week. It was very unnerving.

What was worse was the muddled feelings it swirled in me. Yes there was the fear, but there was something else, something deeper, that felt almost ... appealing.

Intrigued by this curious reaction in my body, I risked another glance at him, but what a mistake that was. He was all half smart, half casual, with that shaved jaw and those dark eyes burning into me. Oh God, he was too handsome to be real, and yet here he was, right in front of me. Again. How could that be possible? It had to beat some serious odds to not only run into him once, but to meet *twice* in the same week. If my luck was running this high then perhaps I should buy a lottery ticket this weekend.

I was staring. I knew I was ... but my body was non-responsive to the orders my mind was yelling at it. Forcing a mental shake, I decided that this incredibly surreal event had gone on long enough, and I ran a shaky hand through my hair and stepped back, not missing the way Jack's eyes zeroed in on the tremble in my fingers and narrowed with curiosity.

Dropping my gaze, I drew in a long breath and cursed myself for my crazy behaviour. I must seem completely neurotic. I *was* completely neurotic. When I finally raised my eyes, however, I was surprised to see a kind smile on Jack's face, and not the pity that I had been expecting, which made me warm to him a little and helped me, marginally, to relax.

'OK, well, you're away from the theatre now. I should get going, can I get my bag back please?' I asked almost stubbornly, determined to put some distance between myself and Jack flipping Felton.

It would definitely be best if I got away while the going was good and my common sense was still intact, but surprisingly, Jack frowned at my words, looking crestfallen at my remark, which threw me completely. In fact, I felt utterly confused, because surely after my near meltdown, he'd be keen to get as far away from me as possible.

Swallowing hard, I glanced over my shoulder again. Catching a brief glimpse of Jen and the other girls from the hostel still bobbing up and down in the crowd, I indicated in their general direction. 'My friends are heading back to bake some cakes and I have some of the ingredients so I need to go.' This was a bit of a lie – they could no doubt survive without the packs of serviettes, plastic cups, and paper plates in my bag, but it seemed a good enough excuse.

As I went to sidestep Jack, he leant down close to me and managed to whisper in my ear, and although he was behaving casually, I noticed just how careful he'd been not to touch me again. 'Walking away from me *again*? I'm wounded. I suppose I should be grateful that you aren't scowling at me this time,' he said, a half smile playing on his lips as he clutched his chest dramatically.

Oh God, he remembered my rude departure from the park, but was being light-hearted about it instead of pissed off. I was so thrown by his behaviour that I ended up mumbling an awkward 'Sorry.' When really, I had nothing to apologise for – although I *was* glad he hadn't made more of my scowling departure, because that childish behaviour was something I wasn't particularly proud of.

'I forgive you, but I'm not letting you get away with it twice. Come for a drink with me.' My reaction was dual: first I was thrown by the fact that he'd just asked me to go for a drink with him, but then I couldn't help but frown at the domineering way that he'd basically ordered me to go. There had been no question in either his words or his tone. He simply expected me to agree. Just like Greg used to.

'Thanks, but I really can't,' I replied, crossing my arms and hoping that my defensive gesture would give him the hint that I wasn't interested. Well, I was interested – my body was, anyway – but it was against my better judgement and self-imposed rules, and not something I would be facilitating further.

'Oh.' Standing tall with a near perfect posture, Jack placed my bag on the ground and tucked his hands into the pockets of his trousers as he continued to observe me. Picking up my shopping bag I prepared to leave, but couldn't help but notice how his new posture made his T-shirt pull tighter across his chest, and I had to forcibly refrain from dropping my gaze to check out his physique.

'I was just hoping to buy you a drink to say thanks for saving me twice,' he said absently as he lowered his eyes and began to nudge at a stone on the pavement with the tip of his shiny dress shoe.

OK, he'd successfully drawn me in, so with my curiosity piqued I tilted my head and watched him, just as he was watching me. 'Saving you?' I queried with an incredulous smile and a raise of my eyebrow.

Looking remarkably pleased that I hadn't left yet, he smiled. 'Yeah, first you saved me from embarrassment in the park by not trying to sue me or go to the papers after I ran you down, and you saved me again from utter boredom tonight by being in the right place at the right time.'

I was weighing up his response with a light frown when he inclined his head like a puppy might, before widening his eyes appealingly. God, those eyes were to die for. A brown so warm and inviting it reminded me of melted chocolate or young conkers, smooth and fresh from their spiky shells. I felt something twang inside my chest and had to briefly squeeze my eyes shut to break the magnetic pull of his gaze.

Predictably, when I reopened my eyes he was still staring at me. 'Please? Just one drink to say thanks? The bar I had in mind is literally just up here,' he added persuasively, pointing over his shoulder. He was like a bloody Andrex puppy, with his innocent, wide eyes and beguiling looks.

Licking my lips, I tried to calm the warring emotions inside me; my protective nature yelled at me to leave, while a tiny, long-buried, curious part of me was starting to try and push to the surface. Oh, sod it. One drink couldn't hurt … could it? Letting out a sigh, I nodded in defeat, causing Jack to grin back at me with his victory, his eyes twinkling with happiness. When he looked at me like that, how could I really refuse?

'Great! The owner of this place knows me so I can always get a drink in peace.'

Jack set off walking, thankfully not linking our arms this time, but instead briefly reverting to his customary hand on my lower back before cursing under his breath and snatching his hand away. Looking down at me as we walked, he gave an apologetic wince. 'Sorry,' he murmured, not ever addressing my obvious fear of contact or prying for details, but simply respecting it, which I found incredibly endearing.

Giving a small nod of acknowledgment, we continued to walk in silence but Jack soon turned to approach a studded metal door that looked more like it belonged to a warehouse or a prison than a bar.

'I'm glad I spotted you, you look quite different from the last time,' he remarked with a roguish smile, holding the door open for me. Wasn't that the truth! Last time I'd been sweaty, red, and dressed in my tatty running gear. At least today I had freshly washed hair, nice clothes, and a little make up on.

'Likewise,' I said, rubbing my chin with a smile to indicate the absence of his beard.

Grinning at me, Jack copied my move and gave his own chin a firm scratch, 'Yeah, they finished filming the beard scenes yesterday, thank God. I cut it off about four hours ago, it feels bloody fantastic.' It looked pretty bloody fantastic, too. Not that I said that out loud.

Still not entirely convinced that this was actually a bar, I tentatively poked my head inside and then smiled in surprise as I stepped over the threshold and into a surprisingly bright, pleasant space. Who'd have thought that behind that rusty metal door would be a bar this cosy? Admittedly it was tiny, but still, it was definitely a premises selling alcohol.

The interior was long and thin, hardly wider than a train carriage, and as I glanced to the right I saw that the bar itself seemed to run along almost the entire length of the wall and was accompanied by a long row of tall, velvet seated, bar stools. The opposite wall was lined with small, high-backed, leather booths that seated the few sole occupants this evening.

A man behind the bar turned to greet us jovially and then burst from behind the counter when he saw who was standing at his door. 'Jack! Great to see you, buddy! Come on in!' He embraced Jack heartily and gave him a good, hard slap on the back which actually made Jack step forward slightly from the impact.

I smiled at his gesture before the barman stood back and smiled at me curiously. He was smartly dressed in a white shirt, gold silk waistcoat, and pinstriped trousers. In fact, in his attire he wouldn't have looked out of place at an upmarket wedding. Feeling myself relax a little, I decided that I liked not only the atmospheric bar, but the smiling barman too – he had a surprising likeness to Laurence Fishburne, except with a little less hair and a lot more body weight.

'Jack, who's your lady friend?' he asked with a glint in his eye. I'd never given Jack my name, but Jack gave absolutely no indication that he didn't know, instead smoothly laughing off the question.

'Get us seated, Joe, and then I'll do introductions.'

Nodding, Joe turned away from us and towards the back of the bar. 'No problem. Your usual booth is free.'

As we began to follow him, I took pity on Jack and leaned up close to his ear with an amused smile. 'My name is Cait.'

Gracing me with one of his show-stopping grins, Jack looked down at me appreciatively and nodded. 'Thanks. Kate as in short for Katherine?' he asked, dropping beside me as we meandered towards our seats.

'No. Cait, spelt C-A-I-T, short for Caitlin. Comes from my grandmother's side. She was Irish, I'm named after her. Technically, I think it's supposed to be pronounced Cat-lin, but I've always been *Cait*-lin.' As he continued to observe me I watched his eyes narrow slightly, his lips twitching in a smile again.

'Caitlin. It's a pretty name … it suits you.' Before I could make too much of his comment, Joe had stopped in

146

front of us and was showing us into the last booth at the bar. Jack slipped in one side and I slid over the soft leather and settled myself opposite, trying to settle my fluttering nerves.

I still couldn't believe I was doing this. I just didn't do this type of thing. And with Jack Felton. God, I must be nuts.

'Nice and private,' said Joe, giving the table a wipe despite the fact it already looked spotless, but his words stuck with me. *Nice and private?* Was this Jack's usual pick-up spot? Or just somewhere he bought women when he wanted to escape being seen by journalists? Neither was a particularly pleasant idea.

Breaking my uneasy thoughts, Joe flicked the cloth over his shoulder and grinned at us. 'So, what can I get you? Beer? Wine? I have some new red in that is fabulously smooth,' Joe addressed his comment to myself and Jack, but both their eyes fell upon me as they waited for my choice.

'Ur, red is great, thanks,' I agreed, my mind still not properly focused as I tucked my shopping bag and handbag onto the seat beside me. Before I could protest that it was only supposed to be a quick drink, Jack ordered us an entire bottle and Joe nodded happily and wandered off to get it.

Clearly savvy to my thoughts, Jack leant back casually in his seat and smiled at me as one of his hands absently traced patterns on the table as he watched me. 'Don't worry, I can always finish it off if you need to leave after your "one drink".' I knew he was mocking me for my hesitation in accompanying him, but even though he was doing it light-heartedly, I decided that two could play that game.

'So, you bring all the ladies here, do you? It is "nice and private", after all,' I stated with a defiant head tilt. As far as I knew, Jack was single, but the thought that he might be rich enough, and famous enough, to get away with bringing lots of different women here for some 'privacy' made my stomach churn uncomfortably. Mind you, who was I to judge? Just because I chose to live my life as a celibate didn't mean that everyone should.

'Actually, I come here alone. It's a good place for a bit of quiet time,' he said simply, not rising to my bait at all.

'Yeah right,' I muttered under my breath, but loud enough for him to hear. Jack opened his mouth to respond but shut it and silenced his reply as Joe arrived back with the bottle of red and two glasses.

'Here's your wine, a French Pinot Noir from 2005. Delicious.' Joe uncorked the bottle and began to pour a glass for Jack to test. 'It's nice to see you with some company at last, Jack. I was starting to worry about you always sitting here by yourself.'

Blinking at Joe and then back to an incredibly smug-looking Jack, my mouth dropped open in shock. I couldn't believe it. Joe literally couldn't have timed his comment better if Jack had actually paid him and scripted it for him, and I watched as Jack grinned at me over the table as if to say 'See? I told you so.'

Apparently I'd been wrong in my assumptions, so all I could do was shake my head in defeat with a rueful, marginally apologetic smile.

'I agree, and I couldn't have asked for better company either,' Jack said smoothly, still looking mighty smug. 'Joe, this is Caitlin, a new friend of mine who has saved me from the hell of attending an awards event tonight.'

Joe turned his face towards me as he poured me a glass of wine. 'It's a pleasure to meet you, Caitlin. Well, enjoy your evening, folks, holler if you need anything.' Then, flashing us a wink, Joe headed back to the bar leaving me to turn back to Jack and swallow nervously.

Jack was smiling across at me pleasantly, his eyes twinkling mischievously as if he were mighty pleased that he'd managed to persuade me to join him, but all I could focus on was that I was sharing a drink with a man for the first time in over four years.

Just me and him. And the wine. In a bar. Did that technically make this a date?

Blinking rapidly at that alarming thought, I only just managed to nod a thank you to Jack as he filled my glass. No, of course this wasn't a date. I *didn't* date. My eyes widened marginally as my brain carried on with its runaway thoughts … Jack didn't know that I never dated, so what if *he* was classing this as a date? Oh God … talk about feeling well and truly out of my depth. What the hell had I got myself into this time?

Chapter Sixteen

Allie

I'd decided to try and burn off my frustration and sadness with a run around the neighbourhood. After pounding the glitzy streets for over twenty minutes I'd swum thirty lengths in the private pool as a cool down, but even after all that exercise I was still edgy and fidgety from my stress.

Bloody man. I'd been better off when I was single. It might have been a touch boring, but at least my heart hadn't felt as shredded as it currently did.

Now I was showered and sitting at the bar in the bungalow with my laptop on the counter and a barely touched bowl of pasta from room service going cold beside it.

Checking my phone for the millionth time I sighed at the empty screen. No calls, no texts, no emails, nada. Without even meaning to I found my finger opening up my contact list and bringing up Sean's number. It would be so easy to call him, just one tiny press of my finger and I could be connected over the airwaves to him within seconds.

Dropping the phone onto the counter as if it were on fire I scowled and crossed my arms defiantly. *I would not call him.* Besides the fact that *he* was the one who should be calling me, there was a tiny part of me that was terrified he might reject my call and leave me hanging. What if he didn't want to speak to me? What would that mean for our relationship?

These were questions I was too scared to contemplate at the moment, so the phone was put aside as I switched my attention to my laptop and prepared to lose myself in my writing.

Drumming my fingers on the counter I stared fixedly at the computer screen and felt rather satisfied at the quantity of text I had produced in the last hour and a half. Considering all the muddled emotions and stress I'd been under, the chapter I'd written was actually pretty good. Flicking my eyes over the final paragraph again – blood, gore, and then a nice cliff-hanger ending – I nodded in approval. Actually, it was really flipping good.

I'd been doubtful that I would manage to get any writing done, but once I'd settled down and placed my fingers on the keyboard the words had just flowed out of me in a torrent. Apparently Sean-related anxiety turned me into a creative genius.

Sighing, I added a full stop to the last line with an overly aggressive punch of my forefinger. As much as I loved my writing, I would much rather have Sean beside me than a literary masterpiece on my screen.

Just as I was about to read through the new text to scan for errors, the screen of my phone illuminated and my heart leapt into my throat. Was it Sean *finally* calling? As the tone filled the room I grabbed the phone only to frown when I saw an unfamiliar number on the screen. Perhaps he was calling from a different phone? Possibly he'd got stuck filming and hadn't been able to call until now, and was using a landline at the studio?

Swiping my finger across the screen to accept the call, I lifted it to my ear and tried to ignore the way my fingers were trembling. 'Hello?'

'Hi there. Is that Alexis Shaw?' The voice was that of an American woman, not Sean, but even as my system flooded with disappointment I couldn't help the way my teeth instinctively gritted at the use of my full name.

'It is. Can I ask who's calling, please?'

'My name is Julie, we met me at LA Digs hostel. I'm one of the assistant managers, but you'll probably remember me from the café.'

Recognition flared in my mind and I couldn't help the small smile that flitted to my lips. 'Oh yeah, you're the amazing cake maker.'

Julie chuckled down the line. 'Yeah, well, that's what everyone keeps telling me, anyway.' There was a pause, and I was just about to ask her why she was calling me when she spoke again. 'I got your name from the hostel records, I hope you don't mind, but I'm trying to track down Cait and I wondered if she was with you?' A frown immediately lowered my brows and I felt my stomach tense. I thought Cait was at the hostel?

'Uh, no. She said she had a meeting at the hostel. Is she not there?' As soon as the words left my tongue I realised how stupid they were, because Julie wouldn't be calling me if Cait was where she was supposed to be.

'No, she was here, but some of the girls went to the shops for me and when they got back they said Cait had just disappeared from the street.'

Disappeared? What the hell?

I was now up on my feet, gripping the phone like a lifeline as I paced across the bungalow to check her bedroom. As expected, I found it empty, and couldn't help but let out a jittery sigh as I walked back to the lounge. 'Apparently there was some event at a theatre and the girls were celebrity spotting, but Cait said she wasn't interested and wanted to wait just along the street for them.' That sounded like Cait; she hated crowds, so I could definitely see her opting for the side-lines. 'When they had finished she was nowhere to be found.'

'Have you tried her phone?' Rolling my eyes, I realised that was my second stupid question in less than half a minute. I really needed to reel in my anxiety and engage my brain.

'Yeah, there was no answer at first, but the last time I called it was switched off.'

Which meant she had either switched it off or it had run out of battery. This was all *very* unlike Cait, and I couldn't help but worry my lower lip until I tasted blood on my tongue. Suddenly my overactive writer's imagination began to get the better of me as a troublesome thought crossed my mind. What if someone had switched it off for her? Narrowing my eyes, I tried to shake off my paranoia as my stomach twisted with apprehension. 'God ... what do we do now?'

Julie huffed out a heavy sigh and then cleared her throat. 'As much as I want to jump on the phone to the cops it's way too early for that. There isn't a great deal we can do. Sit tight and hope she's just gone shopping, I guess.'

Hmm ... Cait wasn't much of a shopper, so I was doubtful, but there was surely some other logical explanation for her disappearance. Unfortunately, I couldn't for the life of me think what it might be.

Trying to quell my rising panic I reassured myself with the fact that Cait had been travelling on her own for three years without any issues. She was independent and sensible and used to being on her own, so she'd probably just gone off somewhere and not thought to let me or Julie know. Glancing at my watch I saw it had just gone nine o'clock. 'She said she'd come back here to join me for a hot chocolate before bed, so hopefully she'll be back soon.'

'Yeah, hopefully. Sorry to worry you, Allie, but I didn't know who else to call. I'll stay in touch, let's call each other as soon as one of us hears anything.'

'Of course. Bye, Julie.'

Talk about adding to my stress. After the nightmare of Sean going silent on me, Cait disappearing was the last thing I needed. Hanging up, I immediately tried Cait's mobile, but just as Julie said, it went straight to answerphone. That didn't stop me trying one more time, before clicking my tongue in annoyance and letting out a curse into the empty room. 'Come on, Cait, where the bloody hell are you?'

Chapter Seventeen

Cait

This bar was great – small, cosy, and with some funky off the wall jazz music playing softly in the background. I'd have to remember where it was and bring Allie, she'd love it.

The wine turned out to be good too, really good, smooth and velvety and far too easy to drink. To my surprise, as the evening with Jack progressed I discovered that the company was equally good. Jack turned out to be laid back and incredibly easy to talk to, and his easy-going demeanour put my worries to rest within no time. I'd even lowered my guard a little and begun to relax– something I assured myself was just a temporary measure for the night – and found that I felt none of the nerves or embarrassment that I had expected when partaking in a conversation with a world famous film star.

Especially a world famous film star that I had to reluctantly admit to being attracted to. Not that I would do anything about it, of course, but the more I looked at him, the more obvious it became that I couldn't deny it any longer. Jack really was gorgeous: those dark brown eyes that seemed to look at me so intently it was almost like he could see through all my oddities and insecurities, the endearing crinkles at the corners of his eyes when he smiled, the way he used his hands as he spoke, the dimple in his cheek when he grinned … Oh, God. Swallowing hard, I shifted in my seat, suddenly rather aware of a throbbing between my legs.

Dragging a breath in through my nose I attempted to engage my usually rigorous defences, which for some reason were totally deserting me tonight. Distracting myself from indulging the physical reactions in my body I instead focused hard on our conversation. Soon I found us easily drifting between topics. We chatted about my travels, the destinations I planned to visit, and shared stories of life growing up in England. It turned out that Jack's father was British but his mother was American, hence the slightly mixed accent he had. I also discovered that when he'd said he and Flynn were in the military together, he'd actually meant the Territorial Army. Flynn had been in the regular army but became a trainer in the TA – one of Jack's superior officers – which was when they had met.

The only awkward moment was when Jack had asked what prompted me to head off travelling and stay away from the UK for such a long time. Instantly, I felt my body tense as thoughts of Greg flooded my mind again like a virus. He was the reason I'd left, him and his overbearing treatment. Not to mention the things he'd done to me on that final night … A shudder ran through my entire body, making my fingers tremble as my glass began to wobble in my hand.

Placing it down, I plucked at my elastic bands several times before wincing at the sore spot on my wrist and deliberately knotting my hands in my lap, staring at the wood grain of the table and trying to buy some time while I composed myself.

Clearing my throat I eventually raised my eyes and met Jack's politely inquisitive look. 'I, um … I just needed to get away,' I murmured, which was the truth, albeit a very minimalistic version. Nodding his head slowly, Jack seemed to be thinking this through as he gazed at me, a multitude of questions floating in his expression.

I tensed all over as I waited for him to pry further and embarrass me, but much to my relief, he didn't follow it up with more probing, and instead changed the subject by telling me about the latest filming he'd been doing for *Fire Lab*. My reaction must have made it obvious that there was more to the story than I was willing to share, but he hadn't tried to push me, and I was so grateful. I was also rather touched by his discretion and let my tension out on a long, low breath.

Maybe I was just a little tipsy, or perhaps it was just my imagination, but just like in the park I began to wonder if Jack was flirting with me. Obviously I was no dating expert, far from it, but the more I looked, the more I noticed his almost affectionate body language – he was leaning across the table with his gaze intent on me, flashing me appreciative signals with his twinkling eyes, and gracing me with endless lopsided smiles as he chatted away happily. Of course, I hardly knew the man, so this could be how he acted with everyone for all I knew.

At age twenty-six, I was single, celibate, and fairly certain that there would never been a man perfect enough to tempt me to crawl out from my defensive shell, but Jack was making me question that. He was just about as perfect as they got. Handsome, kind, funny, sexy, and sensitive when he'd detected that I was feeling uncomfortable. As I sat there opposite him, a small spark seemed to reignite in my belly. I wasn't entirely sure what it was, but it felt a lot like hope, and I realised that this was turning into a decidedly dangerous situation for me.

An ironic smile briefly twitched my lips at the stupidity of my wandering thoughts. It was typical that I should spend years not remotely interested in a man, and then get attached to one who was totally out of my league. Our lives were galaxies apart, not to mention the fact that he'd said earlier he was nearly forty and still single, and had never been married or engaged. As far as I could tell, that either meant he was gay – which given his flirty nature seemed unlikely – or he was merely enjoying a playboy lifestyle too much to settle down.

As I continued to ponder this, I felt an almost overwhelming urge to slap myself around the face to snap me out of this craziness. Why was I even allowing myself to think about this? Having now met Jack in the flesh and felt so comfortable with him I decided that if I wasn't careful, my inexperienced, naïve heart might throw sense to the wind, dump my strict self-disciplined rules out of the window, and fall head over heels for him.

Time to leave. *Right now.*

With this thought floating in my wine-fuddled brain, I drained my glass and stood up rather hastily, bumping the table and sending my handbag falling to the floor. Jack looked up, surprised by my sudden movement, but recovered himself quickly by bending to scoop up my bag and standing up opposite me.

He was respecting my personal space, but close enough that I had to tip my head back slightly to look up at him. It vaguely crossed my mind that he seemed taller than he had earlier. And broader. Mmm. And he really did have a very nice chest. As my mind swirled around with increasingly inappropriate thoughts, I blinked and shook my head. I'd *definitely* had too much to drink.

He stepped marginally closer to hand me my bag, and I jerked my head back when I realised there must be mere millimetres separating us now. He was close – close enough that I could smell his aftershave, but not quite near enough for him to be breaking my request not to touch me. His abrupt closeness made my skin tingle with ridiculous anticipation, like little sparks going off all over my body. When mixed with the warmth in my body from the wine it was actually rather pleasant.

A man was standing well within my personal space and I wasn't backing away, freaking out, or dropping into a panic attack. This was a major breakthrough for me. Perhaps it was to do with the wine I'd consumed? Or maybe it was down to Jack.

Instead of vocalising any of the thoughts running through my mind, I plastered a smile on my face and rolled off an apologetic excuse. 'I've just realised I need to get back … I've … uhh … got some ingredients and the girls at the hostel will be needing it …' My voice faded towards the end of my pathetically flimsy excuse and I felt a blush rising to my cheeks.

Jack's eyebrows rose, and my gaze was drawn to the corner of his mouth as it flickered. He seemed to be attempting to hold back a smile, and as much as I desperately wanted to see another of his grins, I was thankful he held it back – a gorgeous grin in this close proximity could quite possibly cause me to implode.

'They're cooking at twenty to eleven at night?' he asked in a tone dripping with sarcasm.

Twenty to eleven? Where had the time gone? No wonder I was feeling light-headed from the wine; I hadn't eaten since lunchtime and even then I'd only had a small salad. Seeing my shocked expression, Jack graced me with a slightly rueful smile. 'Don't worry, you don't need to make an excuse to leave.'

Wincing, I bit on my lower lip. How mortifying – he thought I was desperate to get away from him, when in reality my traitorous body was set on the complete opposite. This was such an incredibly odd situation that I had no idea what to do. On one hand, I was massively attracted to him, had really enjoyed his company, and would have loved to stay longer, but on the other hand my careful defence knew I should get the hell out of here before I said, or did, something I would no doubt regret.

'It's OK, you stayed for the thank you drink. I enjoyed your company very much, thank you. You're officially free to go, Caitlin.'

He'd been calling me by my full name all night, but this time it registered in my mind to say something. 'Cait,' I corrected. 'Everyone calls me Cait.'

Nodding slowly, Jack gave a small, thoughtful shrug. 'Well, I'm not everyone.'

My eyebrows rose at his cocky attitude, but I couldn't really deny it – he was far from just a usual 'everybody' sort of person.

'Unless you really dislike the full version?'

I usually wasn't too keen on people using my full name, it made me feel like my grandma, but for some reason I rather liked the way it sounded when he said it.

'No, you can call me either,' I agreed, although it was pointless, because after tonight I wouldn't be seeing him again.

'Well, it was very nice to meet you properly, Caitlin,' he added politely. 'Maybe I'll see you again before you leave LA?' he asked, with a tilt of his head that caused a chunk of soft, brown hair to flop across his brow.

If the flushing of my face, hammering of my pulse, and trembling knees were anything to go by, then it really wouldn't be a good idea to see Jack Felton again. I was already dangerously close to breaking my own rules and completely losing my sanity as it was.

'Um, I haven't managed to get a job so I'll probably be moving on soon. I need to book my flight, but I don't think I'll be here much longer.' What I said was true, but I hated the words as they slid from my tongue.

Taking me completely by surprise, Jack's head suddenly began to lower towards mine as if he intended to kiss me and my pulse went from raised to absolutely thundering in the blink of an eye. Talk about an instant way to sober me up, My wine blurriness was now gone and I was more alert than I had been all night. My heart was hammering so violently that I could feel it throbbing in the tips of my fingers and hear the rushing of blood in my ears.

Was I really going to do this? Let a man kiss me?

Jack was immensely careful not to touch me, even his hands stayed firmly by his sides, but his face was now so close that I could feel his warm breath tickling across my parted lips. My eyes were wide as he paused just a few millimetres away from me, looking very much like he was asking for my permission. When I said nothing, he blinked once and then shifted himself closer.

At the very last second, my spiteful mind threw an image of Greg at me from our last night together as he had held my hair and smirked at me before forcing his lips onto mine. He'd been so aggressive that night that he'd split my top lip. In an instant, my walls flew up, my hands tensed into fists by my sides, and I screwed my eyes shut tight and turned my head to the side.

'Please don't …' I whispered shakily.

I'm not sure if I imagined it, but before moving back I could have sworn that Jack brushed the lightest trace of his lips against my cheek. Even this mere touch sent tingling shockwaves running across my skin and I knew my blush must have deepened to almost puce. My eyes flew open, but Jack was already back a few steps with a soft, worried expression on his face, which was almost enough to make me change my mind and pull him back for a real kiss.

'It's OK, Caitlin, you're OK,' he whispered reassuringly as I desperately attempted to get a grip on my spiralling emotions. My fingers were plucking away at my elastic bands so frantically that I was amazed the bloody things hadn't snapped, when suddenly, Jack leant across and tucked one finger under the bands. He didn't touch my wrist, simply held them so I could no longer twang.

'You'll hurt yourself,' he murmured. 'You're OK,' His words were firm, but soft and had me complying and dropping my hand away. Gently letting the elastic band go, he nodded and gave my wrist just the lightest brush with his fingertips, which caused my skin to pop with goose pimples.

I couldn't believe he'd done that. That was twice he'd touched my elastic bands now, and both times had been oddly … reassuring. And his touch? God, it had been just the tiniest brush of his fingers but it had soothed my ragged nerves, making me briefly wonder just how good a kiss from him would feel before I dismissed the idea with a huff.

As Jack continued to watch me, I saw him narrow his eyes and keenly observe my response, which was close to being a jabbering wreck, and then he opened his mouth as if to speak, before promptly shutting it somewhat reluctant. I wondered what he'd been about to say, and what conclusions he'd drawn about me, but then resolutely told myself it didn't matter, because in the long run I would be glad that I'd not let him kiss me. Kissing would eventually lead to other physical things, and there was no way I could do *that*.

Squeezing my eyes shut, I shook my head limply. 'I'm sorry … I just … *can't*,' I murmured pathetically, before summoning up the last of my determination, opening my eyes, and taking a step away from him. Picking up my shopping bag I smiled shakily at him one last time. 'Bye.'

'Wait, it's late. I'll walk you home,' he stated as he tucked some money under the bottle to settle our bill and retrieved his jacket, shirt, and tie from my shopping bag with a small smile.

I had some things for Julie at the hostel, but they could wait until morning, so I dismissed his offer with a shake of my head. 'I'll be fine, I'm staying with a friend at the

Beverly Hills Hotel so I'll need to get a cab,' I mumbled, 'Thanks, for the drinks,' I added politely before absorbing one last image of him and turning hastily to leave.

'Caitlin.' This time Jack's voice had dropped to a low, warning tone that instantly made me pause. 'I *am* getting you home safely. No arguments.' Looking at his resolute face, I sighed in defeat then nodded. To be honest, I always avoided getting a cab late at night when I could, so his company would be preferable to riding alone, although after our near kiss and my subsequent freak-out, I just knew it was going to be incredibly awkward.

Slipping my handbag on my shoulder we turned towards the exit, waving a slightly stiff goodbye towards Joe, who I noticed was watching us with interest. Great, yet another person who'd had the joy of witnessing one of my meltdowns.

For the briefest of seconds, Jack's hand settled on my back again as he guided me towards the door, but once again he removed it almost immediately with a quiet curse. He was trying so hard not to upset me that it might have made me laugh had I not been so in shock from our close encounter.

Instead of getting in a taxi as I had planned, though, Jack instead made a quick phone call and then ushered me outside, where a black car was already pulling up to the curb. Flynn, the large, suited man from earlier, jumped out and came around to open the door for us, and I noticed that while he still looked quite intimidating, he no longer looked angry, which was a relief.

Sliding into the car with a small whispered thanks, I settled myself on the far seat and did up my seatbelt, feeling nervous, and horribly self-conscious about how the night had ended. Women probably threw themselves at Jack on a daily basis, but what did I do when he tried to kiss me? Stress out like some complete social abnormality and practically burst into tears. A heavy sigh slipped from my lips. Perhaps it was time for a few sessions with a councillor again.

The drive took about fifteen minutes, all of which was in complete silence as a strange tension filled the space between us. I was fairly sure Jack spent the majority of the journey looking at me, at least that's what it seemed like in my peripheral vision, but I didn't dare to properly turn my head to find out, instead choosing to stare rigidly out of the window at the passing streets.

As ridiculous as it was, I found myself tempted to reach out and touch him on several occasions, just to see if I got that strange, pleasant tingly feeling again. But thankfully, common sense prevailed and for each minute we drove I sobered up, so that by the time the car pulled up outside the hotel I was feeling certain that I'd made the right decision.

'OK, well, uh, thanks for seeing me home safely,' I murmured a little awkwardly.

'No problem.' Clearing his throat, Jack turned towards me, the movement making me pull my eyes from my lap to meet his. 'Do you have a boyfriend? Is that it? Because if that's the case I would never have made a move. I didn't mean to make you feel uncomfortable.'

Staring at him, I blinked several times, my cheeks reddening as I became aware that Flynn was still sitting in the car and was clearly able to hear every word of our conversation. Jack didn't seem bothered, staring at me intently and awaiting my reply.

Chewing on my lower lip, I met his gaze. He really did seem completely genuine – a regular nice guy, which just made walking away from him even more difficult but still something that I had to do. 'No. I don't have a boyfriend,'

'Is it my age? Am I too old for you?' he asked almost immediately, his body leaning ever closer with his eagerness.

God. He was really persevering with this, wasn't he? 'It has nothing to do with your age,' I mumbled, wanting to get out of the car, but unable to break away from his gaze.

'I see.' He paused thoughtfully, his fingers drumming a brief pattern on his knee. 'Well, I very much enjoyed tonight, Caitlin. Are you sure I can't tempt you into meeting up again before you leave? Maybe lunch tomorrow?'

He was persistent, I'd give him that, but I was more sober now and I found my head shaking and fists clenching as my old defence mechanisms clicked back into place like a well-oiled machine. 'No. Sorry.' I winced as I heard how blunt I sounded, and quickly felt the need to tag more to my refusal. 'I'll be booking flights soon. And, I, um, well, I don't date ...'

His eyebrows rose at this news. 'Never?' he enquired curiously.

'Nope. Never,' I confirmed, before suddenly worrying that that comment might make it sound like I slept around instead. Wondering if I should try to clarify further and explain that what I meant was that I never got romantically involved in any way shape or form, I brought myself up short and grabbed the handle of the door – it didn't matter what he thought about me, because I wasn't going to be seeing him again.

'Thanks again for the drink. Good night.' And with that, I slid from the car and practically ran for the safety of the garden bungalow, before I could turn around and say – or do – something stupid.

Chapter Eighteen

Jack

Climbing from the car, I stood in the warm night air and watched as Caitlin walked away from me towards the hotel reception. After a few steps she sped up, her long hair swaying with the increased pace, before she finally broke into an actual run, jogging around a corner until I could no longer see her.

First she walked away from me in the park, and now she runs? Pursing my lips, I leant on the roof of the car, staring at the point where she had disappeared, tempted to follow her and try to help calm her. Jesus. Was I that bad that she had to run away from me? That wasn't the usual reaction I got from women, that was for sure, but then again, with her nervous twitches and elastic band pinging, Caitlin didn't seem like a usual kind of girl either. God, did she attract me, though. Her tentative, shy personality was incredibly endearing, and she was so pretty that her image was still burned into my mind even though she was long gone from sight.

Shaking my head, I slammed the back door of the car and instead joined Flynn up front.

'Mate, you just got burned!' he taunted, laughing at me when I turned my unamused face to him. He was bloody right too, not only had she asked me not to kiss her – a first for me – she'd also turned down my request for a lunch date. 'Jack Felton snubbed by a woman, never thought I'd see the day,' he chuckled with a shake of his head. 'I could sell that story to the papers for a mint.'

'Piss off, Flynn,' I muttered, his remarks too close to the truth for me to stomach at the moment. 'Let's get one final drink before heading back,' I suggested, needing a strong shot of something to dull the ache that Caitlin's rejection had left. I missed her presence already, which was ridiculous seeing as I barely knew her. What the hell was it about that girl that was affecting me so badly?

Luckily, Flynn let the matter drop and didn't say another word as he drove us the short distance across town to the small community where I lived when in LA. We might not have been speaking, but my mind was in overdrive for the entire journey, replaying the evening and trying to work out where I'd gone wrong. She'd initially been hesitant to accompany me for the drink, but once we'd arrived at the bar she had seemed to loosen up and I could have sworn I was getting positive signals from her body language.

My eyes narrowed as I suddenly recalled her reactions when I'd touched her. Flinching that violently from a touch on the back was not normal. Neither was the way she had sounded almost apologetic as she'd begged me not to touch her again. Not to kiss her. 'Please don't … I'm sorry, but I just can't …' Remembering the tremble in her tone made me clench my teeth so hard that they hurt.

And the elastic band pinging? What the hell had that been about? Her skin had gotten so red from the abuse she was giving it that I'd nearly leant across and ripped the bloody things off on several occasions.

When I'd first signed up to the Territorial Army at eighteen, I'd seen an older colleague around the training ground called Brian using an elastic band in a similar way. He'd just returned from active duty and was suffering from PTSD, using the band to ground him when his flashbacks became too severe. A long breath escaped my lips as I remembered his grim expression when he told me that it was his own self-inflicted version of masochism. Fuck. Did that mean Caitlin was using it for a similar reason? Was it her way to hurt herself when in public? Or did she need the pain like Brian had, to help her fight some nightmares from her past?

Shifting uncomfortably in my seat I tried to quell the growing urge to demand that Flynn turn the car around and take me back to the hotel so I could find Caitlin, and persuade her to let me get to know her. Of course I could be massively exaggerating it in my mind, she might simply flick the elastic bands as a nervous habit. Loads of people had nervous ticks, didn't they? Attempting to persuade myself that that was probably it, I swallowed loudly and tried to clear the suffocating thoughts of her from my mind.

Turning into the gates, Flynn bypassed the road that led to my house and took us down the short, tree-lined boulevard, pulling the car to a stop at a smart, wooden building containing the gym, reception, and a small bar for the residents. This compound was pretty exclusive, consisting of only twenty dwellings, but seeing as we were all high earners paying through the teeth for privacy, the owners had no issues with paying for a barman to remain on site pretty much twenty-four hours a day.

As expected, the bar was practically deserted, with just us, the barman, and one lone figure in the corner frantically tapping away at a laptop. I recognised him as Tim, a computer genius and self-made millionaire. He preferred to work away from his house in the evenings, and was pretty much part of the furniture from eight p.m. onwards.

Taking a seat on a stool towards one end of the bar, Flynn flashed me a quick glance. 'The usual, Jack?'

I nodded my response, still feeling decidedly put out by the frustrating end to my evening with Caitlin.

'A double whisky on the rocks, and a sparkling water, please.'

As Flynn sat on the stool beside me I quirked an eyebrow at his order. 'Water? You're not joining me?'

'Nah, better not, I'm still on duty for another two hours.' He might be a bit of an uptight arsehole at times, but Flynn took his job seriously, and always had done.

Our drinks were served and the barman disappeared again, discreetly leaving us to ourselves. I wasn't really in the mood for talking, but unfortunately, after just a few minutes of blessed silence Flynn shifted on his seat and smirked in my direction.

'I can see why you took a liking to her, mate, she's hot.' I'd guessed that he wouldn't let the subject of Caitlin drop, and I sighed as her image blazed in my mind again. He might be my bodyguard, but Flynn Lawton was in no way, shape, or form my mate. He'd been my main training officer in the TA, which had made us close in a sense, and now he worked for me, so that led to us spending time together on a regular basis, but were we mates? No.

We often shared some laddish banter, but the two of us had very different outlooks on life, love, and ladies. Polar opposites, in fact: he was a user, moving from bed to bed whenever he could, whereas I would rather go home to an empty bed than think I was taking advantage of a woman.

My dad had taught me to always try and treat women right, and as such I believed in proper dating instead of going to bed with someone as soon as you met them. I considered myself a gentleman, or as much of a gentleman as I could be, anyway, and had made it a personal rule that I never used my status to get laid or obtain special perks.

'She's trying to hide herself under loose clothes, but I reckon she's trim underneath those layers.' As much as I hated him passing comment on Caitlin, I had to agree, she had looked pretty tonight, exceptionally so, but her clothes were a bit baggier than they had needed to be, almost as if she were self-conscious or trying to conceal herself.

Grunting my reluctant agreement, I took another sip of whisky and then swilled the amber liquid around the tumbler as I wondered how I could take my mind off the girl now stuck in my thoughts.

'She's got that innocent look about her too,' Flynn pondered, again pointing out something which I too had picked up on. There was something very attractive about Caitlin's slight vulnerability, although it no doubt appealed to me for very different reasons than it did Flynn – it made me want to care for her, and protect her from whatever it was that put that flicker of fear into her gaze every now and then.

Flynn fell silent beside me and after several moments I cast a glance in his direction to see his lips curling into a leer as he took a drink of his water. That look spoke volumes and I immediately felt my body tense.

'What are you thinking?' I asked tightly, fairly sure I already knew exactly his line of thought.

Placing his glass down, he licked his lips and met my gaze as a grin spread across his face. Nudging me with his elbow he then inclined his head and winked at me. 'You probably don't want to know.' Those words combined with his smirk made it perfectly clear that he was thinking of Caitlin in a less than appropriate manner, and I felt anger flood my veins.

Before Flynn could continue with his crude fantasies I found myself on my feet, one of my hands bunching in his suit lapel as I towered over him and glared down at him furiously.

My right fist clenched and unclenched by my side as I got right in his face and spoke in a fierce hiss. 'Don't say one more word about her, Flynn. Don't even fucking think about her, got it?' I ground out my warning through clenched teeth, every muscle in my body taut with the overwhelming emotions rushing around my system.

'Jesus, Ice, calm down. I was just messing with you.' His use of the term 'Ice' made me realise how close I was to losing my control – it was the nickname he'd given me during my army training, because no matter how crazy the situation, I had always kept my cool. Not now. In fact, I felt distinctly unhinged and close to the edge, which was crazy because I barely knew the girl I was getting so wound up about. I couldn't help it though, the very idea of him even thinking about Caitlin sexually was enough to set me on edge.

Holding up his hands in a placating gesture, Flynn wiped the smug grin off his face and raised his eyebrows until I shoved back, let go of his collar, and retook my seat. Back in my TA days, grabbing a superior officer like that would have landed me with a week's worth of shitty punishments, but thankfully these days the tables were turned and Flynn answered to me.

My entire frame was still bristling with tension as he picked up his glass and took a sip. 'You seriously need to get laid.' he muttered, straightening out his suit jacket and sending a frown my way.

He was probably right, but I ignored Flynn's remark and stared straight ahead and tried to steady my breathing. Regardless of how much of a gentleman I might like to think myself, Flynn's comments had sparked several questions that now filtered into my mind. Was Caitlin as slender and sexy under those clothes as I imagined? What would it be like to take her to my bed? A shudder of pleasure ran through my body and I only just contained the moan that rose in my throat as vibrant images sprang my mind. Caitlin's gorgeous chestnut hair splayed across a snowy white pillow like a halo as she lay naked and waiting for me, her wide, hazel eyes staring up at me as I nudged myself between her soft thighs and bent to kiss her parted mouth …

Fuck. I was no better than bloody Flynn letting my thoughts run wild, and as a consequence I was now sporting an impressively speedy hard on, which was thankfully hidden by my seated position and the dim light in the bar.

Shaking my head, I pushed down my lustful thoughts and ground my teeth together in frustration, acknowledging the fact that it was a feeling I probably needed to get used to, because after her adamant refusal of my advances it was clear that Caitlin had no interest in me.

Not that I'd be seeing her again anyway; our two meetings thus far had been completely coincidental, and seeing as she was leaving to continue her travels it looked like she would not be featuring in my future.

That thought disturbed me far more than it should have, and so throwing back the last of the whisky, I abruptly stood up.

'I'm going to walk home, the compound is perfectly safe so take the rest of the night off, Flynn.' I wanted to drown my sorrows a little, but I'd rather do it in the privacy of my own home. With one more look at my bodyguard, I turned and headed out into the warm evening with thoughts of wide, hazel eyes still at the forefront of my mind.

Chapter Nineteen

Cait

Thank goodness I'd gotten away from Jack when I had. My body had been seriously attempting to go against my own rules and say yes to a lunch date with him, which was just insane. I didn't date, and had barely any experience with the opposite sex, and yet I had nearly said yes to an older, more experienced man who was completely out of my league. Letting out a dry laugh I shook my head at my crazy behaviour, and then drew in a breath of the cool night air, hoping to reset my usually sensible brain. It began to work, and I slowed to a walk as I wound through the tranquil gardens of the hotel, feeling calmer now that I was away from his magnetic presence. After a few more lungfuls I felt much more like my usual self and decided that it had probably just been the alcohol that had made me feel so reckless.

No sooner had my foot touched the bottom step of the decking outside our garden bungalow, than I heard a frantic scrabbling from a dark corner of the balcony that caused me to practically jump out of my skin. The dim, automatic porch light clicked on at that second and my eyes flew towards the noise to see a figure struggling to stand up from one of the bean bag chairs.

Confusion swept over me when I registered that the figure was Julie from the hostel. What the heck was Julie doing here? Just as I was about to ask, her thunderous expression caught my attention and stopped me in my tracks.

'I've been calling you all night!' she squawked, appearing from the shadows with her mobile phone clutched in her outstretched hand. 'The girls got back to the hostel after shopping and said you just disappeared from the street! What the hell were you thinking?' Flicking open the front door behind her she stuck her head in. 'Allie? Cait's back!'

As I stood there it suddenly occurred to me just how worried everyone must have been when I had vanished. It hadn't even occurred to me at the time. Oops. Turning back to me and slamming both hands on her hips, Julie glowered at me. Taking in the full extent of her furious posture I began to fidget guiltily on the spot as my forefinger immediately commenced plucking at my elastic bands. At this rate, I'd have an ingrained ring of red skin by the morning.

A second later, Allie burst out to join us, her eyes wide as they settled on me. 'Thank God,' she muttered, giving me a rueful look as she purposefully glanced at her watch and then stepped forward to engulf me in a whole body hug. 'I've been so bloody worried. It's not like you to just disappear Cait.'

I couldn't have felt guiltier if I'd tried. Stepping back, I attempted to give them a placating smile, but it bounced right off Julie as she continued her rant. 'When the girls said they'd lost you I started to think all sorts of awful things ...' Her arms were gesticulating so wildly that Allie had to duck and dodge on several occasions, which on top of my nerves very nearly caused me burst into hysterical laughter. 'Do you know how worried I've been? Sending you off shopping and then losing you? I was on the verge of calling the cops!' she yelled. Except all the words were ground out between her clenched teeth, so it was almost as if each one was a separate statement of its own.

'Luckily Julie remembered my name and knew we were staying together so got my mobile number from the hostel records,' Allie said. Ah, so that was how Julie had come to be here. 'Where *were* you?'

'Uh … I …' I gave a weak smile and hesitated, quickly running all possible answers through my mind. 'I was sharing a bottle of wine with a film star, actually', or 'well, Jack Felton and I just spent the last three hours drinking wine and flirting outrageously', or perhaps 'I nearly let a man kiss me for the first time in four years but chickened out at the last minute …' Hmm, perhaps not. I think I was still slightly in shock, but there was no way I was going to announce to Julie that I'd had drinks with Jack Felton. She'd think I'd gone totally nuts.

Julie was now tapping her foot impatiently as she waited for my answer. Deciding a small lie was easier, I mounted the steps to face Julie's furious gaze and plastered my most dazzling and apologetic smile onto my lips. 'On our way back there were some celebrities at one of the theatres, the girls wanted to watch for a while but I wasn't bothered so I waited off to the side.' Pausing, I licked my lips. So far so good; Julie looked convinced, presumably because this matched with what Jen and the girls must have told her earlier. 'As I was waiting I bumped into a friend from back home. It was completely bizarre, but she's travelling too so I went for a few drinks with her. I totally lost track of time. Sorry.'

I was a terrible liar, and the words sounded flimsy, causing me to flick my glance to Allie. Her eyes were narrowed as she watched me picking away at my elastic bands and I flushed with guilt. She was on to me – she'd seen straight through that lie, which wasn't surprising, really, because it had been totally unconvincing. Praying she didn't push me with Julie there I gave her an intense look accompanied by a tiny raise of my eyebrows, trying to acknowledge that there was more to the story but that I would tell her later. Thankfully, Allie seemed to understand my signal and just gave me a minute nod while staying quiet.

Oblivious to the fact that there was more going on than she realised, Julie's expression didn't lighten at all, so I decided it was time to lay it on thick with a grovelling apology. 'I should have called to let you know where I was, but the time just flew by. We had no idea how late it was, I'm really sorry, Julie.'

'I know I'm not your mother, Cait, but I take on a guardian role at the hostel. You scared the life out of me tonight, the least you could have done was to answer your phone.'

My phone hadn't rung, had it? Digging it out of my bag I realised guiltily that the battery had gone flat. Oops. 'The battery's dead.' Looking back to Julie's irate expression, I prepared to beg forgiveness. 'I'm really, really sorry.'

After another extended pause she tutted, but finally smiled thinly. Thankfully, my grovelling seemed to have worked, because Julie's tone then grew softer. 'You're OK, that's the main thing.' With that, Julie pulled me to her for a tight hug, but leant back after a few moments. 'I need to call the hostel and tell them you're OK,' she murmured, dialling a number on her phone and walking towards the far side of the balcony.

Plonking myself into a bean bag chair, Allie followed suit and then leant in towards me keenly. 'What the heck is going on?' she hissed as soon as Julie was out of earshot. Wasn't that just the question? Chewing on my lip I looked at her expectant face, completely clueless about what to say. Tonight had been so crazy I didn't even know where to start, but shrugging, I blew out a breath. 'Too much to tell you now. Later, OK?'

'Your wrist is really red and your cheeks are flushed …' Suddenly she squinted at me, as if trying to read my thoughts. 'Were you … were you with a guy?' she asked tentatively, her eyebrows drawing into a frown as she watched me frantically chewing on my lip as I tried desperately not to pick at my bloody elastic bands again.

Glancing across at Julie, I saw her still talking, her hands waving around as she spoke.

'Sort of.' In a split second Allie was sitting up, reaching out to touch my forearm supportively. Instead of the curiosity and eagerness for gossip that normal girls would have at news like this, Allie's face was simply full of concern. Bless her, she knew full well what a big deal this would be to me.

'Are you OK?' she asked urgently, understanding how unlike me this was.

I thought back to my near kiss with Jack and found my skin warming at the memory, my lips tingling at what could have been, until I had to purse them to stop the tickly sensation. Swallowing hard, I nodded and gave her hand a squeeze. 'I am.' Before I could elaborate further and tell her about Jack, or the fact that he had been a complete gentleman, Julie had finished her call and was turning back to us with a wry grin on her face. 'After the stress of tonight, this old gal needs a drink. Don't suppose you have anything handy?'

Hiding a smirk I obediently got to my feet and fetched three small beers from the fridge before popping the caps off and handing them around.

Taking a long slug, Julie sat back in one of the bean bag chairs and finally began to look more like her usual, relaxed self.

'There are some leftovers inside if you're hungry?' Allie suggested, but I didn't need to answer verbally because a loud growl from my stomach did all the talking for me.

Chuckling, Julie tipped her bottle back and downed half of its contents before smiling. 'I've got an early start tomorrow so I'm going to head off and leave you girls to it.'

'OK. Again, I'm sorry for being so thoughtless tonight Julie.'

'I'm just glad you're safe.' Giving me a brief hug she finished the rest of her beer, stepped back, and grinned at me. 'See you both tomorrow. Cait, you're on cupcake duty, so get there nice and early.'

Giving a grin, I pretended to salute as she waved us one final goodbye and left.

'She's really nice. I think this social event tomorrow could be quite fun,' Allie commented as we headed back inside and she popped a bowl of food in the small microwave located under the bar.

I was just about to tell Allie about my run-in with Jack Felton, but as I took a seat at the bar I got distracted when I saw notepads, pencils, and Allie's laptop strewn across the surface. Evidence of her evening of writing, which made me recall why she had stayed in. Sean, and his lack of contact.

As Allie placed a bowl of delicious-smelling pasta in front of me, thoughts of Jack faded away as concern for my best friend grew. 'So ... how did the writing go? Did you get much done?' It was my discreet way of asking if she'd heard from Sean, and from the small, sad, knowing smile on her face, Allie knew it too.

Nodding, she gave a shrug, her face looking almost painfully unhappy. 'I did a new chapter. A big fight scene between the two vampire clans, so there was lots of blood and gore.' Flicking at a loose thread in her shorts, I saw a flicker of sorrow cross her eyes. 'Violence was perfect for taking my mind off of Sean,' she finished quietly.

My stomach plummeted at her look. 'He hasn't called?' I enquired softly.

'Nope. Arsehole,' she mumbled before rolling her eyes dismissively. 'Anyway, enough of my depressing day, I have some good news.'

Watching her carefully, I could see Allie was keen to avoid further discussions of Sean for the time being, so I turned my attention to the food before me. As soon as the first spoonful hit my tongue I realised that I was, in fact, ravenously hungry and I greedily wolfed down the meal as Allie fished in her back pocket and pulled out a leaflet.

'So, when I got back to the hotel tonight there was this guy near the gates handing out these ...' Allie dropped a glossy leaflet on the table next to me, where I promptly splashed it with pasta sauce as I enthusiastically scooped up another spoonful.

With a chiding tut, Allie rescued the leaflet and wiped it clean with a tissue. 'You can look at it later ... anyway, he works for a television company that are doing some long-term filming at Dynamic Studios and was offering some temporary work as a runner. I knew you were looking for a job, so I grabbed a flyer. The pay's pretty good for casual labour. Do you think you might be interested?'

Wiping the last of the pasta from my bowl with a chunk of bread, I finally felt replete and sat back to look at Allie with interest. A job at a film studio certainly sounded better than the other options of bar work that I'd got this week. 'A runner, huh?' I'd heard of that job; they were basically the dogsbody who would do errands needed around the set. 'It certainly sounds intriguing,' I said thoughtfully.

Across from me, Allie gave me a hopeful smile. 'If you got the job you could stay here for a bit longer. I'd ... well, I'd really appreciate it if you were here while I sort this stuff out with Sean.' She grimaced as she chewed on a fingernail and I briefly wondered if she'd like to borrow one of my elastic bands. 'If it can be sorted out,' she added softly, her face creasing as if she might be about to cry.

'I'm sure you can, babe, just stick with it until you've spoken to him, OK?' I advised, giving a sober nod and feeling my poor friend's anxiousness.

Briefly weighing it up, I didn't really see any negatives to trying out for the job. I did need to work, being around the television studios sounded pretty fun, and it would be good to support Allie when she needed me the most. 'OK, I'll go for it,' I decided. 'It sounds exciting. Imagine being behind the scenes of a real live television show or film in the making!'

Allie gave me a beaming smile filled with relief and then flashed me a wink. 'I'm glad you said that, because I already put your name down for an interview!'

Chapter Twenty

Sean

It was just gone one in the morning by the time the lights finally went off. About bloody time. My calves were cramping from the awkward position I'd been crouched in for the best part of two hours, but as I looked around me again I felt my lips twitch with dry humour. I was hidden away between a palm tree and a stack of sun-loungers, staring at the windows of Allie's bungalow hoping for a brief glimpse of her. Forget film star, this week I was acting like a stalking nut-job.

Shaking my head, I blew out a long, frustrated breath. The things this woman did to me! I couldn't believe I had been driven to such extreme measures just to satisfy my need to see her. All the effort had been worth it though, because I had managed to see her, even if it had only been from a distance, so at least I knew she was home and safe, which fulfilled the compulsive need within me to protect her.

It was difficult for me to admit just how deep my need for her was. I hated to think that I was obsessed with Allie; it didn't seem healthy, but then all this shit with Savannah had happened and it'd become glaringly obvious that I was. Obsessed. Possessive. Needy. Shit, it made me feel decidedly emasculated to think just how much power she had over me. Enough that I had found myself here, outside her bungalow for the past two nights, just so I could see that she was safe.

Much to my vague amusement, it seemed that my girl was using the bungalow that I was paying through the nose for to socialise with her friends. Cait had been around every night, and earlier I'd watched as Allie and an older woman I didn't recognise had sat on the balcony chatting. Cait had then joined them and to my astonishment, the three of them even shared some beers. Beers? I was so stressed out over our issues that I'd struggled to even eat for the past few days, but my girl was happily chugging back a brew. Jesus. She was either stronger than I'd given her credit for, incredibly skilled at hiding her true feelings, or simply not bothered by the events occurring between us.

Gritting my teeth, I rolled my neck to try and ease the burning tension resting there. Clearly while Allie was up for socialising with her mates, she couldn't be bothered to answer any of the calls I'd made to her today. I must have called at least thirty times, and left messages, but she'd staunchly ignored them all. Like I didn't exist to her. That fact sat in my stomach like a lead weight and pissed me off to the point where dark annoyance welled in my chest, but I closed my eyes and pulled in several deep breaths in an attempt to calm myself.

I knew why she was hurt and pissed off. The situation with Savannah and the fake engagement was insane, and I could understand her need for space to a certain degree, but I'd given her the time she'd asked for, and was now at the point where we needed to sit down and start to work through our issues.

Standing up, I stretched my stiff muscles and began my walk back to the car. Ramming my hands in the pockets of my jeans in frustration I came to a sudden halt as my fingers touched on something flat and smooth. Pulling out the key card I stared at it for a second, and then glanced back at Allie's bungalow as my mind began to speed up.

It hadn't been hard too persuade the woman on reception to give me a spare key card for the bungalow. After all, I'd booked the room and paid an astronomical amount for it. But I hadn't had use for the key. Yet.

Chewing on my lower lip, I stood there for a second, illuminated by the light of the full moon before I made my decision and started toward the bungalow.

Watching her from a distance was no longer enough for me. I needed to see Allie close up. I needed to touch her. Reassure myself that she was OK, and that she was still mine.

As messed up as it was, I'd been in her room before without her knowledge, back when she was snowed in with me in my house in England. I'd even curled up with her in bed that night, and I'd gotten away with it, so there was no reason that I couldn't again. God, I was aching to hold her again. The rational part of my brain knew this was akin to breaking and entering, and was taking my stalking to a whole other level, but rationality flew out of the window where Allie was concerned, and I crept up the porch steps unperturbed.

Pausing for a second, I tried to calm my hammering pulse rate and removed my shoes, hoping my sock-clad feet would be quieter. Gently sliding the key card into the lock I pushed the door open with a soft click and entered the lounge area, engaging my best ninja stealth skills. The room was lit by the light of the moon, making my progress easy, and within three seconds I was across the space and by the bar. Allie's computer and writing notes were scattered across the counter and I paused for a second and rested my hand on the laptop keys. I knew Allie often wrote to escape from stress, so perhaps she wasn't as calm and unbothered about our issues as I'd assumed. The thought pleased me far more than it should have.

Marginally reassured, I turned away from the laptop and padded my way silently down the corridor. Earlier I'd watched as the older woman had made her departure, but I hadn't seen Cait leave, so I could only assume that she had opted to stay the night. The last thing I wanted to do was terrify Allie's sensitive best friend, so I needed to ensure I went into the correct bedroom.

Arriving at the door to the master suite, the one where I'd left the note and rose on my first visit, I was relieved to find the door open just a crack. Phew. No creaky door handles to deal with.

Pulling in a slow breath, I gently eased the door open and stepped into the room.

It was just as well that I had taken the deep breath before entering because the sight before me briefly paralysed my lungs. Allie was asleep, her body naked and sprawled beneath a thin sheet that had rucked up to expose one of her pert, soft breasts and the long, tempting skin of her right leg. The sheet fell across her stomach and thigh so that I could just about see the shadows of the nest of soft hair between her legs.

Fuck. I was instantly solid, my cock throbbing desperately in my jeans.

Closing my eyes for a second, I tried to convince myself to leave, repeatedly telling my brain how wrong I knew this was, but I couldn't seem to help it, and a second later I was pushing the door closed behind me and advancing into the room, seemingly unable to hold back from getting close to her.

She was so fucking beautiful that it made my chest hurt. Allie's hair was spread around her head like a halo, her golden eyelashes fanning onto her cheeks like delicate feathers. There was a small crease between her eyebrows, as if she slept with troubles on her mind, and the possessive part of my nature hoped that it was me she was dreaming of.

Lifting a hand I wiped a small sheen of sweat from my brow. It was really bloody hot in here, and the heat had nothing to do with the mild guilt I felt for invading her privacy. Technically the room was paid for by me, so I was allowed in here. Besides, we might be having a few issues at the moment, but Allie was mine, just as I was hers, so I wouldn't let myself dwell on any potential wrongness in what I was doing.

Looking down to my feet, I saw some discarded pyjamas on the floor, which was unsurprising giving tonight's humidity, so stepping away from the bed I pressed the switch to activate the air conditioning, hoping it might make Allie more comfortable.

Coming back beside my girl I leant over her to absorb her features. Even just lying there as still as she was she drove me crazy with lust. My cock was still pulsating in my jeans and my fingers were itching to touch her.

Willpower had never been a strong point of mine, so giving in to my twisted desires I leant over her and allowed my fingers to gently run across the soft skin of her cheek. Allie didn't wake up, and before I knew it my fingers were exploring her more thoroughly, gently roaming across her collarbone, down the column of her neck until I came to the swell of her breast. A dark, satisfied smile curved my lips as I watched her nipple peak from my touch, and I repeated the motion again, circling the pad of my index finger around the hard nub and loving how soft the skin felt beneath my fingers.

Giving a soft moan, Allie suddenly shifted slightly below me, the sheet slipping from her body as her legs parted in apparent invitation. Christ. She was fast asleep but sopping wet. I could see her juices shining in the moonlight, and without even thinking I found my palms resting on her thighs to further part her legs. Bending down like a starving man, I ran one soft, greedy lick of my tongue up the delicate skin.

The taste of her, salty and floral and deliciously Allie, drove me over the edge and I was suddenly desperately ripping my jeans open and palming the heavy weight of my cock as it fell into my hand, throbbing and ready. Working my palm up and down my shaft with several hard, fast strokes I saw some pre-come coating the tip and knew I was already close. Dropping onto the bed I positioned myself between her parted thighs and brushed the tip of my cock against her swollen clit, the mixture of my moisture and her silky wetness sending tingles of delight up into my balls. The small movement caused Allie to lift her hips and groan below me, but the low, lusty note to her sleep-drenched voice suddenly broke through the crazed fog that seemed to have descended on my brain.

She was asleep.

And I had been on the verge of taking her.

Jesus Christ. What the fuck was I doing? Shooting back from the bed, I ran a trembling hand through my hair as my heart galloped in my chest and my cock instantly softened.

Shock coursed through my system and my legs gave way as I fell onto my arse in the middle of the floor. Had I seriously just been about to plunge into her while she was sleeping? Fucking hell. I might be obsessive and desperate to claim Allie back, but I wasn't a fucking monster.

Shoving my cock back into my jeans I ran my hands over my face to try and bring myself back to reality as my body twitched and jerked with the enormity of my loss of control. I had stopped, though. Thank God.

This had all just been a momentary lapse in my sanity, brought around by my insatiable lust for this woman. That's what I told myself, anyway. I completely lost my mind when she was around, as the last five minutes had demonstrated. It was hardly her fault, but ever since she'd entered my life Allie had driven me crazy in the best of ways.

Standing up, I gently covered her body with the sheet again and lowered my face next to hers to brush a gentle kiss on her cheek. I wanted to wake her up, tell her how much I loved her and needed her to trust me, and then make soft, gentle love to her all night long. But I didn't trust myself. I was so wound up that if she rejected me I would probably have a complete meltdown and end up begging her not to leave me. Allie deserved better than that. She needed a strong, confident man, not a pathetic, snivelling loser with compulsion issues, so I needed to back off, get my shit together, and speak to her when I was more level-headed.

Spinning away from her I walked into the en-suite and felt around in the dark until I discovered the sink. Turning the tap on ever so slightly, I filled my palms with the cool water and splashed it onto my cheeks and back of my neck until I began to feel more normal again.

Tomorrow. I'd speak to her tomorrow. Satisfying myself with that intention I turned and crept from the bungalow, leaving my girl to sleep.

Chapter Twenty-One

Allie

The first thing I did when I woke up was to pull the duvet over myself and shiver, because the room this morning was really chilly. As I felt my nipples harden and the hairs on my arms stand up from the temperature, I readjusted my earlier estimate – it wasn't chilly, it was flipping freezing.

Frowning, I registered a soft hum in the room that hadn't been there on any previous days and looked around until I saw the small red light glowing on the air conditioner. Huh. That was weird. I knew I hadn't turned it on last night because I hated breathing in recycled air. I'd much rather open a window or use a ceiling fan to cool myself down. Blinking several times, I finally braved the cool room and threw back the covers before going to the unit and switching it off. How the heck had it switched on? Shrugging in confusion at the vast array of buttons, I decided it must be automatic and set to switch on when the room got to a certain heat.

Darting back to bed, I pulled the duvet around myself like a cocoon and tried to warm up. I'd had some really vivid dreams about Sean again last night. I licked my lips and blew out a long breath. I still felt aroused, and my breasts and clitoris actually felt sensitive and achy as if they had really been touched by him. A miserable sigh slipped from my lungs – I wished he had been here last night.

My mind was distracted from my potent dreams and longing for Sean when I turned for a drink of water and saw my phone on the bedside table. I was fairly sure it hadn't rung in the night, but I picked it up to check again, and then screwed my face up when I saw there were still no calls or messages from him. Pushing my lower lip out, I blew my bed hair out of my face and shook my head with a scowl. A huge sigh deflated my lungs.

I couldn't believe it. With everything that was going on, our relationship was fragile at best, and I had thought Sean would be keener to sort out our issues.

The fact that he hadn't even lifted his hand to call me yesterday was very telling about just how little Sean valued our relationship, which left me with some tricky decisions to make – did I stay and fight for us, or did I take his disinterest at face value and head back to the UK? I suppose I had a third option to consider, of going off travelling with Cait if she didn't manage to get a job.

It was all a bit much to consider at this time in the morning without a clearer head and significant levels of caffeine in my system, so delaying the horrible task I pulled on a baggy T-shirt and went in search of Cait.

I might be feeling pretty down about the state of my love life, but after her late arrival home last night I was incredibly intrigued by hers.

Since the Greg incident four years ago, Cait had staunchly avoided spending any time with men, and hadn't even entertained the idea of dating, so last night when she had mysteriously hinted that she may have spent the evening in the company of a male, my curiosity had been well and truly piqued. As soon as I'd seen the flush in her cheeks and clouded confusion swirling in her eyes I'd been desperate to get her alone so I could find out more, but the late night talk of Sean, and the job at the film studios had side-tracked me. I felt awful that I'd forgotten it so easily, but I could blame that upon the stress my brain was currently under. Now that I was up and about I desperately wanted to find out where the heck she'd been last night, and more importantly, with whom.

Much to my disappointment, I found the suite empty, and a note on the counter saying that she had headed over to the hostel early to help Julie with the preparation for the meet and greet event. My sceptical side suspected she might be avoiding spilling the beans about last night for some reason – perhaps nerves or confusion – but I supposed I wouldn't know for sure until we spoke about it.

Standing in the centre of the living room, I tipped my head back and stared at the ceiling, feeling a small sting of unshed tears start at the backs of my eyes. Letting out a low, frustrated growl, I swiped at my cheeks with the back of my hand and found myself stamping my foot like a toddler. Damn it, I could really have done with some gossip to distract me from my troubles.

Seeing as that wasn't an option, I blew out a long breath and headed to the bathroom to get ready.

The frustration I felt at Sean's lack of contact yesterday caused me to rub at my hair particularly hard in the shower until my scalp became a little sore. Infuriating man. Not to mention totally out of order. Our entire relationship was on the line and he couldn't even be bothered to call me? Mind you, I was just as mad at myself for letting him affect me like this.

By the time I re-entered the bedroom after my shower I looked down at my phone screen and saw a text message from Sean. So he was finally getting in touch? I knew I was being overly touchy – perhaps it was nearly my time of the month – but for whatever reason I was particularly grouchy today. Gritting my teeth, I felt anger bubbling in my stomach at his belated effort. I swear on all things holy that if his message had been on paper, not my phone, then I would have ripped it up without even reading it. The message alert kept blinking while I dressed though, and curiosity eventually got the better of me as I swiped it to open it.

From: Sean
Please can we meet, Allie? I need to see you. I miss you.
S x

Clenching my teeth until I winced from the pressure I shook my head in disbelief at his cheek. If he missed me so bloody badly he could have called me when he was supposed to. Chewing on a fingernail I grimaced when it broke off far too low and started to bleed. Bugger, that hurt. Feeling bitchy and irksome I typed out a challenging reply, being deliberately difficult just to spite him.

To: Sean P
I'll be at the hostel all day helping Cait prepare for a social event. Come on over.

I missed off my usual kiss from the end, suspecting that it might annoy him, and spitefully hoping that it did. According to Sean he'd been to the hostel on my first night in LA but it seemed unlikely that a Hollywood actor could just walk in there in the middle of the day without causing a riot, so I knew I was goading him, challenging him to do something impossible, but I was feeling so bitterly disappointed that I didn't seem able to help myself.

Predictably, barely a second after my message had sent, my phone began ringing, flashing up Sean's name. I could ignore it and further delay the expected confrontation, but that would only make me as bad as him. Exhaling noisily as I answered, I lifted the handset to my ear and was met by an equally large sigh from Sean.

'Be reasonable, Allie, you know I can't do that.' His husky, almost smoke-roughened voice washed over me and had the same impact on me as it usually did, causing my knees to weaken and my eyes to flutter shut as I tried to soak it into my memory.

Regardless of how much I missed him, how much I craved him, I saw a red mist rise up in front of my eyes at his words. Me be reasonable? He hadn't contacted me yesterday while I'd sat like a sad sack waiting for his call, so I had every right to be touchy.

Besides, he was the one who was suddenly engaged and asking me to hide away like his secret floozy! Reasonable was the very last thing I felt at the moment. Furious, disillusioned, and murderous, perhaps, but reasonable? No.

'Why can't you meet me at the hostel? Because you're famous? Or because you don't want anyone to catch you out cheating on your fiancée?' I retorted, hating the vicious tone resonating through my own voice.

'For God's sake, Allie. She's not my fucking fiancée. It's just a stupid PR stunt until the end of the season. If you'd hear me out you'd understand.'

I didn't even pause for a second, my reply rolling immediately from my tongue. 'Understand what, exactly? That in the eyes of the world you're engaged to her?' I half demanded, half stated. 'Which I assume means you can't be seen in public with me without causing a huge outcry? I'm guessing that's what you meant when you said we'd need to be careful and keep things quiet?'

There was a moment of shocked silence before I heard Sean clear his throat. 'I … uh … yes. But if you'd just let me explain, Allie.'

I barely ever lost my temper, but the depth of my emotions where this man was concerned was leading me to be a seething wreck. 'You had the chance to explain yesterday, but you didn't bother to call, which showed me just how desperate you are to explain.'

There was a splutter of shock down the line, and then a second of silence. 'What? I called you endlessly, but your phone was off so I sent you a message explaining that I couldn't get through. I thought you were ignoring me.' His reply threw me. I hadn't expected him to say that, I'd just assumed that he hadn't bothered to call. There was a scratchy sound down the line as Sean seemed to be moving the phone around in his hand, and I hesitated, suddenly unsure.

Thinking logically, I knew my phone hadn't rung yesterday, so I was about to dismiss his words as more lies, when a loud curse exploded down the line. 'Fucking hell!' I moved the phone away from my head in case further eardrum bursting expletives were about to follow, but instead, Sean's voice slid down the line, low and panicked. 'I just checked my call list. I was phoning your English number by mistake, not your US one. I'm so sorry, I called you endlessly, I swear to God.'

'Whatever, Sean,' I said dismissively, although his obvious panic was allowing doubts to creep in, making my voice a little wobbly. What if he was telling the truth? God, all this emotion was starting to get the better of me and I could feel tears building in my eyes. I needed to stay strong. Thinking back to his earlier words, a question popped into my head, which I promptly threw at him.

'You said this is just until the end of the season. When exactly is that?' I demanded, hoping he might say something short-term, like, oh, I don't know … next week?

'It depends how smoothly filming goes and if we have any extensions, but probably just a few months. Six-ish.'

Six-ish? Six months? Two months apart had just about killed me, but another six? That was half a year! I didn't really absorb his words fully, my brain too wound up to even pause in its train of thought.

'So basically we can't go on dates for at least half a year? Can't hold hands in a coffee shop? Heck, we probably couldn't even go to a coffee shop in the first place, could we? God forbid I should be seen in public with my boyfriend.' I was in full rant mode now, not waiting for his response – I had so many things running around my mind and they needed to come out. 'If I'm understanding your words correctly, Sean, you and I can't do anything together, which makes a relationship between us impossible and officially makes me being in Los Angeles completely pointless.'

What an utterly wretched but accurate summary.

There was a scratchy movement on the other end, as if Sean were pacing restlessly, which given his cool and calm persona was decidedly out of character. 'I'm trying to sort it all out, OK? You're right, we can't meet in public, not yet, but can we meet at your hotel suite later to talk?' There was another wheezy breath followed by several clattering noises. Perhaps he was pacing restlessly. It might be one of his nervous habits. I didn't know him well enough to be sure.

At his mention of my hotel another horrible thought began to occur to me, forming in my mind with greater clarity as each second passed. 'You said I'd have to stay in a hotel because the production team have moved you to a house nearer the set …'

The noises on the phone stopped as Sean stilled, and I could almost picture the look of poised intensity on his handsome face. 'That's right,' he answered, sounding wary.

'Why couldn't I stay with you? I mean I could have stayed hidden so no one knew I was there,' I asked, knowing the answer that he'd told me in the car, but suspecting that there was a whole other reason he didn't want me going there.

'Um … it's for, ah … crew members only.' His hesitation made it immediately clear that I was onto something, and I was beginning to suspect that that something was tall, pouty, brunette, and stick-like.

'Do you live there alone?' My fingernails were digging into my palm by now, the pain only dulled by the fierce hammering of my heart as I waited for his response.

'Why?' he replied, his tone clipped and edgy.

'I just want to know, that's all.'

'No, I share the house, Allie. That's pretty common amongst crew members on long shoots.'

My eyes closed, knowing my suspicions were about to be proven correct. 'You share it with her, don't you?' I whispered, somehow knowing that I was right. He was living with Savannah. I just knew it.

There was a very long pause, so long, in fact, that I pulled my phone away from my ear to check we hadn't been cut off. 'Allie …' He hadn't answered me directly, but it was clear from his strangled, hesitant voice that my suspicions were correct.

So not only was Sean supposedly engaged to Savannah Hilton, but he had dated her in the past, and now he was living with her too. Fabulous. In my books that all stacked up to waaaay too much baggage for me to try and contend with.

'I thought so. Right, well, there isn't really anything else to talk about then.' With that, I hung up, threw my phone on the bed, and then practically ran from the room as it immediately began to ring.

Fleeing to the peace of the private garden I slammed the patio door to close off the incessant ringing and walked to stand beside the pool. I stared at the gently rippling water and realised that my entire body was covered in goose pimples.

He was living with her. It really couldn't get any worse than that, could it? So somehow, against my knowledge I had officially found myself as 'the other woman'. Jesus.

I ran a hand through my hair and scratched at my scalp in agitation. I could really do with talking this over with Cait, but seeing as she wasn't here I'd have to share this new development in the Sean drama with her later. I was well and truly on my own. I don't think I'd ever felt isolation quite so intensely as I did then, and to top it all off I was thousands of miles away from home.

Wrapping my arms around myself I rubbed at my cold skin and tipped my head back toward the sun as I ran through the conversation with Sean. Was I being irrational? Overreacting? Perhaps I had been slightly rash in my decision not to see him sooner, but now that I knew he was living with Savannah I felt completely justified in my actions. I still couldn't quite believe it all.

Swallowing down a lump that rose in my throat, I tried to steady my erratic breathing, but my pulse was hammering so quickly that I felt like it might burst from my chest. I felt on the verge of a panic attack and quickly found a sun lounger that I could fall into as my legs failed me.

Over the next ten minutes, the sun warmed my chilled body and I began to feel more human again. I would recover from this, but being away from home certainly wasn't helping. Perhaps I should try and get a return flight to the UK, but that was something to consider once I'd talked things through with Cait. Sitting myself up, I glanced at my watch and saw that I needed to be heading to the hostel to help with the event. Maybe we'd be able to grab a few minutes there to talk.

I felt so raw that I genuinely thought I might have had a breakdown if I'd had an entire empty day stretching out ahead of me, so it really was a blessing that I had offered to help as it would prove to be a good distraction from my shitty situation and jumbled emotions.

Chapter Twenty-Two

Allie

After leaving my phone at the hotel – it hadn't stopped ringing and I didn't want the constant reminder of Sean looming over me all day – I had jumped in a cab for the fifteen minute journey to the hostel and was now standing on the sunny pavement outside being handed a shopping list by a very flustered Cait.

She looked far from my composed, calm best friend, and I had to hold back a smile as I picked several Rice Krispies from the strands of her long hair. 'Ugh. Thank you. Julie wanted me to make cupcakes, but there's no way my cakes could compare with hers so I thought I'd opt for the easy option of chocolate crispy cakes. The bloody mixture is so sticky that it's getting everywhere.' Running her hands through her hair she blew her fringe from her face and gave me a panicked smile as she glanced at the list in my hand. 'I can't believe we missed so many things when we went shopping yesterday!' she exclaimed, 'Thank you so much, Allie. There's a convenience store on the corner of the next block. Keep the receipt and the hostel will pay you back.'

Barely forty minutes later I was done with the shopping and was now loaded down with bags containing kitchen roll, plastic forks, and various other party stuff that was needed. Even with the Sean situation hanging over me I found that I was actually looking forward to a fun afternoon with Cait at the party, not to mention the prospect of meeting new people.

Just as they had been on the day I checked in, the hostel steps were busy with smokers hanging out and chatting, but as I mounted the top step the handle on one of my plastic bags broke, spewing a tumbling mass of kitchen rolls which cascaded and bumped their way down the steps.

Grimacing, I let out a heavy sigh. As stupid as it was, when I added this little mishap to my problems with Sean, it was almost enough to send tears to my eyes. Before I could bend to begin retrieving my spilt load, a scruffily-dressed man jumped from his perch on the wall and collected them for me.

Surprised by his kind gesture I felt my shoulders sag in gratitude; a knight in shining armour was just what I needed today. 'Thanks. I think I'm overloaded,' I joked lamely, but the laugh died as my saviour straightened up so I could get a closer look at him. He might be hidden below a baseball cap, and several days' worth of stubble, but that jaw and those lips looked all too temptingly familiar.

I doubt anyone else would have guessed it unless they had been carefully examining the man, but beneath a disguise of cap, sunglasses, scruffy trainers, combat shorts, and a crinkled T-shirt was Sean. For a second or two I thought that my emotions might have conjured him up in my cruel imagination, but seconds later, he leaned in close to speak to me and my nose was filled with his delicious scent. He was real, and he was here. Breathing in again, my eyes rolled shut – he might appear scruffy, dirty, and unshaven, but he smelt divine.

A small groan left my lips. Oh, God. I loved him so much it hurt. My chest literally felt as if it was collapsing in on itself and I had to focus really hard not to drop the remaining shopping bags clutched in my shaking hands.

'Please give me five minutes to speak to you, Allie, then if you want me to leave I will,' he murmured against my ear, so softly that his warm breath sent a tingle rushing across my skin.

I began to tremble even harder, my fingers clenching around the handles of the carrier bags and my breath coming more quickly as I struggled to maintain my composure. Various scenarios ran through my head – I could run away and hide somewhere, but however tempting, it would be ridiculously immature. I could make a scene, draw attention to who he was, and then sneak off when a crowd gathered, but that would be unfair and I didn't think I could go through with it either. Throwing my arms around his neck and never letting go was a fairly tempting option, but no matter how much I might want to, I couldn't just forget the Savannah situation.

Seeing my continuing hesitation, Sean leaned in again to press his case. 'Please, Allie. I know this is all a huge mess, but there are some things I need to explain to you, it's really important. I just need five minutes, I promise.' He was pleading now, and I so desperately wanted him to have a solution that I gave one jerky nod and headed inside without another word.

Walking into the kitchen in a daze I handed the bags to Cait, who grabbed my arm and then flashed a concerned looked over my shoulder. 'Who's that?' she hissed, the worry evident in her tone.

'Sean,' I murmured, my voice sounding dry and thick from my shock. Blinking rapidly, Cait gave him another look and then turned her attention back to me. 'Blimey, he looks different dressed like that.'

I didn't know what to say, so I just stood there numbly and nodded until she gave me a shove in the ribs. 'Well, go on then, go and talk to him,' she encouraged, making shooing motions with her hands.

Leaving Cait with a hopeful gleam in her eye I turned back to Sean and tried to find us a quiet place to talk. We could go to my old dorm room, but on second thoughts, perhaps the library would be a better choice – there were no beds to accidentally fall on in there if Sean chose to try and charm me into believing him, because when it came to Sean's seduction skills, I was seriously lacking in self-control.

As I led the way to the library, a growing sense of unease settled in my stomach. Had I made a mistake? I didn't want to be anybody's 'other woman', so perhaps I should have made him leave? Was it too late to do that? It was all so much to take in that my head was whirling by the time I pushed open the library door, but I consoled myself with the thought that it was just five minutes, then he would be gone and I could fall apart in private.

Once I was inside the quiet reading room I instantly became aware of the dimensions of the space and the closeness of Sean's presence. The spacious, airy room suddenly began to feel very claustrophobic, as if the chemistry between Sean and me was somehow eating away at the available oxygen and making the air around us thick and cloying.

My skin began to prickle, all of the tiny hairs on my body suddenly standing to attention. He was right behind me, I knew it. In fact, he was so close that I could smell him – that gorgeous spicy, almost mildly smoky scent that was uniquely Sean.

As expected, when I turned on the spot he was right there, although given his habit of getting well within my personal space, I suppose I should be used to just how close he always stood. Sucking in a nervous breath, I felt a tingle run through my body at his nearness, and my fingers actually began vibrating with the urge to reach out and touch him.

Nerves flooded my system as I fidgeted on the spot. I felt unpredictable, like my body would act without the permission of my brain, so I quickly took a step away to avoid doing something stupid like throwing myself at him, and glanced around instead. We were the only people in the library so I was looking for a safe place to sit – safe away from Sean, that was – because I begrudgingly admitted to myself that even with my good intentions of remaining practical about all of this, the pull between us was too magnetic for me to trust myself.

After scouring the room for a suitable spot I settled on an armchair, and wobbled my way to it. At least he wouldn't be able to sit directly next to me, which would avoid the risk of any direct body contact.

My eyes blinked rapidly at memories of just how good body contact with Sean had felt. Especially when there were no layers of clothing to separate us. Squeezing my eyes shut, I tried to forcibly remove images of Sean's naked body from my mind and focus on the situation at hand. It wasn't easy.

Unfortunately, always one step ahead, Sean outsmarted me, and instead of picking another chair a safe distance away, he assessed me for a second and then dragged the coffee table forward, perching himself on the edge so he was just in front of me. I frowned, annoyed at his close positioning, but then became totally distracted as he pulled off his cap and sunglasses and dazzled me with his handsomeness.

A high-pitched whimper formed in my throat and wouldn't clear as I gawked at his beauty – his dark hair and deep blue eyes hadn't lost any of their appeal in our few days apart, that was for sure, although he did look more weary than usual, and the stubble gracing his jawline only added to the overall appeal. Suddenly talking was the last thing on my mind as I felt our chemistry begin to bubble and sizzle in the gap between us. The stupid whimpering sound was replaced by a lower, lustier noise, almost verging on a growl and my eyes widened in horror at my runaway throat.

Gaining some small semblance of control, I swallowed hard several times, and finally managed to stop the ridiculous noises escaping. Unfortunately, they clearly hadn't been missed by Sean, because after flattening his hat hair he smiled impishly at me as if loving the way I had reacted to him.

'Hi, my gorgeous girl … God, I've missed you,' he murmured, but I merely crossed my arms, not trusting myself to say anything just yet. We sat in silence for a few seconds, the tension between us building and ratcheting until I actually felt annoyed by the fact that I was getting aroused just from being in his mere presence. Raising my eyebrows, I shook my head in exasperation before letting out a sigh from between my teeth. Several more seconds passed and he made no effort to speak. Instead, Sean just sat in silence with his eyes trained on me while I tried to avoid eye contact with his devastating blues by looking around the room at the various shelves and cupboards. As the seconds continued to tick by, we seemed to silently converse via some intense eye contact, which would have been enough to knock me off my feet if I hadn't been sitting down.

My breathing was erratic, wheezing from my lungs, and after I looked at him again – sitting there impassively, looking unfairly handsome – I sighed heavily and averted my gaze again. After several more moments had passed, I could take no more. My pulse was raging so intensely that it was ringing in my ears, so I finally locked my eyes with his again.

'Come on, Sean,' I snapped, frustration mixing with sexual tension and making me erupt. 'I've got the gist of what's going on, and quite frankly seeing as I'm not prepared to share you, I can't see what else we have to discuss. So what is it you're so desperate to tell me?' Sean's lips twisted into an ironic half smile, which got my back up even more, so I tucked my head down with a frown and crossed my arms like a petulant teenager.

From the corner of my eye I could see Sean tilting his head as he contemplated me, but suddenly, and to my complete surprise, he leant forward, his eyes searching mine as he slid a hand to the side of my neck and tangled his fingers in my hair.

Giving a tug, he encouraged me forward to where his lips descended upon mine fiercely, eliciting a yelp of shock from my throat. The response from my body was instantaneous; I accepted his desperate, almost violent kiss, as my anger evaporated and my lips parted with a low, desperate groan. My fingers came up to grip his T-shirt in bunched fists as my tongue eagerly joined with his.

I knew I shouldn't be doing this, but I couldn't stop myself.

My skin burned from his touch, senses alight as I seemed to burst to life after days of barely just existing. Sean's mouth was warm and demanding, and even though my body was screaming at me to stop and ask him the questions I needed to, I registered just how earth-shatteringly good his kiss felt and melted into it like putty in his hands.

After a few dizzying seconds, his hands began to wander down across my body, his thumb brushing across one of my nipples, making me arch into his touch and let out a hot, lusty moan into his open mouth. Clawing at the back of his neck, I suddenly realised that I was out of my seat and practically straddling his lap as he sat on the coffee table. This was quickly spiralling well out of control. The physical bond between us was so incredibly powerful and I knew for sure that if I didn't stop this right now we'd be having sex on the table in a matter of minutes. Or perhaps seconds.

As tempting as that seemed, I grudgingly ripped my mouth from his as I tried to force my common sense to re-engage and stop this while I still could. Images of my dreams of Savannah having sex with Sean instantly popped into my mind, sickening me to my stomach and dousing my arousal as effectively as if a bucket of ice water had just been thrown over me. Just like that, I felt the strength to push away from him and I launched myself backwards into the armchair to put some distance between us.

Licking my swollen lips, I could still taste him. I wanted more. So much more. Squeezing my eyes shut, I drew in several ragged breaths as I avoided the urge to restart our kiss by gripping the armrests until my fingernails hurt. I might have shut out my vision, but I could still hear Sean panting, his reaction to our kiss seemingly as powerful as mine.

After I'd allowed myself several seconds to calm, I opened my eyes, only to be met with such an intense stare that I gasped. Love, desire, pain, determination, and so many more emotions were all swirling in his blue depths as he continued to look at me, his eyes flitting around my face as if committing it to memory.

Resting back into the armchair, I put as much space between us as I could without physically moving my chair. Trying to clear the lingering sensations of his kiss from my mind and body, I dropped my eyes to break our gaze – but what a mistake that was, because they settled on the jutting tent of material at Sean's groin. Oh God. He was aroused, and clearly not attempting to hide it. Swallowing so loudly that he must have heard it, I flicked my eyes away, knowing that my cheeks were flushing bright red with embarrassment and desire, as my own arousal flared up and engulfed me until I had to shift my legs to ease the pressure between them.

'You said you needed to talk, Sean, but it doesn't seem you have much to say.' I ran my hands over my face in exasperation. 'I'm not cut out for this much drama in my life. I think you should probably leave.' The words were thick and mumbled as I stared down at my visibly trembling fingers. Blimey, I would definitely have to keep my wits about me from now on because if Sean chose to kiss me like that again I truly wasn't sure I'd have the willpower to pull away a second time. Morals I might have, but I was only human, after all.

Meeting his gaze, I saw his flushed face and sighed heavily. 'That's got to have been five minutes Sean and you've barely said a word.' And still he remained silent, causing my frustration and agitation to reach its peak.

His eyes were fixed on me expectantly, so I let out a deflated sigh and waved my hands before letting my tongue get the better of me and blab out my feelings. 'What do you want me to say?' I gushed, my irritation making me speak without thinking through my words first. 'Is the connection between us incredible and earthmoving?' I paused with another wild arm sweep. 'Of course it is.' I screwed my eyes shut to avoid his gaze and tilted my head down. 'Do I love you?' I paused again briefly and a small dry sob croaked up my throat. 'Yes, I do. But you already knew that.' Finally, I opened my eyes and looked at him defiantly. 'But that doesn't mean I'm prepared to share you, and even if this engagement is fake, like you claim, I won't hide like some cheap tart. I deserve more than that, Sean, and from what you've said that is our only choice. Well, I'm afraid it's not an option for me.'

Watching his handsome face, I saw Sean's eyes light up at my admissions as he leant forward keenly and licked his lips. 'That's all I needed to hear, Allie. You were trying to run away from us without giving me a proper chance to explain. I just wanted you to admit that what we have together is special, because it is. I've never felt like this about anyone before,' he said in a low whisper. Practically the first words he had uttered since entering the library and they were knockouts. Typical.

Passionate confessions from Sean didn't mean anything if we couldn't actually be together, did they? Letting out a long, slow breath I let my head fall back on the cushion and stared at the ceiling in despair. This was hopeless. We were going round in endless circles and making the wounds in my heart deeper and harder to heal.

'This isn't getting us anywhere, Sean. I don't see how expressing our feelings for each other will help if we can't actually have a relationship. If we were talking about another month, then I could do it, but what do you want me to do? Wait around for six months while you live with that woman, put your hands all over her in public and pretend to be engaged to her?' The very thought made me feel sick to my stomach.

Under different circumstances where Savannah wasn't involved, I could wait for Sean. Of course I could. If it were merely a job pulling us apart, I would find the separation difficult, but I could visit him and would deal with it, but the jealousy boiling inside me would eat me alive if I tried to do that in this situation. He would be going home to her every night, and from the images I'd seen in the press I had a suspicion that Savannah wanted Sean. He said they'd dated briefly, and from the way she was always clinging to him I firmly believed she was hoping to get him back.

'I'm sorry, but I'm not strong enough for that,' I said, shaking my head and hating that it was my jealousy driving us apart in the end. Standing up, I wrapped my arms around myself defensively. 'I hate this.' Closing my eyes, I felt my throat thickening as tears began to threaten. 'I think you should go.' Pulling open the door I stood back, desperately hoping that he would give in and leave me alone – or perhaps pull me into his arms and convince me to change my mind. My thoughts were so muddled that I wasn't even sure what I wanted to happen any more. I waited for Sean to leave, drawing my lips into a tight line, partly to stop myself saying anything I might regret, and partly in an attempt to hold back the tears that were now steadily building.

As I felt a stinging sensation hit the backs of my eyes, I knew I had just seconds to get him out of here before my tears would fall, and I suspected there would be no stopping them once I let the first few escape. I bit into my lip in an attempt to hold them back, feeling so utterly wretched and pathetic that I was seriously tempted to run from the room.

No. I was no coward. He had hurt me, that much was obvious, but I would survive and I would do it with courage and pride.

Standing up slowly, Sean walked towards the door, but instead of leaving he paused next to me, his tall frame seeming to emanate some kind of magical force that made me want to step toward him. Holding my ground, I steeled myself for one last glance at him and then caught his eye with as much of a defiant look as I could.

A heavy sigh escaped my chest – here in front of me was the man I loved, the first man I'd ever loved, and I couldn't quite believe that I was making him leave. But I was, because I would never allow myself to be someone's other woman. Against all my desperate attempts, a droopy, pathetic tear escaped from one of my eyes and I watched Sean's features practically melt as he took in my woefully sad expression.

Sean's eyes crinkled into a frown as he reached up to gently wipe away the solitary tear with the pad of his thumb, my head tilting automatically into his touch as my eyes briefly flickered shut before opening again so I could watch him for one final time. He opened his mouth to speak, but I turned my face away, shook my head, and looked at the floor, still resolute in my decision that he should leave.

'Oh, Allie, please don't cry,' he whispered. 'We're going to get through this. I'm going to sort it out, I've already started the process. I just need you to be patient with me for a short while. Can you do that? Can you give me, I don't know, four weeks?'

What did he mean he had already started the process of sorting it out? Blinking back hot tears, I dared to risk a glance up at his handsome face as a seed of hope tingled in my stomach. Four weeks? That sounded far more doable than six months, but I still needed some facts to be clarified because I had some serious issues where Savannah Hilton was concerned.

'Our relationship is too important to give up on, Allie,' he said, cupping my face gently. 'At least I think it is.' It wasn't said as an accusation, but the tinge of panic in Sean's voice was enough to tell me just how desperate he was for us to work through these issues, and caused my heart to spiral with hope.

'And look at this. I need you to know I wasn't lying about the phone calls yesterday,' Sean murmured, holing out his phone to me. Taking it, I glanced at the screen and saw he had opened up his list of recent calls. Scrolling through yesterday's list I saw at least forty to 'Allie Mobile', except the last one, from this morning which was listed as 'Allie USA'. He'd been telling the truth about dialling the wrong number. He really had been calling me endlessly.

I knew our problems weren't over yet, but just seeing his determination to correct things gave me the confidence that we might somehow turn things around, and my desperation to be with him suddenly overtook me. It was as if a tonne had slid from my shoulders, and in the blink on an eye I was collapsing forward into Sean's arms, gripping at his T-shirt with my trembling hands and burying my head in his solid chest as all my pent-up emotions escaped in a huge rush. God, how embarrassing. Rather annoyingly, I found myself sobbing almost uncontrollably, and within just a few seconds I could feel his shirt becoming soaked beneath my cheek as I wheezed and blubbed like an inconsolable child.

Basically, I was a complete and utter wreck.

'Hey, hey, it's all right, my gorgeous girl, I'm here.' Sean cradled me against him, his strong arms sliding around me with an aching familiarity that made me melt with longing. Before I could really think it through, I was rolling up onto tiptoes and desperately seeking his mouth with mine. My fingers slid to the fine hair at the back of his neck to pull him closer, although it was an unnecessary gesture because he seemed more than keen to return my sudden advances.

Our lips met almost violently, mine open and needy and his warm and inviting as a rushed breath quivered across my lips when they connected. My tongue slid against his, eliciting a low groan from the back of his throat as his arms tightened around me and supported my weight. His fresh minty taste was mixing with a hint of the salt from my tears, but I barely noticed, my tongue continuing to twist and explore with his as my arousal soared.

Chapter Twenty-Three

Cait

Chewing on the skin beside my thumbnail, I winced at the small painful pinch and then looked down at the roughened skin with a frown. Damn it. I knew why I was reverting to this old habit – I was anxious about Allie. She'd disappeared with Sean over twenty minutes ago and I hadn't seen her since.

Even knowing that Allie was more than capable of taking care of herself, it didn't stop me worrying. She'd been in such a state yesterday, and the dazed look on her face this morning when she'd come into the hostel with Sean in tow had really tugged at my heart strings.

Was she OK? That was the question going round and round my mind like a hurricane. What if they'd had a big row and she was sitting somewhere crying and needing my support? I hadn't seen Sean leave, but then again I'd been so busy helping Julie that I hadn't really been keeping a good eye on the door.

Finishing off the final batch of chocolate crispy cakes, I popped the tray in the fridge to set, rinsed my fingers of the sticky mixture, and made the decision to go looking for her.

First I checked the common room, washing room, smoking terrace, and the areas downstairs that might offer them relative privacy to talk in, but my search was fruitless. Perhaps they'd gone for a walk to talk things through? Deciding to do a quick check upstairs just in case, I took my hunt to the large communal bathrooms and coffee area before arriving at the door to the library. It was closed, as it always was, but as I pushed it open expecting to find it empty, I was instead confronted by the sight of Allie and Sean in a heated embrace.

A very heated embrace.

Holy cow. This scene would definitely need an over eighteen rating, because jeez, their hands were everywhere and their tongues were tangling so enthusiastically I could hear the noise from across the room.

So apparently my fears were unwarranted. Allie's continued absence hadn't been because she was upset, but rather because she and Sean were making up so energetically. Blimey. I knew I should turn and leave, but I was frozen to the spot like an ogling idiot. There was something quite fascinating about the passion in their kiss, not to mention the possessive way Sean was gripping Allie against him.

Oh God, as he shifted slightly my eyes suddenly caught sight of why Sean was gripping her against him so enthusiastically – a large bulge was tenting the front of his shorts, leaving me in absolutely no doubt about how excited he was.

That image finally prompted me to shake myself from my gawking. Staggering backwards out of the room I closed the door as quietly as I could before collapsing backwards against the opposite wall.

My cheeks were burning, my breathing raised, and my mind full of images of passionate kisses, with wandering lips and clutching fingers … only this time they didn't feature Allie and Sean, but rather Jack and me.

Is that how Jack would have kissed me if I'd let him? Laying claim to me with his mouth and grip? Or would he have been soft and coaxing, cradling me against him and exploring my mouth with gentle probing flicks of his tongue? Would I have made him as excited as Sean had so obviously been with Allie?

Swallowing hard – so hard that I heard the strangled noise echo in the corridor – I pulled in a deep breath through my nose and ran a trembling hand across my hair as I tried to recover my composure. My hand came away damp and I realised that my brow and neck were sweating.

I was well and truly hot under the collar and all just from some vivid thought. If this potent response to a mere fantasy was anything to go by, then it was probably just as well that I hadn't let Jack kiss me, because I would no doubt have made a complete idiot of myself and done something ridiculous like faint on him.

Pushing away from the wall I began to stumble my way back towards the stairs intent on forgetting any visions that might involve Jack and me caught up in a lip lock. That type of thing was clearly best left to professionals like Allie and Sean.

Chapter Twenty-Four

Allie

Suddenly Sean placed his hands on my shoulders and pushed back from me, breaking our kiss. Sucking in a huge breath he rubbed the end of his nose against mine and gave an embarrassed chuckle. 'Seeing as you're finally willingly back in my arms, I'm seriously tempted to ravish you, but my honourable side is insisting that I sit you down and answer any questions you might have.'

Sniffling the last of my tears away, I used the back of my hand to wipe at my cheeks and smiled up at him sheepishly. 'Sorry … this has been a really stressful few days. I think my emotions finally got the better of me,' I said with a small laugh. Seeing his flushed cheeks and dilated pupils, it was obvious that the kiss had affected Sean just as much as me, but then he shifted slightly and I felt an even more obvious show of his arousal press against my stomach.

'Hmmm. I know exactly what you mean,' he agreed with a subtle thrust of his hips that made me bite my lower lip as I clung to his arms.

'Let's sit,' I said, jerking my chin towards the sofa as I dug up the last remnant of my self-control.

'Good idea. I might just about manage to restrain myself if I'm not pressed against you.' He adjusted his shorts to ease the pressure on what looked to be a rather uncomfortably tight situation, and I couldn't help but grin at his predicament.

Reaching into a back pocket of his shorts, Sean removed a folded white envelope before joining me on the couch. 'I want to share this with you. I'm not supposed to, but I don't care any more. Besides, I've already broken the terms of the contract by telling you most of the details.' Reaching up, he ran a hand through his hair. 'I don't want you to think I'm keeping anything from you ever again, Allie. I was wrong to try and do that, and I'm so sorry. I thought I could protect you from it all, but clearly it backfired big time.'

Looking down at the envelope with narrowed eyes, I glanced back at him before taking it, a frown furrowing my brow as I hesitated and looked at him questioningly. A sigh slipped from his lips as his face formed a similarly grim expression. 'This explains everything, so it might help to make it all clear for you.'

The envelope had obviously already been opened at some point, not to mention folded numerous times. Carefully, I reached inside and removed a single sheet of paper. Scanning it, I saw the familiar logo of the film company Sean was working with at the top, and then traced down to see that it was a letter addressed to Sean. Trying to calm my hammering heartbeat. I allowed myself several moments to read the contents, and then looked up dubiously and wide-eyed at Sean.

I could barely believe what I'd read. 'They actually contracted this farce?' I asked sceptically, my eyes roaming his face and seeing nothing but a grim reality in the hardened angles of his jaw.

'They did. That's how seriously they treat the ratings game over here, Allie.'

'This is … um … certainly a little … unexpected. I thought that maybe you and Savannah had just made it up between the two of you …' I murmured, my eyes flicking to the paper again.

'No, but I can see why you would think that.' He nodded and then sighed. 'I'll explain, as best I can, but it's not something I'm proud of, so I hope you won't think any less of me.' The look of concern that had settled on his face certainly appeared genuine, his big, doe-eyed look pulling at my heartstrings and filling me with the urge to reach out to comfort him. So I did, sliding my hand onto his firm thigh and giving an encouraging squeeze. His gaze dropped to the point of my contact and a sweet smile curled his lips until he covered my hand with his and continued.

'I'll start from the beginning. As you know, I've been out here on and off over the last few years filming the first two seasons of LA Blue.' I nodded, yep, so far so good.

'During the second season the show became really popular, more than we had expected, and as a result the publicity surrounding the actors increased. Some paparazzi snapped Savannah and me out together a few times and a rumour went around that we were dating. The show's ratings soared almost overnight, as did hits on the website. It was crazy, but as you can imagine, the producers were thrilled. People became obsessed with us.' He shook his head and shrugged awkwardly.

'But you were dating,' I reminded him, hating the sour taste of jealousy that popped on my tongue.

Sean shifted on the sofa, scratching anxiously at the back of his neck and leaving the skin red. 'Yes. But only briefly. Because we were filming, Savannah and I were spending an awful lot of time together. I wasn't interested in dating her, but she was incredibly persistent.' I'd never even met the woman, but I already had an irrational hatred for her. 'In the end we went out a few times during the filming of season two.'

Lifting my hand from his thigh, where it had practically cramped up from jealousy, he rubbed some life back into it while fixing his gaze on to mine firmly. 'We never slept together, Allie. Never. I swear to you,' he assured me, with a gaze so intent that it sent a fizzle of connection bursting through me. As insignificant as it might be to some people, the fact that he hadn't slept with her made me feel better about the whole situation and I felt my shoulders relax a little.

'Remember when we were snowed in at my house and I told you the rumours of me sleeping with all my co-stars were lies?' I nodded, remembering the conversation as if it had happened yesterday. 'That is true, Allie, believe me. I didn't sleep with her, or any of my co-stars. Like I told you, I haven't dated for years, not since Elena.' I nodded, wincing as I recalled the awful story of his on-off girlfriend being killed in a boating accident. He hadn't dated since. Until he met me, and apparently our connection had been too strong for him to deny.

'Savannah's a great actress, very professional, but as I came to find out, she's also a completely self-centred bitch.' I couldn't help but smile. 'Once I got to know the real Savannah she began to drive me mad and we split up. Not that we were ever really together.'

Blimey. I was on a seesaw of emotions as my light mood was once again dulled by the pangs of jealousy squirming in my stomach. As irrational as it was, I hated the fact that they had even been together. She would have touched him, perhaps kissed him, and that made me want to do some seriously nasty things to her. Jealousy wasn't an emotion I had ever been particularly familiar with, but since dating Sean I had found that I was becoming rather well acquainted with it. Apparently I was quite the possessive woman where it came to a certain Mr Phillips.

'Even at that early stage it was obvious how popular the show was and Finlay, our director, had already informed us that he planned on doing at least another five seasons if the network agreed.

'Obviously he wasn't thrilled when I told him our brief relationship was over, and being a money-hungry bastard his main concern was the impact it would have on the viewer base and the show's ratings.' Sean raised his eyebrows to show his disregard for the director's attitude, something I couldn't help but share. Did he have no morals at all? 'This is Hollywood in all its greedy glory.' Taking in a heavy breath, Sean smiled thinly. 'This sounds crazy … even to me … but Finlay offered us both a very healthy pay check if we pretended to continue seeing each other. Nothing specific had to be announced to the press, we just had to be seen in public together every now and again to keep the rumour mill going.'

Levelling an apologetic gaze at me, he thinned his lips into a tight line. 'Neither of us was involved with anyone else at the time, and seeing as I didn't ever date I didn't see the harm in it.' Scowling, he lowered his eyes. 'I gave in to the lure of the extra cash. What can I say? I thought I was different, but I'm obviously just a money-hungry arsehole like everyone else who moves out here.' He smiled on the surface, but I could see sadness in his eyes.

'That was it, really. Savannah dated other people on and off during the next year, but we were together enough for filming that there were always pictures of us appearing in the press to keep the fans interested, the rumour mill spinning, and the director happy.'

Blinking rapidly, Sean shook his head. 'You have to believe me when I say it was never supposed to go beyond that. An engagement was not discussed with me at that point, or ever agreed on.' Once again his stare was solid and truthful, so I could do little but sit, nod, and allow him to continue.

'One thing kind of led to another and the longer it went on, the more the press were hounding us for gossip. At the start of this season, Finlay called Savannah and me into a meeting and offered us a bonus cheque if we would pretend to be engaged.' All the air left my lungs at those words. The start of this season was when Sean and I were already together. Did that mean he'd chosen money over me? Before I could draw in a new breath to state my concerns, Sean practically launched himself from the sofa in agitation.

'I was fucking furious at his presumption. I still am!' His big blues met mine, his fury burning into me and laying my previous concerns to rest. He hadn't chosen money over me. That was certainly good to know.

'Obviously things had happened with you by that point and I knew with certainty that you were the one for me.' I was the one for him. There was no way Sean could know how happy those words made me, but my breathing faltered for the second time in less than a minute as they sank in and made something inside my chest heat with love. Even in the midst of this other craziness his words were like a soothing balm. 'I point-blank refused the offer and left the meeting, but as it turns out, Savannah continued talks with Finlay and agreed a deal.'

My eyes widened and my eyebrows made a break for my hairline, immediately causing Sean to raise his hands defensively. Or perhaps it was a proclamation of innocence, I wasn't sure. 'I swear to you I thought that was the end of it. I had no idea they made the deal behind my back.'

As I tried to analysis all of this insanity, my expression morphed into a heavy scowl. This was all so unethical, so unreal I could barely believe it – not to mention it was a complete pack of lies being fed to the fans.

'It was such an utter sham. Still is,' Sean spat with a firm shake of his head. 'Finlay offered me a second, larger cheque later that week and I told them I didn't agree with lying any further and I turned down the offer … unfortunately, Savannah's greed got the better of her and she announced our engagement at a film premiere about three weeks ago. I found the money in my account the same day.' Sean's eyes closed as he shook his head bitterly. 'I wasn't there with her that night, but the next day it was all over the press and people were going wild. I couldn't fucking believe it.' Sean did occasionally swear, but the passion behind his words made me surprised that more expletives hadn't slipped from his lips over the course of the last five minutes.

'I was so torn over what to do. I tried to go to the press and deny Savanah's statement, but Finlay told me in no uncertain terms that my job on the show would have been compromised, and he promised it would affect any future employment in Hollywood.'

My mouth fell open in surprise. 'He blackmailed you?'

A weary sigh heaved from Sean's chest as he nodded. 'Pretty much, although obviously he was careful not to word it that way. He's a big deal in LA, lots of connections to the right people, so I have to take his threat seriously.' Walking back towards the sofa, Sean sank down onto his haunches in front of me and took hold of both my chilled hands. I felt almost frozen from this new, and bizarre, information.

'I was terrified about telling you, Allie. You have no idea.' His eyes were flicking around rapidly now. 'I just couldn't think of a way to say it and make it sound OK, so I avoided it, like a coward. When you kept asking me why I was tense on our Skype calls, this was the reason.'

Dropping down, he rested his forehead on my knee as he took several long, ragged breaths, the air warming the skin below my shorts. His contact helped me loosen up my stiff body, and so I tried to return the favour by gently pulling one of my hands free from his grip and running it soothingly through his hair.

After remaining there for a few seconds, Sean drew in a long breath and looked up, his eyes calmer and more purposeful. 'I went and spoke to Finlay on Thursday, as soon as you ran away from me and nearly gave me heart failure.' I swallowed guiltily and bit down on my lower lip.

'I tried appealing to his softer side and told him about you.' Gripping my hands again, Sean fixed me with his penetrating stare. 'I explained how very important you are to me.' My heart gave a kick of happiness, but then Sean licked his lips, the movement slow and deliberate and somehow changing my happiness to something far lustier. He reached up and cupped my cheek, causing a growing heat to flicker between us and almost scorch my skin where we were connected. No matter how inappropriate the timing, I wanted him.

Sean seemed to agree with my sentiment, but after a second shook his head, apparently intent on finishing his confessions first. 'He wasn't thrilled, but he could see what a state I was in and finally agreed that the engagement farce needed to end. Apparently the man does have a heart after all,' Sean joked mildly before sobering again. 'His acceptance comes with two stipulations – I have to wait until after the new season premiere to make the announcement, and until then Savannah and I have to continue to live together in the same house. He wants the fans hooked in before we "split up". Plus, he thinks that it might cause some extra publicity for the show that way.'

My jaw clenched as I grimaced at his mention of living with Savannah, but there seemed to be an end in sight, which was all I was clinging to right now.

I still couldn't believe people lived like this. How was this make-believe world his reality? It made me feel well and truly boring. 'We have separate rooms, Allie, there is nothing between us.' After finishing his confession, Sean sat still and stared right at me, his eyes large and almost childlike as he awaited my judgement. When I didn't say anything – I couldn't, I'd been stunned into silence – he let out an almighty sigh. 'You probably think I'm a total jerk now.'

I quietly pondered what he'd told me for a second, finding myself totally lost for what to say. My bottom lip took a battering as I chewed on it and thought through all he had told me. Technically, when he'd agreed to the fake relationship, he'd been single, so there was really no harm to that element, and money certainly had a way of making people do crazy things. I dreaded to think what sums of cash had been exchanged for this farce – probably more than my bank account had ever seen in its lifetime.

Nodding to myself, I got to the real crux of the issue – Savannah. She sounded like a grade A bitch, had forced the engagement thing into the public eye, and from what I'd seen of her in pictures, looked more than keen to make fantasy into reality with Sean.

It was a lot to consider so I asked a question that sprang into my head. 'After I left you on Monday, Cait and I did a bit of digging. There were a couple of photographs of you and Savannah out with your families. Have you deceived them too?' I asked, aware that my voice was most disapproving and also wavering from the jealousy still burning inside me.

Sean unfurled his tall frame from his position on the floor and moved to sit back next to me again, his posture decidedly more slumped than earlier.

'Those photos are really old, back when Finlay first asked us to continue the pretence, but no, of course I didn't lie to my family. I told them all the truth.' Running a hand through his hair, Sean shrugged. 'Actually, in the end, it was my parents who convinced me it was the right thing to do. They said the money was too much to turn down. My mum has wanted me to settle down for years so I think secretly she hoped things would work out between Savannah and me and we would end up together for real.' He raised an eyebrow ironically, shaking his head and his eyes sought mine as he searched my face for an indication of my feelings.

I was still basically in stunned silence, but Sean's face crumpled at my continued hesitation. 'Do you think I'm an awful person?' he asked quietly, anxiety written across his handsome face and making him look far older than his years.

Honestly I wasn't really sure what I thought. On one hand I was overjoyed at his proclamation about just how important I was to him, but then on the other I didn't approve of the lie he was living – even though it was supposedly for the good of the show. Fiddling with the hem on my shorts I pondered for a few more seconds. Could I continue to hold it against him? After all, it sounded like he had sort of been forced into the whole thing by Savannah's impulsive public announcement and his director's blackmail.

Beside all of the crappy details, there were also the small facts to consider, such as I was totally in love with him, he was unreservedly gorgeous, and apparently also still deeply in love with me too.

Knowing I had been silent for quite a long time and understanding that my pause must be eating him up with nerves, I finally reconnected our gaze and cleared my throat. 'I don't agree with the lies, Sean,' I stated, giving him a firm look, 'but it seems that you were somewhat forced into a corner.' His face remained impassive as he watched me, but he allowed me more time to form my conclusions.

'And I don't think you're an awful person,' I finished out loud. The relief that flooded his handsome face was immeasurable. In my opinion, Sean Phillips was as far from 'awful' as you could get, a 'caring, delicious hottie with a body to die for', perhaps, but awful? No. Not that I said any of that out loud.

'It seems nobody really got hurt and you turned an incredibly odd situation to your advantage. I wasn't even in the picture until recently, and you couldn't have known that Savannah was going to announce a pack of lies to the press.' Sitting back, I took a few deep breaths to try and calm my reeling brain; I was well and truly overloaded by the bizarre information I had learnt in the last half an hour and needed another moment of quiet. After several minutes, I pursed my lips and gave a marginal nod of my head, actually quite impressed with how calm I was, considering all I had just taken in.

From beside me, I saw Sean shift in his seat as he tentatively placed a hand over one of mine. Heat coursed through me and a shiver of awareness ran from our joined hands right to the tips of my toes and the top of my hairline. The touch shocked me – not the actual contact, but the response that my body had to his warm skin. It seemed even more explosive than usual. When I didn't pull away, he closed his fingers around mine and smiled hopefully.

'Say you believe me, Allie?' he asked hopefully, giving my hand an encouraging squeeze.

'Well, I think so … but you gotta admit it's all pretty far-fetched, Sean.'

He let out a chuckle. 'This is Hollywood, Allie, what did you expect? You wouldn't believe the number of fake weddings I've heard about, not to mention fake divorces, and they are all tangled up with fame or ratings or viewer popularity. It's unreal; actors living in an entirely false world.' His laugh was soft and warming and I found myself chuckling along as my body relaxed back against the sofa.

Suddenly, Sean straightened up and looked me directly in the eyes. The determined look on his face told me he was about to say or do something important, but what? Because secretly, now that the tension had eased between us, I was hoping it might involve another searing kiss.

'Look, let me lay it on the line. This isn't exactly going to be easy for the next few weeks, but I love you. I know I've told you before, but how I feel about you goes way beyond just love. I feel things for you I've never felt before … Can we pick up where we left off? We'll have to be secretive for a while until everything is sorted with the press, so it won't be smooth running, but what do you think?' As he tilted his head, a flicker of tension crossed his face. 'Visiting my house might be a bit tricky when Savannah is home, but I'll speak to her and see what I can sort out.'

His mention of Savannah made my lip curl with distaste. I wasn't looking forward to meeting her at all. Firstly, I had convinced myself that she still wanted Sean, and secondly, after hearing the levels she'd sunk to recently in deceiving not only Sean but the fans too, I wasn't exactly a supporter of the way she lived her life.

Watching me carefully, Sean must have seen my grimace and his shoulders slumped as disappointment flooded his features. 'You still don't believe me, do you?'

I blinked, and decided to be completely honest with him. 'Actually, I do. But I think Savannah is going to cause us problems. I know you said she went to the press with the engagement story because she's greedy, but I can't help but think there's more to it than that. I've seen the pictures in the papers, she's always got her hands all over you. Are you sure she doesn't want you back?'

Tilting his head thoughtfully, Sean considered my question as if it hadn't even crossed his mind before. 'I don't think so. She flirts with me, but then she flirts with any man that has a pulse. I'm almost positive it's nothing more than that,' he said confidently.

225

Hmm. We'd have to agree to disagree on that for now, because from the body language she'd displayed in the various pictures I'd seen I'd place money on the fact that she still held a torch for him. Shaking his head, Sean frowned, tilting his chin to give me an assessing look. 'It's more than that, isn't it? What else is on your mind?'

I met his gaze and hesitated, not wanting to share yet more doubts with him after the already emotional revelations of the last fifteen minutes. 'If I'm being honest, I'm still not entirely convinced that a relationship between you and me will ever really work.' Seeing his brow lower defiantly I quickly continued before he could interrupt me. 'A film star and a teacher doesn't seem the most practical in the long run, does it? We live in totally different worlds, not to mention different countries for half the time.'

To my surprise, and bitter disappointment, Sean didn't immediately argue with me, instead choosing to chew on the inside of his cheek while still staring at me. After an age where he simply sat there, he licked his lips and drew in a long breath. 'We can make it work, Allie,' he said quietly, but not as forcefully as I'd hoped. Seeing my continued hesitation he gave my hands a tighter squeeze, sending warmth rushing around my body. 'Besides, you've finished teaching; all you need to do is make a go of your writing and you could live anywhere you wanted.' Licking his lips, he gave a tentative smile. 'You could live wherever I was. If you wanted to, that is. We both need to want this to work though, Allie.'

There were no long, drawn out pauses or thinking time required this time – my answer literally rolled from my tongue. 'I want it, Sean, of course I do,' I whispered keenly, and I really did. When I recalled the four weeks we'd spent together in the UK, I thought of nothing but how blissfully happy we'd been. I couldn't think of anything in the world I wanted more.

His shoulders sagged in relief, his lips curling into that roguish smile that I so loved. 'Me too, my gorgeous girl. I understand your concerns, of course I do, but will you at least give me a chance? We have to be careful for the next few weeks anyway, which will limit the amount we can see each other so maybe we could call it a trial of sorts?' Raising a hand he gently brushed some loose strands of hair behind my ear, his expression softening and melting my heart along with it.

'Actually, given how we met, we sort of skipped the proper dating phase, so maybe we can do that now. I'll court you properly, win you over again. We'll take it slow …' Narrowing his eyes, he pursed his lips and slid a hand down, flicking his thumb across one of my nipples and causing it to instantly harden against his touch. 'Well, slow-ish …' he conceded with a cheeky grin. 'I'm not a saint.' If he felt even one tenth as horny as I currently did, then we weren't going to manage to take it slow for long, but as I gasped my pleasure, I gave an accepting nod of my head.

I met his gaze and saw the hope and desperation there that I had also heard reflected in his voice. He was still waiting patiently for me, and as I saw the love and longing in his expression I realised that my brain, and body, were fast moving away from his phoney engagement and mass deception and towards a much more selfish destination. We could still be together. Maybe. If we could find a solution to the other issues that seemed to loom over our relationship, but I'd grab this moment and go with it. I could always worry about the issues later.

Sean Phillips, the man I loved and basically the man of my dreams, could once again be my boyfriend.

My wandering thoughts must have caused my smile to broaden considerably, because Sean looked at me quizzically, a confused smile twitching at the corners of his lips.

'What?' he asked with a slightly nervous lilt.

Nodding my head frantically, I smiled. 'Deal. A trial it is. I think I can cope with you "courting me" while we keep it quiet until you sort things out.' Giving in to the urge to be closer to him, I leant toward him and buried my face into the warmth of his neck. 'Please don't think my hesitation was because I don't love you, Sean, because I do ...' as good as it felt to be snuggled against him, I needed him to see how serious I was about this, so I leant back and connected our gazes, '... more than you could ever know. It's just quite a bit to take in and I wasn't sure how I'd deal with it ... I'm still not, but if you're willing to fight for us, then so am I.'

Saying it out loud suddenly made me feel quite overwhelmed again, and extremely, well ... ordinary, especially sitting here next to Sean with his exquisite tan, beautiful body, and tousled good looks as his face began to dip towards mine for a kiss.

Suddenly the library door burst open, causing us to jump apart as I practically had a coronary on the spot. Within a split second I'd instinctively grabbed Sean's tatty baseball cap from the sofa between us and rammed it on his head, causing him to jerk forward sharply. Looking at the offending door, I watched as two young guys entered with laptops in their hands, apparently heading to the desks that held the hostel's Wi-Fi hotspot. The first gave us a cursory glance and a nod by way of greeting, but the second looked so sleepy, or perhaps hungover, that he didn't even bother to look at us.

My heart was hammering in my chest at our near escape and I flashed Sean a concerned glance. 'We should go,' I whispered. 'I need to get back and help Cait, the event starts soon and I've basically abandoned her.'

Lifting up a hand, Sean winced dramatically and rubbed at his neck. 'I think you gave me whiplash,' he murmured, causing me to blush. I may have been a little over exuberant when I'd put his hat on him. He flashed me a wink to show he was joking, donned his dark glasses, and stood up before offering me a hand.

Placing my palm in his, I stood and followed him from the room, feeling like I was breaking some invisible law just by holding Sean's hand. Once we were in the empty corridor he stopped, removed his sunglasses, and turned to face me. I wasn't sure if he saw the way I was staring at our joined hands, or perhaps just feeling it too, but he chuckled and squeezed my palm before leaning in to whisper in my ear. 'Exciting, isn't it?'

When I raised my eyes to meet his gaze I saw he was grinning at me with a very naughty twinkle in his eyes. 'Sneaking around, the risk of being caught, the almost illicit feeling of all this … it's quite a turn on, wouldn't you agree?' he murmured, inching even closer as his hot breath fanned across my cheek and made me draw in a shaky gasp. As wrong as it was, I couldn't deny his words. My heart was still thundering in my veins and from the way my body was tingling at his closeness and thrumming in all the right places, I knew I was most definitely aroused.

Adjusting my stance, I pressed my thighs together and found myself biting on my lower lip at the pleasant sensation in my groin. Nodding slowly at Sean, I stood rooted to the spot as he shifted his hips forward so his lower body was pressed against mine. As his very obvious excitement pressed against my belly I couldn't help but let out a low moan and slide my hands around his waist to yank him more firmly against me, which immediately had the desired response when he growled and dipped his head for a desperate kiss.

Our lips met frantically, warm skin moving against warm skin as my mouth instinctively parted to allow his probing tongue to explore. The narrow hallway soon became filled with our breathy sighs as our hands joined in and groped through our clothing, but Sean suddenly pulled back before I'd even managed to get my hand down his shorts.

Reaching for me, Sean took hold of my wrists and guided me one step backwards so I was pressed against the wall with his body caging me in. His face was mere centimetres from mine, his breaths ragged and short and I found myself pinned by his desire-laden stare. 'I want to fuck you against this wall right now,' he muttered, giving a hard accompanying thrust to prove his point.

That sounded so wrong and so dirty, but God, did I want him to follow through. Before meeting Sean I'd never been one for dirty talk or public sex acts, but when Sean swore or suggested illicit activities, they immediately sent a jolt of lust straight to my throbbing core. A huge sigh escaped his lips and Sean gave me a rueful smile before reluctantly shaking his head. 'But we can't. It's way too public, and even I'm not that much of an exhibitionist.'

Disappointment and frustration pounded in my core, but he was right. To be honest, we were lucky we hadn't already been caught: this was the main corridor running through the hostel and always seemed to be busy with people. Seeing as we'd been at it like a couple of horny teenagers, it was a frigging miracle no one had come past. 'Besides, I'm not sure that fucking you against a wall exactly fits with my quest to take it slow and date you properly,' he murmured with a dark chuckle that made me sputter out a shocked giggle.

Pulling in several steadying breaths, I couldn't help but join him in smiling as he gradually pulled himself away from me and rearranged things inside his shorts with a wince. 'I'm going to have one serious case of blue balls after all this waiting,' he muttered, before grinning at me boyishly. 'Soon though, my gorgeous girl, I promise I'll find a way for us to be together. Good luck with the event. Message me tonight before bed, OK?' And as soon as he'd seen my answering nod, Sean replaced his glasses, landed one quick kiss on my lips, and murmured the words, 'Message. Bed time. Don't forget,' into my mouth, before disappearing down the corridor and leaving me feeling breathless, wobbly-legged, and horny as hell.

Chapter Twenty-Five

Sean

So far, two nearly two weeks had passed since Allie and I had agreed to a trial relationship, but due to my crazy schedule and the need for secrecy, we'd only managed to see each other three times. All three meetings had been quick, snatched moments in the privacy of her hotel suite when I had managed to grab an hour or two free, and so far I had managed to remain a gentleman and keep sex out the dates. I wanted Allie to know that it was her that was important to me, but bloody hell, had it taken some serious restraint to hold back.

On our first 'date', I'd arrived for lunch bearing a bag of smoked salmon and cream cheese bagels, and Allie had been just as excited as me, her eyes twinkling as she giggled the entire time.

Unfortunately, on my last two visits I'd started to detect her reticence at our enforced secrecy. She'd insisted she was fine, but had clearly underestimated how well I knew her. In our short time together, I paid attention to my girl in all things. Had done since we'd met. Allie had breached my heart in ways I'd not thought possible, and by doing so had unwittingly made herself my fixation. I wouldn't quite go as far to say that she was my obsession, because that sounded a little too stalker-like, but she was certainly on my mind more than I cared to admit. In all honesty, I probably knew her traits and body language better than she did.

Instead of being the carefree, radiantly beautiful, slightly scatty girl I had grown to love in England, Allie had been increasingly withdrawn from me. Her smiles didn't quite reach her eyes any more and, despite the sunshine in LA, her cheeks hadn't held their usual healthy flush. She'd looked sad, and the knowledge that it was all my fault just about made my heart wither up and die in my chest. I'd also caught her watching me intently on several occasions, as if she was trying to deduce what was going on in my mind. Perhaps she was trying to work out if I was worth all this hassle. I hoped she would decide I was. I would just have to prove that I was.

So it was this determination that had led me to tonight. I felt like a complete idiot, and probably looked like one too, but if helped prove to Allie how dedicated I was, then so be it.

Christ, my head was itchy. And my eyes were still stinging. I really hoped she appreciated all the effort I had gone to. Blinking several times to ease the unfamiliar sensation in my eyeballs, I cleared my throat and knocked on the door to her garden bungalow as my pulse began to hammer in my chest.

Here goes nothing.

Chapter Twenty-Six

Allie

I was sitting on my bed reading when a soft knock at my door pulled me from the storyline. It was another vampire novel by one of my favourite authors, so as well as proving to be an enjoyable pastime, I could technically class it as research for my own writing too. An effective and satisfying double whammy.

Looking up, I saw Cait's head bob around the doorframe with a smile. 'Hey, Allie, there's someone here to see you.'

Frowning, I placed the book on my bedside table as I slid from the bed and walked towards her. 'Who? Sean?' We didn't have plans, but then again, we never officially had plans any more; he would just turn up whenever he had an hour free. So much for his promise that he was going to 'date me properly'.

'Not quite,' Cait replied cryptically with a wink, before spinning on the spot and practically skipping into her bedroom without another word.

Completely confused and not really in the mood for visitors, I made my way through the bungalow. There was no one around, but the front door was ajar so I made my way towards it and pulled it open before squinting in confusion at the blond, flower-laden stranger before me.

'Hey, my gorgeous girl.'

Whoa. Time. Out.

What the heck? That was definitely Sean's low, raspy voice, but it was coming from a man that looked nothing like Sean. Instead of his deep brown hair this guy had long, blond hair and where I would have expected Sean's bright blue eyes, I was instead being assessed by green pools.

'Sean?' I whispered, completely baffled.

'Yep, it's me, baby,' he confirmed, and as I focused in on his oh-so familiar lips I began to see through the unfamiliar traits to Sean below: the crinkle at the corners of his eyes that I loved, his jawline – that for once was immaculately clean-shaven – not to mention that roguish smirk which was pulling at his lips. This was some seriously good disguise work.

'What do you think?' He gave a spin so I could get a full look at his silly, stubby ponytail and then faced me again, smiling broadly.

'It's amazing.' I gave the new him a close inspection and decided that he was just as breath-taking as ever. My reactions to his handsomeness were just the same; my heart was pounding a furious rhythm, and my body was super-heated and sensitised as if it knew exactly what pleasures this man could bestow upon it if he so chose.

I couldn't help but reach up and gently touch at the hair, which I suppose was some sort of wig. It was a bloody good one because I couldn't see where it joined his head. 'Is it for filming?'

'Nope. It's for you,' he replied, tilting his head. 'As are these,' he added, holding out the huge bunch of beautiful flowers that I'd almost forgotten about in my shock.

'Wow. Th … they're beautiful. Uh … thank you.' I was stuttering like an idiot, but this was all really, really weird.

'I know I promised to court you properly, Allie, and I'm so sorry that I haven't been able to do it as I'd like. But if you're free tonight I was hoping to start making it up to you. Would you like to come out to dinner with me?'

The bizarreness of this just soared several notches higher, but I couldn't help the warmth that rose in my chest at his words or the huge grin that plastered itself all over my face.

'I would love to.'

A breath left Sean's lips, I think one of relief. Did he seriously think I would turn him down? Perhaps he had picked up on my concerns about our relationship in our last few meetings and was worried. 'Shall we go, or do you want to change?' he asked, returning my grin and looking mightily pleased with himself.

'I'll change. Just give me five minutes. Come in. Could you put the flowers in some water for me, please?' As Sean took the bouquet from me I jogged back to my room on cloud nine, thankful that I hadn't removed my make up yet. All I needed was a quick change of clothes and I'd be ready for my date with Sean. Jeez. A date with Sean. I was way more excited than I should be, and quite nervous too, which was silly given how well we knew each other, but this was a big deal – he was taking my concerns seriously and had made a huge effort with his crazy disguise to help get our relationship back on track.

Pulling open my wardrobe, I smoothed my hair as I considered my options. Sean had been quite smartly dressed in a crisp grey shirt and black suit trousers, so I should make an effort too. Selecting a pretty, pale blue summer dress and high heels, I caught sight of my reflection in the mirror and saw happiness pouring from my features. I was practically glowing. I had a date. With Sean. Here in Los Angeles. It was amazing the difference just a few days could make.

As I returned to the lounge I found blond Sean waiting for me with a huge grin on his face. 'You look gorgeous,' he murmured, sliding an arm around my waist to pull me up against him for a heated kiss. Within seconds his tongue was rolling across mine, exploring my mouth with a thoroughness that left me breathless. I could feel his hardness developing against my stomach and couldn't help but press myself closer.

'The thing you do to me,' he muttered, planting a hot kiss on my temple as he recovered his breathing. Leaning back and panting, I stared up into his face and still couldn't quite get over his new look. The hair I could just about deal with, but those green eyes were going to take some getting used to. Apart from the familiarity of his smell and the way he had so capably held me and kissed me, it was almost like being in the arms of a different man.

'Ready to go?'

'Let me just grab a quick glass of water.' I needed some liquid to try and douse the heat he had so skilfully ignited within me.

My closed laptop was sitting on the bar and Sean gave it a tap as I filled my glass. 'I've seen this out surrounded by notes quite a few times. Have you got much writing done since you've been here?'

I took my drink of water and turned to him. 'A little. Probably not as much as I should have,' I admitted with a shrug. There seemed to be an odd, almost panicked look on his face for a brief second, before he blinked and relaxed again. The look completely vanished. What had that been about?

'Shall we go?' he asked, extending a hand to me with a smile. He seemed completely normal again now, so it must just have been the new blond hair and green eyes that made me think he was panicked. Brushing my concern away, I took his hand and let him lead me out of the bungalow and into the warm early evening.

As we strolled through the beautiful tropical gardens, I noticed him wincing and scratching beside his ear.

'Is it uncomfortable?' I watched him run a finger around his forehead just below the hairline and decided that it must be horribly warm wearing a wig in this humid weather.

Giving a shrug he glanced at me again, still looking content and relaxed and I decided that if he were dressed more casually in a shorts and a T-shirt, he'd look quite a lot like a surfer. 'My eyes have adjusted to the contact lenses now, but my head is hot and itchy as hell. I have no idea why people would ever choose to wear these things.' Seeing my guilty glance, he flashed me a wink. 'Don't worry, you're totally worth it, Allie.' My heart just about melted at the purposeful look he gave me. Oh, this man and the things he did to me! Just a few simple words and I felt like a pile of mushy, loved-up female hormones. 'The guy in the make-up department must have thought I'd completely lost it when I asked him to do me up like this, but it works pretty well, I think. At least this way we can go out together tonight.'

We came to the car park and Sean approached a black, open-top muscle car – a Dodge, I think – and held the passenger door open for me. 'Wow. Nice ride,' I commented, realising that this was the first time I'd actually seen the car he drove while in LA.

Just as I lifted my leg to step into the car, Sean caught my eye, a wicked smirk lingering on his lips. 'I could say the same about you,' he murmured softly, his tone low and rough and full of sexy intent. My eyes popped open and I wobbled on my one leg until Sean had to reach out and steady me while I lowered myself into the car. Bloody cheeky bugger. But there was no hiding my blushing cheeks at his compliment.

Blinking down at me smugly, Sean wiggled his eyebrows and closed the car door before walking around to the driver's side. 'Actually, this isn't mine. Some of the really persistent journalists know my car, so I figured a hire car would help us blend it.' Blend in in an open-top, muscle car? Hardly! Although I suppose they were commonplace over here. But the fact that he'd hired a car stuck with me – he'd really put a lot of effort into this date. The thought made me warm inside as a huge smile pulled at my lips.

I had just opened my mouth to ask what car he usually drove, when he distracted me by sliding into the driver's seat and asking one of his own. 'How do you feel about sushi?' he asked, watching my reaction carefully. 'I know it's not everyone's cup of tea so, I have a back-up plan if you don't like it.'

His remark made me realise just how much we still had to learn about each other, but I smiled at his thoughtfulness before nodding. 'I love sushi, and it's been ages since I ate it so that sounds perfect.'

'Great, I was hoping you'd say that because this place is amazing.'

We drove for about ten minutes before Sean pulled the car into an underground car park below a huge, towering skyscraper on Wilshire Boulevard. Frowning, I looked around what appeared to be a business park area. It seemed more like the commercial district than a location for a restaurant. Seeing my confusion, he smiled. 'The restaurant is on the top floor. Trust me, it's good.'

Top floor? Blimey. Once parked, Sean jumped out and dashed around the car to open my door for me. I couldn't help the smile that broke on my lips. Bless him, he really was going all out to 'court' me. His strange green eyes flashed me a wink as he linked his fingers with mine and led me to the lift.

'This feels really weird. Being out in public together, I mean,' I mumbled, fighting the odd sensation of guilt about being out with him, which was ridiculous. I knew the engagement to Savannah was fake, so taking a deep breath I forcibly shoved my silly concerns aside and gave his hand a squeeze, determined to enjoy the evening.

'It doesn't to me. It feels right. Perfect,' he replied softly, his face free of his grin and looking decidedly solemn. Wow. Swallowing loudly, I added that to the list of lovely remarks he had made tonight. In less than an hour, Sean had managed to push away almost all the doubts I had about our relationship. We could do this. It could work.

Once we were safely enclosed within the confines of the reflective elevator, he pressed a button labelled 'Takami Sushi & Robata' then turned to me with a purposeful look that made my stomach clench.

'Twenty-first floor. I think that probably gives me just enough time for this …' I didn't get a chance to ask what 'this' was, because Sean promptly showed me by sliding a hand to the nape of my neck and lunging forward, pressing his lips firmly against mine. Staggering backwards into the wall, the small, silent space was filled with an 'ompf' as the breath was squashed from my lungs in a rush. Using my gasp to his advantage, Sean twirled his tongue with mine, his hands clutching me to him fiercely as he groaned deep into my mouth and thrust his hips urgently against me several times.

His loss of control was such a turn on that I found myself forgetting about our public location and hitching one leg around his hips to join us more intimately at the groin. A strangled cry filled the air, from him or me, I wasn't sure, and Sean pulled back on a curse. 'Stop … for the love of God, make me stop …' I couldn't break the intense eye contact or form words to demand he cease, but I did at least manage to lower my leg back to the ground.

He stared down at me for a few seconds, his eyes awash with emotion before letting out a wry chuckle and soothing my bruised lower lip with a gentle lick. 'You have no idea how close I was to fucking you right here, Allie.' He then placed a peck on the end of my nose which was so chaste it was at complete odds to the heated action of a second ago.

I was an utter mess; my brain was fogged with desire, my legs trembling from the intensity of our kiss, and my heart was still hammering wildly against my ribs. 'I want you so badly,' he muttered, adjusting the bulge in the front of his trousers and raising his hands to help me smooth down my hair.

Jeez. I was aroused beyond my comprehension and I was panting. Hard. I sounded like I was having a flipping asthma attack. Suddenly there was a quiet 'ping', and before I could properly prepare myself, the doors opened to reveal an elderly couple waiting for the carriage.

We all stood still. The only sound filling the space between us was my ragged breathing and it drew the attention of both of them as their pale eyes turned towards me.

Rather abruptly, the pressure of the moment got to me – their peering, beady eyes staring at me, Sean's silly disguise, my panting, not to mention the fact that if we'd pulled apart just a few seconds later they would have gotten a right eyeful of our lusty embrace – and I giggled. It was one of those half giggles, where you know you aren't really supposed to laugh so you try and catch it in your throat like a cough. Unfortunately, that just made me snort like a pig.

Turning desperate eyes on Sean, I saw him squeezing his lips together too, clearly having a similar reaction to me. Or perhaps it was my giggles that had prompted his.

The cherry on the cake came when he casually moved his hands to cover his groin. My eyes darted down with the movement, and the knowledge that he was definitely sporting a hard-on sent me over the edge as more giggly-snorty noises escaped from my throat and wouldn't stop.

'Is she all right?' one of the couple asked as Sean raised one hand to grip my shoulder in an attempt to guide me from the lift.

'She's fine, thank you, just very excited about trying the sushi.' Of course his silly answer did nothing to ease my giggles and by the time we were alone in the small foyer, both of us were laughing.

As we composed ourselves, Sean placed his hands on my shoulders and gazed down at me as his thumbs massaged the bare skin. 'I feel so carefree tonight,' he blurted. 'Being here with you, it's so perfect. I feel like nothing else exists.'

Joining in his soft smile, I had to agree. That was no doubt the reason for my giggling – I felt on top of the world. Sean, who was still looking highly amused, raised a hand, and used his thumb to wipe away the sole tear that had escaped during my laughter. 'Better now, my gorgeous girl?'

'Yes, thank you.' I was still grinning like an idiot, but at least I was a happy, head-over-heels-in-love idiot.

'I'm glad I amuse you,' he murmured with a roll of his eyes. 'Although that wasn't the exact reaction I had been aiming for when I kissed you.'

Oops. Perhaps my giggles had dented his ego, although seeing as this was Sean, sex god extraordinaire, I highly doubted it. Flashing me a wink, he linked our fingers together and led me to the counter in the entryway. Absorbing the lovely warmth from his palm I glanced up at him and shook my head – it was really weird to see him with the blond ponytail.

'Good evening, I have a reservation under the name of Dean Waters.' Oh God, he was using a fake name as well. That was almost enough to make me laugh again, but thankfully my moment of madness seemed to be behind me and I managed to maintain my composure.

I was brought further down to earth as we were guided to a private booth by the window and I saw the stunning views across downtown LA. We were surrounded by shimmering skyscrapers twinkling with lights as the evening darkened around them. Glancing around, I could see why Sean had dressed up too, because although this place wasn't screamingly posh, it was certainly beautifully elegant.

'This is amazing,' I murmured, awed by the place, delicious smells, and peculiar sight of him sitting opposite me. He was still handsome as sin even in a disguise.

Pushing a menu toward me, he pointed to the drinks section. 'I don't drink spirits, but I've been reliably informed by my sister that this place does the best lychee martinis. She always wants to come here when she visits because she reckons this is the best sushi she's ever tasted, and that the martinis are "out of this world".' As he drew out the words I wondered about his sister. I was curious about her, and knowing that she had been the one to pull him out of his self-destructive drink phase I was keen to meet her one day too.

I'd never really tried lychees – they looked a bit too much like eyeballs for my liking – but as the drink came so highly recommended by Evie I could hardly resist, so I ordered one from the pretty waitress who arrived at our table to take our order.

Once Sean had ordered for us – a sharing platter of various Japanese delights – he leant forward and casually began to fiddle with his chopsticks. 'Now, before we eat, I need you to go to the toilet and remove your panties for me.' A small choked noise escaped from my mouth as my eyes darted to Sean in shock. Where the hell had that come from? He was now relaxing back against the booth, looking completely calm and relaxed as if he hadn't just directed me to do something ridiculously naughty in this high-end restaurant.

'What?' I spluttered. Even though I'd heard him perfectly I was doubting whether my ears were actually working.

'You heard me, Allie. Go. Now.'

His commanding tone had me instantly standing up as my core clenched and flooded with arousal, but then I paused and looked down. 'But … but … my dress is really short.' It might have sounded a flimsy excuse, but I wasn't convinced that it would hide my modesty, and the thought of flashing the other posh diners filled me with horror.

Narrowing his eyes on my legs, Sean pursed his lips and then let out a throaty noise of disapproval. 'Shit. You're right.'

Lowering myself into my seat, I was surprised to feel a pang of disappointment at the abrupt end to his planned naughtiness. I'd never really considered myself much of an exhibitionist, but in the lift I'd barely been able to stop myself, and now I was seriously considering throwing caution to the wind and removing my knickers regardless of who saw my pale, white arse. But before I could do anything reckless, Sean stood up, dropped a kiss on the top of my head, and disappeared.

Following his retreating figure, I assumed he was heading to the bathrooms and shook my head as a smile flitted to my lips at his sexy playfulness tonight.

A minute or so later, the waitress arrived at our table with our drinks order. My martini was a pale, creamy, green and decorated with half a lychee still in its pink shell. It looked beautiful. I was taking my first sip when Sean arrived back and stopped beside me instead of re-taking his seat.

'Is the drink good?' he enquired mildly, causing me to nod as I took my first sip of the delicious liquid. 'Good, I'm glad.'

Leaning down, he casually placed a small rectangle of grey material next to my chopsticks and then slipped into his seat opposite with an odd expression on his face that was somewhere between desire and extreme smugness.

Placing my fingers on the material, I found it warm, and looked to Sean in confusion. I already had a napkin, so what was this?

'You can go to the bathroom now and swap your underwear for that,' he said quietly giving a flick of his fingers towards the grey cloth. Still mystified, I picked up the soft material and was about to open it up when Sean leant across and stopped me. 'Uh-uh … not here. Trust me, you'll want to do that in the bathroom. Don't be long.'

Taking his words as my dismissal I left for the toilets and didn't unfold the grey cloth until I was safely inside one of the posh marble cubicles. Holding a corner, I flapped the material open, unsure what I would find, and let out a squeak of surprise.

Pants! The material was his boxer shorts, and I could barely believe it. One of my favourite Calvin Klein pairs, too. Seeing as I was now holding them in my hand, that meant that Sean was going commando in the restaurant, a thought that thrilled me immensely and had me squirming on the spot. Smiling broadly at how ridiculous – yet arousing – all of this was, I relieved myself on the loo and tugged my knickers off.

Holding my underwear in my teeth I turned his boxers around, not convinced that they would fit me, and then stepped into them. A girlish giggle escaped my throat as I had to turn the waistband over twice to get them to stay up, but after faffing for a few minutes, I was in, and they seemed relatively secure and hidden by the length of my dress.

Folding up my own knickers – a very small, lacy pink thong – I held them balled in my hand and walked back to the table hoping that I didn't end up with his boxers around my ankles. Knowing my tendency for clumsiness, I'd place bets on the possibility of falling flat on my face with his pants flapping in the air around one foot and my arse on display to the entire restaurant.

Realistically, I knew that wouldn't happen, not if I walked carefully. I also knew that none of the other diners would know I was holding my knickers and wearing my boyfriend's pants, but by the time I got back to the table, my cheeks were absolutely flaming anyway.

Slipping into the booth, I licked my dry lips then deliberately took my time and had a sip of my drink. I could play at sexy games just as well as him if I put my mind to it, so I decided that if Sean wanted my panties he was going to have to ask for them.

The martini really was delicious, the sweet, cool liquid bolstering my courage as I hummed appreciatively and placed my glass back down, adjusted it on the placemat, and casually raised my eyes to meet his gaze.

What I found were two lust-filled green pools staring back at me with a look so intense that I shuddered from desire. The contacts still seemed odd, but the look he was giving me was so familiar that I managed to overlook them. I could almost see him vibrating from his barely contained excitement until finally, Sean rose to my bait and leant forward, extending one hand, palm upwards.

'I believe you have something for me.'

This was completely crazy. We were in a posh restaurant and I was holding my knickers in my hand, for goodness' sake, but being pulled in by Sean's confident tone I lifted my hand and placed it in his. 'Indeed I do. Hot off the press.' To an outsider it would simply look as if we were sharing an affectionate hand hold during our meal, whereas really, I was handing him a pair of illicitly removed knickers.

Instead of grabbing them immediately, Sean took a second to run his thumb across the side of my hand, the soft, tender action warming me to my core. He looked positively gleeful, not to mention sexy as hell.

'My gorgeous girl. You do have a naughty streak, don't you?'

Chewing on my lower lip, I felt my cheeks heat even further as I gave a shy nod. God knows why I suddenly felt shy – we'd done all manner of things to each other in the past so removing my knickers in public shouldn't be such a big deal.

'Don't look embarrassed, I love that you're adventurous,' he murmured as he took the knickers from my hand and drew his arm back into his lap.

I was about to tell him that I was only adventurous when I had him to guide me, but he surprised me by standing up. 'Right, I'll just go and put these on,' he murmured, his face a picture of utter seriousness. What? My mouth dropped open so fast that my jaw audibly clicked, and then Sean was doubled over with laughter so loud that it briefly drew the attention of a passing waiter.

'I'm kidding!' He dropped back in his seat, chuckling. 'Jesus, can you seriously imagine me wearing these?' He tugged on the thin string that made up the majority of the thong and winced. 'They'd cut my nut sack in half.'

Squashing up my panties into his fist, he lifted his hand and took a sniff. Jesus. I was fast losing count of the number of times my eyes had bulged from their sockets tonight, but no matter how shocked I was I couldn't drag my eyes away from his. He looked so raw, so masculine, and so utterly into me that it felt like the biggest compliment I'd ever been paid.

'You smell fucking amazing, Allie,' he growled heatedly. I had no reply, so I just sat there gawking at him as my body thrummed with arousal. Playing with the lacy material, he smirked at me. 'These are damp. Were you wet for me in the lift? Are you wet for me now?'

Oh. My. God. So we were now officially partaking in dirty-talk slap bang in the middle of a restaurant. His eyebrow raise told me he actually expected an answer, so with a loud swallow I nodded and replied, 'Yes, and yes.'

His cheeks flushed slightly as he tucked my knickers into the pocket of his trousers with the sexiest, darkest smirk on his face.

To my horror, the waitress then arrived with our meal, placing down two large platters of sushi and sashimi, a bowl of pickled ginger, and a bottle of dark soy sauce. Bowing, she retreated and placed a screen across the entrance to our booth to give us some privacy as we ate.

The food looked delicious, but as I caught Sean's gaze I saw that he was completely ignoring the meal and staring fixedly at me instead.

'I want you to touch yourself, Allie. I want to watch you come. I need it. Do you think you could do that for me, here in this restaurant?'

Ho-ly shit. Any thoughts of eating disintegrated at his words as my mouth went dry, but my sex flooded with arousal. It was as if all the moisture in my body had listened to his words and pooled at my core.

This was one of those moments where I effortlessly found myself bowing to his dominance again, and jerkily, my head nodded, causing him to grin in response. 'You don't have to speak, just follow my guidance. Keep your eyes on me at all times, understand?' I was so deeply under his spell that I was only vaguely aware of nodding before he let out a deep, satisfied breath.

'Good girl. Lower your hand now. Dip under that ridiculously short skirt of yours and slip your hand inside my boxers.'

I did as I was asked and sucked in a breath at how sensitive I was. It felt like every nerve ending in my body was pulsing through my groin. My flesh was slick, swollen from arousal and my fingers skated easily down and back up to my clit.

'I ... I'm close already, Sean,' I gasped, my words breathy and thin.

'That's OK, baby, I can see in your face how turned on you are. As you touch yourself I want you to pretend it's me.' I whimpered, desperately wishing that it was him touching me, and knowing that no matter how good this felt, Sean could be making it feel a hundred times better.

'I'm going to talk to you right until you climax, but I don't want you to come without my permission, OK, baby?'

Really? I was so hot for him that I'd almost come just from the first touch of my fingers, and I seriously doubted my ability to control it or hold off my release, but to please him, I nodded.

'Feel those boxers against your hand now? Do you know how hard I was in them earlier? How hard I still am now?' His eyes were burning into me, his posture tight and coiled with expectation. 'In the lift when you were clawing at me with your nails and sucking on my tongue, I was so fucking stiff I nearly came there and then.' A small, soft gasp left my lips as I felt more moisture saturate around my fingers. 'Think of my cock now, Allie, it's so hard again, baby, hard for you. Imagine it touching you, resting against your quivering body.'

It was almost too much, the carnal tone of his voice combined with the vivid images it was creating in my mind were nearly driving me insane. My free hand gripped the edge of the table like a vice in a vain effort to hold back my impending climax. 'Oh God, Sean … please.' I wasn't sure what I was begging for … him to let me come, to stop with dirty talk, or what … but the words just slipped out.

'I'd fuck you so hard, Allie, I'm so turned on that there's no way I could be gentle. Would you want that? Me to take you rough and hard? Fuck you until you begged for release?'

'Oh God … yes …' I was damp with sweat, my skin overheating from the closeness of my release and my attempts to control it, when he finally leant further across the table and peeled my fingers from the wood. Clutching my free hand he nodded, long and slow. 'You need to be quiet now Allie, but you can come. Let it go, baby.'

And I did. Boy, did I. I came like a frigging freight train, my hand gripping Sean's so tightly that he winced, my body clenching and jerking as I came in a series of bone-jarringly deep contractions that had me both breathless and completely exhilarated at the same time. I did somehow manage to remain relatively quiet, although I think a small, needy whimper escaped because at one point, Sean grinned and whispered, 'Shhh …' I just hoped that if anyone had heard it, they might pass it off as a moan of appreciation at the quality of the food.

When my mammoth public climax finally ended, I blew out a breath and released some of my vice-like grip from his hand with an embarrassed giggle.

'That was so fucking hot. Give me your fingers,' Sean ordered in a low tone, holding out his spare hand.

Blinking rapidly, I lifted my hand up – complete with glistening digits – and watched as Sean proceeded to suck them into his mouth and give them a very thorough clean with his tongue. He didn't break his eye contact at all, not the entire time his tongue worked tirelessly around my fingers. It was such an intimate act, and so sensual that if he carried it on for much longer I would soon be ramping up to climax number two.

Finally he deemed my fingers clean enough, and released them from his mouth before taking both of my hands and holding them firmly. 'Holy shit, Allie, you taste so good.' Sean's voice was choked and raspy, as if he was struggling to contain himself, and we both sat in stunned silence for several minutes as we tried to get ourselves back under control.

Glancing sideways at the food, Sean wiggled his eyebrows at me, released my hands, and chuckled. 'I think we might have diverted a little off course there. Just as well sushi is served cold, eh? Shall we get this date back on track and eat?'

After my enormous orgasm I suddenly felt ravenous, but I couldn't help but wonder about Sean's condition, surely after all that he was in need of some release?

'Don't you need to … I mean, shall we … uh … sort you out?' Seeing my flummoxed state, Sean smiled and shook his head.

'No, that was just for you, sweetheart. I enjoyed it immensely, Allie. Watching you come is such a thrill.' He licked his lips and I instantly wanted to lean over the table and kiss the trail of moisture his tongue had left. 'Besides …' He leant in, giving me a conspiratorial look, '… it gets a bit messier for me, especially when I'm as horny as I currently am, so it's probably best not to let it shoot in a restaurant.' If possible, my blush got even deeper, but I nodded in heated agreement and couldn't help but smile when he winked at me and grinned. He looked so happy and carefree, and it was hugely contagious.

'Come on, tuck in. The sushi here is the best I've ever eaten.'

I had to say, the spread did look delicious, and after having another sip of my cocktail I tucked in with gusto.

By the end of the meal, our lusty start had been pushed aside as we enjoyed the opportunity to spend some time together. Sean was chatty and entertaining as always, and I had such a good time that I was thoroughly loved up by the time we got the bill.

Sean's sister had certainly been right about both the martini and the restaurant, because the meal and drinks had been delicious and needless to say, I was now a fan of lychees.

All things considered, this was one of our first real dates since we'd got together. We hadn't ventured out together much in the UK because it had been cold and snowy, and since arriving in LA, our time together had been spent in my hotel suite. After practically living with Sean for the four weeks in the UK I had really missed his company in our months apart, and then this strained time in LA had put further pressure on us as a couple. Just being with him again tonight had made me feel invigorated and alive. I finally felt positive about the future.

Great food, drink, and company. I couldn't think of a better way to spend an evening, and by the time Sean paid the bill, I was drunk with happiness and looking forward to what else the night might hold for us. As Sean took my hand and led me to the lifts, I felt my cheeks flush in anticipation, and as the usual frisson of desire surrounded us in the elevator's enclosed space again, I realised that I couldn't wait.

Chapter Twenty-Seven

Sean

As I drove Allie home with the top down and the warm evening breeze in our hair, I couldn't help the smug curve that came to my lips as I thought over how well our meal had gone.

I had nearly made one fuck-up at the beginning when I'd mentioned seeing her bloody laptop, because the times I'd seen it out were when I'd snuck into her room at night without her knowledge. Luckily she hadn't seemed to realise. Thank God. I wasn't sure how Allie would react if she knew I'd crept in several times to watch her sleep. She probably wouldn't mind, not really, not if I explained how worried I'd been about her back then, but it would certainly give her a clue about just how deep my obsession for her ran, and I wasn't sure that was something she needed to know.

Apart from that one near blip, Allie had been completely relaxed and happy all night, which made me feel on top of the world. Her beautiful face had been alight with joy, reminding me of just how great we'd been back in the UK when we hadn't had all the Savannah shit hanging over us. As well as feeling content, I felt real hope blooming in my chest. We could do this. It would work between us. Thank God for that, because now I'd experienced life with Allie I wasn't sure I could go back to the lonely, insular existence I'd once had.

As I accelerated, Allie's long hair flipped up from her shoulders and across her face, causing her to giggle and smooth it down. The sound of her light laughter brought a grin to my lips. I loved that sound, but more than that, I loved being the cause of it. Yeah, I think I had done pretty well tonight.

Top points, Phillips, for a job well done.

Parking at the hotel, I once again jogged around the car to open the door for Allie. My dad would be proud – I was killing it on the gentleman stakes tonight: I'd opened doors, helped her from the car, and bought flowers. Except for the part where I'd jumped her in the lift and shoved my tongue into her mouth and thrust my groin against her. That wasn't perhaps the most gentlemanly of acts … but I'd needed to do it.

My smile spread to a full grin as I remembered her face when I demanded she take off her knickers. It had been touch and go, and I'd thought I might have gone a step too far for a few seconds, but no. My girl had stepped up to the challenge like a pro. Fuck. She was so sexy it was unbelievable. I couldn't get enough of her, and watching her come had been fucking incredible.

All in all, it had felt liberating to be out in public with Allie tonight. As good as the wig had done me, I couldn't wait until this mess with Savannah was cleared up so I could take Allie out for real. That thought caused a smile to split on my lips as I pulled her door open and held out my hand.

As Allie stepped from the car and stood beside me, she treated me to another of her gorgeous, shy smiles. I loved her smile. She was so beautiful. And all mine. Linking my hand through hers, I took great pleasure in the way her fingers tightened around mine, and then added yet another gentlemanly act to my list by walking her through the lush gardens to her bungalow.

Once we had reached the door she turned to me with pink cheeks and a seductive twinkle in her eye that sent a jolt straight to my groin. 'Will you stay? I would love to wake up in your arms, Sean, it's been so long.' Licking her lips she seemed to flutter her eyelashes almost bashfully. 'Too long,' she added persuasively, her tone low and husky.

God, I wanted to. Right now I was so loved up that I would like nothing more than to flip her over my shoulder, carry her to the bedroom, and throw her on the bed before having my wicked way with her. But I couldn't.

Reluctantly, I shook my head, knowing that with my early start tomorrow I really needed to head home and sleep. If I stayed with Allie in her bed, there was no way I would be sleeping. 'I can't, Allie, I'm sorry.' The disappointment I saw springing to her eyes made me feel like such a shit, but it was soon gone as she schooled her features into a more neutral expression. My heart sank. Shit, right before my eyes Allie was pulling away from me again.

'Oh, OK,' she murmured, her eyes flickering away as her expression became oddly bland. This was the same detached look she had given me when I'd been trying to explain about the situation with Savannah. Fuck. 'I understand. I'm sure you have to get back,' she murmured, her lip curling as if in distaste. Get back? Oh shit ... did she think I was leaving to go back to Savannah? 'Its fine, Sean.' But her voice didn't sound fine. At all.

'I have an early shoot, I didn't think you'd want me to wake you up in the middle of the night ...' But my voice faded off as I saw the accepting melancholy on her beautiful face. Damn. Had I blown all of my good work this evening by saying I wasn't staying over? I had been trying to be considerate, I didn't think Allie would appreciate my 3:30 a.m. alarm, but maybe I should have stayed anyway.

Was it too late to change my mind? Probably – it was ten already, so if I stayed I'd get barely any sleep and then turn up at the studios tomorrow with bags under my eyes that would make my director freak out.

Desperate to make things right, I reached out for her hand and pulled her limp fingers toward me, but when she continued to stare off over my shoulder, I used my free hand to cup her chin and angle her face towards mine.

Locking eyes with her, I hit her with my most sincere, honest look. 'I'm not going back to her, Allie. That's not what this is about. I have a really early shoot, that's all. I'm on set for four a.m.'

Allie's eyes remained fixed with mine and finally, after what seemed like an eternity, she nodded.

'Believe me, I want nothing more than to spend the night with you, my gorgeous girl, but right now I want you so much that I know I wouldn't get any sleep if I stayed, and I have a twelve hour shoot tomorrow.' I couldn't believe I was once again putting work above my girl. Thank God my night shoots would be over soon, cutting my schedule down and allowing me to spend some proper quality time with her. 'This is my last manic week, then my hours lessen and we'll be able to see more of each other, I promise.'

My words must have sunk in, because the fragile, uncertain expression began to melt from Allie's face as a small smile curled her lips. 'OK, I'm sorry,' she murmured. Cutting off any further words, I lowered my head and felt the familiar, exciting tingle of our connection as our mouths joined and I relaxed against her, causing her hands to slide up and around my neck.

After a moment or two of heady kisses I pulled back, well aware that my libido was moments away from guiding me into her bed for the night regardless of my schedule tomorrow. 'I'll find a way for us to be together soon, I promise.' As I lowered my head for one final kiss, an idea occurred to me and I leant back and grinned. 'Actually, how do you feel about art?'

Seeing her confused expression, I raised a hand and smoothed some wayward hairs back from her face. 'The studios I work with are joining with some fancy art gallery Downtown for an exhibition next Wednesday. I have to attend with the cast, but I have two spare tickets. Would you like to come?' Watching her carefully I could see from the twinkle in her eye that my girl was tempted. 'Perhaps you could bring Cait? I couldn't talk to you a great deal while we were there, but I could arrange so we could sneak off together afterwards? I'm not working the following day either, so maybe we could spend it together?'

My girl chewed on her lower lip for a moment or two before an excited glint entered her eyes and she nodded. 'OK, sounds interesting.' It certainly did – perhaps the idea of sneaking around thrilled Allie as much as it did me.

Phew. It seemed that I was forgiven.

That had been a close one. Bloody hell. Relationships could be such a fucking nightmare at times.

Chapter Twenty-Eight

Cait

Sipping the deliciously cool glass of champagne that had just been thrust into my hand by an over-eager waitress, I narrowed my eyes on Allie. 'How the hell did you blag entry to this?' I asked in bewilderment, as I watched yet more Hollywood greats float past me towards the rear of the art gallery. This event – whatever the heck it was for – was flooded with famous people. I'd never seen so many diamonds, Rolexes, and flashy fake smiles in my life.

God, we were so out of place it was almost laughable.

Giving a casual shrug, Allie smiled secretively and sipped her champagne. She wasn't saying, but I suspected Sean had sorted out tickets for us.

Thinking of Sean, my cheeks heated. I had barely been able to look him in the eye since I'd accidentally walked in on him and Allie playing tonsil tennis in the library. The image of his excitement straining at his shorts seemed to be ingrained into my mind, causing me to blush like a tomato whenever I saw him and making me feel like a right perv. Rather annoyingly, every time I had seen Sean since it had also triggered me to remember the colourful visions about Jack I'd had in the corridor, which invariably led to my cheeks heating even more. It was a bloody nightmare.

Catching another glimpse of Sean though the crowd I quickly looked away and sipped my drink as a distraction. He must be behind this, I couldn't see any other way that two nobodies like Allie and me would manage to get entry. Ever since they had had their heated make-up session, Sean had been trying to smooth the issues in their relationship by creating opportunities for the two of them to spend some time together; it had been a sushi date last week, and a bagel delivery the week before, so I suspected this was his latest attempt. If he was trying to impress Allie with his star-studded lifestyle, then this was a pretty good way to go about it.

Looking around again I noticed that the crowd of guests had grown significantly, and I tried to supress my panic and look as if I fitted in. Even with my back straight as a rod and with my floor-length dress, fancy shawl, and heels on, I still felt decidedly like the odd one out surrounded by such opulence and glamour.

Glancing towards the door, I felt my eyes widen as my mouthful of champagne seemed to get stuck my throat. Oh God, this was all I needed. The traitorous bubbles began flooding up my nose and burning the roof of my mouth until I finally managed to force it down with a very inelegant splutter.

Following my line of sight, I heard Allie chuckle next to me. 'Ah, the next batch of A-listers are arriving,' she murmured, obviously misreading my shock and thinking I was just reacting to the big shot celebrities now entering the gallery. I couldn't care less about most of the new faces, but one stood out as all too familiar. Jack Felton.

I suppose his arrival shouldn't have surprised me. Given the other famous faces I'd seen tonight it seemed like all the elite of Los Angeles had turned up. Against my will I felt a shimmer of reaction as I looked at him dressed up in a tux again. My mouth dried and I practically downed my entire glass of champagne. Clearly the time that had passed since I'd last seen him had done nothing to ease my crush, because my body was practically thrumming with alertness, and it was a feeling that I found particularly unnerving.

Leaning in closer to my ear while still keeping her gaze on the crowd of familiar faces from magazines and films,

Allie lowered her voice to a soft whisper. 'Don't worry, they still have that effect on me. Sean thinks I'm stupid, but they're famous people, aren't they? It's crazy.'

Finally ripping my gaze away from Jack – the man who had featured in several of my dreams this week – I turned to Allie with wide eyes as my nerves immediately kicked in and my forefinger began to go to work on my elastic band at hyper-speed. 'It is, totally crazy. But I'm not staring at them, I'm looking at him,' I said, tipping my chin at Jack as he took a glass of champagne from a server and began to gaze around the room.

Allie frowned, her gaze flicking to my hand and the furious tugging of my elastic band and then slapped my wrist before narrowing her gaze on me. 'Stop picking. What's got you so wound up?' Rubbing my wrist, I frowned, but almost immediately felt my body dying to turn around and look at Jack again. Not that I would indulge it. I needed to end this stupidity right now and forget that he was even here. I would not turn around.

'That's Jack Felton. Why are you looking at him?' Allie asked, before grinning, 'Oh yeah, I remember! He's the one you like in that TV show, isn't he?' She commented curiously as she peeked over my shoulder towards the group.

'Yep. The very same.'

'I can see why you like him. He is rather handsome.'

Handsome? Yes, there was no denying he was definitely that. He was also my 'Mr Flirty' from the bar the other week. A man whom I never dreamt I would actually meet, and now, not only had I literally run into him one week and shared a drink with the next, but he was now at the same bloody event as me. Fate clearly had it in for me, although I suppose I could blame Allie's relationship with Sean for tonight's Jack sighting. Obviously by socialising with Sean we had inadvertently slipped into the circle of famous people he was friends with.

I just couldn't believe it. Half of me was horrified, but the other half – clearly my reckless side – was practically dancing a can-can of joy at his unexpected arrival.

Angling myself so he wouldn't be able to see me, I looked back at my Allie and decided that it was probably time to come clean with her. 'Umm. You remember the other week when I came back to the hotel late and Julie rang you because I'd vanished from the hostel?'

Allie paused for a second, thinking back, and her eyes widened. 'Oh my God, yes! We never got around to talking about where you were! And then all that stuff with Sean happened and I kinda forgot … I feel terrible now. What a rubbish friend I am. You still want to talk about what you were doing?'

Swallowing loudly at the thought of confessing, I felt my heart accelerate in my chest. 'Him.' I jerked my thumb over my shoulder. 'Although obviously I wasn't actually doing him! But I was with him,' I whispered, not even daring to say his name out loud. Thinking of the looks he gave me and how close I'd come to kissing him, I tilted my head thoughtfully. 'I probably could have done him though, if I'd wanted.'

'You and Jack Felton? Yeah right,' Allie replied with a grin. 'Dream on, Cait. Come on, what were you really doing?'

She didn't believe me? She thought I was joking? This was priceless…

'I was with him, honestly. I bumped into him while out running when I first arrived, and then he was at some premiere thing at the theatre and recognised me so we went for a drink.' It sounded too far-fetched, so I could see why Allie wouldn't believe me, but what else could I say? It was true. End of.

261

'So now you're saying you've met him twice?' She clearly didn't believe me. Perhaps she thought I'd finally lost my marbles. Perhaps I had.

'Umm … yeah. I guess tonight makes three.' Glancing briefly to the spot where he'd been, I frowned when he was no longer there, and found my eyes skimming the room to see where he'd gone.

To my surprise, I saw he was making his way through the crowd, seemingly making a beeline for us. Once he was only a few feet away I swallowed nervously and watched in stunned shock as his gaze lingered on me for a second before he turned to Allie with a polite smile.

'Allie? Am I correct?' he said, quickly checking out the visitor pass around her neck. They had our full names on them, which I had thought was overkill at first but now I'd had a look at all the A-listers present I could understand the security measures.

Shooting me a confused look, Allie turned back to Jack and nodded. 'Uh, yes.'

'I'm Jack, a close friend of Sean's,' he said in a conspiratorial whisper, as if she wouldn't know who he was. 'He wanted me to pass on a message to you. He says you look gorgeous, and that the plans for seeing you are all set. He'll call you at ten, so have your phone on.'

I watched as Allie's cheeks flushed crimson, and she nodded her thanks while trying – and failing – to wipe the gigantic grin from her face. So I'd been right; our attendance this evening had been set up by Sean.

'Caitlin, it's a pleasure to see you again,' Jack said, turning those dark eyes on me and hitting me with a megawatt smile that made me feel a little bit breathless. I heard Allie gasp, and almost wanted to turn to her with a smug grin for being proven right, but I didn't. I kept my full attention on the handsome man gazing at me. It didn't escape my notice that he also checked out my name badge.

'You both look stunning tonight,' he added in a low murmur, and though he was supposedly addressing both of us, Jack's eyes never left mine, causing my skin to heat and prickle under his close inspection.

After several seconds where some tension seemed to build between us, Jack broke the spell by turning his gaze toward Allie with a pleasant smile. 'Well, it's a genuine pleasure to meet you, Allie. Sean has told me an awful lot about you.'

'All good I hope,' Allie replied, preening and blushing and causing Jack to nod. After a second, his eyes flickered back to me curiously as he tilted his head, 'I have to admit, after you said you'd be flying out soon I didn't think I'd see you again. I thought you'd be long gone by now, off to some far flung destination,' Jack said with a quick wink, which knocked me completely off balance. Never before had I had such bizarre reactions to a man, but with Jack I felt like I was constantly floundering. My face was now burning from his undivided attention and his scent, spicy and sweet, was invading my senses and making me dizzy.

'Um ... no. Not yet.'

As if that wasn't bad enough, Allie chose that moment to wiggle her eyebrows and then excuse herself to go to the toilet, leaving me alone to cope with Jack. Marvellous. Some best friend she was! I couldn't believe she had deserted me.

With Allie now gone, I took a shaky sip of champagne to wet my parched throat and gave myself a quick telling off. After all, he wasn't touching me or intruding on my personal space, and he had proven himself to be a perfect gentleman more than once, so I really needed to relax.

'So, how are you, Caitlin?' How was I? Pretty much on the verge of a panic attack, that's how I was. Our near kiss was suddenly at the forefront of my mind, and my eyes kept drifting to his mouth of their own accord, wondering for the millionth time if he would have been gentle, or rough like Greg used to be. Much to my relief he didn't seem to notice.

'I'm fine thank you, feeling a little out of place here but OK,' I joked. He didn't try to probe further into my reasons for declining his date, thank goodness, and after several minutes alone with him exchanging small talk, I began to feel slightly more stable and even managed a weak smile or two in his direction.

'Jack!' The sound of his name being called caused us both to turn in the direction of the voice, and I saw a photographer waving at him.

Looking back at me with a grimace, he rolled his eyes. 'Well, duty calls. I'd better go. It was lovely talking to you again, Caitlin.' I'd felt nervous about being alone with him, but now he was leaving I stupidly didn't want him to go.

'OK, bye Jack.'

After one more lingering glance, he turned and left and I immediately dumped my glass on the bar and sagged against the rail as I tried to steady my hammering pulse. Blimey, that man was handsome. Allie must have been hiding out and watching our interaction, because no sooner had Jack left than she was rushing back to my side with eyes like saucers.

'Ohmygod!' Her words came out as one long exhalation as she grabbed hold of my upper arms and practically shook me. 'You were telling the truth!' Her face was flushed, eyes wide, and a grin was curving her mouth to the point where she actually looked a bit manic.

Leaning to the side so she could see round me again, she stared over my shoulder for a second before focusing her eyes back on mine.

'He could barely take his eyes off of you. Ho-ly. Shit. Cait.' Her response was drawn out, as if each separate word was its own sentence, then blinking back to reality she jerked her thumb toward the back of the gallery. 'We need to talk. Right now.'

As we made our way towards a quiet corner, I was suddenly stopped by a hand on my wrist, and my first thoughts were that it was Jack again. 'Hey, beautiful. You seem to be empty-handed. Can I get you a drink?' That wasn't Jack's voice, and instinctively I felt my entire body tense as I tried, and failed, to get my wrist back. Turning my body, I had to look up to see the face of my unwanted companion because he was surprisingly tall, but I recoiled even more as panic swiftly gripped me – I didn't recognise him, but the stranger had exactly the same colour hair as Greg, and the memories it jerked in my brain immediately made me want to vomit.

'Get off me,' I demanded, hoping he didn't hear the slight desperation in my voice.

My breathing had risen to short, sharp pants, but seeing the frown settle on his brow as he looked towards my hands I glanced down and realised belatedly that he had already let go. How embarrassing. My mind had gone into overdrive and as a result I was overreacting and had been on the verge of making a scene in the middle of this fancy gallery.

'I just wondered if you wanted a drink,' he said defensively, now looking decidedly like he wanted to get away from me, and to be honest I couldn't really blame him.

'I … uh … sorry. I have to go,' I mumbled, stepping back and spinning in the direction that Allie had gone. God, I felt like a wreck. Seeing a server with a tray of champagne, I swiped two with my trembling hands and handed one to Allie as I joined her.

Apparently oblivious to my close encounter she leant forward with her eyes twinkling. 'Jack Felton? I want details, woman,' she said, her face a mixture of concern, excitement, and downright shock.

Trying to settle myself, I thought back to Jack and how best to explain it all. Starting at the beginning I recounted my run-in with him in the park weeks ago, and went on to explain about the night at the theatre where the hostel girls had been celebrity spotting. I told Allie how I'd sat on the side-lines until Jack had literally vaulted off the red carpet and persuaded me to go for a drink with him. The vaulting part had caused Allie to squeal almost gleefully.

When I finished my story by giving her the details of how he nearly kissed me and how I'd nearly let him, Allie downed half of her champagne and stared at me with huge eyes.

'So why did you stop him?' she asked quietly, but the tone of her voice told me she already understood.

Blinking slowly, I sighed and looked at her with a resigned expression. 'Same old reason,' I whispered. Allie touched my shoulder supportively and gave a small, sad smile. 'Yeah, apparently all that counselling hasn't exactly cleared up my issues with men,' I summarised, trying to keep my tone as light as I could.

Allie nodded, but I could see the underlying disappointment in her features. To be honest, I was disappointed in myself. I'd not been remotely interested in any man for years, but last week some part of me had actually wanted Jack to kiss me – perhaps even wanted more – and yet I'd stopped him.

Giving me a playful nudge in the ribs, Allie winked at me. 'Well, knock me down with a feather. Cait Byrne went out for drinks with a man. I never thought I'd see the day,' she joked, apparently noticing how I was mentally beating myself up and trying to lighten the mood.

Nodding, I allowed myself to swivel marginally and scan the room for Jack. He was now standing with Sean involved in what appeared to be a rather jovial conversation because the two of them were both grinning broadly.

'He's a good looking guy,' Allie murmured, mirroring my own thoughts. 'He looks a bit older than Sean. Is he?'

Nodding, I sighed and turned away from him again. 'Yeah, but not by much. I think he's nearly forty. To be honest, I didn't really think I'd ever see him again,' I remarked quietly. For my sanity it would probably have been better if I hadn't.

'He's got that calm, handsome maturity thing going on. I can see why you like him.'

Defensive instinct very nearly had me claiming that I didn't like him, but that would have been a lie. From what I'd learnt about him the other night, which admittedly was limited, I did like Jack, and there was no denying that I was attracted to him, but what it really came down to was one single fact – I was scared.

Scared of opening myself up to the vulnerability of getting hurt again, scared that he might treat me like Greg had, but mostly, scared to give up the fierce independence that I'd built up over the last four years.

I would no doubt get emotional if I confessed those feelings to Allie, which wouldn't be ideal in the middle of a swanky gallery, so instead I closed the door on them – something I was particularly good at – and grinned at her.

'How crazy have our lives become? You dating Sean Phillips, and me getting asked out by Jack Felton!'

The mouthful of champagne that Allie was currently sipping was suddenly spraying very inelegantly from her mouth and dribbling from her nose. 'He asked you out?' she hissed, frantically wiping her face with the serviette in her hand.

'Uh … yes. I might have left that part of the story out,' I admitted with a small smile.

'You definitely bloody did leave that part out!' Getting rid of her empty glass and scrunched up napkin, Allie turned back to me with raised, expectant eyebrows, so with a roll of my eyes I filled her in.

'At the bar he said he'd enjoyed himself, and asked if we could meet up before I left. I said no. Then, later in the car when he dropped me back at the hotel he asked me to go for lunch with him the following day.' I gave a casual shrug, as if getting asked out by a movie star (twice) was a regular, run-of-the-mill occurrence.

'And you obviously said no again,' Allie concluded, looking thoughtful. After a few seconds, she chewed on her lower lip and then took my hand, giving it a squeeze. 'Do you not think that maybe it's time to try and trust a man again?' she asked gently. 'I know what Greg did to you was evil, but that's the past now. Travelling has been so good for you, Cait, you're so much stronger.' But even with her soft approach and complimentary words I felt my throat tightening.

'I know …' I agreed. I was stronger in my confidence and mental attitude, but still, this was Jack Felton we were talking about. 'You're right, and I have moved on. Actually, the way I felt with Jack was kind of an eye-opener – I'd almost thought I'd never feel a connection with a man again.' Turning my gaze across the room, I caught a brief glimpse of him posing for a photograph with Sean, their faces illuminated by the flash of the camera, both looking composed and handsome beyond words.

My stomach tightened as I watched him, but shaking my head, I looked back at Allie. 'But he's hardly an ideal target for my first steps back into dating, is he? It's unlikely that a man with such a busy career would be looking for anything more than a quick fling, and seeing as I have cartloads of baggage, not to mention how inexperienced I am, that's not exactly the type of guy I need.' Suddenly, a chuckle rose in my throat. 'Not forgetting the fact that he's a flipping movie star and I'm a travelling hippy searching for my destiny.'

'Hey, relationships with famous people can work out,' Allie interjected defensively, and I only just refrained from commenting how her time with Sean hadn't been hassle-free up to now and still wasn't exactly on a smooth path.

Drawing in a deep breath, I composed myself and pushed my shoulders back. 'I don't think I'm ready for a relationship yet. Anyway, I need to work on lowering my defences and building up trust.' Seeing Allie's disappointed look I shook my head confidently. 'It's fine. I'm going to use this experience as a positive step in the right direction, maybe start to see if I can build up some friendships with guys I meet travelling. Take it one step at a time.'

Narrowing her eyes, Allie finally gave in with an accepting sigh. 'OK, I suppose you have a point. I think the idea of getting some male friends is a really good one.'

Allie and I continued our conversation, gradually drifting away from me and towards the subject of Savannah and Sean. Allie said she was fine with the fact that Savannah was due to arrive at the gallery at any point, but as time wore on, I could see her eyes flicking towards the door whenever anyone entered, and couldn't help but worry about how my friend would cope with this first, real life sighting of her boyfriend's fake fiancée.

I let out a small, dry chuckle at how strange our lives were. Allie was attempting to deal with the imminent arrival of a woman that she was basically considering as her competition for Sean, and I was almost thrumming with the knowledge that Jack Felton, movie star, and my recent new acquaintance, was standing somewhere in the same room as me.

'I'm going to see if I can sneak a quick word with Sean. I'll be back in a bit.' Allie murmured, apparently keen to speak to him before Savannah arrived.

I wandered around the exhibits, rather drawn to some of the works but quietly appalled by others. The painting I was currently standing by was ghastly, not my taste at all, comprised of messy swirls of brown, red, and orange. In my mind it resembled an unwashed wall from a slaughterhouse.

The hideous painting distracted me so much that I didn't even notice anyone coming up beside me until Jack's low, raspy voice washed over me. 'So, are you enjoying the exhibition?' he queried softly, his sudden appearance making me jump.

Whipping my head around, I found him watching me intently, but still giving me space. The hairs on my arms stood up at his close proximity and I frowned, not liking the way my body kept reacting to his presence.

'Uh … yeah, it's great. Although this piece is a little …' I stopped myself, cautious in case he somehow knew the artist.

Leaning closer, he grinned. 'It's monstrous, isn't it?' A relieved giggle rose in my throat and I nodded, sharing a small smile with him before turning my gaze away. This was crazy. My stomach was turning somersaults and I suddenly felt clammy and hot. Jack just made me feel things I wasn't equipped to deal with, at all. Worse than that, he made me want things I wasn't equipped to deal with. I really needed to create some distance between us, so perhaps if I just stayed quiet he'd eventually lose interest and move away.

Thankfully, Jack seemed more than happy to lead the conversation with small talk about the event and the pieces of art he most admired, most of which also appealed to my tastes, while I simply averted my eyes and studied the champagne flute clutched in my hand with great enthusiasm.

After several minutes where I had barely looked at him or uttered a single word, Jack paused. 'I'm not that boring, am I?' he remarked quietly, trying to draw my attention. Wincing, I knew my silence had probably come across as rude, but my politeness wouldn't allow me to flat out ignore him no matter how strangely he made me feel, so taking a deep breath I summoned some inner courage, straightened my back, and looked straight at him.

I decided to do what I'd watched Allie do all night when conversing with celebrities: talk politely for a few minutes, boost their ego a bit with some flattery, and then escape. Probably to grab a large recovery vodka.

'Not at all. Sorry, I'm just tired and my mind wandered off for a second.' I knew I was being far less friendly than on the night we'd spent in the bar, but I was tense and my defences were up now. I needed to be cool, calm, and confident, avoid all talk of our near kiss, and then excuse myself from his company.

The near kiss. Oh, God. Why had I even thought about it? Because now it was all I seemed to be able to focus on. That and my vivid imaginings of what Jack would have been like, the feel of his breath whispering across my lips as he'd leant closer, the spicy, sweet smell of his aftershave, the way my body had instinctively wanted to lean into his, the gentleness with which his tongue might have explored my mouth …

'You've gone rather pale, Caitlin, are you all right?' Jack asked, breaking me from my trace with a jolt. Flicking my panicked eyes to his I found concern etched on his face as he studied me and I felt my cheeks flame.

I didn't feel sick, but I could well believe that I might look it after those potent visions. Being here with him and trying to act nonchalant when my body was vibrating with

271

the need to move closer to him was draining beyond all belief.

'I'm just tired,' I replied, and I really was. Tired of being an emotional freak. I still wasn't entirely sure why I felt like this towards Jack, but obviously nothing could, or would, ever come of it, so I really needed to find an excuse to move away from him.

As if answering my prayers for help, my phone suddenly started to ring in my handbag. Flashing an apologetic look at Jack, who looked slightly perturbed that I was even bothering with my phone when I had him to talk to, I dug it out and saw Julie's number flashing up. My escape route. Thank God. I'd planned this phone call earlier tonight; my get-out plan in case the exhibition was dull or stressful and I'd needed a way to leave. The exhibition hadn't been dull, far from it, but flashing another look at Jack's devastatingly handsome profile, I swallowed hard. I definitely needed an escape route … just for different reasons than I'd expected.

'I'm sorry, I have to take this …' I mumbled, hoping I sounded apologetic. Jack frowned slightly, but almost immediately regained his manners, cleared his face, and nodded. 'Of course.'

Almost sagging with relief, I turned away and accepted the call. 'Hi, Julie,' I said in a rushed breath, but before I could take a step away, I felt a hand on my lower back. My eyes immediately closed as a pleasant warmth shot up my spine, and I sucked in a huge lungful of air. How the hell did he do this? Instead of making me feel uncomfortable as physical contact always did, Jack's touch somehow transferred a reassuring heat into my skin. I could almost say I was starting to enjoy it … which terrified me.

Turning to Jack warily, I saw him snatching back his hand and seeming to chastise himself for touching me as he bit back a curse. Frowning as I watched him shove his hands into his pockets, I swallowed hard as it became apparent that he'd remembered my anxiety towards physical contact.

I was fighting against the peculiar reactions that I had to Jack, but there was no denying it; at the five points where his fingers had been there were still fizzing tingles shooting across my skin, causing my already troubled thoughts to spiral. Glancing down at the phone still clutched in my hand, I heard Julie's voice squawking through the hand piece and lifted it to my ear. 'Hang on, I'll just be a second.'

There was no way I was hanging up. Julie was my route out of here and with my body reacting so strangely I knew I had to get away as fast as I could.

Now that I had paused, Jack dug into his jacket pocket, removed his wallet, and extracted what looked like a business card before holding it out to me. Wow. After refusing him already I hadn't expected this move. He was certainly persistent, which really wasn't helping with my determination to create distance between us. Staring mutely at the card, I noticed it was classy-looking, printed on thick, cream paper with simple black italics across the centre stating just his name and two phone numbers.

'In case you need me for anything,' he murmured. There seemed to be a strange twinkle in his eye as he spoke. Was he coming on to me? I had so little experience with dating, flirting, and seduction that I wasn't sure. Maybe he was just used to being so attractive that women always made the first move and he found my reluctance a challenge? That idea annoyed me, and even though it was just my own assumptions, it instantly dulled any lingering curiosity.

Glancing at the business card still held in his outstretched hand, I schooled my features to be as blank as possible and looked to Jack's face. His very, very handsome face. It almost killed me, but I levelled my voice and delivered the best cut-off line I could manage.

'I can't see why I'd need you,' I stated, then without accepting his card or even saying goodbye, I turned on my heel and strutted out of the gallery with the phone clutched in my hand and my heart racing behind my ribs.

Did I really just say that? To him?

By the time I finally put the phone to my ear again, Julie was calling my name loudly, trying to get my attention. 'I'm here, sorry about that.' I was speaking to Julie, all the while debating whether I'd just been incredibly rude, incredibly stupid, or perhaps both, by declining Jack's number.

'Your voice sounds funny,' Julie said curiously. 'Who were you just talking to?'

Images of Jack popped instantly into my mind and I struggled to push them away as I rolled my lips between my teeth almost to the point of pain. 'No one. Thanks for calling, I'm outside now, so the call worked. I'll pop by the hostel next week and see you for a cuppa at some point.'

'OK. You sure you don't need me to come and get you?'

'Nah, I've got a cab number, but thanks, Julie.'

After I hung up, I took a few steps down the street before pausing and digging into my handbag for the emergency flip-flops I kept there. Easing my protesting feet from the ridiculously high heels I'd managed to survive in all evening, I let out a sigh of relief and sent Allie a text to tell her I was leaving.

Stepping into the trusty flats, I heard my phone beep almost immediately with a message from her telling me she was still intent on meeting Sean.

Dialling a cab number – a company that could guarantee a female driver if you requested one, which I always did – I stood gazing at the rush of cars speeding by and thought back over the last few minutes.

Had I really just walked away from Jack Felton, heartthrob and all-round sex symbol? A small bubble of near hysterical laughter rose in my throat as I recalled how

I'd described him to Julie as 'no one'. He was about as far from a 'no one' as you could get.

The evening might have added more confusion to my already muddled emotions, but one thing was sure in my mind – from the almost violent way I'd reacted to his touch, it was clear that he would be way too easy to fall for. Nothing good could come of spending more time with Jack Felton. I was damaged goods. A freak. Nodding my head decisively, I leant against the wall to wait for my taxi, knowing I'd been sensible to walk away.

Jack

I hated events like this, full of stuck-up, prissy arseholes air-kissing the cheeks of their bitter rivals, fawning over directors in the hopes of landing the next big role, and basically being utterly obnoxious. Thank God Sean was here. At least that was one face I knew I could converse with normally.

After Caitlin's abrupt departure, I stopped off at the bar to gather myself for a few minutes. I hadn't in a million years expected her to be here – in fact, I hadn't expected to ever see her again – and it had floored me. Completely. Not to mention how gorgeous she'd looked in that long, jade dress. As well as showing off her fabulous figure the colour had made her hazel eyes stand out and sparkle even more than usual. With her perfect posture, light make-up, and beautiful attire, she had screamed elegance and I'd been so desperate to get to know her better that I'd very nearly followed her out of there.

Fuck. I ordered a single malt whisky on the rocks and leant on the counter as I steadied my erratic breathing. That girl just kept getting better and better. The first time we'd met I'd liked what I'd seen and she'd only been wearing her sweaty gym gear. Then at the theatre she'd had on that tunic dress which had hinted at a toned body underneath it, but tonight in that sleek dress … Wow. Even with the thin shawl she'd used to cover her arms, there was no disguising how the dress clung to her figure, and it had been enough to get my imagination going wild. She might try to hide it, but now I knew for sure she had a fabulous figure. It had nearly done me in.

Frowning, I stared down at my drink and swilled the amber liquid slowly in the glass. She had rejected me. Again. And pretty harshly too. As I recalled her final goodbye to me, I winced. I can't see why I'd need you. Christ, that had been a pretty big knock back.

Regardless of the battering my ego was taking at her hands, there was something about her that drew me in. It was a shame she obviously had some sort of issue with men. Or was it just me? That was an irksome thought that I didn't like in the slightest. The other week in the bar when I'd placed my hand on her back, I'd felt her entire body freeze. It was almost as if she had been repelled by me, and the panicked tone in her voice when she asked me not to touch her had made me feel instantly guilty.

As I recalled tonight's events, I relaxed marginally. It couldn't just be me, because I'd watched a random man try to get her attention by taking hold of her wrist and I had seen the reaction again first-hand. Real fear had crossed her features for a second or two before she managed to gather herself, and then although she hadn't looked scared, she'd definitely remained rigid and cold.

It was just as well he'd let go of her, really, because some possessive part of me had been on the verge of barrelling over there to intervene. She'd been fine a second or so later when a female server had brushed against her, so I could only deduce that something had happened to her to make her wary of men.

As much as she presented a challenge, that wasn't what was drawing me to Caitlin. Her fragility was very endearing, making me want to take care of her, which was absurd because she could clearly do that herself, but still, it was there, a definite and powerful spark between us. I was almost certain Caitlin felt it too. I could see it in her eyes, and at the bar I'd known she'd wanted me to kiss her. Not that I was helping matters, because I kept on slipping up and touching her. I just couldn't seem to help myself.

Sighing, I slung back the fiery liquid in my glass and ordered another. I hadn't felt a connection like this in a very long time. If only Caitlin had been willing to open herself up and let us explore that connection. But that thought wasn't worth dwelling on; she was off travelling soon so it was highly unlikely that I'd ever see her again. I'd lost my chance.

From the corner of my eye I could see a bleach blonde woman sidling her way along the bar towards me. Casting a brief glance in her direction, I saw fake breasts, a Botoxed brow, and some seriously white teeth. Crikey, those things were so bright they probably glowed in the dark. Time to make a break for it. Grabbing my glass, I pushed away from the bar and thanked all things holy when I saw Sean standing on his own by a high table staring out across the crowded room.

'No plastic surgery. No enhancements. She's not even got fake nails and Allie is still the most gorgeous woman here,' he said, not even looking my way when I approached. Following his line of sight I saw Allie talking to a small group of people, none of whom I recognised.

Looking back at my friend, I raised an eyebrow at his smitten expression, but seeing as I also had one woman taking up residence in my mind, I could hardly criticize him for it.

I knew I shouldn't pursue my unhealthy interest in Caitlin, but now I knew she was friends with Sean's girlfriend, I didn't seem to be able to help myself. 'What do you know about her friend Caitlin?' I enquired. Her surname was Byrne, I'd learnt that much from her name badge, but I wanted more. Knowing she'd be leaving soon, I begin to question just how sensible it was for me to indulge this line of questioning, but I couldn't stop myself.

Even knowing that it was bad to snoop, I found myself waiting for Sean's reply with my breath held in anticipation.

Sean shrugged, finally turning his attention back toward me. 'Allie's talked about her a little, but I don't know a great deal. They're best friends but Cait's been travelling the world for a while, so they decided to meet up here. I think she's applied for a temp job at your studios, actually.'

That certainly got my attention, Caitlin might be staying here for work? The very idea caused the hairs on the back of my neck to rise. 'Oh, really? What job?' As hard as I tried to sound unaffected, I failed, and my voice came out an octave or two higher than usual as excitement began to pour through my veins.

'No idea, mate, Allie didn't say. I just remember her saying it was Dynamic Studios.' Interesting, if Caitlin got a job at the studio then there was a high chance that I would get to see her again – regularly – and this news absolutely thrilled me to the core.

Perhaps I could ask Jason in recruitment which jobs were coming up. Rubbing at my chin I made a mental plan just in case I did see her – tread carefully, respect her space, and hope that she might learn to trust me. Somehow I had to make her trust me. The anticipation made my heart speed up. There was just something about that girl that made me desperate to get to know her.

Suddenly looking at me with narrowing eyes, Sean smiled knowingly. 'Why so curious? Are you interested in her?'

Trying my best to feign a casual look, I shrugged and dug one hand into my pocket. 'Perhaps. I'm certainly intrigued.' Sipping my whisky, I relished the burn as it slid down my throat. 'We bumped into each jogging a few weeks ago and got talking. I had no idea she was friends with Allie.'

'She's very pretty,' Sean commented, giving me a playful punch to the shoulder as he wiggled his eyebrows. 'And very young.'

I shrugged. 'I have no idea how old she is, but we seem to get along well.'

'I don't know exactly, but she must be around Allie's age. Twenty-seven or so.'

'Hardly any worse than the gap between you and Allie then,' I commented, aware that while a thirteen year gap didn't bother me, it might well put Caitlin off. Not that she seemed interested in me, anyway. Although she had said her rejection of me had nothing to do with my being older, which gave me a flicker of hope.

'You want me to ask Allie if her friend wants to go on a date with you?' he joked, a broad, teasing grin spreading on his face.

Not rising to his bait, I sipped my drink and leant on the high bar table to my right. 'She doesn't date.'

Sean's expression lost some of its earlier playfulness. 'You've already asked her out?'

It was a little hard on my ego to admit out loud that she'd turned me down, but Sean was a close friend, so I did, with a shrug. 'Yep. She said no. Told me she doesn't ever date.'

'Wow. It's been a while since you've shown interest in anyone, what's changed?'

'Just been too busy, and never felt enough of a connection to bother following anyone up. Work is beginning to ease now, and I felt a real spark with her.' As much as I was trying to keep up my bravado, a small sigh slipped from my lips, giving away my frustration. 'I thought it would have been fun to take her out, but she didn't agree.' I shrugged, trying to hide my bruised pride. 'I was just curious about her.'

Before Sean could continue, I saw his eyes flash to the door and then close in a long, slow blink, accompanied by a low groan. 'Here comes the circus. Let the acting begin. Wish me luck.' Sean gestured to the door with a jerk of his chin. Following his line of sight, I saw Savannah Hilton making a grand entrance, tossing her hair over her shoulder and pouting like a trout at the cameras.

Savannah Hilton was a prime example of the kind of woman I detested the most – fake, greedy, and conceited, and I wondered how on earth his poor girlfriend would cope with the spectacle that was no doubt about to ensue.

'Good luck. From the look on Savannah's face, you're going to need it.'

To my surprise, as I glanced at Savannah making her entrance I also saw Caitlin re-entering the bar with a frown on her face. She looked in a foul mood, but seeing as she was making a beeline for the coat cupboard, I could only assume she had left her jacket behind.

As much as I knew I shouldn't, I couldn't help myself from watching her. She handed her ticket to the woman behind the counter who then disappeared to get the jacket. Just a second or so behind Caitlin, a pair of men were staggering their way in her direction, also with their coat tickets in their hands. As I observed their progress, I watched in horror as the first guy tripped over his own feet and stumbled into Caitlin's back.

From the way she'd responded to my touch, and with what I'd witnessed tonight, I knew this was going to freak her out, and sure enough, as the clumsy man's hands landed on her shoulder and back to steady himself I saw her entire body go rigid. Swivelling on the spot, she practically recoiled into the wall in an attempt to get away, but the arsehole was so drunk that as Caitlin moved, he fell with her, basically cornering her.

As my feet began moving instinctively in her direction, I got a look at the pale, drawn expression on her face as she pushed uselessly against his swaying body. Her eyes were wild and unfocused and there was a sheen of sweat forming on her brow. She looked on the verge of a panic attack. The man's friend was in hysterics by this point, apparently finding his mate's drunkenness amusing, but I was the complete opposite, and felt murderous.

'Get away from me,' she ground out, causing the man to lift his head and grin blearily at her, but he still made no move to get away.

Not even bothering to stop and wonder if she wanted my help, I grabbed the collar of the guy's suit and hauled him back, tossing him sideways into the opposite wall and glaring at him with my fists bunched at my sides.

'She said get away, you bloody idiot.' The man and his friend took one look at my furious face and staggered away giggling, leaving me to face Caitlin. She was frozen in place, leaning on the wall with her eyes closed, lips rolled tightly between her teeth, and one hand picking furiously at the elastic band on her wrist as she drew in long, shaky breaths. That bloody elastic band. I was tempted to rip it off, but instead, I tried to calm my temper.

The urge to pull a woman into my arms had never been stronger, but I resisted. Just. 'Are you OK?' I murmured softly, which caused her to jerk, open her eyes, and stare into the distance. She was basically non-responsive, the only movement in her body an occasional blink and the constant flicking of the elastic band.

'Caitlin?' Not wanting to touch her in case that fuelled her panic, I tried again, using a firmer tone, which would hopefully snap her out of it but not freak her out. 'Caitlin? Look at me. Are you OK?' My voice seemed to permeate her consciousness, and after drawing in several ragged breaths she blinked again, her eyes finally focusing and turning to me. God, she was as white as a sheet.

'I ... I am now.' A loud swallow forced its way down her throat and she looked as if she finally realised it was me stood beside her. 'Uh ... Thank you. Looks like I did need you after all.' She was stuttering slightly, but she certainly seemed calmer, and had attempted a vague use of humour, which was good.

'Do you want me to see you home?' I asked, half out of concern and half hoping that she might say yes and give us a little more time together.

'No.' Her response was immediate, and the tone harsh enough to make me wince and get the message – she wanted to get away from me pronto. 'I mean ... I'll be fine, thank you.' At that moment, the cloakroom attendant reappeared with a black jacket, which Caitlin accepted and slid into, folding her shawl over her arm. 'I'd better go. Thank you again, Jack.' And with that she was turning to leave. Again. What was it with this woman and walking away from me?

My stubborn ego just wouldn't accept her repeated rejections, not when I knew I'd seen interest in her body language. She liked me, I was sure of it, but something was holding her back. Knowing this I just couldn't let her go. I couldn't. Every molecule within my body was screaming at me to follow her and make sure she really was OK. 'Caitlin, wait ...'

Her retreating figure tensed, then paused and slowly rotated toward me. My stomach sank when I saw that her eyes were almost blank again, clouded only with caution and fear as if she were still living through the encounter of a few minutes ago.

Her arms wrapped tightly around herself, making her look so defensive that I knew if I pushed her now then I would lose any future chance of getting to know her.

Tensing my fists, I held back from moving towards her, and instead tried to smile at her reassuringly. 'It was good to see you again. Goodnight.'

She gave one slow blink and a faint nod before turning and heading toward the door again. Letting her walk away was the hardest thing I'd done for a long time, but as Caitlin pushed through the exit, all I could do was stand there and let her go.

Allie

There was a definite possibility that my heart actually stopped for a few seconds when I saw Savannah Hilton, Sean's wafer-thin, willowy, and utterly stunning co-star (and fiancée, as far as the world was concerned), as she elegantly entered the gallery and strutted straight through the crowd to join him. I say strutted because there is no other way to adequately describe the way that woman moved her hips. It was like liquid sex moving through the room.

Unable to tear my gaze away, I watched in sick fascination as her fingers immediately sought Sean's hand and intertwined with his, but took some small satisfaction from noticing how his smile was tight and strained.

Letting out a long, loud sigh, I took a large swig of my champagne as I continued to watch them. Savannah looked beautiful, obviously. She did on screen and it seemed no different in real life. In fact, I suspected that if you knocked on her door at four in the morning, she would still look as perfectly groomed as she did now. Bloody bitch.

I instinctively found myself looking for any signs of chemistry between them. Savannah was certainly playing up nicely for the cameras, and seemed keen to be as close to Sean as physically possible, although she definitely looked a little edgy. Sean, on the other hand, was a wholly different story; his entire being radiated tension. Apart from the fact that he was allowing her to drape all over him, which irked me no end, he seemed completely ambivalent towards her.

A muscle flickered along his jaw as Savannah slipped her arm through his, wrapped her other across his stomach, and plastered herself to his side, and in response I felt my heartbeat rise with jealousy. Bitch. But why was he letting her touch him so intimately? Surely a cursory handhold would have been enough. But no, he was standing back while she practically humped him in public.

Narrowing my eyes I watched them closely, unable to tear my gaze away as they were approached by a photographer for some sort of interview. My observations were disrupted by a man who stepped almost right into my line of sight and beamed at me.

'Hey, I'm Austin. I saw you standing on your own and wondered if you'd like a little company?' I was about to knock him back but then I caught a glimpse of Sean looking our way, shooting the guy a death stare, and I paused. I'd never been one for manipulating situations to my advantage, and I'd certainly never considered the possibility of using one man's advances to snare the attention of another … until now. Sean looked livid, barely managing to keep his attention on the photographer, but as mad as he might be, his flipping arm was still curled around Savannah's waist and that was enough to spur me into being a little reckless.

'Uh, OK, that would be nice,' I said, smiling at the guy. He was good looking, if you liked them well preened and clean cut, but he was perhaps a little too groomed for my liking. His blond hair was parted and slicked back, chin cleanly shaven, and he had bright green eyes the colour of moss.

Over the course of the next few minutes, Austin managed to get closer and closer to me until the only way he could have closed the gap further would have been to actually climb on top of me. I tolerated it, because although it was immature (and not very fair) I hoped it was giving Sean a taste of his own medicine.

He'd touched my shoulder several times during our talk, and brushed his fingers on my forearm at one point, but I tensed when Austin slid a hand around my waist. This was getting a little beyond a casual flirt to make Sean jealous. The feel of Austin's fingers lightly caressing my hip gradually increased in pressure until it made me feel so guilty that I actually felt a little sick.

Making my excuses, I escaped to the bar for some space, but no sooner had I leant my elbow on the cool marble surface than I became aware of an angry wall of heat advancing to my right. I didn't even need to look to know it was Sean. I could feel him in every molecule of my body as they united in the joint desire to reach out to him.

Glancing at him, I felt my stomach drop when I saw the hard, bitter expression on his face. He wasn't even looking at me. Instead his eyes stared straight ahead, paying me no heed whatsoever. I was so stunned by his dismissal that it took a second or two to work out that Sean actually was looking at me, via the mirror mounted above the bar.

Connecting my gaze with his in the glass, I saw his furious glare and felt my hackles rising as I replayed the last half hour's worth of memories, all of which involved him having his arm around, or touching, Savannah as she fawned over him like a doe-eyed, love-sick teenager.

'What the hell are you doing?' he ground out between clenched teeth.

He was annoyed. Good, he bloody deserved a bit of payback for tonight. 'I'm ordering a drink,' I replied coolly, not rising to his bait.

'I meant with that dickhead who had his hands all over you.'

Turning marginally so I could see Sean in person, I saw the murderous expression on his face and flinched, but still managed to force out a shrug, acting as nonchalant as I could.

'I have no idea what you mean. He's talking to me. I'm talking back. It's called polite conversation. He might have put his hand around my waist briefly, I don't really remember.' I knew I was playing with fire, but I just couldn't help myself.

'He definitely did put his hands on you, and not just on your fucking hip,' Sean snarled, his head snapping away from the mirror and making direct eye contact with mine.

We might have been mad at each other, but the chemistry between us was just as intense as ever, and as our eyes met unflinchingly, tension seemed to crackle in the small gap that separated our bodies. I was fairly sure that if we had been alone, there would have been some magnificent angry sex taking place right about now.

The strength of his stare made my heart accelerate, but I was so angry with him that I tried not to let it faze me. 'Well, it looks like we're even, doesn't it? He has his hands on me, and you have your hands on Savannah,' I spat, our heated glowers clashing as our whispered row threatened to escalate into a full-on shouting match.

My remark was met with complete silence from Sean as some of the anger seemed to slip from his face to be replaced with ... something I couldn't quite name. His eyes flickered around my face before he blinked, long and slowly, an action I found mesmerising.

'Is this just a game to you?' he asked quietly, shaking his head. It was then that I recognised his new emotion – disappointment. He was disappointed in me. That was so much worse than anger and I felt my earlier bravado wither and die.

As this horrible realisation sank in, I watched as Sean ripped his gaze from mine and stared down at the counter.

'Because it certainly isn't a game to that guy you've been flirting with for the last half hour.'

I was suddenly feeling on the back foot, not liking the way his judgement was making me feel, because deep down, I knew he was right, and I was disappointed in myself too.

'Nothing happened, and nothing will happen. We were just talking,' I murmured, trying to justify my actions and knowing that my inner turmoil showed in my trembling voice.

'Yeah? You might want to tell that to the fucking hard on he's been rocking for you,' Sean said in disgust as he began to turn away from me. 'I'll let you get back to him. If you're lucky he'll still have a semi, so that'll save you some work later on.'

I knew his disgusting words were thrown at me out of hurt and jealousy – or maybe he really was disgusted with me – but either way they made me panic and I quickly tried to reach out for his wrist. 'Sean ...' He flinched slightly, but then with a brief flick of his arm he disengaged my hand and continued away from me.

Shit. Shit. Shit. What the hell had I just done? Flashing my eyes around wildly, I saw Sean was now back at Savannah's side, his arm firmly around her waist and her body practically tucked against him.

What a sight. It made me feel so sick that I ended up grimacing. I bet perfect Savannah would never make a face like this. On top of his blatant display of supposed affection, he also appeared to be pointedly ignoring me, his body angled away and fully focused on Savannah and the man they were currently talking to. Not that I could really blame him; I'd been a complete cow.

God, talk about a major backfire – it seemed that somehow instead of tempting him to come to me, I'd actually managed to push him firmly into her arms, which Savannah was clearly loving.

So Sean was in the perfect, possessive arms of his waif ex-girlfriend who obviously wanted him back, and I was standing on the side-lines with an ugly, scrunched-up face like a complete spare part.

To make matters worse, I saw Austin moving in towards me again with a narrow-eyed smirk on his face, so sending him a quick apologetic wince across the gap between us, I turned to make my escape. Dashing haphazardly through the crowds, I bumped into random elbows and spilt at least three people's champagne until I finally saw the sanctuary of the exit looming ahead of me and made a dive for it.

Chapter Twenty-Nine

Allie

Bursting from the gallery door and into the cool of the night air, I stumbled forward almost blindly as tears blurred my vision. Before I could take more than a few steps away from the gallery, I found myself being yanked sharply backwards by a tight grip on my elbow that had me staggering around in my high heels as if I were drunk. Which I wasn't.

Idiotic, yes. But drunk? Sadly, no.

'Careful, Allie! Bloody hell, you nearly ran straight into the traffic. What the hell is the matter?' Cait. My shoulders sagged in relief. After basically throwing my love life down the toilet, my best friend was a welcome sight right now and I promptly threw myself into her arms and began to sob loudly.

'Whoa! Hey … hey, shhh, it's OK,' she said soothingly, patting my back.

Poor Cait, I'm sure she didn't know what had hit her, but I proceeded to snivel, hiccup, and cling to her as I tried to cry out my stupidity and the ever-growing fear that I'd just royally screwed things up with Sean.

When I was finally able to speak, I leant back and drew in a shaky breath. 'It's not OK, but thank you for trying to make me feel better.' Giving her a watery smile I licked my lips and checked the road for any signs of a taxi. 'I want to get away from here. Can we go back to the hotel?'

'I'm just waiting for my cab, but they just texted to say it'll be at least twenty minutes because there's a traffic delay.' Giving me an assessing look, Cait jerked her thumb across the road and towards a bar. 'Want to go and get a drink and you can tell me what's wrong?'

Blowing out a huge breath, I ran my hands over my hair to smooth it, but grimaced. 'I must look a right state.' Pulling a small packet of wet wipes from her handbag, Cait set about cleaning under my eyes for me and then stepped back with a satisfied smile.

'You look fine. We'll find a quiet corner and I can tell you about the huge mistake I probably just made.'

Her words made my composure crack and I laughed, loud, and hard and slightly manically. 'You made a huge mistake? That makes two of us, because I have just majorly fucked things up with Sean.' Seeing the expectant concern on her face, I rolled my eyes. 'Let's get inside and I'll tell you.'

I linked my arm through Cait's elbow, and we made our way across the road and into the bar. It was small, but thankfully relatively empty. As promised, she settled me into a quiet corner and disappeared to get us some drinks before returning with two glasses of house white just a minute later.

'You want to go first?' Cait asked, a sad smile twitching on her lips.

Shaking my head adamantly, I took a sip of my wine and practically sighed with delight as the liquid parched my dry throat. 'No. Whatever you've done can't be as bad as mine, you go first.'

'OK … well, I talked to Jack,' she started tentatively, and I nodded. 'Again.' She emphasised this word and began to fiddle with the stem of her wineglass. 'I kept thinking about our near kiss, so it was a bit awkward at first but not too bad.' Cait sighed.

Reaching across, I gave her hand a gentle squeeze before asking the question I'd been dying to know since I'd watched them in the bar. 'Did he ask you out again?'

She was chewing on her lower lip, yet another sign of her anxiousness. 'No. But he did try to give me his number,' she confessed much to my excitement, until I picked up on her use of the word 'try'.

'Try?' I questioned, already sensing with a heavy heart where this was going.

'Mmm-hmm,' Cait confirmed with a nod. 'I declined it.'

Although I'd given the excuse of going to the toilet to leave them alone together, I had watched the interaction between Cait and Jack for a while. Well, what good friend wouldn't snoop just a tiny bit if their mate was being chatted up by a celeb? It had seemed pretty obvious that he was interested in Cait, and that she reciprocated, even if only tentatively, so it was really disappointing to see her so stubbornly walking away from it.

'He said I could have it in case I needed him for anything, and I believe the exact words I used were "I can't see why I'd need you."' Cait used her fingers to make speech marks in the air and grimaced. 'Then I walked away. I barely even say goodbye,' she confessed, now looking unsure and embarrassed.

'You said that? To Jack Felton?' I gawked, trying to picture the shock on his face when she said it, not to mention the fact that she had dismissed him by walking away. Jeez, talk about brave. Or stupid. Or stupidly brave.

'And then, to add insult to injury, as I was leaving some drunk guy fell on me ...' Cait paused, a shudder running through her body. 'Jack dragged him off me, so I kind of did end up needing him. Talk about ironic.' Taking a long, deep breath, Cait seemed to shake herself and then smiled at me weakly. 'So that's my mess up. I basically just turned down a date with a film star that most women would kill to be with, which probably makes me the world's biggest prize idiot.'

Cait raised her glass in an ironic toast, but I could tell her humour and bravado were to cover the insecurity she was feeling. She was avoiding Jack because she was scared, which, given her history, I couldn't blame her for, but it was still incredibly frustrating to witness. I understood her reticence – he was older and more experienced than she was, but just the fact that she had admitted to feeling something towards Jack was a step in the right direction, and it seemed a shame not to pursue it.

'You said you thought you'd screwed up with Sean. What did you do?'

Groaning, I dropped my head into my hands and hid my face. The more I thought back over my pathetic stunt, the more I wanted the ground to open up and swallow me. Explaining what had happened, I described Austin's attention and the jealousy it had sparked in Sean, and then reluctantly told her about my angry encounter with him at the bar.

'It was such an immature thing to do,' I moaned, shaking my head and picturing the look of fury and disgust on his face as he'd walked back to Savannah. 'To be honest, I wouldn't be surprised if he's off somewhere rekindling things with her. At least Savannah is his age and probably acts like a grown up, unlike me.'

Seemingly lost for words, Cait gave me a consoling smile and rubbed my arm. Glancing at my watch I saw it was now half past ten, and there had been no call from Sean, so obviously he'd had second thoughts about meeting me tonight – further evidence of how much of a fuck up I'd made.

'We're a right pair, aren't we?' Cait mumbled, but before I could agree, her mobile flashed up a new message and she began to pull on her jacket. 'Taxi's here. Let's continue this conversation back at the hotel.' Grabbing my things, we made our way outside where a yellow taxi was waiting. As I clicked over the pavement in my heels, Cait turned to me.

'Don't rule him out yet, Allie. It seems that between you and Sean you've both made your fair share of mistakes. Call him tomorrow and see how the land lies.'

I nodded, but deep down I couldn't stop thinking of how repelled he'd looked, and feared my stunt tonight might have been the final nail in the coffin of our relationship.

Pushing open the door to the bungalow, Cait turned to me with a frown. 'I don't remember leaving the lights on,' she commented warily, before spinning to me with a look on her face that seemed to push aside some of her earlier melancholy. 'Oh! I bet room service has been around and put those chocolates on our pillows again! Chocolate is just what I need right now!' Kicking off her flip flops, she flung her handbag onto the sofa and grinned at me. 'You put the kettle on and I'll go and get them,' she yelped excitedly before disappearing in the direction of the bedrooms.

Rolling my eyes, I wandered to the bar area and ran the tap for a few seconds before filling the kettle and switching it on, then sat on one of the stools to release my tortured feet from the confines of my shoes. I wasn't exactly a great high heel wearer at the best of times, but going out for drinks in a celebrity-studded art gallery I'd had very little choice. I could hardly have worn my trusty Converses.

Cait reappeared a few seconds later, walked over to where I was sitting, and placed just one chocolate down on the table with an odd expression on her face. I frowned and looked at her in confusion. 'Who got left out?' I asked in disappointment as I dumped my high heels down with a sigh of relief.

'No one, yours is still on your pillow.' As she spoke, I noticed that Cait definitely looked a bit strange; her cheeks were flushed and her eyes kept darting between me and the bedrooms in a decidedly twitchy manner. 'There was, uh, something extra on your bed you might want to see,' she said cryptically.

Giving me another odd look, Cait pursed her lips between her teeth, her eyes wide and unreadable. I couldn't decide if she was trying to hold back a laugh, or just felt extremely uncomfortable, because her expression was downright bizarre. Sliding from my stool I decided to investigate, but as I walked down the corridor I heard Cait give a nervous giggle behind me.

Making my way towards the wing that housed the master bedroom, I sighed heavily. What a night. Perhaps room service had made a mistake and left an entire box of chocolates on my bed – now that would make me feel better.

But as I arrived at my room, I saw something else that made my spirts soar. Sean. More accurately, Sean, sprawled on his back, on top of my bed, asleep, and wearing not a stitch of clothing. Blimey. His head was closest to the door so his manhood wasn't in my direct line of sight, but Sean didn't exactly have a teeny-weeny, and I got a pretty good view of his package, so there was no doubt Cait would have had a bit of an eyeful too. Oops. I stifled a giggle – poor girl, no wonder she had looked so flustered.

Closing the door behind me I turned, licked my lips, and began to advance into the room as quietly as I could so I didn't disturb him.

Pausing by the side of the bed I gazed down at him and allowed my eyes to roam across his sleeping form. A small sigh slipped from my lips as I took in the sight. Physically speaking, he was about as perfect as a man could get: toned, but not bulky; tanned, but naturally; perfectly proportioned in the tackle department; and with a nice sprinkling of hair in all the right places. For me, he was the epitome of masculinity and I found that just looking at him was getting me aroused.

Trying to ignore the fact that I now had a rather pleasant throbbing between my legs, I crossed them at the ankle and tried to decide what his presence here meant. Presumably he'd forgiven me? Or even if he hadn't, at least he was here with me and not in bed somewhere with Savannah.

Lowering myself gently onto the side of the bed closest to his head, I tentatively lifted a hand and gently stroked some hairs back from his brow. His skin was warm under my fingertips, making me smile like a lovesick fool. My expression promptly turned to a grin a second later as he made a small, happy grumble before his head tipped sideways to rest heavily in my palm. It was as if even in his sleep he wanted to be as close to me as possible.

My chest suddenly felt really tight as my heart accelerated, and then seemed to try to burst from the confines of my ribs as if it had been set on fire with a kind of burning, all-consuming love. God. I really did love him so much, and I couldn't believe I had nearly messed that all up with my stupid, childish games.

Suddenly feeling almost desperate to make things right, I gently rolled his head off my hand and stood up. Raising my hands to the thin straps at my shoulders I flicked them to the side and let my dress slide from my body and pool at my feet.

We might've been going through a bit of a tough patch, but I knew one thing that never seemed to go wrong between us – sex. Unclasping my bra I let it fall down my arms to join my dress on the floor, my nipples tightening in the cool of the room and sending a delicious tingle to the heated flesh between my thighs. Gazing at Sean I tried to formulate a plan, and then wearing just my lacy panties I climbed on the bed and positioned myself next to his hips.

Using one finger I gently circled its tip on the hollow of his hip bone. In the past this simple action was enough to give Sean a hard on within a minute, even while he slept. I'd discovered it by accident one morning when I'd woken up before him and had been absently – and innocently – trailing my fingers across his skin. Needless to say, once I'd seen his morning wood, things hadn't stayed innocent for very long.

Hoping it would work tonight, I continued for a few more seconds and watched in satisfaction as his peacefully sleeping cock began to rouse from its slumber. Seconds later, after several twitches and jerks it began noticeably growing in excitement, causing a smug grin to pull at my lips. Adding just a few gentle strokes to the soft skin on the underside, I checked his steady breathing, and saw he was definitely still asleep but now with a quickly developing hard on and an endearingly confused frown fluttering on his brow.

Suddenly, rather like a jack-in-the-box, his cock went from lolling sideways to springing upright as if standing up to look for whatever had disrupted his sleep. Grinning like a kid at Christmas, I made sure to be quick before he woke up, and lowered my head to lick the top like a lolly, causing it to bob and jerk under my tongue. I gripped my right hand around the base of his shaft and encased as much of the top as I could in my mouth.

Running my tongue around his length, I began a gentle rhythm with my hand then sucked him into my mouth again. Beneath my ministrations I felt his stomach tense as Sean began to wake, and in my mouth he grew even harder as his hips gave a gentle upward thrust. Continuing with my movements, I saw his hands fist in the sheets as his head moved and his eyes finally opened.

'Fuck … oh, fuck … that's so good, Allie …' One of his hands moved to my hair and tangled in the strands as his hips thrust upwards again, a little more firmly this time so he went deeper into my mouth.

'Oh, my gorgeous girl …' His words faded off as his eyes darkened and his brows lowered, and then suddenly the hand in my hair moved to my shoulder and gripped. Before I could do anything, Sean had managed to remove himself from my mouth, flip me onto my back, and was leaning over me, pinning my arms to my sides as he stared down at me.

His face was flushed with pleasure, but his eyes were stormy and definitely glowing with a darkening emotion. Uh-oh. 'Pouncing on me while I'm asleep, eh? That was very sneaky, Allie. Don't think you're going to get away with distracting me from the fact that you have been very bad this evening.'

I stared at his face, unsure what to say or do. Frustration, desire, and lust were zinging between us, making it hard to focus on anything other than the desperate urge to have him inside me.

Running his words through my mind, I knew I'd been stupid to flirt with Austin but I was still harbouring some annoyance at Sean's actions. Before I could vocalise this, his lips crashed down upon mine, sending pleasure bursting across every molecule in my system. Eagerly joining in with his ferocious kiss, my tongue lashed with his, soaking up his taste and the way he had me pinned below him, which he knew was a position I got quite a thrill from.

When his head finally lifted, I dragged in a breath and lifted my chin defiantly, reluctant to give in just yet. 'I thought you said I was the one trying to use distractions …' I panted, licking my bruised lips and immediately wanting more of his demanding kisses.

'I decided two could play at that game,' he said, parting my legs by jamming his knee between them and forcing them wider. Wedging himself between my thighs he then delivered a wicked thrust of his hips that had his cock jammed up against my panties in just the right place. A low groan of approval left my throat, and caused Sean to laugh darkly. 'So, do you have anything to say about your behaviour tonight?'

So this was going to be discussion sex, was it? Or perhaps angry sex. Who knew? To be honest, I didn't care what type it was as long as it sorted out our issues and helped get us back on the straight and narrow.

Still, his words made me sputter with irritation. 'Me? What about you? Why the hell did you organise tickets for me to go to that stupid event? You must have known Savannah would be there fawning all over you!'

Leaning on his elbows, Sean took one of my wrists and pulled it above my head. 'Of course I knew she'd be there, but I thought you wouldn't be bothered because it's – all – fake.' His last three words were ground out between clenched teeth.

Following suit with my other wrist, Sean moved it above my head so that he was holding them both in one of his large palms. 'OK? Not uncomfortable?' he murmured, clearly intent on checking my willingness even if he was pissed off with me.

'Fine,' I replied, my petulant tone immediately dropping away as I began to squirm under him as he lowered his free hand and began to tease one of my nipples with the pad of his thumb. 'What wasn't fine was seeing you all over her,' I panted. 'Surely just holding her hand would be enough …' But I was stopped from further complaint as he pinched my nipple hard, causing my back to arch from the bed. 'Oh God!'

Desire was hazing my ability to think straight as he lowered his face to within an inch of mine. 'I did nothing tonight but fulfil my contractual obligations, Allie.' He swapped his attentions to my other breast, rolling the wanton nipple between his forefinger and thumb until my head began to swim. 'You, however, let a random man put his hands on you, and seeing as you're mine that is simply unacceptable.' Lowering his head, he dropped his hand away and greedily sucked my nipple into his mouth, laving it with his tongue and sending sparks of desire spiralling through me.

'You're mine too, and you still had your hands on her!' I gasped. 'You're a fucking hypocrite, Sean!' In response, Sean gave my nipple a sharp bite, pulling at the sensitive flesh and causing me to simultaneously yelp from the sting and push it back into his mouth for more.

'Oh God ... I'm supposed to be angry with you, but, please, Sean ... fuck me. Please,' I begged, wanting the talking to stop so we could get down to what we both obviously wanted. Needed. I needed him inside me so I knew we were OK.

Moving his hand between us, Sean took less than a second to dig his fingers into the lace of my panties and rip them from my body, jerking my hips into his abdomen with the force of his movement. He threw the ripped material to the side and I nodded my head eagerly, uncaring that he had just ruined my knickers.

'Take me, Sean ...' I wasn't into anything particularly kinky, but Sean was quite a dominant lover, often liking to take charge, something I'd discovered I also rather liked, and as a result our lovemaking was frequently quite rough and ready. In fact, I think I'd lost count of the number of knickers Sean had ripped his way through in our time together, but he had always replaced them with a new pair and a rueful smile a day or so later.

Lining up his cock with my entrance I groaned in relief as I felt his soft skin touch mine, but he frustratingly stopped just as the tip entered me. 'But actually, no, not quite yet. I think an apology might be in order, don't you?' Sean murmured teasingly as I desperately tried and failed to thrust my hips up against him.

'Yes … you definitely need to apologise to me,' I gasped, taunting him while tugging uselessly at my pinned wrists in the hopes that I could free one and use it to grip his bum and pull him down into me.

Barking out a short laugh, Sean kissed me again, his tongue surprisingly soft and gentle given the situation, not to mention at complete odds to the rest of his actions so far. 'Uh-uh, that's not what I meant and you know it. What you did tonight was childish, Allie.' He gave a small, sharp jolt of his hips that sent his cock plunging halfway into me and immediately back out again, like an ultimate temptation that left me writhing below him desperately, and seconds away from begging.

I knew he was right. I had been stupid and I did need to apologise, but I held off for just a few more seconds, deciding to make one final point. 'I might have been stupid, but my actions were driven by your behaviour. Letting her touch you all over and reciprocating? That was inconsiderate, selfish, and unbelievably hurtful …' Sean paused in his teasing, his head lifting up and eyes seeking out mine before blinking several times. I felt the tension beginning to leave his body as I saw the anger melting from his features, replaced by regret.

Our angry lovemaking had momentarily stopped, but even with arousal pulsing in every pore of my body I knew that this moment was more important than connecting ourselves physically, and I stared up expectantly into his eyes.

A heavy breath fell from his lips. 'You're right. OK … I'll speak to Savannah and set some ground rules. Hand holding only from now on, you have my word.' It wasn't an apology using the word 'sorry', but it was what I needed to hear.

'You've really never had sex with her?' I asked, my voice suddenly sounding pathetically weak and reedy.

Lowering his damp brow, Sean rested it on my forehead so our noses were touching. 'No. Never. I promise.' As he spoke, our quickened breaths mixed and tickled across my lips. 'As much as I disliked the way you responded to Savannah, and I do understand, I was so jealous when I saw you with that fucker,' Sean admitted in a rush, his eyes darkening with displeasure and his fingers tightening marginally around my wrists still pinned above my head. 'I can't tell you how close I came to striding over there and ripping his hands off for daring to touch you.'

He was opening up, so I really should too – although admittedly, perhaps it would be easier to do so if I wasn't pressed below him with his solid erection laying heavily on my stomach and my arms pinned above my head, but I suppose needs must.

'I was wrong to try and wind you up, Sean. I'm so sorry. I was such an idiot. It was stupid jealousy from seeing you with her in the flesh … touching. It nearly killed me …' I admitted on a shudder, closing my eyes to briefly escape from his intense blue gaze.

'It's not real, my gorgeous girl. None of it,' he whispered, releasing my wrists so that he could prop himself onto both elbows and cup my face in his hands. Lowering my arms, I rested my hands on his waist and bravely opened my eyes again, loving the way his features were completely sincere. 'She'll never see me gaze at her like this,' he murmured, his eyes seeming to burn into my soul as he ground his hips against mine temptingly.

Surprisingly, even given the pause in proceedings and the serious nature of our discussion, he was still completely hard against my thigh and swelling by the second, and I couldn't help but shiver with expectation.

'She'll never get to kiss me like this …' His lips moved to mine, pressing against my mouth in a soft, warm demand, before his tongue gently ran along the seam of my lips. My mouth opened and he wasted no time plunging his tongue inside, probing and exploring so tenderly that I was soon straining off the mattress, moaning my appreciation and clawing at his back in my desperation to ease the throbbing heat between my legs. Pulling his head back for a second he locked his gaze with mine as he marginally shifted his hips to the right.

'She'll never feel me inside her like this.' With one smooth thrust, Sean filled me to bursting point, causing me to throw my head back and cry out from the pleasure of being so utterly consumed.

'And she'll never hear me tell her that I love her.' Sliding out of me, Sean paused with just the tip of his straining erection inside me and looked deep into my eyes. 'I love you, Allie. Possibly more than you can even comprehend,' he murmured, before a smooth downward thrust had him buried to the hilt again as I craned my neck up to capture his lips.

'I love you too, Sean,' I panted breathlessly.

A silent agreement was suddenly forged between us, stating that conversation time was over and I gasped as Sean began to move purposefully within me, drawing back only to plunge inside me again and again, and seeming to hit my g-spot with each and every beautifully timed thrust until I felt like I was coming undone from the inside out.

Transferring his weight to one arm, Sean continued to move within me while tweaking and rolling one nipple between his thumb and finger. My nipples were so sensitive that each tug sent a burst of tingling heat directly to my groin and almost made my eyes roll back in my head from the pleasure of it.

'I'm close. Allie, come with me,' Sean requested softly. Almost rearing up, he then thrust harder and deeper than before, giving a far sharper pull to my nipple which sent me cascading over into a climax so powerful that I cried out and clutched him to me. Giving one more thrust, I felt Sean growl as his erection begin to jerk inside me, the heat of his release filling me as he collapsed on top of me.

'You want to know the best thing?' he panted, lifting his head to look at me. Nodding my head, I saw Sean grin. 'Apart from an hour at the studios tomorrow morning, I'm free to spend the entire day with you, which means I can stay over and we can do this all over again. Preferably without the arguing part.'

My eyes must have lit up as my hands cupped his face and dragged it to mine for a grateful kiss. Caging my body with his arms so I didn't have to take all his body weight, Sean burrowed his head in the crook of my neck, breathing heavily and repeating my name against the skin below my ear, occasionally muttering the word 'mine' for good measure.

Feeling possessive, was he? Well, if that was how Sean made love to me when he felt the need to express a little ownership, then that was just fine by me because that had been in-cred-ible.

Chapter Thirty

Cait

Today was the day. Job interview day. Not just any job interview either, but an interview at the actual, real life, massively famous Dynamic Studios. Some of the biggest blockbusters of the last century had been filmed there, not to mention the plethora of successful television series that had started out behind their doors. I might only have applied for a temporary position, but I was nervous. Really flipping nervous. My right leg was bouncing endlessly and I was flicking the elastic bands around my wrist to the point of pain as I sat on the sofa in silence. Mind you, the copious amounts of caffeine I'd ingested in the hour since waking probably weren't helping my twitchiness either.

The non-stop torrent of possibilities and questions running through my mind suddenly came to an abrupt halt as my eyes widened and I very nearly choked on my tongue.

Sean Phillips, rubbing his sleepy face and completely oblivious to my presence, was wandering towards me clad only in a pair of black boxer shorts. *Very* tight black boxer shorts. Blinking in embarrassment but somehow unable to turn away, I grabbed my coffee mug as a mild distraction just as he lowered his hands, saw me gawking at him, and froze in the doorway.

God, I couldn't believe I'd seen him undressed twice in less than twenty four hours. I mean, he clearly had an amazing body, but sheesh, that man needed to get some less fitted boxers if he was going to be strutting around the place. Blushing, I thought back to last night when I'd seen him asleep on Allie's bed minus the boxer shorts. I hadn't exactly hung around, but it had been more than obvious he had been naked. Seeing the full view I'd had then, I supposed I should be grateful that he was at least wearing some form of clothing today.

Sean looked completely shocked: wide eyes, tense stance, and a what-the-hell-do-I-do-now vibe emanating from his every pore. Seeing as I'd known about him being here last night I appeared to be marginally more prepared for this encounter. But only marginally. My cheeks were definitely burning now and my tongue seemed to have frozen in my mouth, rendering me speechless.

Fidgeting on the spot, Sean seemed to be debating what he should do when I finally managed to regain control of my tongue. 'Uhh … good morning.'

Looking totally blindsided by my presence, Sean still appeared to be floundering, 'I … uh …' Finally relaxing, Sean chuckled, although he still looked decidedly sheepish. 'Morning. I was going to make some coffee. I don't suppose there's any going?'

'Sure. I'll pour you two,' I murmured, glad of the excuse to go to the coffee maker and turn my eyes away from his half-naked body.

'Thanks.' Bless him. For a man with a body as good as Sean's, the poor guy seemed a bit embarrassed about his state of undress, and didn't quite seem to know what to do with his hands, alternating between hanging them at his sides and swinging them nervously in front of his groin.

'Here,' I said, chucking him the towel from the radiator beside me that I'd used after my swim this morning. 'Sorry it's bit damp.'

Immediately wrapping it around his waist, he grinned at me in relief. 'No, it's perfect. Thank you, Cait.' Securing the towel, Sean came closer and began to add milk to the two cups while I fiddled nervously with my elastic band and avoided further eye contact.

'Allie mentioned you have a job interview today, good luck with it.' Then, picking up the cups with a final smile, he disappeared from view, leaving me to sag onto the bar in relief.

That encounter had certainly kick-started my adrenaline and got my pulse racing – not to mention erased my earlier nerves about the upcoming interview. Smiling at the bizarre start to my day, I jumped from the stool and headed to my room to change – it was time to get myself a job in television.

I knew Dynamic was one of the biggest names in the film and television industry, but I was totally unprepared for just how huge their site was. After arriving early at the front gates, I had filled in a visitor entry form and then been ushered towards a guide who took me back outside and loaded me and six other applicants into a large golf cart. He then drove us through various avenues, past large warehouse-type buildings each labelled as stages with different numbers on them, before pulling up beside a structure called the Executive Building.

From there, we left the warmth of the day to be herded inside a large, cool, busy seating area to await our name call. My heart sank when I saw the crowds, because there must have been at least fifty people applying for these jobs. Needing some space to calm myself I chose the least crowded side of the room and found a seat.

As I sat there clutching my CV and surrounded by pictures of the famous names who had worked here over the years, I felt my stomach reeling with excitement. Even if I didn't get the job this would go down as a memorable day.

Before I'd had any time to calm my nerves my name was being called for the interview by a trendily dressed woman waving a clipboard. Jeez, talk about swift. Trying to steady my galloping pulse I stood up, straightened out my clothes, and left the safety of the waiting area as I followed the woman along a corridor towards an office.

Pausing at a door, she turned to me with a smile. 'Mr Mathers will be interviewing you today. Good luck.' Smiling my thanks weakly, I watched as she walked away before drawing in a calming breath and knocking on the closed door.

The door swung open and I was met by a surprisingly young-looking man who waved an arm to usher me into the office space. Hmm. A small, enclosed space containing just me and a strange man. This wasn't exactly on my list of great situations to be in, but I tried to distract my paranoia by taking in a deep breath and skimming my eyes over his appearance. His steel-rimmed glasses and casual jeans, T-shirt, and blazer made me and my suit look positively overdressed. He had an efficient air about him, and I could only assume that the casual outfit meant that he was perhaps an executive of some sort who no longer needed to dress to impress.

'Good morning, Miss Byrne. I'm Jason Mathers, head of recruiting. Thank you for coming today – please take a seat.' Relief washed through me when he left the office door ajar and I immediately felt myself relax.

As I propped myself on the edge of the chair, I watched him sort through some papers on his desk. Picking up some pages that I recognised as my CV, he waved it briefly in the air.

'I looked over the CV you emailed us last week, but I'm afraid I don't think that you'll be suited to the role of runner.'

Talk about getting straight to the point. Disappointment landed in my stomach, squashing all my earlier excitement like a hammer blow. The leaflet had said these positions basically involved running errands like fetching and carrying, basically the lowest of the low, so how could I not be suitable? Irritation niggled at me as I replayed his words – if he'd realised this last week, he could have emailed me then and saved us both the bother of this pointless interview.

'Oh. OK then, well, thank you for seeing me,' I replied, courteous to the end even if I was slightly put out.

As I went to stand he held up a hand that stopped me in my tracks. 'Actually, Caitlin I was impressed by your credentials ...' he said, causing my heart to give a kick at his use of Caitlin, and not Cait. Jack was the only other person who had used my full name recently, and his image immediately sprung to mind. It also occurred to me that I much preferred the sound of my name falling from his tongue. Wincing, I replayed the way I had walked away from him at the gallery yesterday. I still couldn't quite believe I'd done that, but sitting in a job interview was hardly the time to dwell on it, so I pushed thoughts of Jack away and focused my attention back on Jason.

He flicked through the copy of my CV until he got to the previous employment page. 'I was hoping you might consider a different role with us.' Now my heart was hammering for an altogether different reason. 'I see that you worked at the Sydney Opera House in the props department.'

'Yes, that's right.' My eyebrows rose with excitement at where this might be leading. I had loved that job, and had stayed there nearly a year before reluctantly deciding that I wanted to see more of the world. Partly, I had also left because I'd been concerned that my ex might find me if I stayed in one place for too long. I couldn't be sure if he was actually trying to track me down or maybe just freak me out, but he occasionally sent letters to my parent's house just to remind me of him. Whether it went beyond that I didn't know, but to be safe I still didn't stay in one place for long, or do any social media.

'I actually took the liberty of emailing the contact you have listed as a reference, and they speak very highly of you. Would you be interested in working with us on the props for *Dark Blood*?'

'Oh my gosh, yes' were the first words that sprung to mind, but attempting to maintain at least some vestige of professionalism I instead nodded and smiled broadly. 'That sounds like an amazing opportunity.' Matching my grin, Jason leant back in his chair, observing me intently.

'Do you know much about the show?' he enquired, and I smiled wider, pleased that my penchant for a little television watching was finally proving useful.

'Some; it's set on a university campus, and follows the lives of a group of students, some of whom are secretly vampires.'

'Great, that's exactly it. Look, I'll lay it on the line, Caitlin, the things you did in Sydney – especially the specialist work with silicone masks you worked on – that's exactly what we're going to be needing for the next season, and I want you doing it.' He leant forwards on his desk and gave me an intense look. 'I know you came here to apply for the temporary runner work, but for this role we'd be looking for a more permanent position, say a six month contract to start.

I see you already have the correct work visa, so we could set off with a three month probationary period and go from there? How does that sound?' he asked, as he dug through a tray to his left and pulled out a brown envelope which he then slid across the desk toward me. 'I have a contract drawn up in preparation, actually. Take a read.'

Seeing my shocked face, he smirked. 'Time waits for no man, Caitlin. I always like to be prepared.'

Wow. He was certainly keen, and I couldn't deny that his enthusiasm was very complimentary.

Pausing, I read the contract twice through and tried to weigh it up. This was all rather flattering, and six months was doable. With Greg's occasional letters still landing on my mum's doormat I certainly wasn't in a rush to go back to the UK, that was for sure, and I was enjoying my time in LA so far – it was warm and friendly and I could happily see myself living here for a while. And now Allie was here, it seemed even more perfect.

If I could get a job I really loved again it would be utterly amazing. 'I don't see that would be a problem. I'd probably need to find somewhere to live, because I'm in temporary accommodation at the moment,' I added, thinking out loud more than asking.

Jason looked exceptionally pleased by my response, nodding happily. Pausing for a second he looked thoughtful and then pursed his lips, as if something had just occurred to him. 'There are some cheap apartments that Dynamic rent out to employees for a percentage of your wage. They're pretty small and basic, but they're just across from the studio site in a private compound, so they're very safe, and convenient for work. I could see if any are free if that might help persuade you to accept the contract?' Jason offered, looking hopeful.

Gosh, this was all moving incredibly quickly … but I was excited, more so than I could remember being for a long time, and couldn't really see any reason not to take this job.

'Wow. OK, um … that could be really good.' With my reply, Jason grinned, and not wasting a second he pulled a spiral phone book towards him and flicked through the cards. Picking up the phone on the desk he made a brief call, nodding several times as he listened and then hung up, looking smug.

'You're in luck. They have a small two-bed available. What do you say, Caitlin? Can I add you to the Dynamic's payroll?' He waved the contract papers at me, his eyes twinkling hopefully.

'Um …' I paused briefly, but then decided to grab the opportunity I'd been presented with. 'Yes. I'd love to. Thank you.'

'Great! People with your specialism don't come along every day.' Handing me a pen, Jason flicked the contract to the signature page where I squiggled my name, and then handed it back to him.

Standing up, Jason suddenly seemed full of energy as he filed my contract and practically bounced on the spot. 'I tell you what, I have a few minutes free. Why don't I show you around the facilities? I think you'll be impressed.'

'OK, great. Thank you, this is all very exciting.'

Jason led me back down the corridor to the reception and then out into the bright morning sun. 'When you start I'll sort you out with a site map – this studio complex is spread over more than fifty acres.'

Fifty? Holy crap, I'd thought it was big, but not that big. I had a dreadful sense of direction, so I'd definitely be in need of a map.

'In general, the *Dark Blood* set is based in stage number five, right at the far western side, but they also use some of the back lot locations when filming outdoor scenes. They film on location in the city too, Dynamic have a deal with the University of California to use their campus.'

Nodding, I remembered particular scenes on the campus. It had some seriously impressive buildings within the grounds. Jason led me to another golf cart, and upon seeing my smile, he grinned. 'Get used to these, Caitlin, it's the best way to get around the site.'

Arriving at stage five we entered the huge warehouse and then moved into a smaller, windowless room containing the set. Grinning like an idiot, I looked around as I followed Jason closely. 'Like I said, we don't start the next shoot for two weeks, but there's still rehearsals going on. It's always busy in here, night and day.' He was right about that – even at this relatively early hour it was buzzing with noise and movement as crew members busily dashed around with cameras, prop trolleys, and carts loaded with sound equipment.

Immediately I felt excitement start to sizzle in my veins. Right in front of me was a set-up of one of the most common scenes in the show – the university dorm room. Ironically, one of the few sets not shot on campus. Wow, I'd seen it on TV so often that it was strange to see that the walls were just chipboard.

Opening a door to a side room, we stepped into some sort of TARDIS as I stood and gawked at the rows and rows of clothing that I could see disappearing into the distance. My God, it was huge in here. 'We keep specific costumes for the show on the rails, and the props are all boxed on the racks down this side. If there's something we need but don't have, we can request it from Dynamic's main costume department.' With a room this size crammed this full, I couldn't see that there would ever be anything they would not have, but I kept my mouth shut and followed Jason as he led me back outside again.

'So, that's about it for today. I'll get the props manager to do you a full tour of her department when you start, as she's not in today. I'll be in touch with an official start date and a copy of the contract.' Jason loaded me back into the golf buggy and drove me to the building where we'd started, and once we were both out, he extended his arm out for a handshake. Panic briefly gripped my chest as I stared at his hand, frozen to the spot. Swallowing hard, I gave myself a stern talking to – Jason had been nothing but professional, making me feel quite at ease, so a simple handshake would be fine. I would be fine. Drawing in a breath, I held the air in my lungs and accepted his palm, keeping it as brief as possible before pulling my hand back and letting out my breath in a low hiss. That wasn't so bad. Maybe I was getting better.

'I'm going to have to get back and help out with the other interviews, but it was great to meet you, Caitlin, I just know you're going to fit in here.'

'Yeah, me too. Thank you again, I can't wait to start.' Jason disappeared, leaving me standing in the sun with a huge smile plastered on my face. The prospect of this job was really exciting, right up my street, and in the world-famous, massively acclaimed Dynamic Studios, of all places. It could lead to some seriously good links for my future and I couldn't help the grin that was now glued to my lips.

Gazing around, I took in the sights of the large warehouses around me and smiled. This was my new workplace. How amazing was that? The buildings all looked so plain and boring from the outside, and yet inside all sorts of magic was taking place.

My stomach was tumbling with excitement, and there was a huge, goofy grin on my face as I wandered along not properly looking where I was going. Suddenly a door to my left swung open, only just missing me and I stepped back with a gasp as a tall, broad, grey-haired man strode through, followed closely by a group of harassed-looking crew members.

The scowling man shot a glare in my direction then began to bark orders to the people with him. As I watched the group rushing to catch up with him, my eyes landed on the last person exiting the building and my mouth fell open.

Jack Felton. My eyes rolled in my head as I drew in a stuttering sigh. This guy was like a bloody bad penny, always popping up when I least expected him. Actually, scratch that – he was just always popping up. I didn't seem to be able to put my foot down anywhere in this flipping city without bumping into him.

Glancing my way, Jack caught my eye and I saw him register brief surprise before smiling at me cautiously. At least it looked cautious. Perhaps he was still smarting from the way I'd rudely dismissed him last night.

As I blinked rapidly and tried to process seeing him again, my brain suddenly slowed as one horrifying conclusion began to formulate … did he work here? At these studios? Wouldn't that be just marvellous? My emotions were already screwed up where that man was concerned – the last thing I needed was to see him daily.

Daily. Oh my God. And I'd signed the contract, so there was no going back on it now. I was suddenly hyperventilating, my breath tight and wheezing from my lungs like a sixty a day smoker. Seeing as LA was chock full of film companies it had never even occurred to me that Jack might film at this one …

Drawing in a breath, I forced my face to remain neutral as I tried to calm the panic threatening to overpower me. My traitorous body wanted to smile back, but if I were to be working here then this weird connection couldn't carry on between us any more. It was ridiculous, and definitely bad for my heart's health, so as much as I could, I schooled my features to a bland mask and merely gave a small nod of my head before turning and continuing towards the exit.

What was that man doing to me? I'd never been so rude to anyone in my entire life. He seemed like a genuinely nice guy too, and I'd practically blanked him. Again. I couldn't believe I'd done it, but I knew perfectly well why I had – I was scared. Scared of how he made me feel, and scared that I wasn't in control of myself when he was around.

Grimacing as I walked on, I felt an overwhelming urge to look back at him gnawing at my stomach until at last I gave in and turned with a small, apologetic smile on my face. As I met his gaze all I saw was a deep frown creasing his brows. Even as our eyes met, he didn't smile, merely blinked, shook his head in apparent resignation, and then turned back to the men he was with.

My stomach plummeted so quickly that I felt a little sick. God, talk about getting slighted. Mind you, after the way I'd walked away from him on multiple occasions, I'd be a complete hypocrite to complain. Swallowing hard, I tried to ignore the churning emotions burning in my stomach. If I felt this guilty and this rejected by a mere frown then I already liked him way more than I should, so this could only be for the best. That's what I needed to convince myself of, anyway.

Distance. A normal, Jack-free life was what I had wanted. Needed. I needed distance from him. That way I could return to my usual withdrawn, but calm, life. I would be in charge, which meant I would be safe.

Good. That was that settled then.

As I carried on walking, I digested the fact that the moment didn't feel half as victorious as I'd thought it would. In fact, I felt distinctly like I'd just made a huge mistake, and that was cutting me to the core and leaving me more confused than ever.

Chapter Thirty-One

Allie

The feeling of something tickling my jawline woke me up. Grumbling my complaint I tried to itch it away, only to discover it was actually Sean's head as he lightly rubbed his stubble-covered chin repeatedly back and forth across my cheek.

'Good morning, my gorgeous girl,' he murmured, a smile clear in his tone.

A matching smile pulled at my own lips as I stretched and opened my eyes to find him perched on top of me, looking handsome as sin, but disappointingly fully clothed. Mmm ... from the smell of my shower gel on his skin and the dampness of his hair, he was freshly showered too. Scrummy. Clean, fresh Sean in my bed. Perfect. Mind you, I didn't mind him when he was dirty in my bed, either.

'You off to work?' I mumbled, sleepily remembering that he'd mentioned he needed to go to the studio today.

'Yeah. Sorry to wake you, but I wanted to check we're definitely OK after last night.'

Last night. The art gallery. *Savannah*.

Images of her pawing over Sean flooded my brain and I felt instantly more awake as my body tensed below his. The unpleasant thoughts didn't last long though, as I replayed my arrival back at the bungalow and the angry, delicious make-up sex we had shared. Blinking slowly, I felt my cheeks heat at memories of Sean's intensity. He'd been like a man possessed. Not that I had complained in the slightest.

Pulling in a long breath, I smiled and nodded. 'We are.'

His shoulders relaxed before he lowered his head and nuzzled into my neck. 'OK, good. I'll leave you to sleep. Don't eat, I'll pick us up some breakfast on my way back.'

Sliding my hand into his damp hair, I pulled him down for a quick kiss and my smile transformed into a grin at the thought that he would be at the studio this morning smelling like my shower gel. Mine. He might like to get possessive, but it went both ways. This man was mine. After one chaste kiss he was gone, leaving me feeling sleepy, content, and brimming with happiness.

Sean really was a gem. He'd stuck to his word like glue, only being gone for a single hour this morning before arriving back with warm chocolate croissants, fruit salad, coffee, and the promise that he was now free to spend the rest of the day with me.

It was a pretty fantastic start to the day. The energy was palpable as the bungalow transformed from just being a luxurious suite into our own little bubble of happiness. Our spirits were understandably high: me thrilled by the prospect of some time with Sean, and him seemingly buoyant because of my good mood.

We lounged by the bungalow's private pool, enjoying the heat of the noon sun, chatting, reading, and appreciating the fact that he had a rare day off. We'd breakfasted out here, not wanting to miss a minute of the warmth, and the remnants of our earlier meal were still beside us – empty coffee cups and a few missed flakes of croissant – but both of us were feeling too lazy to move.

Sighing contentedly, I reached the end of a chapter, put my book down, and glanced across at Sean. My breath hitched a little in my throat and a small smile curled the corners of my lips at the sight beside me – he was just gorgeous. He didn't have any swimming trunks at the bungalow, so he was lying there in just his tight boxers –

Calvin Kleins, which seemed to be his preference – which wasn't a sight I minded in the slightest. This particular pair was quite small, and an incredibly good fit, making them, rather, er … well packed, shall we say. And not leaving a great deal to the imagination. Not that I needed imagination to know what was under the cotton – I had Sean's body committed to memory.

One change since I'd last seen him in the UK was his chest hair, which had been trimmed down so it was shorter and neater. This just made his muscular chest look even more defined though, so obviously I wasn't complaining. Apparently in the new season of LA Blue he'd have to get his top off quite a few times, and the producer hadn't liked his untamed state – he'd called him 'a hairy British bear' – and immediately demanded the ladies in the hair and makeup department trim him down. I'm sure it made their day. Possibly their year.

I was very fond of Sean's chest hair – his fur, as I referred to it. I saw it as manly and a huge turn on, and even in this trimmed state I still found myself itching to run my fingers across it.

Tilting my face toward the sun, I couldn't help but hum happily to myself – this was blissful. It almost felt as if we were a regular couple again, sunning ourselves on a foreign holiday somewhere exotic, and I was loving every minute of it.

Thankfully, last night's argument was now firmly behind us, although I'm fairly sure we'd both taken on board the points made, and learnt from our mistakes. Hopefully things would be a little smoother between us from now on.

'You're too far away. Come here,' Sean grumbled, one hand patting the gap between us on the double lounger while his other held up an e-reader. This sunbed was amazing, it was like a four poster bed, with light gauze draped across it to cut out the glare from the sun, and a huge mattress big enough for two.

Rolling onto my side, I shuffled closer to his bronzing skin. His closest arm took hold of me possessively and I relaxed, allowing him to do his thing and tuck me close to his side with a contented sigh. 'That's better,' he said, giving my waist a brief squeeze just above the ticklish spot at my hip.

Squirming under his teasing touch, I let out a small giggle and when he relented and moved his hand, I gave in and flopped lazily onto him. 'It's hot today, I didn't want to get you sweaty.' Resting my cheek on the sun-warmed skin of his chest, I now had a perfect view over his near perfect body and found a smile tugging my lips again. Possibly a slightly smug one too, because let's face it, having this guy lying beneath me made me a very, very lucky girl.

'You didn't seem to mind getting me sweaty last night,' he commented teasingly, his hand sliding back to my hip and resuming its earlier caress. He had a point, and I couldn't help but smile as I recalled last night's lovemaking. Once we'd gotten the talking part over with, it had been mind-blowing.

Sex with Sean had been great from the start, always intense and passionate, but it seemed that adding in the highly-strung emotions of anger and jealousy had made last night somehow even more explosive. I was still reeling from it.

Just thinking about how possessive he'd been got me hot under the collar and I felt a stirring of interest flutter in my belly as my libido began to wake up. To be honest, if Sean kept rubbing my hip like this I'd either pounce on him right here in the open, or need to jump in the pool to cool off my growing arousal.

'By the way, you could have told me you decided to bring Cait along to the bungalow,' he murmured, his e-reader lowering for a moment as he spoke.

Oops. He had a point there. Seeing as Sean was footing the bill for this luxurious accommodation I probably should have told him. Mind you, on the night I moved here and invited Cait along for the ride I had only just found out about the fake engagement and had been furious with him. It hadn't crossed my mind since then. 'I needed some company. Sorry, I didn't think to tell you.'

My voice was a little weak, and in response, Sean placed his book down and gave me an understanding squeeze, as if he knew exactly what I was thinking, but didn't want to mention it either. I felt his head twist as he dropped a kiss on my hair and I nuzzled closer.

'I don't mind in the slightest, but I walked out in my boxers this morning and nearly scared the shit out of Cait.'

Propping myself up on my elbow, I raised my sunglasses onto the top of my head so I could look at him properly. His eyes were shaded by a pair of Aviators, but he didn't look overly bothered by his near flashing. In fact, judging by the way the corners of his lips were tweaking, he appeared quite amused by it all.

'You did?' Giggling, I placed a hand on his chest and trailed my fingers towards his belly button, watching in fascination as the skin tensed and rippled with my movements. 'Sorry. Cait is quite shy so you probably did scare her, but I'm sure she'll get over it.'

'It could have been worse, I nearly walked out stark naked. That would really have given her a fright.' Grinning, I decided not to tell Sean that Cait had probably gotten an eyeful of his tackle last night, just in case it made him feel uncomfortable around her. Not that he had any reason to be shy when it came to his privates – he had more than enough going on in the trouser department to make any man envious.

Gosh, with the heat from the sun combining with my wandering (and increasingly heated) thoughts about Sean's lower anatomy, I was starting to feel like I might melt.

Peeling myself from Sean's one-armed embrace, I sat up. Stretching out my arms, I yawned and eyed the tempting pool. 'It's so hot today. I'm going to cool off in the pool, you coming for a swim?'

'In a minute, let me finish this chapter,' Sean said, lifting up his e-reader again. He was a man after my own heart – I hated to leave a book mid-chapter, always getting to the end of one before putting it down. It was a small obsession of mine.

'OK.' Dropping a kiss onto one of his nipples I gave it just the tiniest nip with my teeth, enough to make him jerk and yelp, but as he went to reach for me I jumped up and ran giggling to the far side of the pool, towards the ladder. Seeing Sean giving me a rueful smile across the glittering water as he rubbed his abused nipple, I grinned and waved teasingly at him before approaching the side.

I'm a bit of a wuss when it comes to introducing my body to cold water. I never jump straight in, always choosing to climb slowly down the ladder until I have acclimatised enough to brave the act of immersing myself. As I lowered my foot onto the first step, I gasped at the chill that surrounded my skin. The sun was hot today, so I'd thought the water might have warmed slightly, but no, it was still flipping freezing.

It took me a while, and several loud gasps, but after a few minutes I was about halfway in, the water now lapping around my belly button. To my astonishment, I was suddenly hit with the most gigantic wave of freezing cold water splashing all over my back and head, causing me to scream, flail one arm wildly, lose my grip, and promptly fall from the ladder and under the water.

Plumes of bubbles surrounded me for a second as I sank down under the bright surface, before pushing off the bottom and popping up sputtering out a mouthful of water. To my embarrassment, I then briefly flailed around like a drowning hippopotamus before coming to my senses and swimming to the side to hold on.

Lifting a hand, I rubbed at my eyes to remove the water and then pushed my sopping wet hair away from my face to see, and hear, Sean laughing loudly as he trod water in the middle of the pool.

'Cannonball!' he said with a grin and a wicked wiggle of his eyebrows.

'You're supposed to shout as you jump into the pool, not afterwards!' I scolded him, flopping my drenched hair over my shoulders in a decidedly huffy gesture.

'Yeah, but you deserved it.' Seeing my affronted look, he grinned even wider and shrugged. 'After biting my nipple you proceeded to tease me by standing on the ladder and wiggling your delectable arse from side to side as you fannied about being too scared to get in the water.'

Faking outrage, I dropped my mouth open. 'I was not fannying! And I wasn't scared! I was making a ladylike and elegant entrance!' I exclaimed, now struggling to hold back the laughter. 'Or at least I was trying to,' I muttered, feeling far from elegant, and more like a half drowned rat.

'It looked like you were fannying to me,' he said with a grin, giving a shrug which caused a chunk of his wet hair to fall across his forehead somewhat distractingly. 'I was just being helpful and assisting you in your entry to the pool.'

He continued to tread water as he raised a hand and pushed his hair back from his brow so it was slicked neatly away from his face. Watching him, I felt my eyebrows rise in appreciation. What with his tan, the sun twinkling in his blue eyes, and his near perfect hair Sean now resembled something like a GQ model, and I couldn't help but grin back. How could I stay mad at him when he looked like that?

I couldn't, and I wasn't really mad at him – we were in a swimming pool, it was designed for fun, so messing around and getting me wet was sort of expected.

Pushing off from the side, I swam out to him and found that he wasn't actually treading water, but standing, so I lowered my legs to follow suit and immediately managed to dunk myself under the water again. While the water was shallow enough for Sean's six foot something body to stand, my five foot six frame could not reach the bottom.

Warm hands enclosed around my upper arms, bringing me to the surface where I sucked in a shocked breath and locked my gaze with Sean, who was openly laughing at me, his blue eyes sparkling and making him look ridiculously boyish and handsome.

'You seem to rather like it under the water,' he commented as he helped me tuck my legs around his waist. Looping my arms behind his neck, I grinned back and blinked several times to clear the droplets of water from my eyelashes.

'I like it here even more,' I murmured, locking my ankles behind his back and squeezing my thighs to bring myself as close as possible to his muscular abdomen.

He hummed an agreement, adjusting me so I slid marginally lower on his body until I could feel the stirrings of his arousal developing against my bum. 'Agreed. This is certainly an improvement on you trying to drown yourself,' he replied in a tone which had suddenly dropped far lower than before, but with his lips still twitching with amusement.

His gaze lazily lowered towards my lips and stayed there, causing my heart rate to rocket as a familiar, and much missed, throbbing heat settled in my groin. 'You have water on the tip of your nose,' he murmured, leaning forward to kiss it away. 'And your cheek.' His sinfully soft lips trailed from my nose across to my cheek, licking and kissing as he went and eliciting a small moan from my throat. 'And on your lips …' His mouth finally found mine and I seemed to lose all sense of time as I happily gave myself over to his delicious attention.

The idea of the swim had been to cool myself off, but with Sean's tongue now teasing me by tickling along the edges of my lips and tracing the seam with deliberate slowness, I was hugely aroused and quickly becoming overheated again. Moaning my appreciation, I opened my mouth to grant him access, which he immediately took, his tongue plunging past my lips to claim mine as his initially slow and lazy movements became far more demanding.

Sucking my bottom lip between his teeth, he gave it a nip as his hands slid to my waist. Oh God, I was moaning like a wanton hussy but couldn't stop myself. Even though there was barely a shred of space between us, he gripped my hips and pulled me against him even harder, causing him to curse against my lips and grind his erection against me. I thrust my pelvis forward, trapping his excitement between our bodies where I could feel the heat pulsing against my stomach. 'Christ, Allie. The things you do to me.'

The things I do to him? Hah! Likewise, buddy – the effect was most definitely mutual. I'd literally never been so affected by a man in my life.

Turning in the direction of the bungalow, Sean walked us toward the shallower water until it was lapping at waist level, and gently rested me back against the side of the pool. 'One second. Wait here,' he said, detaching me from his body. He didn't need to tell me, I was frozen to the spot as I watched him use the pool edge to swiftly hoist himself from the water like a bronzed water god. Mmmm, his skin was glistening in the sun and his shorts were clinging oh-so perfectly to that delicious bottom of his. Nope, I certainly wasn't going anywhere.

My eyes remained latched on his retreating figure as he headed towards the towel stand, grabbed some large fluffy towels, and turned to come back to me. Water dripped from his muscular body, running over his muscles in rivulets that drew my gaze and had me licking my lips greedily. God, he was just so sexy. The water had left his hair slick and ruffled deliciously, and the wet material of his boxers moulded around his straining erection to utter perfection. Blimey, what a sight. My mouth was practically watering. As if reading my thoughts he paused, glanced down at his tented shorts, grinned at me, and disposed with his boxers before continuing back towards me completely stark naked. 'Just as well we're not overlooked, eh?' he murmured cheekily.

I was so horny I'd been rendered speechless. Forget a bronzed Adonis, he was sex on legs. In fact, he looked too good to be true and I shivered all over from the sight. With a purposeful expression, Sean winked at me and reaching the poolside behind me, laid the towels down so they hung over the edge and formed a makeshift backrest. Even in the midst of a saucy seduction he was thinking of me. He really was incredible.

Sliding gracefully back into the water, Sean waded in front of me again and gently laid his hands so they cupped my neck. Trailing his hands from my shoulders, down my arms and onto my waist, they finally settled on my bottom and gently massaged the flesh as he gazed at me intently.

'Now, where were we?'

Gripping my bum, he lifted me so I could wrap my legs around him again, and once we were firmly entwined he lowered his mouth to mine for a fierce kiss which almost consumed me whole. Now his erection had been freed from the confines of his boxers it stood up keenly and ended up well and truly squashed between our bodies, showing no signs of shrinkage from the cold water and pressing urgently along my opening, causing me to groan impatiently and grind myself against him.

'Don't be so impatient ... I'm savouring you, my gorgeous girl.' A smirk curled his lips as he watched me huff out an impatient breath, which quickly turned to a satisfied moan when he lowered his lips to mine again. 'I'm leading this. You can't rush me,' he murmured into my mouth. Damn him! I was aroused and needy and wanted him buried inside of me right now. Unfortunately, experience had taught me that nothing would sway Sean once he'd made his mind up about something, and seeing as he really did lead all things sexual so bloody well I tried to settle my swelling urgency and simply enjoy the moment.

Separating our mouths, Sean used one hand to trail up my body until it rested at the base of my throat, his fingers splayed across the delicate skin. A flicker of a smile crossed his handsome face as he stared down at me, no doubt because he could feel the effect he had on me reflected in my pulse fluttering wildly against his fingers. 'Let me know if you get uncomfortable,' he told me, before pressing against my throat and encouraging me to curve my spine backwards.

'Unloop your arms, gorgeous girl, and hold the pool rail.' Doing as I was told, I leaned my head and shoulders against the soft towel on the poolside and stretched my arms out on either side of me so I could grip the rail, my legs still firmly wrapped around his waist for support. With his left hand still gently encasing my throat I felt almost owned by him, and the surrender of the position made my arousal soar. God, he was good. Outside the bedroom we were complete equals – Sean had even commented that he liked my feisty side – but in bed he was a dominant lover. It was just how he worked. Seeing as he always made me feel so bloody good, I had to say I loved it.

With me under his control, Sean now had easier access to my upper body, which he immediately took advantage of by reaching around me with his free hand and untying my bikini top with one quick flick of his fingers. Freeing my breasts, he chucked the top onto the poolside and moved both hands so they were circling my lower ribs. 'Hmm. So beautiful, Allie. And all mine.'

I was so drowsy from arousal that all I could manage in reply was to briefly let go of the pool rail, raise my hand to cup his cheek, and whisper, 'Likewise.'

Nodding intently, Sean guided my hand back to the rail. 'Keep them here, gorgeous girl,' he murmured, before replacing his hands on my waist and beginning a teasing massage. Using the lubrication of the water he slid them up until his thumbs were making circling patterns on the lower swell of my breasts, just below my nipples. The sensation was so good that I practically gargled my delight as I arched my back further, my eyes facing upwards but squeezed shut in bliss.

After tormenting me by touching every part of my breasts except the desperate nipples, Sean finally put me out of my misery and bowed his head, giving each nipple just the barest lick with the point of his tongue. A garbled shout of frustration left my mouth as I attempted – and failed – to thrust my chest against his mouth and my hands once again flew from the rail, this time burrowing into his hair and trying to shove his head down.

'Uh, uh. Naughty, naughty,' Sean murmured, peeling my hands away and placing them back on the rail. Holding them there for a second he leant in to kiss my neck, running his heated tongue along my jugular and chuckling against my skin. 'Naughty girls have to wait longer for what they want.' Gah! He was driving me insane! But no matter how frustrated I was, I immediately wrapped my fingers around the pool rail and gripped on to it as if my life depended on it. I was a quick learner, and I desperately wanted to come, so there would be no more breaking the rules. Not today, anyway.

'Better.' Nuzzling his face between my breasts, Sean trailed his fingers away from my now obedient hands, resting his grip on my ribs again, and finally, blissfully, took one swollen nub into his mouth. Thank God. It felt so amazing I cried out in pleasure, my head thrashing from side to side in bliss. The contrast of my skin, chilled from the water, and his hot mouth made me gasp, the sudden inhalation merely forcing my breast further into his mouth and helping increase the pressure from his skilful touch.

Sean circled his tongue around my nipple, nibbled and licked until I felt like I was going insane from the pleasure, before he gave a sharper bite which sent a jolt of lust to my clit so strong that I felt it pulse spasmodically. Christ, the alluring mixture of pleasure and pain had very nearly made me come.

'I felt that,' Sean chuckled against my skin, clearly well and truly proud of himself as he languorously moved his attention to my other aching breast, almost causing me to release the pool rail before I realised what I was doing and held it in an iron grip. 'You like a touch of pain, hmm? I'll have to remember that.'

I think his question was rhetorical – or at least I hoped it was, because there was no way I could formulate an articulate response now. I was almost out of my mind; my body was on fire for Sean, my core spasmodically clenching and unclenching in its desperation to be filled by him. In fact, my body was writhing so frantically that I was causing the water around us to slap against the side of the pool and flood the concrete behind us.

'Sean … Please …' Never ever had I begged a man for sex, but with Sean I seemed to do it all the time. The power he held over me was incredible, but even more astonishing was the way I seemed to wholeheartedly embrace my submission to him.

'I told you I'd make you wait. All in good time, my gorgeous girl,' he murmured against my nipple, the vibrations of his lips causing me to buck wildly against him in protest and let out a pathetically needy groan. Trailing a finger across my stomach he tickled and teased before eventually arriving at my hip, where he set about untying the string holding up my bikini bottoms. At last! I almost yelled my relief.

Once both sides were undone, Sean gave a tug, pulling it from between us and dragging it roughly over my throbbing clit in the process. As soon as it was free from my body, Sean dropped it, the material falling away from me and no doubt sinking to the bottom of the pool – not that I cared in the slightest. We could retrieve it once Sean was done having his wicked way with me.

Shifting me, Sean used his strength to hold us apart as he pressed the broad tip of his arousal against my core, but just as he was about to push inside me, I lifted my head and spoke. 'Wait!' He actually did pause, one of his eyebrows rising in surprise.

'You've been writhing against me in desperation for the last ten minutes but now you want me to wait?' he asked in frustrated amusement.

'Can we shift a bit shallower? It's just that I read somewhere that having sex in a pool isn't good for a woman. All that chemical-laden water being shoved inside can cause infections …' Giving a grunt, Sean was prompted into motion immediately, grabbing the towel from behind me and clutching me to him so I was caged against him like a limpet.

'Of course. Actually, I have an idea …' he murmured against my ear, those final five words somehow laden with salacious intent and causing my skin to quiver with anticipation.

Chapter Thirty-Two

Sean

Walking us far shallower than Allie probably expected, I paused at the low, flat steps where there was only a centimetre or so of water lapping the edge. This should be perfect for what I had in mind. Gently lowering my girl from my arms, I landed a scorching kiss on her lips which prompted a very satisfying gasp to rumble in her throat. The gasp melted into a moan as I explored her mouth with deep, sweeping lashes of my tongue, and a smile curved my lips at the sound. I didn't think I'd ever tire of hearing how much I affected her – it was the best fucking feeling in the world knowing that I was the one making her feel that good.

Bending down, I placed the towel on the second step, where it immediately began to soak up water, and then jerked my chin at it. 'Kneel down.' The command in both my intent and tone was obvious, and yet I couldn't help but add a softer note to my instruction. 'Let me know if it's too hard under your knees.'

Allie dropped immediately to her knees for me and my pulse leapt at her easy, trusting compliance. Maybe I had some inbuilt dominance, because I fucking loved to see her on her knees.

Standing back to admire her, I couldn't help but sigh with contentment. Fuck me, she looked glorious. Her back was ram rod straight, causing her breasts to jut forward perfectly, the sun was warming her back, making it glow with health, and her gorgeous hair that I so loved was wet, making it look even longer than usual. Licking my lips as I focused on the long, tempting strands I just knew I was going to have to wrap it around my wrist soon.

Suddenly just looking at her wasn't enough, and so I knelt behind her and began to run my hands all over her beautiful body. Kneading her shoulders, arms, and buttocks I gave her a firm, relaxing massage then wrapped my arms around her to cup her breasts and repeat the treatment.

By this point Allie was writhing in my arms, letting out an almost constant string of soft whimpers, and in response my cock was practically screaming to take her. I wanted to, desperately, but not quite yet; I wanted to be sure she was ready for me first. Reluctantly I let her go and placed one hand on her shoulder to give a gentle push. 'Lean over, baby, on all fours.'

Once again Allie followed my lead immediately as she leant forward and placed her hands on the higher step so she was on her hands and knees before me. My cock was now nudging at the crease of her bottom, desperately searching for its release, but I was so turned on that I tried to hold off to make sure I didn't hurt her.

This position was perfect for me to explore her opening with my fingers, so I immediately did, running a finger along her delicate skin before dipping into her centre with a heated groan. She was so ready for me that I simply couldn't hold back any longer.

'You look so beautiful like this, Allie, skin flushed and body waiting for me … Christ, I love you.' As soon as the words were out of my mouth I removed my fingers and used my hand to position the head of my cock at her entrance. Pulling in a deep breath to try and help my restraint, I gripped her hips and began to slowly press forward. Looking down, I bit my lip as I watched the first inch disappear inside her. Seeing her body accept me had always turned me on, whether it be my fingers or cock, but holy fuck, seeing it in the bright sunshine was so erotic. The muscles of her channel were visibly quivering, gripping around the tip of my cock like a fist and trying to pull me in further.

'Sean … deeper, please.' Allie's plea was uttered in a hoarse, desperate tone, and I began to comply, nudging deeper inch by inch until I was buried to the root and my stomach was flush against her buttocks.

My head tipped back and eyes flickered shut from the incredible depth I got in this position. Pleasure was shooting around my system, and my cock was jerking wildly, demanding that I start to move, but I didn't. Instead I paused, with us joined as intimately as possible. Allie let out a garbled exclamation about how good it felt, but after several moments she tried to shove herself backwards into me, presumably attempting to speed up the proceedings.

Grinning at her impatience I quickly stopped her by pulling out completely and tutting quietly. 'Uh-uh.' Allie tried to thrash around in complaint, but my fingers quickly put a stop to that by gripping her hips like a vice to prevent her from moving. 'Slow down, I'm making sure you're ready for me, baby.'

Twisting her head to the side Allie managed to make eye contact with me, her blue eyes flashing with arousal and determination. 'I'm ready, Sean, believe me. I feel like I'm going to implode if you don't let me orgasm soon.' I sucked in a breath at her words. The way she used the phrase 'If you don't let me' had been ridiculously arousing, appealing to the side of me which craved control, and my cock suddenly felt even thicker and harder than before.

Christ, I had a feeling that this was going to be some monumentally good sex.

Clearing my throat, I tried to hold back from thrusting with abandon and follow through on my intentions to make sure she was definitely OK. 'You say that, but last night I was ... less than gentle.' Wasn't that just the biggest ever understatement? I had thrust into her so hard I'd seen stars. 'I'm trying to make sure I don't hurt you. Are you not sore?'

'I'm a little tender but in a good way, nothing that a good orgasm from you won't ease. I'm fine, Sean, but thank you.' Blinking several times I reeled in my control and then began to push inside her. Again I went slowly, and again she tried to demand I went faster, but once I had fully reunited us her complaints lessened and began to morph into lusty moans.

Beginning to move with more purpose, I placed one hand on her left shoulder and slid one around to rest over her right breast. The nipple hardened against my palm and I couldn't resist tweaking and pinching it as I used the hand on her shoulder to pull her onto my thrusts. As my control began to lessen my contact became harder and deeper, and just what I had wanted all along. Clearly it was just what Allie had wanted all along too, because her body was willingly accepting my harder movements, clutching me with her muscles as she groaned heatedly.

God, this woman was amazing.

The water around our knees and calves was splashing with our movements, slopping onto the pool side and leaving patterns on the sun-bleached stone. My ego took great pleasure in the sight, seeing the wildly splashing water as a reflection of the power with which I was taking her. Mine.

I felt my orgasm building in my balls and my eyes briefly rolled shut. Desperate to make sure Allie reached her climax with me I let out a groan of pleasure and tangled my fingers in her beautiful hair.

'Touch yourself, Allie.' My girl must be familiar with those words by now, as I frequently found myself uttering them purely because I often couldn't bear to give up the hold I had on her hair. Don't get me wrong, I bloody loved touching her between her silky thighs – I was a red blooded male, so of course I did. But her hair? Fuck, something about seeing it twisted around my fist just did me in every single time.

Wrapping a huge swath of her golden locks around my wrist, I absorbed the sight for a second and then tugged gently, causing her to arch her back and let out a long, low moan as she moved one hand towards her clit.

Gripping her shoulder with more force I helped her balance as I really began to move. My pace had sped up, but I was determined to maintain my control for long enough to bring Allie to the brink with me. I continued to drive my throbbing cock into her over and over again until I was once on the brink of my release.

Thankfully, after just a few seconds of this increased tempo I felt Allie's channel beginning to clench as her release also neared. Thank God for that, because I was about ready to burst at the seams with the need to shoot my load.

'Sean, I need to come …'

Her tone almost seemed to be asking my permission, which caused me to smile as I groaned out my reply. 'Yes … come, Allie. My gorgeous, gorgeous girl, come for me.'

My pace remained relentless, abdomen slapping furiously against her on each thrust and causing her to rock violently back and forth, her gorgeous breasts swinging below her, and then suddenly she exploded, her channel going into spasm around my cock, clamping down on my length hard enough to cause a strangled cry to grate from my throat. 'Fuck, so tight …'

As I continued to push in and out of her, Allie's orgasm rolled on and on, seeming to last forever as each of my thrusts caused her to grip around me again and again like a vice.

Even as I buried myself to the hilt and came with a loud, animalistic shout, I could feel regular aftershocks of pleasure spiralling throughout her body. Holy shit. That was possibly one of our best efforts yet, and just as monumental as I had thought it might be.

Dropping my head forward I rested my sweaty brow on her heaving back and ran a trail of kisses across her shoulders and neck. I tried to steady my panting breaths, but it was a losing battle at the moment, so instead I concentrated on tending to my girl and helping to support the weight of her exhausted body. I didn't seem to be able to keep my hands off her, so as I trailed my palms lovingly across her skin it served a dual purpose – inflaming my love and helping to ease her down from her climax.

Wanting to stay joined with her for as long as possible, I didn't pull out, but instead knelt up and began to gently massage her scalp in case I had hurt her by tugging too hard in the heat of the moment. As I trailed my fingers through her damp hair to loosen the tangles, Allie moaned with pleasure, the sound sending a jerk straight to my softening cock. Jeez, the things this woman did to me.

Once I was satisfied that Allie was replete and relaxed, I placed one more kiss on her shoulder and only then began to ease myself out of her. I winced as my over-sensitised length finally slipped from her body, immediately wishing that I could slide it back and stay there forever.

'Stay here,' I murmured, rubbing her lower back once more before standing and heading to the pool side bathroom. Cleaning myself off, I then grabbed some tissues and towels and hurried back outside to Allie.

Blinking in the bright sunshine I saw our reflection in the windows of the bungalow and bit on my lower lip in arousal. Fuck, she looked sexy as hell kneeling there waiting for me. As potent as our love making had been, I still felt my cock give a twitch of approval at her positioning.

Catching my eye in the reflection, Allie smiled shyly and then grinned. 'Thank goodness Cait didn't come home. Can you imagine the shock she would have got seeing us?' My eyes immediately shot to the bungalow windows again and I joined Allie in a broad smile. The pool steps were directly opposite the lounge's floor to ceiling windows, so Cait really would have got an eyeful of me mounting her best friend from behind like a randy dog. I was so satisfied that a loud laugh slipped from my lips as I grinned cockily.

Stepping back into the shallow water, I gently reached between her legs and began to clean her off with some tissues. Tending to Allie after sex was like an addiction now. It had started off as a way for me to ease the guilt I'd felt after our first few sexual encounters where I had been less than pleasant in my treatment of her, but now it was for purely selfish reasons. Looking after her was one of the best feelings I'd ever experienced in my life.

As I bent lower to make sure I'd been thorough I saw the evidence of our joint climaxes shimmering on her thighs. Holy fuck. That image sent another jolt to my cock and I had to suck in a sharp breath to stop me from grabbing hold of her and immediately initiating round two. God, I never wanted to go two months without her ever again. Only the thought that she might be sore now persuaded me to hold back from taking her – I might be addicted to Allie, but I wasn't a monster.

Reaching out a hand I helped Allie to her feet, and then scooped up the wet towel that we had knelt on before tossing it onto the pool side where it landed with a loud splat.

Wrapping my arms around her I pulled Allie against me and closed my eyes in contentment as she nuzzled into my neck and let out a long, satisfied sigh. I had my girl in my arms, the sun warm on my back, and I was utterly replete from our love making, this day really couldn't get much better.

'That was incredible, Sean,' she murmured, and I agreed with a humming noise. Lowering my lips, I planted a kiss on the top of her head just as she lay a kiss directly over my heart. 'I love you too, Sean. I was too overwhelmed to manage to say it earlier.'

Smiling down at her, I guided us from the pool, through the patio doors to her room, and across the wooden floor to the en-suite bathroom where we had a quick shower. Allie's wandering hands indicated that she was quite happy to initiate round two while we stood under the heated water, but as tempting as that was I didn't want her to be too sore, and so instead side-tracked her by washing her from head to toe. Once I was done, Allie returned the favour, lavishing me with attention and seeming to enjoy the opportunity to get up close and personal with every inch of my body.

Every. Single. Inch.

The cheeky minx must have spent a good five minutes soaping my groin area, which predictably ended up with me gritting my teeth, clinging to the shower wall, and sporting a gigantic hard-on. God, we'd had vigorous sex twice in less than twenty-four hours but I was completely ready to go again.

When Allie next looked up at me I could see from the twinkle in her eyes that she was going to try and coax me into changing my mind about round three, and then, just as I had anticipated, she reached up and wrapped a soapy palm around the base of my cock. Groaning, I clenched my teeth as I struggled for control, and then gently pushed her backwards with a wry smile.

Stepping from the shower I picked up two fluffy towels, slung one loosely around my waist so it hung from my hips and shielded my erection from her wandering hands, and then moved forward, intent on drying my girl.

'You're no fun,' she pouted.

Allowing her sulk, I smiled, and set about drying her shoulders and back. 'That's not what you said a few minutes ago in the pool,' I murmured dryly, causing her shoulders to shake as she giggled.

Once she was dry I began to quickly wipe the fluffy cotton across my body, but Allie surprised me by snatching the towel from my hands and raising it to dry off my chest with a smirk.

'My turn,' she murmured as she ran the material across my taut nipples, eliciting a hiss from my lips. Hmmm. So she wanted to reciprocate? Well, that was just fine by me, so I gave in without a fight, lowering my arms and tilting my head as I merely observed her. I watched her every move with a small smile on my face, wondering if I looked half as blissed out when I was caring for her as Allie currently did.

She gave my biceps a small tap, and I obediently lifted my arms so she could dry my sides. Once she was satisfied, Allie moved around in front of me and gave the towel around my hips a gentle tug, grinning cheekily as it fell to the floor to reveal my privates in all their glory.

Fuck, I'd only just managed to get my erection under control after her shower escapades, but now that I was buck naked with Allie's greedy gaze staring straight at my groin I gave in with a sigh and watched it harden again before my eyes.

I was fully erect and rock solid in less than three seconds. Which even with my high sex drive was pretty impressive.

The temptation of my twitching erection was obviously too great for Allie to resist and instead of continuing with her drying regime she went to reach for my shaft again.

Fuck … my resolve was seriously depleted now, so as she gazed up at me, seeking my permission I gave in with a groan and thrust my hips towards her mouth.

I was only human, after all.

Looking like she'd just won the lottery, Allie leant forward and flicked her tongue across the tip of my cock, causing it to jerk up against my belly as I staggered back and rested against the counter.

Crawling forward, she looked up at me from under hooded eyes and made a show of licking her lips before taking hold of me in her fist and pumping her hand up and down. 'You don't have to do this, you know,' I murmured as my fingers curled fiercely around the counter top.

Widening her eyes, she smiled impishly at me, sucked the tip of my cock into her hot mouth, and then leant back, still working me with her hand. 'I know. But I want to.'

Well, when she put it like that, who was I to stop her?

After that all talk ceased as Allie really got into her rhythm, sucking me deep into her mouth, rolling her tongue around the crown, and working the base of my shaft with her fingers. My head rolled back briefly before I brought my heavy-lidded gaze forward again and watched her work my cock with huge enthusiasm. Man, she was so fucking good at this.

After our recent pool sex I knew I wouldn't last long, especially not with the power Allie was using on me. She was sucking me like a woman dying of thirst. Moments later, when she raised a hand and began to fondle my balls, I felt my insides tightening, and then before I'd even properly realised it, I was coming, my climax flooding her mouth with such force that some escaped her lips and dribbled down her chin.

After working me down for several seconds, Allie knelt back on her knees and gazed up at me, and I couldn't help grinning down at her. Leaning down, I lazily wiped away the come trailing from her mouth and blew out a long, satisfied breath. Forget about Allie needing a rest to stop her getting sore, at this rate it would be me needing to give my tackle some lengthy recovery time.

Finishing me off with a final gentle lick, she rolled back onto her knees and then placed a brief kiss right on the tip of my cock before meeting my eyes. 'Thank you.'

She was thanking me? God, this woman never failed to surprise me. Grinning at her like the lovesick idiot I was, I reached down and lifted her until Allie understood what I wanted and stood up before hopping up and wrapping her legs around my waist.

Smashing my lips onto hers, I plunged my tongue into her mouth, still able to taste my release on her tongue, and kissed my girl hard, trying to express to her just how much she meant to me. 'No, my gorgeous girl. It is definitely me that needs to be thanking you.'

Chapter Thirty-Three

Allie

This all felt so normal. We'd shared the bed, chilled out round the pool, showered together, had some incredible sex, and declared our love for each other. Having Sean here with me again felt so natural that a contented smile curved my lips as I began to brush out my hair. Glancing across at him, I found Sean watching my every move in fascination. 'I love your hair. Here, let me.' Striding behind me, he relieved me of the hairbrush and began to gently brush out my tangles before picking up the hairdryer from the counter. My smile was now a grin as I watched in the mirror as Sean concentrated on the task of methodically drying my hair section by section. The focused look on his face was almost comical. Bless him.

Once the hairdryer was off and Sean was running the brush through my dry hair with ease, I caught his gaze in the mirror. 'You being here, and us enjoying the day together, it feels like a dream.' Even with my upbeat words, I couldn't hold back the heavy sigh that suddenly slipped from my lips as I remembered that this was just one day and that Sean would be going back to his work tomorrow. And more depressingly, back to Savannah.

Hearing my sigh, Sean placed the brush down and gave my shoulder a squeeze. 'Hey, why so glum all of a sudden?' Sliding an arm around my waist he turned me and effortlessly lifted me to sit on the vanity unit between the two sinks. Stooping down so he could look deep into my eyes, he raised a hand and cupped my cheek before gently rubbing it with his thumb.

I immediately felt stupid for ruining a great day with my insecurities and petty jealousy. 'Sorry, I'm fine, it's just the stuff with Savannah is still on my mind ...' I paused, hating the way that her mere name made jealousy bubble in my stomach. 'Plus all the secrecy and hardly getting to see you, it's hard. Really hard.' I paused before saying what was really on my mind. 'Sometimes I feel like it would be easier for you if I weren't here. It's like we're in a weird alternate reality that's pulling us apart and never going to end. You'd be better off if I wasn't in your life.'

'No.' His voice was almost harsh, his eyes flashing with some unreadable pain, but his face immediately softened as he gazed at me, his beautiful blue eyes crinkling with concern at the edges. 'I want you here, Allie, but beyond that, I need you in my life,' Sean implored, as he pulled me to the edge of the unit, edged himself between my thighs before resting his head on my shoulder.

I could feel his accelerated breathing on my neck, fast, short pants as if he was struggling to breathe. 'Don't say things like that, Allie.' We were so close that I could smell my shower gel still fresh on his skin and I wanted to keep him locked there forever.

I really wanted to believe him, bury my head in his reassuring warmth, and forget all about Savannah flipping Hilton, but the more I considered our reality, the more I couldn't. Instead, all I managed was to nod unconvincingly and sit limply on the unit as he leant back and considered me with an ever-growing frown on his face. 'The craziness will end, I promise. Don't give up on me.' Tilting my chin upwards, he hit me with the full blast of his intense blue eyes. 'Don't run again, please.'

A sliver of guilt worked its way into my chest as I recalled how easily I'd run from him when the going had got tough. 'OK. I'm sorry. I didn't mean to bring a downer on our day.'

Taking a deep breath, I forced a smile and reached up to place a quick peck on his lips. 'Let's forget it and have some lunch, I'm starving.' Trying to look, and sound, reassured, I slid from the counter and went in search of some clothes so Sean could shave in peace. He clearly wasn't convinced by my act, because I spotted him watching me cautiously in the mirror as I walked around the bedroom. He became quieter from then on, barely speaking a word as we ordered some food from room service, and I repeatedly cursed myself for ruining an otherwise lovely day.

His thoughtful silence lasted through lunch, and the tension between us completely took away the enjoyment from my prawn salad until his head shot up abruptly and he jumped from his stool. 'I just need to make a quick call.' He seemed suddenly perkier as he dashed from the room with his mobile and I wondered what on earth had come over him as I picked unenthusiastically at my food.

Returning a few minutes later with my cap and sunglasses in his hand and a huge grin on his face, Sean held his spare hand out for me. 'Come with me, I've had an idea of how I can put your mind at ease.' It was so good to see him smiling again that I didn't hesitate. As soon as I'd placed my palm in his, Sean gave enough of a tug to send me stumbling into him and I was immediately aware of the tempting warmth and firmness of his chest.

Even with my mood, I immediately found my earlier lust reigniting at the feel of him under my fingertips. It was almost pathetic how easy I was for him. God, I was insatiable at the moment. It was like having sex with Sean again had given me some sort of addiction.

Looking up at him with wide eyes, I licked my lips, almost positive he would be able to read my mind and be just as up for it as me, but to my mild annoyance he looked completely together and calm as he smiled at me.

'Easy, tiger, let me put your mind at rest about our future together then you can rub my chest as much as you want.' It couldn't have been possible for me to flush any redder, and I hastily looked away as he chuckled and placed a kiss on the top of my head.

Handing me my cap and glasses Sean donned his own, pulling the cap down low over his eyes and I suddenly realised to my horror why he'd gone to fetch mine – this was his version of a disguise so we could make a rare excursion outside. Except instead of the blond hair and contact lenses he'd used last time, he was settling for a simple cap.

Nerves exploded in my stomach hard and fast as it finally perforated my mind that we were about to venture out in public. Together. With no real disguises. Which considering he was contracted to appear engaged to Savannah and therefore not dating me, almost made it against the law, didn't it? It was certainly enough to get him sacked, which terrified me. If he ended up losing his job because of me, that would surely be the end of our relationship too, wouldn't it?

Gulping hard at the reality of what we were about to do, I took the items from his outstretched hand. Sean must have seen my hesitation, or perhaps felt the tremble in my hand, because he stopped and dipped his head to look in my eyes. Either way, he whipped his cap off and wordlessly pulled me into his arms so I was firmly pressed against the impressive chest that had ignited me with lust just a few minutes earlier. This time, however, instead of wanting to rip his shirt off, I was clinging to it for dear life.

'Hey, hey, it's all right, my gorgeous girl, we're just going for a short drive. No need to worry. OK?'

Giving a little shudder, I suddenly felt really stupid. After all, I had been the one to make a fuss about us not being able to go out together. I had been the miserable, moaning girlfriend going on and on about how we couldn't be a normal couple. And now we were finally about to go out, I was the one freaking out. I was such a mess.

Pulling in a deep breath, I leant away, braced myself on his forearms, and nodded. 'Sorry, I freaked myself out for a minute there. Are we OK doing this? I mean, are you going to get into trouble?'

Grinning and looking thoroughly amused, Sean shook his head slowly, his blue eyes twinkling. 'Not if we're careful. We're not going far. Stick your hat on and we'll head off.'

I was about to ask where we were going but I was distracted as he donned his sunglasses and hat and before my eyes, transformed into a totally different person. I'd always scoffed at how no one recognised Clark Kent as Superman when he put his glasses on, but to be honest, with his reflective glasses and cap pulled down low, I think even I would have struggled to recognise Sean at first glance. I was fairly sure he would simply blend in with the other guys walking about on the streets of LA in the sunshine.

Even so, as we walked out of the bungalow, I was practically shaking all over. The phrase 'must not look nervous' was running round and around my mind, but of course, that was easier said than done. Swallowing loudly, I glanced around nervously, wondering if anyone was watching – which of course they weren't, because we just looked like two regular people walking in the hotel. It was only me who felt nervous, but I was so tense it almost felt like I had a neon sign flashing above my head.

Holding Sean's hand and absorbing his calm strength would have eased some of my nerves, but I figured that probably wasn't exactly ideal as we were trying to be secretive, so I held off, pushed my shoulders back, and tried my hardest to act casual and nonchalant. In reality, this probably just made me look severely constipated, an impression no doubt strengthened by the tense, slightly wincing expression on my face.

Crossing the car park, I did a double take as I heard Sean whistling a decidedly happy tune under his breath. My eyes flew open at his ease – I was so tense and nervous I must've surely looked like I had something rammed up my arse, but Sean was happy as Larry? Marvellous. Stopping beside a dark green Jeep I glanced at it in relief. OK, so that really hadn't been anywhere near as taxing as I had imagined, and I felt my posture relaxing now we had made it to his car.

Taking a little longer to look at it, I nodded my head in appreciation. It was one of the old-style Wranglers, with an exposed frame and a leather cover that had seen better days instead of a roof. I loved it, but I was a sucker for old-school Jeeps. I always had been, ever since watching an episode of *The A-Team* as a kid where Hannibal had driven one through a wall of fire. Hopefully our journey today would be a little less stressful than that though.

Climbing up into the cabin, I pulled the door closed and looked around. There were no luxuries or soft touches, it was all exposed dials, switches, and metal surfaces. It was nowhere near as flashy as I thought Sean's car would have been, especially considering how much money he must have made, but knowing Sean had a bit of a rough and ready side and liked to get out and explore the great outdoors, I supposed it suited him perfectly.

Once we were buckled up, Sean flashed me a grin and what looked like a wink from behind his Aviator sunglasses, and then started the car. We drove through the streets of Downtown LA, passing areas which were becoming increasingly familiar. I was even able to point out my favourite pizza restaurant and a few of the bars I had been to with Cait. The longer we drove, the less tense I became, but no matter how many times Sean leant over and gave my knee a reassuring squeeze, I still couldn't fully relax.

How strange was this? Cruising along with the sun blazing. We must have looked like a couple with not a worry in the world, whereas in reality, my stomach was doing cartwheels. Where were we going? He still hadn't told me, and with every mile travelled I felt slightly sicker from anxiety.

I was far from an expert on the city, but I soon recognised that we were heading away from Downtown Hollywood and the hostel, and in the direction we'd gone when visiting Venice Beach.

As it was, we didn't quite make it to the beach this time. Instead, Sean pulled off the main highway at what I remember Cait calling the Cheviot Hills. In a matter of seconds, the main road was forgotten, to be replaced by tree-lined avenues, broad roads, and gorgeous sprawling houses and I was practically hanging out of my window and drooling in appreciation. Cait had said it was posh, and blimey, had she been right. I'd never seen such opulent properties or well-manicured gardens in my life. The lawns looked like they had been trimmed with fingernail scissors. Perhaps they had; maybe that was what sack loads of cash could buy you over here.

As we pulled alongside a large park, Sean drew the car up to the side of the road, pulled off his glasses, and turned to look at me with an unreadable expression in his eyes. 'We're nearly there, Allie. You might want to slip your hat down a little lower unless you fancy being in all the papers tomorrow.'

What? More than slightly confused, not to mention suddenly terrified, I did as Sean asked and yanked my hat down as low as it could go, folding one of my ears over in the process. Frowning at him, I felt my patience wearing thin. 'Where exactly are we going?' I asked as he pulled the car back onto the road.

'My house,' Sean said. 'You can meet my fiancée.' He finished, exaggerating 'fiancée' so it was dripping thick with sarcasm. 'That way you can talk to her and see first-hand that there's nothing between us except work links.' No matter how lightly he seemed to be taking this, I was fast falling into panic stations.

'What?' I yelped, my voice full of panic as I felt little icy slivers of fear running through my veins. He was taking me to his house? Oh my God, my stomach felt like it had dropped out of my body, rolled from the Jeep, and fallen hard on the roadside.

Dressed in faded jeans, a scruffy T-shirt, and wearing no makeup at all, I was completely not ready to be introduced to sleek, sexy Savannah as Sean's romantic interest. I opened my mouth to protest but all I could manage to utter were a few garbled noises.

Then, before I could reconnect my mouth and say anything, Sean was pulling the car up to the entrance of a gated housing lot, where we instantly caught the attention of a couple of journalists sitting on the grass verge. Before I could even register what was happening, flashbulbs began to pop around the car and to my embarrassment I screamed like a small child.

'Oh, my God!' I exclaimed, slithering down in my seat so far that I was practically taking residence in the foot well. 'I am totally not ready for this, Sean!' I shrieked, clinging to my hat and trying my best to cover my face. Thank God the canvas roof was up so they couldn't get a good look inside, but that didn't stop them getting close to the windows and snapping several pictures. Shit, all I could think about was what would happen to us if he lost his job because of this.

Looking highly amused, Sean glanced over at me – or should that be down at me – and laughed, a lovely rumbling chuckle that briefly made me forget about the photographers as my heart did a little flip. I really loved the way he laughed. 'If you had acted casually, they would probably just have thought you were my sister or a friend. But lying down there? That makes you look guilty as hell.' Annoyingly, he was right. He also seemed very calm about it, which was pissing me off no end.

Thankfully, at that moment a tall, tanned, blond guy wearing a dark security uniform glanced into the car then pressed a button which started the gates rising. The bloody things seemed to take forever to rise, but eventually Sean was able to pull his car in away from the journalists. Thank God for that. Drawing in a huge, shaky breath I clambered out from my hiding place and lifted my hands up to see just how badly I was shaking. My hands looked like they were experiencing a major earthquake. Bloody hell, I could barely control my own fingers.

Trying to calm myself, I attempted a distraction by looking around. After my performance in the car I needed to get a grip, otherwise Savannah and Sean were going to think I was completely neurotic.

'So, this is where I'm living. Temporarily,' Sean emphasised as he drove up a curved driveway towards a large, white, low-level house. Once we pulled to a stop I climbed from the car and pulled in several breaths to calm myself. Running my eye over the house again, I was vaguely reminded of my childhood holidays in Spain because it resembled a villa, with arched windows, tiled steps, and terracotta roof slates. It was lovely, and huge. Obviously.

Now we were well away from prying eyes, Sean came around the car and pulled my cap off, chucking it in the back seat along with his. Placing his hands on my shoulders, he grinned, not seeming at all bothered by his hat hair, but then again, it looked all ruffled and spiky and basically gorgeous. Mine, however, felt like I'd just spent the last hour in a wind tunnel, and I quickly ran a hand through it, hideously conscious of the fact that I was about to meet a virtual supermodel. Stopping my agitated movements, Sean gently smoothed my hair for me, running his fingers through the long strands until my eyes fluttered closed from the pleasure spiking through my scalp. If he was trying to relax me by targeting my soft spot, then it was working.

'I can't wait until all this is sorted and I can show you the place I bought over here. You're going to love it, Allie.' As soon as Sean's fingers stopped their wondrous touch, I opened my eyes and immediately felt my nerves return when I eyed the house behind him.

'Mmm-hmm,' was all I could manage. Yes I was excited about seeing his new place, of course I was, but right now my focus was on the impending meeting with Savannah.

Chuckling, Sean took my hand in his and began to lead me towards the house. 'Come on, Savannah won't bite. Plus she's expecting us, I called ahead to check she was home.' Using some fancy key fob to open the front door, Sean led me from the heat of the day into a large, bright, cool entrance hall. The floors were polished marble, and the scattered furniture was all expensive-looking, but it felt quite sterile, and lacked any warmth or homeliness. There were no knickknacks, photographs, or personal belongings, no coats over the ornate bannister, nothing. It felt very much like a show home. Which I suppose it was; they were 'showing' the world they lived together, even though it was a sham.

Leading me through the extensive property, we passed a large lounge fitted out in beiges and creams, past several closed doors, and then into a huge, brightly-lit kitchen.

Wow. This part of the house was amazing – a beautiful, modern kitchen complete with granite work surfaces and shiny black cupboards that ran seamlessly into a dining area. This section had a wooden table large enough to seat ten, and continued through to a small seating area with leather sofas. All this was lit by daylight flooding in from the wall of windows that ran along the entire rear of the property, almost making it feel like we were in the garden. It was incredible.

'Savannah must be out on the deck,' Sean commented, pointing at the opening in the glass that led to a wide decking area strewn with loungers, and then down to an immaculately kept garden. I was quite speechless. Talk about how the other half live – this place was stunning.

'Would you like a drink? Coffee, tea, perhaps some juice?' Sean questioned as he opened the fridge.

'Water please,' I replied, and then I heard padding footsteps behind me and turned to see Savannah Hilton – clad only in a tiny leopard print bikini and knee-length see-through sarong – making her way through the doors towards us. She gave me a cursory inspection before sweeping her face towards Sean and smiling broadly. 'Something cool for me too, darrrling, it is so hot out there today.'

Frozen to the spot. That's how I felt, because I had gone totally rigid from head to toe. Even my scalp felt taut. First of all, if she knew we were coming then she was clearly displaying her perfect body on purpose, and secondly, the way she called him 'darrrling' with that irritating roll of her tongue made it sound overtly intimate, and I immediately wanted to punch her.

So here she was in the flesh. Savannah, Sean's co-star, but more important in my mind – Sean's ex. Even if they hadn't actually slept together, they had dated, which probably meant they had kissed and maybe fooled around a little. Ugh. The thought of their hands being on one another made me sick with jealousy.

Turning from the fridge with a bottle of juice, Sean took one look at her lack of attire and sighed heavily, as if he was used to her flaunting displays. Placing the juice on the counter he walked over to the sofas, picked up a white shirt, and tossed it to her, barely sparing her a glance in the process. 'We have guests, put some clothes on.'

Rolling her eyes – her perfectly made up eyes, complete with smoky eyeshadow – Savannah shrugged into her shirt, closing just one button over her stomach, and then finally turned her attention towards me, her eyes narrowing a fraction as she soaked in my appearance.

'You're probably right. I'm all sweaty, I must look such a state.' From the snide look she gave my outfit, I took that comment to mean that she thought I looked a state. Which I probably did.

Even with the slight sheen of sweat on her skin from the sun she looked flipping perfect. In fact, it probably just improved her overall sexiness. Her waist was miniscule, stomach flat, arms and legs toned and tanned, and hair as sleek and shiny as if she had just walked out of a salon. If I were being bitchy, which clearly I was, then I'd have said that her boobs were almost definitely fake.

I'm a laid back person, and can usually get along with pretty much everyone, but Savannah? I took an immediate dislike to her that was so strong it was causing my stomach to roil and churn and my skin to prickle with the urge to move away from her. She practically reeked of falseness.

Coming around the counter, Sean handed me my water and Savannah a glass of orange juice, slid his free hand around my waist, and made the introductions. 'Allie, this is Savannah Hilton. Savannah, Allie Shaw, my gorgeous girlfriend I've been telling you about.' Savannah's expression was unreadable, slightly pouty and sour-looking,

355

but perhaps that was just what Botox looked like. My insides warmed from his words, and the feel of his fingers sitting possessively on my hip grounded me to the point where I could actually manage words.

'Savannah, it's a pleasure to meet you.'

Her eyes noticeably ran up and down my body a few times before returning to my face. For a second, it looked like she was decidedly unimpressed with what she saw, before her expression suddenly cleared, becoming almost friendly. 'And you, Allie. I've heard a great deal about you.' OK, well that was polite enough, perhaps I'd misread her initial look.

Sipping her drink, Savannah suddenly screwed up her face and almost retched. 'Eww. God, Sean, how many times do I have to tell you I drink the low fat juice, not this sugar-ridden stuff?' Turning to me, she rolled her eyes conspiratorially as if we were best friends and then sashayed across the kitchen and towards the sink. I'm fairly sure the exaggerated roll in her hips as she walked was for Sean's benefit, but rather satisfyingly I noticed that his eyes were still glued to me. Dumping her juice down the sink, she refilled it with the right juice, giving another eye roll and an irritated click of her tongue as she did so. What a diva!

'So, how are you finding LA, Allie?' Savannah asked, slipping her lean body up onto one of the bar stools and giving a nod of satisfaction when she took a drink of her new juice. I noticed this new positioning allowed one of her long, lean legs to escape from the sarong, and couldn't help but wonder if the display were accidental, or once again for Sean's benefit. My inner bitch suspected the latter.

Polite conversation with Savannah Hilton in a mansion in the LA hills was not how I'd expected this afternoon to pan out, but I did my best to appear calm and casual, even if my insides were still a little clenched at the forced nature of our meeting. 'It's great. Nice and warm compared to the UK.'

And so it went from there – we all talked pleasantly for the best part of half an hour, Savannah and Sean briefly discussing their busy schedules over the coming weeks but making me feel very much a part of the conversation until I was surprisingly relaxed. This was turning out to be fairly pleasant. Savannah was a bit over the top with some of her mannerisms, but the more we chatted, the more I started to think that perhaps I'd been too quick to judge her. She was a drama queen, yes, but she seemed to like me, and her intentions towards Sean appeared friendly, and not overtly territorial as I'd expected.

'I'm just popping to the toilet,' Sean said, placing a quick kiss on my shoulder as he left the room.

'Would you like any snacks?' Savannah asked, standing up and coming around the counter towards me where she opened a small cupboard to my left.

Sipping my water, I shook my head and smiled. 'I'm fine, thanks.'

Closing the cupboard door empty-handed, Savannah looked down at me and returned my smile, but this time it seemed tinged with sympathy, which confused me. 'I think you're taking this all very well,' she said, her face softening with almost exaggerated concern and her tone consoling as if she were speaking to an injured child.

Assuming she meant having to hide my relationship with Sean, I shrugged and nodded. 'Thanks. It is what it is, we won't have to hide forever.'

Laughing dryly, she crossed her arms, suddenly seeming to loom over me because she was standing really, really close. 'Oh, I didn't mean that darrrling. I meant me and Sean.' Her and Sean? What? Now I really was confused. And I still really disliked the way she rolled her r's. It sounded so condescending.

'You mean living together?' I asked cautiously, not really sure where she was going with this.

'Noooo.' She drew the word out long and slow, as if I was stupid and couldn't understand her. 'I mean you're very good for overlooking the fact that he and I still fuck.'

It took several seconds for her words to infiltrate my mind, and as they did I simply sat there staring at her and blinking rapidly. Still fuck? I didn't think they had ever 'fucked' in the first place. I instantly wanted to vomit all over the sickly sweet smile on her face as she towered over me, her height advantage suddenly that much more noticeable.

'We work together so much, go to events together, and now live together, so it's understandable, really, that our sexual urges sometimes get the better of us.'

Urges? Understandable? Flipping understandable? None of this was understandable, what the hell was she talking about? I'd asked Sean this very question and he had stared into my eyes as he promised me that they'd never slept together. He'd looked so solemn, so truthful … had that been an act? Just my fabulously talented actor boyfriend using his skills to deceive me?

My head was spinning. If it wasn't for bloody Little Miss I-Fuck-Your-Boyfriend standing in front of me, I probably would have fallen to the floor, but there was no way I was giving her the satisfaction of seeing me crumble.

'I should be thanking you, really,' she continued, taking advantage of my shocked silence. 'When you first arrived in LA and had that falling out? Christ, Sean was like a man possessed that night. I don't think he's ever taken me that roughly before, or so many times. It was incredible … don't you just love how dominant he is?'

She knew about his preference for control? And about our argument? Sean had told her? And then fucked her? That was it. I couldn't take any more. Jumping up so suddenly that my stool tumbled backwards and crashed onto the spotless marble floor, I stared at her in open-mouthed shock, still unable to formulate words.

Savannah blinked at me several times before her mouth popped open in a silent 'o' shape and she dramatically raised a hand to cover it. 'Oh God ... you didn't know. Fuck. Allie ... I thought he'd told you darrrling ...' Wincing as her irritatingly-rolled word ground its way into my brain, I squeezed my eyes shut for a second just to check that I wasn't imagining this.

Sean wouldn't have slept with her, would he? But if he hadn't, then how did she know about his tendency for dominance? Suddenly all my insecurities about us, and his celebrity lifestyle, came crashing down upon me. Hard. Really, when it came down to it, I barely knew him. Our entire relationship had been based upon a week of snowbound fucking followed by secretive meetings and forbidden liaisons. I knew the façade he had presented to me, the slightly neurotic, intense, but ultimately caring man, but was that the real him or just a front? Now he was back in the comfortable surroundings of Hollywood, perhaps he'd slid back into his old ways.

Opening my eyes, I found Savannah reaching out for me, her hands flying up towards my shoulders in a supportive gesture, but the evil glint in her eye completely gave away her glee. She was *loving* this.

Despite the fakeness and ugly smirk, I could see that men would find her beautiful. Sean surely would, too. He was impetuous and passionate when it came to sex, he'd proven that with me, so with her constantly around him I'm sure it would have been easy for him to give in to his 'urges', just like she'd said.

The need to vomit reared up my throat again as I stepped out of her reach, half tripping over the bloody stool as I clutched at the kitchen counter for stability. I couldn't breathe. I was so panicked I was lightheaded, lights bouncing before my eyes until I could barely see.

Hot tears were burning my eyelids, my nose clogging with the need to release them, but I would not give this bitch the satisfaction of seeing me cry.

Knowing that I was about to do the one thing I had promised Sean I wouldn't, I turned from Savannah and prepared to run.

I had to get away, and I had to get away now.

Author's Note

Thank you for reading!

I write for my readers, so I'd love to hear your thoughts, feel free get in touch with me:
E-mail: **aliceraineauthor@gmail.com**
Twitter: **@AliceRaine1**
Facebook: **www.facebook.com/alice.raineauthor**
Website: **www.aliceraineauthor.com**

When I write about my characters and scenes, I have certain images in my head. I've created a Pinterest page with these images in case you are curious. You can find it at **http://www.pinterest.com/alice3083/**

You will also find some teaser pics for upcoming books to whet your appetite!

Alice xx

The Untwisted Series

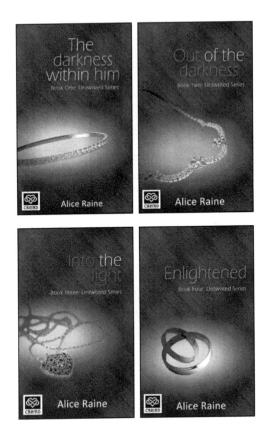

By Alice Raine

For more information about **Alice Raine**

and other **Accent Press** titles

please visit

www.accentpress.co.uk

Printed in Great Britain
by Amazon